SPOONBENDERS

ALSO BY DARYL GREGORY

NOVELS

Pandemonium

The Devil's Alphabet

Raising Stony Mayhall

Afterparty

We Are All Completely Fine

Harrison Squared

SHORT FICTION

Unpossible and Other Stories

SPOONBENDERS

DARYL GREGORY

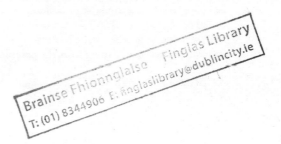
riverrun

First published in Great Britain in 2017 by

riverrun

an imprint of
Quercus Editions Ltd
Carmelite House
50 Victoria Embankment
London EC4Y 0DZ

An Hachette UK company

A CIP catalogue record for this book is available
from the British Library

HB ISBN 978 1 78648 275 4
TPB ISBN 978 1 78648 276 1
EBOOK ISBN 978 1 78648 278 5

10 9 8 7 6 5 4 3 2 1

Printed and bound in Great Britain by Clays Ltd, St Ives plc

"You'd think that whatever causes these things to happen doesn't want them to be proved."

—URI GELLER

1995

JUNE

I

Matty

Matty Telemachus left his body for the first time in the summer of 1995, when he was fourteen years old. Or maybe it's more accurate to say that his body expelled him, sending his consciousness flying on a geyser of lust and shame.

Just before it happened, he was kneeling in a closet, one sweaty hand pressed to the chalky drywall, his right eye lined up with the hole at the back of an unwired electrical outlet box. On the other side of the wall was his cousin Mary Alice and her chubby white-blonde friend. Janice? Janelle? Probably Janelle. The girls—both two years older than him, juniors, *women*—lay on the bed side by side, propped up on their elbows, facing in his direction. Janelle wore a spangled T-shirt, but Mary Alice—who the year before had announced that she would respond only to "Malice"—wore an oversized red flannel shirt that hung off her shoulder. His eye was drawn to the gaping neck of the shirt, following that swell of skin down down down into shadow. He was pretty sure she was wearing a black bra.

They were looking at a school yearbook while listening to Mary Alice's CD Walkman, sharing foam headphones between them like a wishbone. Matty couldn't hear the music, but even if he could, it was probably no band *he'd* heard of. Someone calling herself Malice wouldn't tolerate anything popular. Once she'd caught him humming Hootie & the Blowfish and the look of scorn on her face made his throat close.

She didn't seem to like him as a matter of policy, even though he had proof that she once did: a Christmas Polaroid of a four-year-old Mary Alice, beaming, with her brown arms wrapped around his white toddler body. But in the six months since Matty and his mom had moved back to Chicago and into Grandpa Teddy's house, he'd seen Mary Alice practically every other week, and she'd barely spoken to him. He tried to match her cool and pretend she wasn't in the room. Then she'd walk past, sideswiping him with the scent of bubblegum and cigarettes, and the rational part of his brain would swerve off the road and crash into a tree.

Out of desperation, he set down three commandments for himself:

1. If your cousin is in the room, do not try to look down her shirt. It's creepy.
2. Do not have lustful thoughts about your cousin.
3. Under no circumstances should you touch yourself while having lustful thoughts about your cousin.

So far tonight the first two had gone down in flames, and the third was in the crosshairs. The adults (except for Uncle Buddy, who never really left the house anymore) had all gone downtown for dinner, someplace fancy, evidently, with his mom in her interview skirt, Uncle Frankie looking like a real estate agent with a jacket over a golf shirt, and Frankie's wife, Aunt Loretta, squeezed into a lavender pantsuit. Grandpa Teddy, of course, wore a suit and the Hat (in Matty's mind, "Hat" was always capitalized). But even that uniform had been upgraded slightly for the occasion: gold cuff links, a decorative handkerchief poking up out of his breast pocket, his fanciest, diamond-studded wristwatch. They'd be back so late that Frankie's kids were supposed to sleep over. Uncle Frankie mixed a gallon of powdered Goji Go! berry juice, placed a twenty-dollar bill with some ceremony next to the jug, and addressed his daughters. "I want change," he said to Mary Alice. Then he pointed to the twins: "And you guys, try not to burn down the fucking house, all right?" Polly and Cassie, seven years old, appeared not to hear him.

Uncle Buddy was technically in charge, but the cousins all understood that they were on their own for the evening. Buddy was in his own world, a high-gravity planet he left only with great difficulty. He worked on his projects, he marked off the days on the refrigerator calendar in pink crayon, and he spoke to as few people as possible. He wouldn't even answer the door for the pizza guy; it was Matty who went to the door with the twenty, and who set the two dollars' change very carefully in the middle of the table.

Through some carefully timed choreography, Matty managed to outmaneuver Janelle-the-interloper and the twins to score the chair next to Mary Alice. He spent all of dinner next to her, hyperaware of every centimeter that separated his hand from hers.

Buddy took one piece of pizza and vanished to the basement, and the high whine of the band saw was all they heard of him for hours. Buddy, a bachelor who'd lived his entire life in this house with Grandpa Teddy, was forever starting projects—tearing down, roughing in, tacking up—but never finishing.

Like the partially deconstructed room Matty was hiding in. Until recently it and the adjoining room were part of an unfinished attic. Buddy had removed the old insulation, framed in closets, wired up lights, installed beds in both rooms—and then had moved on. This half of the attic was technically Matty's bedroom, but most of the closet was filled with old clothes. Buddy seemed to have forgotten the clothes and the empty electrical sockets behind them.

Matty, however, had not forgotten.

Janelle turned a page of the yearbook and laughed. "Ooh! Your lover!" she said.

"Shut up," Mary Alice said. Her dark hair hung across her eyes in a way that knocked him out.

"You want that big thing in your mouth, don't you?" Janelle asked.

Matty's thighs were cramping, but he wasn't about to move now.

"Shut the fuck up," Mary Alice said. She bumped her friend's shoulder. Janelle rolled into her, laughing, and when the girls righted themselves, the flannel shirt had slipped from his cousin's shoulder, exposing a black bra strap.

No: a *dark purple* bra strap.

Commandment #3, Thou shalt not touch thyself, began to smolder and smoke.

Twenty feverish seconds later, Matty's back arched as if yanked by a hot wire. An ocean roar filled his ears.

Suddenly he was in the air, the studs of the slanted ceiling inches from his face. He shouted, but he had no voice. He tried to push away from the ceiling, but realized he didn't have arms, either. In fact, no body at all.

After a moment, his vision swiveled, but he felt no control over that movement; a camera panning on its own. The floor of the room swung into view. His body had fallen out of the closet and lay stretched out on the plywood.

That's what he looked like? That chubby belly, that pimply jawline?

The body's eyes fluttered open, and for a vertiginous moment Matty was both the watcher and the watched. The body's mouth opened in shock, and then—

It was as if the strings holding him aloft were suddenly cut. Matty plummeted. The body screamed: a high-pitched, girlish squeal he had time to register as deeply embarrassing. Then consciousness and flesh crashed into each other.

He bounced around inside his body like a Super Ball. When the reverberations settled, he was looking out through his eyes at the ceiling, which was now the appropriate distance away.

Thumps sounded from the next room. The girls! They'd heard him!

He jumped up, covering his crotch like a wounded soldier. "Matty?" Malice called. The door began to swing open.

"I'm okay! I'm okay!" he shouted. He launched himself into the closet.

From somewhere the blonde laughed. Mary Alice appeared at the closet doors, hands on her hips. "What are you doing in here?"

He looked up at her, the bottom half of his body covered by women's apparel, the topmost dress an orange striped number that looked very seventies.

"I tripped," he said.

"Okay . . ."

He made no move to get up.

"What's the matter?" Mary Alice asked. She'd seen something in his expression.

"Nothing," he said. He'd just had a bad thought: These are

Grandma Mo's dresses. I've just despoiled my dead grandmother's clothes.

He propped himself on an elbow. Trying to look comfortable, as if he'd just discovered that twenty-year-old frocks made the perfect bedding material.

Mary Alice started to say something, then she glanced at the wall behind him, just over his shoulder. Her eyes narrowed. Through force of will, Matty did not turn around to see if she was looking at the empty electrical box.

"Okay then," she said. She backed away from the closet.

"Right," he said. "Thanks. All good."

The girls left the room, and he immediately turned and covered the hole in the wall with the orange gown. He began to rehang the dresses and coats: a waist-length rabbit fur coat, a bunch of knee-length skirts, a plaid raincoat. One of the last items was covered in a clear plastic dry-cleaning bag. It was a long, shimmery silver dress, and the sight of it rang chimes somewhere far back in his brain.

Oh, he thought. That's right. It's what Grandma Mo wore on the videotape. *The* videotape.

〳〵

Uncle Frankie had shown Matty the tape at Thanksgiving four years ago. Frankie had been drinking a lot of red wine, hitting it hard as soon as his wife, Loretta, unwrapped the shrimp cocktail appetizers, and his sentences had turned *emphatic* and *urgent*. He was railing about some guy named the Astounding Archibald, who'd ruined *everything*.

"Think what we could've had," Frankie said. "We could have been kings."

Irene, Matty's mom, laughed, making Frankie scowl. "Kings of what?" she asked.

Irene and Matty had driven in from Pittsburgh the night before, and they'd woken up to find that Grandpa Teddy had bought a bird and not much else; he'd been waiting for his daughter to conjure the rest of the meal. Now that they were finally on the other side of dinner, the table turned into a postcombat battlefield: pumpkin pie destroyed,

Rice Krispies Treats in ruins, all wine bottles depleted. Matty was the last kid left in his chair. He'd always liked hanging out with the adults. Most of the time he stayed under the radar, not speaking, in the hope that they'd forget he was there and start saying interesting things.

"That no-talent hack just couldn't stand to see us win," Frankie said.

"No, he was a talented man, a talented man," Grandpa Teddy said from the head of the table. "Brilliant, even. But shortsighted." As usual, he was the most dressed-up person in the house. Shiny black suit, pink shirt, riotous paisley tie as wide as a trout. Grandpa always dressed like he was about to go to a wedding or a funeral, except in the mornings or just before bed, when he walked around as if he were alone in the house: wife-beater T-shirt, boxer shorts, black socks. He didn't seem to own "sportswear" or "work clothes," maybe because he never did sports and didn't work. He was rich, though. Irene said she didn't know where the money came from, but Matty imagined it was all poker winnings. Grandpa Teddy, it was understood, was the greatest cardshark of all time. He taught Matty seven-card stud, sitting at the kitchen table for hours until Matty's pennies ran out. (Grandpa Teddy always played for money, and never gave it back after a game. "You can't sharpen your knife on a sponge," he'd say, scripture that Matty believed in without entirely understanding.)

"Archibald was a necessary evil," Grandpa Teddy said. "He was the voice of the skeptic. If your mother had shown him up, the audience would have loved us for it. We could have gone to the stratosphere with that act."

"He was evil," Frankie said. "A damn liar and a cheat! He wouldn't take Communion without palming the wafer."

Grandpa Teddy chuckled. "It's all water under the bridge now."

"He was just plain jealous," Frankie said. "He hated our gifts. He wanted to destroy us."

Matty couldn't stand it any longer. He had to ask. "What did this guy do to us?"

Frankie leaned across the table, looking Matty straight in the eye. "What did he *do*?" he said in a low, emotion-choked voice. "He killed Grandma Mo, that's what."

A thrill went through Matty. It wasn't just this dramatic declaration; it was the electricity of being noticed by his uncle. Of being seen.

Uncle Frankie had always been kind to Matty, but he'd never talked to him as if he mattered.

"Can we drop this, please?" Irene asked.

"He did kill her," Frankie said, leaning back but keeping his eyes on Matty. "Sure as if he'd put a gun to her head."

Matty's mom frowned. "You believe that, don't you?"

Frankie swiveled his head to stare her down. "Yes, Irene. Yes, I do."

Loretta got to her feet. "I'm going for a smoke."

"I'll join you," Grandpa Teddy said. He rose from the table, straightened his cuffs, and took her arm.

"You're not supposed to smoke, Dad," Irene said.

"Loretta's smoking," he said. "I'm secondary smoking."

Uncle Frankie gestured to Matty. "Come on, it's time you saw something."

"I'm not doing these dishes alone," Irene said.

"Have Buddy help you." He slapped his brother on the shoulder— a little too hard, Matty thought. Buddy's eyes fluttered, but his gaze never moved from the middle distance. He had a way of sitting very still, slumping lower and lower, as if he were turning to pudding.

"Leave him alone," Irene said.

Buddy remained unperturbed. He'd been in one of his trances since finishing his pie, staring into space, occasionally smiling to himself or silently mouthing a word or two. His muteness was a mystery to Matty, and the adults wouldn't talk about it, a double silence that was impenetrable. Matty's mom would only give him variations of "That's the way he is." Once Matty worked up the courage to ask Grandpa Teddy about why Buddy hardly spoke, and he said, "You'll have to ask him."

Frankie led Matty to the front room, where a huge console television was parked against the wall like a Chrysler. His uncle dropped heavily onto his butt—holding his wineglass aloft and managing to keep most of the wine inside it—and opened up one of the cabinets.

"Now we're talking," Frankie said. A VHS machine sat on a shelf, and in the space below was a jumble of videocassettes. He pulled one out, squinted at the label, and tossed it aside. He started working his way through the stack. "I gave Dad a copy," he said under his breath. "Unless Buddy threw it out, that fuckin'—hey. Here we go."

It was a black cassette box with orange stripes. Frankie ejected the current tape from the machine and jammed in the one from the box.

"This is our history," Frankie said. He turned on the television. "This is your heritage."

On the screen, a store clerk madly squeezed rolls of toilet paper. Frankie pressed play on the VCR, and nothing happened.

"You have to turn it to channel three," Matty said.

"Right, right." The TV's dial was missing, exposing a naked prong. Frankie reached up to retrieve the set of needle-nose pliers Grandpa Teddy kept on top of the console. "That was my first job. Grandpa's remote control."

The tape had the swimmy look of something recorded off broadcast TV. A talk show host in suit and tie sat on a cramped set, with a brilliant yellow wall behind him. "—and they've been thrilling audiences around the country," he was saying. "Please welcome Teddy Telemachus and His Amazing Family!" Matty could hear the capitals.

The applause on the recording sounded metallic. The host stood up and walked over to an open stage, where the guests stood awkwardly, several feet back from a wooden table. Father, mother, and three children, all dressed in suits and dresses.

Grandpa Teddy looked pretty much like himself, only younger. Trim and energetic, the Hat pushed back on his head, giving him the appearance of an old-time reporter about to give you the straight dope.

"Wow, is that Grandma Mo?" Matty asked, even though it could have been no one else. She wore a shiny, silvery evening dress, and she was the only member of the family who looked like she belonged onstage. It wasn't just that she was Hollywood beautiful, though she was that, with short dark hair and large eyes like a 1920s ingénue. It was her stillness, her confidence. She held the hand of a sweet-faced, kindergarten-age Uncle Buddy. "She's so young."

"This was a year before she died, so she was, like, thirty," Frankie said.

"No, I mean, compared to Grandpa Teddy."

"Yeah, well, he may have robbed the cradle a bit. You know your grandfather."

Matty nodded knowingly. He did know his grandfather, but not in whatever way Uncle Frankie was talking about. "Oh yeah."

"Now, this is the number one daytime show in the country, right?" Frankie said. "Mike Douglas. Millions watching."

On-screen, the host was pointing out various things on the table:

metal cans, some silverware, a stack of white envelopes. Beside the table was a kind of miniature wheel of fortune about three feet tall, but instead of numbers on the spokes there were pictures: animals, flowers, cars. Matty's mother, Irene, looked to be ten or eleven years old, though her velvety green dress made her look older. So did her worried expression; Matty was surprised to see it already set in place on such a young face. She kept her grip on the arm of her younger brother, a wiry, agitated kid who seemed to be trying to twist out of his suit and tie.

"Is that you?" Matty asked. "You don't look happy to be there."

"Me? You should have seen Buddy. He got so bad that—but we'll get to that."

Maureen—Grandma Mo—was answering a question from the talk show host. She smiled bashfully. "Well, Mike, I don't know if I'd use the word 'gifted.' Yes, I suppose we have a knack. But I believe every person has the capability to do what we do."

When she said "every person," she looked at Matty. Not at the camera, or the audience watching at home—at him. They locked eyes, across a gap of years and electronic distortion. "Oh!" he said.

Uncle Frankie glanced at him and said, "Pay attention. My part's coming."

Grandpa Teddy was telling the host about keeping an open mind. "In the right kind of positive environment, all things are possible." He smiled. "Even kids can do it."

The host crouched awkwardly next to Frankie. "Tell the folks your name."

"I can move things with my mind," he said. Visible at Frankie's feet was a line of white tape. Everyone except the host was standing behind it.

"Can you, now!"

"His name is Franklin," his sister said.

The host held his microphone to her. "And you are?"

"Irene." Her tone was guarded.

"Do you have a special ability, Irene?"

"I can read minds, sort of. I know when—"

"Wow! You want to read my mind right now?"

Grandma Mo put a hand on Irene's shoulder. "Do you want to try, sweetie? How are you feeling?"

"Fine." She didn't look fine.

Teddy jumped in to explain that Irene was a "human lie detector—a divining rod, if you will, for the truth! Say that we use these cards—" He reached toward the table.

"I'll get them," Mike Douglas said. He stepped over the taped line and picked up a large stack of oversized cards.

"Fucker," Uncle Frankie said.

"What?"

"Wait for it," Frankie said.

On-screen, Teddy said, "Those are ordinary playing cards. Now, Mike, shuffle through the deck and choose a card, then show it to the camera for the folks at home. Don't show it to Irene, though."

Mike Douglas walked to one of the cameras and held up a five of diamonds. He goofed around a little, moving it in and out of focus.

"Here's your chance to lie to a little girl," Teddy said. "Let's put your card back in the deck. Excellent, Mike, excellent. And a couple of shuffles . . . all-righty, then. Hold out your hand, if you please. I'm going to start dealing cards, faceup. All you have to do is answer Irene's question. And don't worry, she always asks the same thing, and it's a very simple question."

Grandpa Teddy dealt a card onto the host's palm. Irene said, "Mr. Douglas, is that your card?"

"No-siree, little miss." He mugged for the camera.

"That's the truth," Irene said.

"It's that simple," Grandpa Teddy said to the host. "You can say yes or no, whatever you like." He dealt another card onto his palm, and another. Mike said "no" to each new card, and Irene would nod. Then Mike said, "That one's mine."

"You're lying," Irene said.

Mike Douglas laughed. "Caught me! Not the queen of spades."

They went through more cards, Mike saying "no" each time, but after the tenth Irene shook her head.

"That's your card," she said.

The host held out his palm to the camera: on the top was the five of diamonds. Then he addressed Grandma Mo. "What do you say to people who say, Oh, those are marked cards. They taught the girl to read them!"

Grandma Mo smiled, not at all upset. "People say all kinds of things." She was still holding Buddy's hand. He was so small his head was barely in the frame.

The host reached into his jacket pocket and brought out an envelope. "So what I've done is brought some pictures. Each of them is a simple, geometric pattern. You've never seen into this envelope, right?"

Irene looked worried—but then, she'd looked worried from the start of the show.

"Ready?" the host asked. He picked a card from the envelope and looked hard at it.

Irene glanced at her mother.

"Simple geometric shapes," the host said.

"You don't have to prompt her," Grandma Mo said.

"Tell me if I'm lying," the host said. "Is it a circle?"

Irene frowned. "Um . . ."

"Is it a triangle?"

"That's not fair," Irene said. "You can't ask me questions, you have to—"

Uncle Frankie pressed a button and the image froze. "Take a look at the bowl." He pointed at a small, round-bottomed stainless steel bowl. "It's got water in it. Ready?"

"Sure," Matty said.

Frankie pressed play. On-screen, Irene seemed angry. "He's not doing it right. There's no way I can say yes or no if he keeps—"

From offscreen, Grandpa Teddy said sharply, "Frankie! Wait your turn!"

The bowl on the table seemed to tremble, and then the whole table began to vibrate.

The camera swung over to little Frankie. He was sitting on the ground, cross-legged, staring at the table. The pile of silverware rattled, and the bowl began to rock back and forth.

"Careful now," Grandpa Teddy said. "You're going to—"

The bowl tipped a bit more, and water sloshed over the edge.

"—spill it," Grandpa Teddy finished.

"Holy cow!" the host said. "We'll be right back." A band played, and then a commercial came on.

"You did that, Uncle Frankie?" Matty asked. "Cool."

Frankie was worked up. "You see that shit with the pictures? That was Archibald's idea, too, trying to fuck us over. Told Douglas not to let us use our own material, gave him those Zener cards."

Matty wasn't sure how that would throw off his mother's power. He knew that she couldn't be lied to, just as he knew that Grandpa Teddy read the contents of sealed envelopes, that Grandma Mo could see distant objects, and Uncle Frankie could move things with his mind, and that Uncle Buddy, when he was small, could predict the scores of Cubs games. That they were psychic was another Telemachus Family Fact, in the same category as being half Greek and half Irish, Cubs fans and White Sox haters, and Catholic.

"It gets worse," Frankie said. He fast-forwarded through the commercials, overran the resume of the show, rewound, then went forward and back several more times. Grandma Mo and Buddy were no longer onstage. Grandpa Teddy had his arm around Irene.

"And we're back with Teddy Telemachus and His Amazing Family," the host said. "Maureen had to take care of a little family emergency—"

"Sorry about that," Teddy said with a smile. "Buddy, he's our youngest, got a little nervous, and Maureen needed to comfort him." He made it sound like Buddy was an infant. "We'll bring them back out here in a sec."

"You're okay with going forward?" the host asked.

"Of course!" Teddy said.

"What happened to Buddy?" Matty asked his uncle.

"Jesus, he broke down, crying and wailing. Your grandmother had to take him backstage to calm him down."

The host had his hand on young Frankie's shoulder. "Now, just before the break, little Franklin here seemed to be—well, what would you call it?"

"Psychokinesis, Mike," Uncle Teddy said. "Frankie's always had a talent for it."

"The table was really shaking," the host said.

"That's not unusual. It can make dinnertime pretty exciting, Mike, pretty exciting."

"I bet! Now, before we continue, I want to introduce a special guest. Please welcome noted stage magician and author the Astounding Archibald."

A short bald man with a ridiculous black handlebar mustache strode into the shot. Teddy shook his head as if disappointed. "This explains so much," he said. The bald man was even shorter than Grandpa Teddy.

"Good to see you again, Mr. Telemachus," Archibald said. They shook hands.

"G. Randall Archibald is not only a world-renowned magician," Mike Douglas intoned, "he's also a skeptic and debunker of psychics."

"This explains so much," Teddy said again, more loudly.

The host didn't appear to hear him. "We asked him here to help us set up these tests for the Telemachus family. See this line?" The camera pulled back to show the full extent of the white gaffer tape. "It was Mr. Archibald's idea that we do not allow Teddy or members of his family to handle the silverware, or approach the table in any way."

"Perhaps you noticed," Archibald said to the host, "that Irene had no problem reading the cards when they were the ones that Teddy provided for you. But when you used the Zener cards—which Teddy had no advance access to, and was not allowed to touch!—she hemmed and hawed."

"Not true, not true!" Teddy said. "Mike was doing it wrong! But worse, *someone* filled with negativity was causing interference. Severe interference!"

"You mean my mere presence caused her powers to fail?" Archibald asked.

"As I told you, Mike," Teddy said, "you gotta have an open mind to allow these abilities to work."

"Or an empty one," Archibald said. Mike Douglas laughed.

Archibald, looking pleased, addressed the audience. "While Irene was concentrating *so* hard, we had a camera focused on her father. Mike, can we show the television audience what we recorded?"

Teddy looked shocked. "Are you mocking my daughter? Are you *mocking* her, you pipsqueak?" This from a man barely two inches taller.

"I'm not mocking her, Mr. Telemachus, but perhaps you are mocking the audience's ability to—"

"Let's bring my wife out here," Teddy said. "Maureen Telemachus is, without a doubt, the world's most powerful clairvoyant. Mike, can you bring her out here?"

The host looked off camera and appeared to be listening to someone. Then to Teddy he said, "I'm told she's unavailable. Tell you what, let's just look at the videotape, and we'll see if she can come back out after the next break."

"I think you'll notice something very interesting," Archibald said. He had a showy way of speaking, punching the consonants. "While everyone was distracted by the little girl, the table began to move and shake."

"It sure did," Mike Douglas said.

"But how did that happen? Was it *psychokinesis* . . . or something a little more down to earth?"

The screen showed the stage from minutes before, but from a side angle, slightly behind the family. At first the camera was aimed at the host and Irene, but then it swung toward Teddy. He had stepped across the strip of gaffer tape, and his foot was pressed against the table leg.

Archibald spoke over the playback. "This is an old trick. Just lift the table slightly, and slip the edge of your shoe's sole under the leg."

Teddy's foot was barely moving, if it was moving at all, but the table was undoubtedly shaking. Then the screen showed Archibald and the host. Teddy stood off to the side, looking into the wings, grimacing in frustration.

"I can teach you how to do it," Archibald said to the host. "No psychic powers required."

Mike Douglas turned to Grandpa. "What do you say to that, Teddy? No powers required?"

Teddy appeared not to hear him. He was staring offstage. "Where the—" He stopped himself from swearing. "Where is my wife? Could someone please bring her out here?"

Irene grabbed Grandpa Teddy's arm, embarrassed. She hissed something to him that didn't make it to the microphones.

"Fine," Grandpa Teddy said. He called Frankie to him. "We're leaving."

"Really?" Archibald said. "What about Maureen? I'd really like to—"

"Not today, Archibald. Your, uh, negativity has made this impossible." Then to the host he said, "I really expected better of you, Mike."

Teddy and his children walked offstage—with great dignity, Matty thought. Mike Douglas looked flummoxed. The Astounding Archibald seemed surprisingly disappointed.

Uncle Frankie pressed the eject button and the screen turned to static. "See what I mean?"

"Wow," Matty said. He was desperate to keep the conversation going, but he didn't want Frankie to get fed up and stop talking to him. "So Grandma Mo never came back onstage?"

"Nope. Never got to do her part of the act. It would have shut Archibald up, that's for sure, but she never got the chance. Buddy got worse and we all went home."

"Okay, but . . ."

"But what?"

"How did that kill her?"

Frankie stared at him.

Uh-oh, Matty thought.

Frankie hauled himself to his feet.

Matty hopped up, too. "I'm sorry, I just don't—"

"You know what chaos theory is?" Frankie asked.

Matty shook his head.

"Butterfly wings, Matty. One flap and—" He made a grand gesture, which brought his almost-empty glass into sight, and he drained it. "God damn." He studied the front window, perhaps seeing something new in the old houses. But the only thing Matty could see was his uncle's reflection, his shiny face floating like a ghost over his body.

Frankie looked down at him. "What was I saying?"

"Uh, butterflies?"

"Right. You have to look at cause and effect, the whole chain of events. First, the act is wrecked. We're dead as far as the public is concerned. Gigs get canceled, fucking Johnny Carson starts making fun of us."

"Carson," Matty said, affecting bitterness. Everybody in the family knew that Carson had stolen Grandpa Teddy's envelope act.

"Once they isolated us, we were sitting ducks." Frankie looked down at him with an intense expression. "Do the math, kid." He glanced toward the dining room; Matty's mom had moved into the kitchen, and no one was in sight, but Frankie lowered his voice anyway. "Nineteen seventy-three. Height of the Cold War. The world's most famous psychics are discredited on *The Mike Douglas Show*, and just a year later, a woman with your grandmother's immense power just *dies*?"

Matty opened his mouth, closed it. Immense power?

Frankie nodded slowly. "*Oh* yeah."

Matty said, "But Mom—" Frankie put up a hand, and Matty lowered his voice to a whisper. "Mom said she died of cancer."

"Sure," Uncle Frankie said. "A healthy woman, a nonsmoker, dies of uterine cancer at age thirty-one." He put his hand on Matty's shoulder and leaned close. His breath smelled like Kool-Aid. "Listen, this is between you and me, right? My girls are too young to handle the truth, and your mom—you see how *she* reacts. As far as the rest of the world is concerned, your grandmother died of natural causes. You follow me?"

Matty nodded, though he wasn't quite following, starting with why he could be told this secret, and Mary Alice, who was two years older than him, could not. Though maybe that was because she wasn't a Telemachus by blood? She was Loretta's daughter from a previous marriage. Did that make a difference? He started to ask, and Frankie put up a hand.

"There's more to this story, Matthias. More than's safe to tell you right now. But know this." His voice was choked with emotion, his eyes misty.

"Yes?" Matty asked.

"You come from greatness," Uncle Frankie said. "You have greatness in you. And no jackbooted tool of the American government can—"

Matty would never know what Uncle Frankie was going to say next, because at that moment a loud bang sounded from upstairs. Mary Alice screamed, "Fire! Fire!"

"God damn it," Frankie said softly. He squeezed his eyes shut. Then he hustled up the stairs, shouting for everyone else to stop shouting. Matty followed him into the guest bedroom, which served double duty as a kind of utility room, crowded with boxes and laundry baskets. The padded cover to the ironing board was on fire, and the iron sat in the middle of the flames, its black cord dangling over the side, not plugged in. The three-year-old twins stood in a corner, holding hands, looking wide-eyed at the flames; not afraid so much as surprised. Mary Alice held one of Buddy's huge shirts up in front of her, as if she was shielding herself from the heat, though she was probably thinking of smothering the flames with it.

"Jesus, get Cassie and Polly out of here," Frankie said to Mary Alice. He looked around the room, didn't see what he was looking for, and then said, "Everybody out!"

The twins bolted for the hall, and Mary Alice and Matty moved only as far as the doorway, too fascinated to leave completely. Frankie crouched beside the ironing board and picked it up by the legs, balancing the iron atop it. He carried it toward them as if it were a giant birthday cake. Mary Alice and Matty scampered ahead of him. He went down the stairs, moving deliberately despite the flames in his face. This impressed Matty tremendously. Mary Alice opened the front door for him, and he walked to the driveway and dumped the ironing board on its side. The smoking, partially melted iron bounced twice and landed bottom-side down.

Aunt Loretta appeared from around the corner of the house, followed a moment later by Grandpa Teddy. Then Matty's mom burst through the front door, followed by the twins. The whole family was standing in the front yard now, except for Buddy.

"What happened?" Loretta asked Frankie.

"Whaddya think?" Frankie said. He turned the ironing board so that it was upside down, but flames still licked at the sides. "Pack up the hellions and Mary Alice. We're going home."

For months Matty couldn't get that videotape out of his mind. It seemed to be a message from the distant past, an illuminated text glowing with the secrets of his family. He desperately wanted to ask his mother about it, but he also didn't want to break his promise to Uncle Frankie. He resorted to asking his mother oblique questions about *The Mike Douglas Show* or Grandma Maureen or the government, and every time she cut him off. Even when he tried to sneak up on the topic—"Gee, I wonder what it's like to be on TV?"—she seemed to immediately sense what was up and change the subject.

The next time he and his mother returned to Chicago, he couldn't find the cassette in the TV cabinet. Uncle Buddy caught him pawing through the boxes, trying each tape in the machine, fast-forwarding to make sure Mike Douglas didn't pop up mid-tape. His uncle frowned and then slumped out of the room.

Matty never found the tape. The next Thanksgiving Frankie didn't seem to remember showing it to him. At holidays Matty sat around the dinner table, waiting for the adults to talk about those days, but his mother had placed some kind of embargo on the matter. Frankie would bring up something that seemed promising—a reference to Grandma Mo, or "psi war"—and Mom would fix him with a look that dropped the temperature of the room. The visits became less frequent and more strained. A couple Thanksgivings Frankie's family didn't show up at all, and some years Matty and his mom stayed home in Pittsburgh. Those were terrible weekends. "You've got a melancholy streak," she'd tell him. If that were true, he knew where he got it from; his mother was the most melancholy person he knew.

It *was* true that he was unusually nostalgic for a kid, though what he pined for was a time before he was born. He was haunted by the feeling that he'd missed the big show. The circus had packed up and left town, and he'd shown up to find nothing but a field of trampled grass. But other times, especially when Mom was feeling good, he'd be suddenly filled with confidence, like the prince of a deposed royal family certain of his claim to the throne. He'd think, Once, we were Amazing.

Then his mother would lose another job, and they'd have to eat Kraft macaroni and cheese for weeks straight, and he'd think, *Once*, we were Amazing.

))))

And then, when he was fourteen years old, his mother lost the best job she'd ever had, and they moved back in with Grandpa Teddy, and soon afterward he found himself sitting in a closet full of his dead grandmother's clothes, recovering from the most interesting thing that had ever happened to him. His embarrassment had faded, which made space in his body for other emotions, a thrumming mix of fear, wonder, and pride.

He'd left his body. He'd floated eight feet off the ground. Some ceremony was called for.

He thought for a moment, then lifted the silver dress by its hanger and addressed it. "Hiya, Grandma Mo," he said, quiet enough that Mary Alice and her idiot friend couldn't hear him. "Today, I am—"

He was going to say, "Today, I am Amazing." It was going to be a poignant moment that he would someday tell his children about. He was young Bruce Wayne vowing to avenge his parents, Superman promising to uphold his Kryptonian heritage, a Jewish boy doing whatever Jewish boys do on their Bar Mitzvahs.

Then he noticed the shadow at the door.

It was Uncle Buddy. He held a hammer in one hand, and a staple gun in the other. His gaze slowly moved from Matty to the closet, then back to Matty—and the dress. His eyes widened a fraction. Was he about to smile? Matty couldn't take it if he smiled.

"I was just putting it away!" Matty said. He thrust the gown at him and ran, frantic to escape his uncle, the room, and his body.

2

Teddy

Teddy Telemachus made it a goal to fall in love at least once a day. No, fall in was inaccurate; throw himself in was more like it. Two decades after Maureen had died, the only way to keep his hollowed heart thumping was to give it a jump start on a regular basis. On summer weekends he would stroll the Clover's garden market on North Avenue, or else wander through Wilder Park, hoping for emotional defibrillation. On weekdays, though, he relied on grocery stores. The Jewel-Osco was closest, and perfectly adequate for food shopping, but in matters of the heart he preferred Dominick's.

He saw her browsing thoughtfully in the organic foods aisle, an empty basket in the crook of one arm; signs of a woman filling time, not a shopping cart.

She was perhaps in her mid-forties. Her style was deceptively simple: a plain sleeveless top, capri pants, sandals. If anyone complimented her, she'd claim she'd just thrown something on, but other women would know better. Teddy knew better. Those clothes were tailored to *look* casual. The unfussy leather bag hanging to her hip was a Fendi. The sandals were Italian as well. But what sent a shiver through his heart was the perfectly calibrated shade of red of her toenail polish.

This is why he shopped at Dominick's. You go to the Jewel on a Tuesday afternoon like this, you get old women in shiny tracksuits looking for a deal, holding soup cans up to the light, hypnotized by *serving size* and *price per ounce*. In Dominick's, especially in the tony suburbs, your Hinsdales and your Oak Brooks, it was still possible to find classy women, women who understood how to accessorize.

He pushed his empty cart close to her, pretending to study the seven varieties of artisanal honey.

She hadn't noticed him. She took a step back from the shelf and bumped into him, and he dropped the plastic honey jar to the floor. It almost happened by accident; his stiff fingers were especially balky this afternoon.

"I'm so sorry!" she said.

She stooped and he said, "Oh, you don't have to do that—" and bent at the same time, nearly thumping heads. They both laughed. She beat him to the honey jar, scooped it up with a hand weighted down by a wedding band and ponderous diamond. She smelled of sandalwood soap.

He accepted the jar with mock formality, which made her laugh again. He liked the way her eyes lit up amid those friendly crow's-feet. He put her age at forty-five or -six. A good thing. He had a firm rule, which he occasionally broke: only fall in love with women whose age, at minimum, was half his own plus seven. This year he was seventy-two, which meant that the object of his devotion had to be at least forty-three.

A young man wouldn't have thought she was beautiful. He'd see those mature thighs and overlook her perfectly formed calves and delicate ankles. He'd focus on that strong Roman nose and miss those bright green eyes. He'd see the striations in her neck when she tilted her head to laugh and fail to appreciate a woman who knew how to abandon herself to the moment.

Young men, in short, were idiots. Would they even feel the spark when she touched them, as he just did? A few fingers against his elbow, delicate and ostensibly casual, as if steadying herself.

He hid his delight and assumed a surprised, concerned look.

She dropped her hand from his arm. She was ready to ask what was wrong, but then pulled back, perhaps remembering that they were two strangers. So he spoke first.

"You're worried about someone," he said. "Jay?"

"Pardon?"

"Or Kay? No. Someone whose name starts with 'J.'"

Her eyes widened.

"I'm sorry, so sorry," he said. "It's someone close to you. That's none of my business."

She wanted to ask the question, but didn't know how to phrase it.

"Well now," he said, and lifted the honey jar. "Thank you for retrieving this, though I'm sure it's not as sweet as you." This last bit of corn served up with just enough self-awareness to allow the flirt to pass.

He walked away without looking back. Strolled down one aisle, then drifted to the open space of the produce section.

"My oldest son's name is Julian," she said. He looked up as if he hadn't seen her coming. Her basket was still empty. After a moment, he nodded as if she'd confirmed what he suspected.

"He has a learning disability," she said. "He has trouble paying attention, and his teachers don't seem to be taking it seriously."

"That sounds like a tough one," he said. "A tough one all right."

She didn't want to talk about the boy, though. Her question hung in the air between them. Finally she said, "How did you know about him?"

"I shouldn't have brought it up," he said. "It's just that when you touched my arm—" He tilted his head. "Sometimes I get flashes. Images. But that doesn't mean I have to say everything that pops into my head."

"You're trying to tell me you're psychic?" Making it clear she didn't believe in that stuff.

"That's a much-maligned word," he said. "Those psychics on TV, with their nine hundred numbers? Frauds and charlatans, my dear. Con men. However . . ." He smiled. "I do have to admit that I misled you in one respect."

She raised an eyebrow, willing him to elaborate.

He said, "I really have no need for this honey."

Her low, throaty laugh was nothing like Maureen's—Mo's rang like bells over a shop door—but he enjoyed it just the same. "I didn't think so," she said.

"It seems you've loaded up as well."

She looked at the basket on her arm, then set it on the floor. "There's a diner in this strip mall," she said.

"So I've heard." He offered her his hand. "I'm Teddy."

She hesitated, perhaps fearing another joy-buzzer moment of psychic intuition. Then she relented. "Graciella."

□

Teddy became a convert to the Church of Love at First Sight in the summer of 1962, the day he walked into that University of Chicago classroom. A dozen people in the room and she was the only one he could see, a girl in a spotlight, standing with her back to him as if she were about to turn and sing into a mic.

Maureen McKinnon, nineteen years old. Knocking him flat without even looking at him.

He didn't know her name yet, of course. She was thirty feet from him, talking to the receptionist sitting at the teacher's desk at the other end of the big classroom, which was only one chamber in this faux-Gothic building. The lair of the academic made him edgy—he'd never recovered from two bad years in Catholic high school—but the girl was a light he could steer by. He drifted down the center aisle, unconscious of his feet, drinking her in: a small-boned, black-haired sprite in an A-line dress, olive green with matching gloves. Oh, those gloves. She tugged them off one finger at a time, each movement a pluck at his heartstrings.

The secretary handed her a sheaf of forms, and the girl turned, her eyes on the topmost page, and nearly bumped into him. She looked up in surprise, and that was the coup de grace: blue eyes under black bangs. What man could defend himself against that?

She apologized, even as he removed his hat and insisted that he was the one who was at fault. She looked at him like she knew him, which both thrilled and unnerved him. Had he conned her in the past? Surely he'd have remembered this Black Irish sweetheart.

He checked in with the receptionist, a fiftyish woman wearing a young woman's bouffant of bright red hair, an obvious wig. She handed him his own stack of forms, and he gave her a big smile and a "Thanks, doll." Always good policy to befriend the secretary.

He took a desk a little behind the girl in the olive dress so he could watch her. He assumed she was here because of the same newspaper advertisement that had drawn him to campus:

RESEARCH SUBJECTS NEEDED FOR STUDY OF PSYCHIC PHENOMENA

Then in smaller type:

$5 HONORARIUM FOR INTAKE SURVEY, $20 PER DAY FOR THOSE CHOSEN FOR LONG-TERM STUDY. CENTER FOR ADVANCED COGNITIVE SCIENCE, UNIV. OF CHICAGO.

He figured the study was the usual academic foolishness, preying on the two types of people who'd answer such an ad: the desperate and the deluded. Those four yahoos in shirtsleeves and dungarees, laughing as they hunched over their desks, egging each other on? Desperate for the dough. That mole-faced student in the cheap suit, knee bouncing, all greasy hair and thick glasses: deluded into thinking he was special. The black kid in the shirt, tie, and Sunday shoes: desperate. And the old married couple helping each other fill out the paperwork? Both.

Teddy was here for the cash. But what about the girl? What was her story?

Teddy kept checking on her while he filled out his paperwork. The first few forms asked for demographic information, some of which he made up. It only got interesting a few pages in, when they started asking true-false questions like "I sometimes know what people are going to say before they say it." And "Watches and electrical devices sometimes stop working in my presence," which was followed twenty items later by "Watches and electrical devices that were broken sometimes start working in my presence." Pure silliness. He finished quickly, then carried his clipboard to the front of the room and handed it to the red-wigged secretary.

"Is that it?" he asked.

"The five-dollar check will be mailed to the address you put on the form," she said.

"No, I mean, the rest of the study? What happens after this?"

"Oh, you'll be contacted if you're one of the ones chosen."

He smiled. "Oh, I think they're going to want to talk to me."

"That's up to Dr. Eldon."

"Who's he?"

She seemed a little put out by this. "This is his project."

"Oh! Wait, is he a big guy, kinda heavy, with Einstein hair and big square glasses?"

A hit. A palpable hit. "Have you already met with the doctor?" she asked.

"No, no. It's just . . . well, when I was filling out the forms I kept getting this image. Somebody who was really interested in what was happening here today. It kept popping up, so I started doodling. May I?" He held out his hand for the clipboard he'd just given her. He flipped back a few pages. "Is that him?"

Teddy was no artist, but he could cartoon well enough for his purposes. In fact, it helped if you weren't too good, too accurate. What he'd drawn was little more than a circle to suggest a fat face, a couple of squares for the glasses, and a wild scribble of hair above.

The receptionist gave him the look he liked to get, confusion taking the slow elevator to amazement.

He lowered his voice. "And the weird thing is? I kept picturing me in a meeting with him. Him, me, and that girl—" He nodded toward the girl in the olive dress with the black hair and the blue eyes. "All of us sitting around a table, smiling."

"Oh," the receptionist said.

"This is why I need to be in this study," he said earnestly. "This kinda thing happens to me all the time."

He didn't mention that this kind of thing happened usually in bars, when there were a few bucks on the line. Fleecing fivers out of drunks was easy, but no way to earn a living. It was time to upgrade his act.

When he saw that ad in the *Sun-Times*, he realized that his first step should be to get certified as the real thing by real scientists. He made sure to do his homework before he showed up: a visit to the U of C library; a few questions about the Center for Advanced Cognitive Science; a quick flip through the faculty directory to see a picture of Dr. Horace Eldon; and voilà. One soon-to-be psychic flash, complete with doodle. The last bit, adding the girl into his precognitive vision, was a late improvisation.

He left the classroom without saying another word to the girl. Yet he knew, with an unexplainable certainty, that they'd meet again.

□

Graciella was a woman ready to talk. While their coffees steamed in front of them he asked many questions, and she answered at length, which seemed to surprise her; he got the impression of a tightly wound woman, normally guarded, who was playing hooky from her internal truant officer.

She was, as he'd guessed, a stay-at-home mom—or, given the size of some of the homes in Oak Brook, the suburb where she lived, a stay-at-mansion mom—whose primary duty was to arrange the lives of three school-age sons, including the problematic Julian. Her days were entirely set by their needs: travel soccer, math tutoring, tae kwon do.

"Sounds stressful," he said. "To do that alone."

"You get used to it," she said, ignoring the obvious question. "I'm the rock." She still had not mentioned her husband. "But why am I telling you all this? I must be boring you."

"I assure you, you're the furthest thing from boring in months."

"Tell me about you," she said decisively. "Where do you come from, Teddy? Do you live near here?"

"Just up the road, my dear. In Elmhurst."

She asked him about his family, and he told her of his grown children, without mentioning grandchildren. "Only three, two boys and a girl. My wife was Irish Catholic. If she'd lived, we'd probably have had a dozen, easy."

"Oh, I'm sorry to hear that," Graciella said.

"She was the love of my life. She passed when the kids were young, and I raised 'em on my own."

"That was probably unusual at the time," she said.

She made it sound like it was so long ago. And he supposed it was, though he didn't want her to dwell on their age gap; where was the fun in that? "Difficult, sure, very difficult," he said. "But you do what you have to do."

She nodded thoughtfully. He'd learned not to rush to fill the silence. He saw her notice the Rolex on his wrist, but instead of commenting on that, she said, "I like your hat."

He'd set it on the edge of the table. He'd been absentmindedly stroking the crown as they spoke. "It's a Borsalino," he said. "The finest maker of—"

"Oh, I know Borsalino."

"Of course you do," he said, with pleasure. "Of course you do."

"So," she said. Finally getting to it. "Do something psychic."

"It's not something that you can flip on like a switch," he said. "Some days it comes easily for me, easy as pie. Other days . . ."

She raised her eyebrow, egging him on again. She could do a lot with an eyebrow.

He pursed his lips, then nodded as if coming to a decision. He plucked a napkin from the dispenser on the table and tore it into three pieces.

"I want you to write three things you want for your family."

"What do you mean?"

"Just two words, two words on each piece, something like 'more money.' Call them wishes." He doubted she'd wish for money. That was clearly not her problem. She opened her purse to look for a pen and he handed her the one he kept in his jacket pocket. "Take your time, take your time. Write forcefully, in all caps—put some emotion into it. This is important."

Graciella bit her lip and stared at the first slip. He liked that she was taking it seriously. Taking *him* seriously. When she began to write, he turned in his seat and looked out across the empty plastic booths. It was afternoon, the dead zone.

"Finished," Graciella said.

He told her to fold each slip in half, then fold it again. "Make sure there's no way for me to read what you've written." He turned over the Borsalino and she dropped in the slips.

"The next part's up to you, Graciella. You need to think hard about what you wrote. Picture each of the things on the paper—all three wishes."

She gazed up at the ceiling. "All right."

The front door opened behind him, and she was distracted for a moment. A man in a black coat took a seat at a table kitty-corner from them. He sat just behind Graciella's left shoulder, facing away from them. Jesus Christ, Teddy thought.

"Concentrate," he told her—and himself. "Got all three?"

She nodded.

"Okay, let's see what we've got." He shook the three slips onto the table, then arranged them into a row. "Take the nearest one and put it in my hand. Don't open it. Just cover it up with your hand."

They were palm to palm, with the paper between them.

"Graciella," he said. She looked into his eyes. She was excited, yes, but nervous. Scared by what she'd written. By what was going to be said aloud.

"*School*," he said. "*New* school."

A puff of surprise escaped her.

"I guess that's about Julian," he said. "Turns out you'd decided after all, yes?"

"That one's too easy," she said. "I told you all about him. You could have guessed that."

"It's possible," he said. "Quite possible. Still—" The man behind Graciella coughed. He was big, with a crew cut like a gray lawn that rolled over the folds in his neck fat. Teddy tried to ignore him. He opened the slip and read it. " 'New school.' It's a good wish."

He set the paper aside and told her to pick the next slip. Again she covered his palm. His fingers touched her wrist, and he could feel her pulse.

"Hmm. This one's more complicated," he said.

Her hand trembled. What was she so afraid of?

"The first word is 'no.' " He closed his eyes to concentrate. "No . . . rabbits?"

She laughed. Relieved now. So he hadn't hit the slip she was worried about.

"You tell me," she said.

He looked at her. "I'm seeing 'No rabbits.' Are you writing in code? Wait." His eyes widened in mock surprise. "Are you pregnant?"

"What?" She was laughing.

"Maybe you're worried about the rabbit dying."

"No! I definitely want them to die. They've eaten my entire garden."

"This is about gardening?" He shook his head. "You need bigger wishes, my dear. Perhaps this last one. Put this one into my hatband. There you go. Don't let me touch it."

She tucked it into the front of the band. "How are you doing this?" she asked. "Have you always been able to do this?"

The man behind her snorted. He made a show of studying the plastic menu.

"Let me concentrate," Teddy said. He put on the Borsalino, but kept his fingers well away from the band. "Yes. This one's definitely a big one."

The man laughed.

"Jesus Christ!" Teddy said. "Would you mind?"

The man turned around. Graciella glanced behind her, then said to Teddy, "Do you two know each other?"

"Unfortunately," Teddy said.

"Destin Smalls," the man said, offering her his hand.

She refused to take it. "You're a cop, aren't you?"

Ding! Teddy's heart opened like a cracked safe.

"I work for the government," Smalls said.

"Is this a setup?" Graciella asked. "Is this about Nick?"

"Who's Nick?" Smalls asked Teddy.

"My husband," said Graciella.

"I have no idea why he just showed up," Teddy said to Graciella. "I haven't seen this guy in years."

"Don't be taken in," Smalls told her. "It's called billet reading. An old trick, almost as old as he is."

That was hurtful, trying to embarrass him in front of a younger woman. But she didn't seem to be listening to Smalls, thankfully. "I have to go," Graciella said. "The boys are getting dropped off soon."

Teddy rose with her. "I apologize for my acquaintance here."

"It was a pleasure meeting you," she said to Teddy. "I think." She started for the door.

Teddy scowled at Smalls, then said, "Graciella, just a second. One second." She was kind enough to wait for him.

"The last wish," he said, his voice low to keep Smalls out of it. "Was that about you? Are you going to be okay?"

"Of course I'll be okay," she said. "I'm the rock."

She marched across the parking lot. He had so many questions. The two words she'd written on the last slip were NOT GUILTY.

Destin Smalls, to Teddy's annoyance, took Graciella's seat.

"Still running the Carnac routine, Teddy?"

"You look like death's doorman," Teddy said. It had been four years since he'd seen the government agent, but he looked like he'd aged twice that. A bad patch. That's the way it happened. A body could hold the line for a decade, one Christmas photo just like the ten previous, then bam, the years zoomed up and flattened you like a Mack truck. The last of the man's football-hero good looks had been swallowed by age and carbohydrates. Now he was a blocky head on a big rectangular body, like a microwave atop a refrigerator.

"You have to know you'll never get past first base," Smalls said. "You're an old man. They talk to you because you're safe."

"I'm serious, your color looks like hell. What is it, ball cancer? Liver damage? I always took you for a secret drinker."

The waitress reappeared. If she was surprised that an attractive suburbaness had been replaced by a seventy-year-old spook, she didn't show it.

"Coffee for my friend here," Teddy said.

"No thank you," he said to her. "Water with lemon, please."

"I forgot, he's Mormon," Teddy told her. "Could you make sure the water's decaffeinated?"

She stared at him for a moment, then left without a word.

"I take it back, you can still charm them," Smalls said. "So how are the hands?"

"Good days and bad days," Teddy said.

"Good enough for the billet trick," Smalls said.

Teddy ignored that. "So what are you doing in Chicago? D.C. too hot for you?"

"They're trying to force me out," Smalls said. "They're closing Star Gate. They cut my funding to nothing."

"Star Gate's still running?" Teddy shook his head. "I can't believe they hadn't already chased you all out of the temple."

"Congress is shutting down every project in the SG umbrella. Too much media blowback."

"You mean media, period." Teddy leaned back, relaxing into it now, the old banter. "You guys never liked it that any honest report had to mention your complete lack of results."

"You know as well as I do that—"

Teddy held up a hand. "Excepting Maureen. But without her, you had nothing."

The waitress returned with the water and the coffeepot. She refilled Teddy's cup and vanished again.

"Here's to Maureen," Smalls said, and lifted his glass. "Forever ageless."

"Maureen."

After a while, Teddy said, "Too bad about the job. Nobody likes to be the last one to turn out the lights."

"It's a crime," Smalls said. "A strategic mistake. You think the Russians shut down the SCST?"

"Why not? They just shut down their whole country."

"Ex-KGB are still running the place. Not five years ago, we had intelligence that the Ministry of Agriculture was ahead of us on developing a micro-lepton gun."

"Jesus, are you still trying to build one of those? How much government dough have you spent on that?"

"That's classified."

"But somebody in Congress knows, don't they? No wonder they're shutting you down. Nobody but you believes in remote viewers and psychokinetics."

"Speaking of which, is Frankie staying out of casinos?"

"Leave Frankie out of it."

Smalls raised a hand in surrender. "How is he, then? And Buddy and Irene?"

"They're fine," Teddy lied. Frankie kept borrowing his money, Irene was depressed, and Buddy—Jesus, Buddy got worse every year. A mute and a recluse. Then a few months ago he started taking apart the house like a man who knew only half a magic trick. *Observe, ladies and gentlemen, while I smash this watch! Okay, now I'll, damn it . . . what was it?* "Buddy's turned into quite the handyman," Teddy said.

"You don't say. And the grandchildren? You have how many now?"

"Three and a half," Teddy said.

"Half?" Smalls looked surprised. "Is Irene pregnant again?"

"God I hope not. No. I mean Loretta's girl, Mary Alice."

"You shouldn't do that. Categorize like that. There's no such thing as a step-grandchild."

"You didn't come all the way to Chicago to ask me about my grandkids," Teddy said. "Strike that. That's exactly why you came out here, isn't it?"

Smalls shrugged. "Are any of them . . . showing signs?"

"I thought they were shutting down your program, Agent Smalls."

"It's not dead yet."

"Well, until it's dead or alive, keep the kids out of it. That was the deal you made with Maureen and me. That goes double for our grandchildren."

"There are two ends to that deal," Smalls said. "You're supposed to keep them out of trouble."

"You mean, keep them from using their great and terrible powers for evil."

"Or at all."

"Jesus, Smalls. Those grandkids, none of them can do so much as read a menu unless it's in front of them. Besides, the Cold War's over."

"Yet the world's more dangerous than ever. I need—*we* need—Star Gate and people like Maureen."

Teddy wasn't used to Smalls sounding desperate. But a desperate government agent, even one barely in the game, was a useful thing. "Fine," Teddy said. "Give me your number."

The abrupt capitulation surprised Smalls. He took a moment to pull a business card from his wallet. The face of it was blank except for Smalls's name, and a number. D.C. area code.

"They paid for you to fly all the way out here just to talk to me for ten minutes? I thought they cut your funding."

"Maybe I thought it was worth doing."

"Like you could convince them to—" Teddy stopped. The frown on Smalls's face told him he'd hit the mark. Teddy laughed. "You're robbing your own piggy bank for this? Jesus, you need to save for retirement. What's Brenda have to say about that?"

Smalls rubbed a thumb across his water glass.

"Oh Christ," Teddy said. "I'm sorry. She was a good woman."

"Yes. Well." He stood up, and pocketed the slip of paper. "You and I both married better than we deserved."

□

If nothing had happened after the day he first saw Maureen McKinnon—if Dr. Eldon hadn't seen his cartoon and flagged his application for inclusion in the study; if he hadn't also chosen Maureen; if he hadn't found himself side by side with her a few weeks later—well, her spell might have worn off.

First, though, had been his solo audition for Dr. Eldon. Two weeks after the initial survey, Teddy had been invited back on campus to discuss "his gift" and found himself in the doctor's weirdly shaped office, a bent L intruded upon by support beams, ductwork, and plumbing.

"I just see things," Teddy said. Not making too big a deal of it. "Especially on paper—there's something about the way people concentrate when they're writing or drawing that lets me see it more clearly."

Dr. Eldon nodded and scribbled in his notepad. Eldon was at least ten years older and fifty pounds heavier than his already unflattering picture in the faculty directory. "Do you think you could, ah, demonstrate something for me?" the doctor asked. His voice was soft and earnest, almost wheedling.

"Okay, sure," Teddy said. "I think I'm feeling strong enough to try. Do you have a piece of paper?" Of course he did. "Just make three drawings that are simple to visualize. Something famous, or a simple cartoon figure, or geometric shapes, whatever you like."

Teddy got up from his chair, walked a few feet away, and turned his back to him. "I'll cover my eyes," he said. "Just tell me when you're finished."

Dr. Eldon frowned in concentration, then drew his first figure. Teddy couldn't believe how well this was going. He'd been sure Eldon would insist on doing *his* tests, under all kinds of laboratory controls, but instead he was letting Teddy run the show. This was *easier* than bar work, where the marks were always looking up his sleeves—or into his cupped palm, where he currently held a tiny mirror that allowed him to watch the academic. It never crossed Eldon's mind to wonder why a guy with his back to him also needed to cover his eyes.

When the professor was done, Teddy slipped the mirror back into his pocket and told him to fold the papers into squares.

"I'm not going to do these in order," Teddy said. "I'm just going to sort through the images as I get them, and you'll tell me if I'm in the ballpark."

Teddy pressed the first square to the front of his hat. Pretended to concentrate. Then he put that square down and picked up the next one, then the next, squinting and wincing his way through each one.

"I'm receiving images," Teddy said. The first thing Dr. Eldon had drawn was a Mickey Mouse face. Typical. Tell somebody to draw "a simple cartoon figure" and that was the first thing that came to mind. The other drawings were straightforward enough. The second one was a pyramid. And the third was an airplane.

"So many things," he said. "I'm getting a bird flying over a mountain. No, it's a triangle. A triangle mountain? And a big circle, maybe the moon? No, there's more than one circle. They're kind of stacked up around each other, and the bird . . ." He shook his head as if confused. "The bird is . . . metal? Oh!" He all but snapped his fingers. "It's a plane. A triangle and a plane. But what's with the circles?" He tapped his forehead. "There are two of them behind one middle circle. Like the Olympic rings, but not as many, you know? It seems so familiar, so . . ."

Teddy slumped in his chair, looking defeated. Dr. Eldon stared at him, his face stiff with the effort of hiding his delight.

"I'm sorry, Doc," Teddy said. "That's all I got."

"It's quite all right," the professor said softly. Then: "You did very well."

"Did I?"

Dr. Eldon passed him the pages, and Teddy pretended to be as amazed as the academic felt. "Mickey Mouse! Of course!"

Dr. Eldon grinned in satisfaction. "So would you be willing to participate further?"

Teddy could almost hear the sha-ring of a cash register. He didn't respond right away. "I have to work most days," he said apologetically. "I can't afford to skip too often."

Eldon said, "There will be a stipend for all research participants."

"Enough to lay off a day's work?"

"A significant stipend."

"Well then, that sounds fine," Teddy said.

Dr. Eldon said, "I'm afraid we have to stop now; there are other participants waiting. When you go back to the room, could you, ah, send the next person in?" Then with a wry smile he couldn't repress: "I think you can guess who it is."

Teddy played dumb, even as his heart tightened in his chest. "I'm sorry? Is this part of the test?"

"You mentioned to Beatrice—that's my secretary—that you got a flash of a young woman meeting with me."

"Oh, right!" Teddy said. "Is she back there?" He was proud at how steady his voice was. "Who do I ask for?"

Dr. Eldon glanced down at a list of names that lay on the desk in front of him. All but the last three had been checked off. "Her name's Maureen McKinnon."

This was the first time he'd heard her name spoken aloud. He liked the music of it. "No problem, sir." He bent over the list as if making sure of her name. "Miss McKinnon. Got it."

He walked to the classroom down the hall, the same room where he'd filled out the application forms two weeks earlier. It had been empty and dim before his interview, but now three people were there: the young black man, wearing the same tie and maybe the same shirt; the white, slick-haired mole boy; and the girl of his dreams. She sat in the first row, legs crossed under a blue skirt with yellow polka dots, one dainty yellow shoe like a ballet slipper kicking nervously.

The black man sat several rows back, but mole boy was right next to her, talking eagerly. See what happens? Leave a girl alone in the room, and some pimply-faced kid immediately starts bird-dogging her.

The kid held a copper-colored key in his hand, and he was saying, "It's all about concentration. Imposing your will."

"Whatcha doing?" Teddy asked Maureen. Ignoring the boy.

She looked up and smiled. "He's trying to bend a key."

"With my mind," the kid said.

"You don't say! Is your name Russell Trago?"

"That's right."

Teddy had read his name off the list, and took a guess that this was Russell. Which made the black man Clifford Turner. "You're up next, Russell. Good luck in there."

"Okay! Thanks." He put the key on the desk, then said to Maureen, "Remember what I said. Impose your will."

Teddy slid into the seat he'd vacated, and picked up the key. Weird that he'd left it behind. Usually a man liked to keep his props with him. "Still flat," he said.

"He barely got started," Maureen said.

"That's too bad; it looked fascinating, just fascinating. I'm Teddy, by the way. Teddy Telemachus."

"I'm—"

"Don't tell me. Mary. No. Something like Mary, or Irene . . ." A pen and a piece of paper sat on the desk in front of her—the invitation from Dr. Eldon. He could use that paper if it came to it. Maybe do the Three Wishes routine for her. "Wait, is it Maureen?"

"Aren't you a clever one," she said. He liked that gleam in her eye. "It's not really Russell's turn, is it? They sent you out here to get me."

"Ah. You're too smart for me, Maureen McKinnon."

"What did he have you do?"

He told her about the guess-the-drawing game, but refrained from explaining how he'd done it—or how easily.

"They seemed quite excited when I picked the first one," he said. "I thought it was a triangle, but it turned out to be a pyramid."

"Oh! Really?" She seemed a little *too* surprised.

"Why, you think ol' Trago is the only one with powers beyond those of mortal men?"

"It's not that," she said. "It's just that—"

He picked up the key and said, "Let me give it a try."

"You bend keys, too?"

"Among other things," he said. He closed his fist around it. "But I may need your help with this one." He scooted the desk closer to her. "It's not about imposing your will. You just have to *ask* the object to bend. The object wants to listen to you. All you have to do is think, Bend . . . Bend . . . And you know what happens?"

"I hope 'explode' isn't on the menu," she said.

He laughed. "Only if you yell at it. You have to ask sweetly."

It was a simple trick. He'd already passed the key to his left hand.

When he'd moved the desk, he'd jammed the tip beneath the desk lid and pushed down. The bend wasn't much, just twenty or thirty degrees, but all the best magic tricks started small.

"Let's see how we're doing," he said. He began rubbing the closed fist, which let him pass the key back into his right palm. He allowed the tip of the key to appear between thumb and index finger.

"You say it now," Teddy said. *"Bend."*

"Bend," Maureen said.

"Please bend," he said.

"*Please* bend," she said.

He slowly pushed the key up, between thumb and index finger, letting more and more of it appear, exposing the bend.

"Oh no," Maureen said.

"What's the matter?"

"I might have trouble getting back into the house."

"It's *your* key?"

"I thought you realized—"

"I thought it was his! You gave that kid your only house key to play with?"

"I didn't think he could actually *do* anything," she said.

This seemed hilarious to both of them. They were laughing when Russell Trago returned to the room, looking wounded. Maureen covered her mouth. Trago seemed to sense he was the target of their laughter.

"They said they wanted Maureen," he said. Looking at Teddy.

"Oh," Teddy said. "Sorry. My mistake."

Maureen slid out from her desk, then held out her hand. He pressed the warped key into her palm.

"What happened?" Trago said. His eyes widened. "Did I bend it?"

Teddy saluted her as she walked away. "Knock 'em dead, Maureen McKinnon."

She'd left behind the pen and paper. She'd folded it over, hiding it from Trago maybe when he sat beside her. Teddy unfolded it. There were three drawings:

Pyramid.

Airplane.

Mickey Mouse.

"Holy Christ on a stick!" Teddy exclaimed.

He ticked through the usual methods, then ruled them out one by one. Yes, he'd told her about the first drawing, but not the other two. The distance to Dr. Eldon's office made eavesdropping impossible. Plus, Trago had been in the room with her during most of Teddy's interview, trying to bend her God damn house key, with Clifford Turner as witness. There was no method that Teddy knew of to see those drawings, from this far away.

There was only one explanation. Maureen McKinnon, nineteen years old, was the best damn scam artist he'd ever met.

☐

Teddy drove home from the diner thinking about amazing coincidences. He didn't believe in them unless he engineered them himself. But how to account for meeting Graciella, the most interesting woman he'd talked to in years, on the same day that Destin Smalls strolled back into his life? Like Graciella, he smelled a setup, but it wasn't Smalls who set it up. Not his style. The agent moved in straight lines like a righteous ox.

Teddy parked his Buick in the garage, went out the side door, and stopped dead. A hole had appeared in the backyard, and Buddy was in it, thigh deep, and shoveling deeper.

"Buddy!"

His son looked up at him, curious. Naked from the waist up, which only made him look fatter.

"What the hell are you doing?"

Buddy looked down at the hole, then back at Teddy.

"It's a God damn hole in the middle of the yard!"

Buddy didn't say anything. Of course. Buddy had decided he was Marcel Marceau.

"Put it back." He waved at the mounds of dirt all round him. "Put it back *now*."

Buddy looked away. Jesus Christ. The kid used to be so talented. Could have made them all rich, just by sitting around writing numbers with his crayons. Now he'd turned into a God damn golden retriever, digging holes in the lawn.

Teddy threw up his hands, marched into the house. There were dishes in the kitchen sink, but at least all the appliances were still in one piece. In the front room, Matty sat cross-legged on the couch, swami-style, his eyes closed.

"What the hell are *you* doing?"

Matty's eyes snapped open. "What? Nothing!" Then: "Thinking."

"You're doing a hell of a job." Teddy placed the Borsalino atop the rack. "Why aren't you at school?"

The kid hopped up. "School's over."

"What?"

"Half day for the last day of school. It's summer vacation." He was chubby, pale like Maureen's side of the family, short like Teddy's. Poor bastard. Literally. His mom was broke, and his dad had abandoned the family years ago.

"And now what?" Teddy asked.

Matty blinked up at him.

"You're going to be around here all the time?"

"Uh . . ."

How had he lost all control of his house? Home is a castle my ass. More like a refugee camp. He picked up the pile of mail on the front table, started shuffling through the envelopes. Bill, bill, junk mail. Another one of those computer disks. America Online. Got one every damn day, sometimes two in the same day.

"Why don't you clean up the kitchen," Teddy said. "We'll start cooking when your mom comes home." That was the best thing about having Irene back in the house. When it was just Teddy and Buddy, it was Chinese takeout three nights a week. Takeout or omelets.

Matty moved past him, and Teddy put out a hand, a five-dollar bill between his fingers. "Say, kid. You got change for a five?"

Matty put his hands in his pockets. Too early and too obviously, but they could work on that. "I don't know, mister. Let me check." A little telltale smile. They'd have to work on that, too. "Yeah, I think so." Plucked the fiver from Teddy's fingers, started folding it.

"Hey, I said I needed change," Teddy said, playing the gruff customer.

"Oh, I'll change it." Teddy had taught him the patter, too. Matty unfolded the bill carefully, then stretched it out between his hands. "How about that?"

The five had turned into a two-dollar bill.

"Give it a little snap," Teddy said. "Like a towel. Make 'em hear it. And don't smile till the end. Tips 'em off." The kid nodded, then went off to the kitchen without offering to return his five. At least he'd learned that much: never give the money back.

Teddy looked at the last envelope in the pile and felt a pinprick in his heart. Recognized the handwriting, that graceful, quick hand. Say what you will about Catholic school, those nuns knew how to teach cursive. Above the house address it said simply "Teddy." No return address.

He dropped the rest of the mail back onto the table, then walked upstairs to his bedroom, gazing at the envelope, feeling heavier with every step.

God damn it, Maureen.

He went into his bedroom and shut the door. As always, he was tempted to leave the letter unopened. But as always, he couldn't stop himself. Slit open the envelope, and read what she'd written. Then he dialed open the door to the little safe in his closet.

Inside, above the velvet tray that held his watches, was a stack of older envelopes. He used to get one every week. Then every few months. The last one had come a little over four years ago.

He held the envelope to his nose. Breathed in. Couldn't smell anything but the old paper. Then he tossed it onto the stack with the rest and shut the door.

3

Irene

Nothing killed nostalgia for your childhood home like moving back into it. She'd come limping back to Chicago in her eight-year-old Ford Festiva, a teenage son in the passenger seat sprouting and stewing from every pore, dragging a U-Haul crammed with the entirety of her possessions: a mattress and box spring; a wood-veneer coffee table; two sturdy kitchen chairs; and two dozen wet cardboard boxes labeled HUMILIATION and DISAPPOINTMENT.

She was thirty-one years old. She'd failed to achieve escape velocity, and the crash landing was brutal.

There'd been a few Christmases, back when things were going almost okay in Pittsburgh, that she'd feel a thrill of warmth when she turned the corner into her old neighborhood and saw that pale green house, the hedges glowing with fat red and green lightbulbs, and the little square window on the second floor that marked her bedroom. Behind the house loomed the huge weeping willow, and when she saw its naked winter limbs she'd think of five-year-old Buddy up there, fearless in those years before their mother died, swaying in the high branches.

Now the first look at the house when she came home from work made her chest tighten in something like despair. She'd pull up after a nine-hour shift at Aldi's, feet aching and brain punch-drunk with boredom, and realize, again, that the house was a trap.

Lately it had been a trap under construction, and today was no exception. She couldn't even get into the driveway because of a stack of lumber. Annoyed, she parked on the street and went in through the front door. In the front hallway were three white boxes of various sizes, each splotched with black Holstein patches.

"Mom!" Matty shouted. He practically threw himself down the stairs. "Is this ours? Did you buy this?"

"I don't even know what it is."

"It's a Gateway 2000! And a monitor. And a printer, I'm pretty sure." He squatted beside the biggest box. "It's got a built-in modem, with a *Pentium*." The back of his head was matted and greasy.

"Don't touch it. We might have to give it back. What time did you sleep to?"

"Uh, pretty late."

"Did you take a shower today?"

"Sure."

She looked hard at him.

"I mean, not *yet*. I was about to, then the computer—"

"You're fourteen, Matty. You can't walk around like a caveman." And he should have known, too, that he couldn't lie to her. Was he hoping that someday she'd be so distracted she wouldn't notice?

"Can't I just look at it?" Matty asked.

"Where's your grandpa?"

"Out back, talking on the phone. Somebody called Smalls? Deep voice. He wanted Grandpa."

"*Destin* Smalls?"

Matty shrugged. She started for the kitchen and the back door.

"I promise, I won't even break the packing material," he said.

"Do *not* open anything," she answered.

Out on the patio, Teddy sat in a lawn chair reading a newspaper, his knees crossed, shoes gleaming. He wore his suit jacket despite the heat. The air smelled like cigarette smoke, but there was no cigarette in sight. His left hand rested mock-casually on the aluminum arm of the chair. The cordless phone lay on the cement beside him.

"Why is Destin Smalls calling you?" Irene asked.

Teddy didn't look up from the news. "It's none of your business."

"Is he going to arrest you?"

That got him to lower his paper. It was the *Tribune*, which was weird. They were a *Sun-Times* family. "Don't be ridiculous," Teddy said. "He's practically retired."

"Then why'd he call?"

"Old friends check in, Irene. That's a normal human activity."

"Since when is he your friend?"

"Jesus Christ." He raised the paper again—and immediately dropped it. "And could you get those boxes out of the front hall? Nearly broke my neck."

"They're not mine. Did Buddy order a computer?"

"Who the hell knows what Buddy does."

"Where would he get the money? That's, like, two thousand dollars."

"Two grand? For a computer? What do you do with it?"

"You can go on the Internet," Matty said. "Or do homework on it." He'd appeared in the doorway, keyed up as a puppy.

"I'm not having you sit around this house playing computer games," she said.

"Can we ask Uncle Buddy if we can open them?" Matty asked.

"What's for dinner?" Teddy asked.

"I'm not making dinner tonight," Irene said.

"I didn't ask you to."

"I think you just did. I'm busy enough, making a cake."

"A cake? Why would you—oh. Maureen's birthday."

"Buddy would have a fit if we didn't celebrate."

"Did I say I didn't want to celebrate? Of course I do."

"Good, because Frankie and Loretta are coming over."

"Hey, maybe Buddy bought the computer as a birthday present," Matty said.

"For his dead mother?" Irene said.

"It's Buddy," Matty said reasonably.

"You make the cake, I'll take care of dinner," Teddy said, as if it was his idea. "I was thinking pizza."

"You hate pizza," Irene said.

"No, I hate *most* pizzas. I have high standards. I used to stop by this restaurant in Irving Park. Nick Pusateri ran it. He could do this crispy crust, just snap in your mouth like a God damn cracker. I used to bring them home for you guys."

Irene had forgotten all about them. He'd carry them in on a cardboard bottom with a puff of white paper over them, no boxes. You'd break open that paper and delicious steam would bathe your face.

"He had a son, Nick Junior," Teddy said. "Not the brightest bulb. Somehow managed to become a real estate developer and get rich."

"You don't say," she said.

"So last week, I run into this woman at Dominick's. Never met her before. Her name's Graciella, has three kids. And guess who her husband is?"

"If it's not Nick Junior, then you're shitty at telling stories."

"I'm going to ask Uncle Buddy," Matty said, and vanished back inside.

"Small world, right?" Teddy said. "Small God damn world." He put aside the paper and pushed himself out of the lawn chair. "I'll be back for dinner." He set his hat on his head, then adjusted the angle. He stepped out the side gate just as Matty came sprinting up. The kid had run all the way around the house.

"Buddy says I can open it!" Matty said.

"He did?" Irene said.

"Well, I asked him if I could, and he nodded."

"Fine. You can set it up in the basement—*after* you take a shower. And do *not* install the Internet!" He ran inside again.

She watched her father back the car out of the garage, going extremely slowly. She wondered how many years were left before they had to take away his keys. It was a certainty that she'd have to make the call alone. Buddy was oblivious and Frankie was too much in the sway of the Legend of Teddy Telemachus to take action.

She picked up the newspaper Teddy had been reading. A headline was circled in black marker: PUSATERI OUTFIT MURDER TRIAL BEGINS. She read the first paragraph, then the second.

"God damn it," she said.

"What is it?" Matty said from behind her.

"Your grandfather's hanging out with mobsters," she said. "Again."

"Really?" He sounded more excited by this than she liked. She looked up and saw that he was wearing only a towel.

"The water's turned off downstairs," he explained. Matty and Irene had been using the downstairs shower, ceding the upstairs bath to Dad and Buddy.

"Use the other one," she said, and walked into the kitchen, reading.

Nick Pusateri Jr. may take the stand in his own defense, his legal team said Monday. This continues weeks of speculation about whether Pusateri, accused of the 1992 slaying of Willowbrook businessman Richard Mazzione, would testify. Pusateri is thought to be a high-ranking member of the Chicago Outfit, and the son of alleged crew boss Nick Pusateri Sr. Prosecutors are eager to implicate other members of the organization.

She finished the article and dropped the paper into the garbage. Murder, mobsters, and Destin Fucking Smalls. Whatever was going on with her father, she didn't like it.

☆

The death of her mother was the landmark by which Irene navigated her memories. The day she first met Destin Smalls was only seven months before Maureen's death. It was early in February, on the morning Irene found her mother crying.

Irene couldn't remember why she'd gone upstairs to look for her. It was a school day, so perhaps Irene wanted to complain about Buddy or Frankie not getting ready. When she pushed open the door to her parents' bedroom, she found her mother sitting on the edge of the bed, palms on her thighs, eyes closed. Tears had traced a line down each cheek.

There was something obscene about the sight. It was not just that her mother rarely cried; it was that the tears were falling and she was doing nothing to wipe them away, nothing to hide them. It was the most naked she'd ever seen her mother.

Perhaps Irene gasped; something made her mother's eyes snap open. And still she didn't wipe at the tears. She glanced at Irene, but then her attention moved somewhere else, somewhere inside.

Irene said, "Are you divorcing Dad?"

Her mother seemed to take a moment to parse the words. "What?" Then: "Why would you say that?"

There were so many reasons Irene could name. The fact that Dad slept on the basement couch now. That when he woke up he stalked the house in silence, scowling at every noise the kids made, barking at them, *For Christ's sake go play outside!* He was not a drunk, Irene decided later, when she'd come to know a few, but he had the alcoholic's tunnel vision, the addict's hollowed wound. This was the winter Dad got into a car accident and spent weeks with bandages on his hands, the winter after the summer of *The Mike Douglas Show* and the family's public humiliation. Somehow he made the house feel as small as one of those hotel rooms they'd stayed in when the Amazing Telemachus Family had been on tour.

"You didn't say no," Irene said, as if catching her in a trick.

Anger flashed on her mother's face, raw and fierce. Her hands had not moved, but Irene felt as if she'd been slapped. For a long moment, no one spoke.

Irene realized that Buddy had come up behind her. His sixth birthday would be soon, but he looked younger, a big baby head on a skinny body, no hint that he'd someday be the tallest of them.

Her mother, finally, wiped one cheek with the knuckles of her hand. "You're a bright girl, with a great talent, and I love you." She stood up. Her mouth was set in a hard line. "But you've got to learn some manners. And no, I'm not divorcing your father."

She walked out of the room and downstairs. Irene followed her, and Buddy trailed silently after. Her mother took her winter coat from the coatrack and pulled it on.

"Where are you going?" Irene asked. It was not yet eight in the morning.

"To work. Walk Buddy to the bus stop. Make sure Frankie gets out of bed."

"You have a *job*?" Irene was outraged that she hadn't been told this.

"Don't wake your father." Her mother opened the front door. Cold rushed in and circled Irene's bare legs like a frantic dog.

Outside it was gray on gray, snowflakes hovering in the air, the world rendered as a pencil sketch. Her mother walked toward a dark sedan parked in the driveway, its exhaust puffing clouds. A man in a long coat stepped out of the driver's side. He said something to her mother that Irene didn't hear, and opened the passenger door for her. He touched the small of her back as she stepped around him, and then closed the door behind her. Then he turned, and saw Irene standing in the doorway, Buddy holding on to her legs.

"You two will catch cold!" he said in a friendly tone. He was square-jawed and tall, twice the size of her father. And twice as handsome. His black hair was parted with Ken doll precision.

Irene shut the door—and immediately stepped to the picture window and pushed aside the drapes. The car backed out of the driveway, leaving tracks that she was sure her father would notice when he awoke. But no: by the time she escorted Buddy to his bus stop a half hour later, the snow had already filled them in.

☆

Here's a question of etiquette that could only come up in the Telemachus family: Who should blow out the candles on a dead woman's cake? They used to let Buddy do it, but then Cassie and Polly started begging for the honor, and not even Buddy could turn down the twins when they were in Full Cute mode.

"Go to town, girls," Irene said to the twins. There were seven candles on the cake. There should have been fifty-two, but Irene didn't dare have that much fire around the girls. So five yellows, one for each decade, and two reds for remainder. Buddy watched anxiously until each candle was extinguished.

Maureen Telemachus had died twenty-one years ago, when she was thirty-one, the same age as Irene was now. This is the last year I have a mother, Irene thought. From now on she'll be younger than me.

Hardly anyone talked as they ate. Loretta, usually in a good mood, seemed subdued. Buddy's silence was no mystery, but Teddy's was. He'd brought home the pizza—a pair of Giordano's, thick as motorcycle tires, not the crispy style that he'd been rhapsodizing about earlier—but wouldn't say where else he'd been for the rest of the two hours since he'd left the house. He was distracted, and picked at his cake as if he couldn't decide what it was.

Frankie's silence, however, was aggressive, peppered with grunts that begged for someone to ask what was the matter. Irene already knew. Two weeks ago Frankie had taken her and Dad out to dinner at the Pegasus, all on Frankie's dime, he said, because he had some *fantastic news* to share. It wasn't until they were done with the meal that he came clean. His *fantastic news* was that Teddy and Irene could become distributors in something called UltraLife, which he claimed was *the fastest-growing multilevel marketing company in the United States.*

At the Pegasus, Teddy had said, "When you say multilevel marketing—"

"He means pyramid scheme," Irene had said.

That comment pretty much ruined the rest of the night. And the rest of Frankie's month, evidently. But why did he think he could convince Irene or Teddy to invest in such an obvious scam? Irene was broke, and Teddy, though he had plenty of money (from sources he would not identify), refused to bankroll his kids. *He'd* grown up poor, and clawed his way out of poverty on his own, which in his mind was the ultimate test of evolutionary fitness. How many times had he told his children: Never lend chips to someone who can't buy their way into the pot.

Irene blamed her father for Frankie's crooked little heart. Dad had filled his head with tales of gambling and gangsters, schemes and scams, con men and ex-cons. On the road, he'd sit eight-year-old Frankie on a hotel bed and teach him how to do a false cut. (Not Irene, though, not a single card trick. That stuff wasn't for girls.) He'd constantly say to Frankie, You're going to go far, kid! And Frankie would eat it up. He'd spend hours trying—and failing—to levitate pencils and spare change and paper clips. By the time the family got booked onto TV, Frankie was planning his solo career as a Vegas headliner, despite having no ability with either psychokinesis or sleight of hand. It wasn't until Mom's funeral that he showed a hint of talent, and by then it was too late to help the act.

Once Mom died, there were no adults driving the bus. Teddy closed his eyes and refused to take the wheel. Frankie became a free-range malcontent, and Buddy became, well, Buddy.

Matty said, "We got a computer."

He wasn't looking at Mary Alice, who sat beside him, but that's who he was addressing. She didn't seem to notice. She stared at her uneaten cake as if it were an unmoving clock.

Frankie squinted at Irene. "You can afford a computer?"

"I didn't buy it. Buddy did."

"Buddy?"

"I set it up downstairs," Matty said. "If, uh, anybody wants to look at it."

Frankie turned to his brother. "What the hell do *you* need with a computer?"

Buddy sought out Irene's eyes with a classic Buddy look: mystified and sorrowful, like a cocker spaniel who'd finally eviscerated his great enemy, only to find everyone angry and taking the side of the couch pillow.

"He bought it for Matty," Irene said, even though she was not at all sure about that. "He's going to pay him back, when he gets a job."

"I am?" Matty said.

"He can't sit around all day," Teddy said. It was the first thing he'd said since the cake came out. Thanks for that, Dad.

"I could help Uncle Buddy," Matty said.

"Ha," Frankie said. "Have you seen the way he works? I'm surprised he hasn't electrocuted himself. Keep your distance, kid. It's bad enough Buddy's going to kill himself."

Buddy's eyes widened.

"Figure of speech," Loretta said kindly.

"No, he'll work with me," Frankie said.

"At the phone company?" Irene asked.

"He'll be my apprentice."

Loretta said, "Maybe you shouldn't promise anything until—"

"Nobody tells me who rides in my van," Frankie said. "It's settled. He starts Monday."

Irene lay on top of the covers, exhausted but unable to quiet her brain. When she'd gone to bed that night she'd plummeted into unconsciousness, and had disappeared into two hours of dreamless sleep before being hauled up into the waking world, her thoughts wrapped up like seaweed on a fishhook.

In other words, the usual. Wide awake in the thin hours of the night, her mind churning along on the All-Star Tour of Embarrassments and Mistakes. The tour could visit any decade, and feature any number of characters from her past, from middle-school girlfriends to strangers she'd never known the names of. She'd remember a conversation or, more often, an argument, and try desperately to get her previous self to say something smarter, or kinder, or nothing at all. Yester-Irene's behavior, however, was almost willfully resistant to modification.

Lately the tour had been returning again and again to the most disastrous period in her life: the last year in Pittsburgh. In that time she'd gone from dream job (or at least, the best she could hope for with only an associate's degree) to alleged criminal. It had broken her financially and emotionally. Matty had caught her more than once sitting at the kitchen table, hate-crying into a pile of bills and overdue notices. Which only made her feel worse. A child shouldn't see his mother worrying about money. It made the kid into a figurehead parent, with all the responsibility and none of the power. She knew this from personal experience.

She pulled on her robe and went into the hall. The house was quiet except for Buddy's snore. Her usual insomnia treatment was to read until the book dropped out of her hand, but when sleep seemed impossibly out of reach, she'd do penance for her wakefulness by performing some onerous task: cleaning out the refrigerator, balancing the checkbook, verifying the date of each canned good in Dad's basement pantry. (Scariest find: a can of kidney beans purchased by her mother twenty-five years ago.) Some nights Irene came dangerously close to pitching in on one of Buddy's renovation projects.

None of that appealed to her tonight. She went downstairs and drifted through the first-floor rooms, her eyes growing wide in the dark. Surfaces caught errant light and became strange. Objects trembled with arrested motion, waiting for her to glance away. Every chair and table became a wary animal. Don't be afraid, she thought. It's just me.

Irene had realized at her mother's funeral not only that she had inherited her position as Sole Responsible Adult, but that she'd been training for the job since she was ten. She was the one who'd managed Buddy's tantrums. She was the one who'd poured water onto Frankie's bed to get him up and out to school. (Only had to do that twice, but it worked.) Most of all, she learned how to keep Dad out of her way. She resented the job, but she was secretly proud of it. She knew that if she had not grabbed the wheel, they would have all gone over the cliff.

It wasn't until the winter after she'd graduated high school, in the wide backseat of the Green Machine, that she was asked the question she'd been waiting to hear all her life. Lev Petrovski, half naked and beautiful and sweating despite the frost outside the windows, pressed his forehead to hers and whispered, "But who's going to take care of you, Irene?"

This was not a statement she could weigh for truth. It was a question, and her heart shouted the answer: *You*, Lev. You will.

What a stupid, stupid girl she was.

On her second circuit of the first floor, she became aware of a faint, shifting light emanating from the basement. She went down the stairs and saw that Matty had left the new PC running. Multicolored lines zigzagged across the screen.

She sat at the desk (a battered hulk that had once occupied a corner of Frankie and Buddy's bedroom) and touched the keyboard. A field of blue appeared, and icons popped up like square flowers. It was a new version of Windows, and everything seemed shinier and somehow more insistent than what she'd used at her old job. Back then she'd been considered the office computer expert, not because of any actual expertise, but because her immediate supervisor had abdicated all technological responsibility. It fell to Irene to print out the electronic mail (or else how could the partners read it?) and become the guru of Word-Perfect and Lotus 1-2-3.

She bent to look for the computer's off switch, and noticed that Matty had already hooked it up to a phone jack. *It's got a built-in modem!*

Irene got up without turning off the machine. The little clock on the screen said that it was 12:32.

She went upstairs and found the stack of mail that had accumulated over the past couple of days. There were five AOL CDs, each one promising 50 FREE HOURS! Well, she thought, if there was one thing she had, it was free hours.

A few minutes later, the modem squealed loud enough to wake everyone in the house—or so it seemed; the night made the house seem both larger and smaller than it was in daytime. Soon the screen filled with a wall of colorful, rectangular buttons: "Today's News," "Clubs &

Interests," "Personal Finance," "Entertainment." And this one: "People Connection," with a picture of two men and two women, laughing and smiling with their arms around each other. Her mouse cursor hovered over it, then slid away to safety. Who were these people? What the hell were they so happy about? And why should she connect with them?

She went exploring elsewhere, reading new stories she wouldn't have bothered with if not for the novelty of them being on-screen, and looked through the "Education" section in case there was anything that might be of use to Matty. It was like wandering her house, except that everything was bright and blinking and pixelated.

Eventually, though, she returned to the "People Connection" button. She stared at it for ten, fifteen seconds. Then clicked.

She was presented with a page of "Chat Room Listings" that gave her another batch of online metaphors to unravel. She could chat (which meant type), in a room that didn't exist, to people she couldn't see. The number of categories was overwhelming: Friends, Gay & Lesbian, Town Hall . . . Romance. She could almost hear their desperate clamoring behind the screen. *Do you like me now? Am I funny? Oh, sure, I work out all the time . . .*

No. Nope. Nada. She was not going to become one of those lonely people sitting up all night bleaching their eyes against a computer monitor. She signed off, turned off the PC, and went upstairs to find a junk drawer to clean out.

It took all of two days for Matty to notice. He met her at the front door as she walked in from work, his voice quaking with indignation. *"You installed AOL?"* Then: *"Without telling me?"*

Irene flushed with embarrassment. "It was an experiment. We're not paying for it, so forget it."

"I'll pay! Frankie's giving me a job."

"Frankie says a lot of things that don't happen. And even if you paid, I wouldn't let you on AOL."

"What are you afraid of? It's just the Internet!"

"The Internet is made out of people," Irene said. "Terrible people." She'd gone back online a second night, and had quickly learned that the AOL interface was little more than a colorful picnic blanket thrown over a seething pit of sex. She was not going to tell him how much time she'd spent staring into that tawdry abyss. Matty was at an age at which dirty talk would be kerosene thrown on an already burning crotch.

Last week the inevitable happened. Long after he'd headed up to bed, she'd gone into his room to deliver a load of laundry and found him rigid on the mattress, holding himself, staring up at the ceiling. She said a quick "Sorry!" and backed out of the room—and then was struck by the fact that he hadn't moved a muscle, or even covered himself. Had the shock paralyzed him?

She knocked on the door. "Matty? Are you okay?" Then: "Of course you're okay, it's fine, it's natural." He didn't answer. "I know you're embarrassed, but I really need you to answer me right now."

She pushed the door open an inch, not looking in. "Matty?" She heard a heavy thump.

"Matty?"

"I'm here!" he yelled. "Everything's okay!"

I'm here? She left him alone, and told herself she'd talk about this later with him. She'd already put him through a sex talk that left him mortified and mute. She didn't want to go further. That's what dads were for.

Except Matty's. Lev Petrovski was somewhere in Colorado, she'd heard, living in the woods where the postal system was so primitive that child support payments could not make their way out. Evidently.

Sometimes she worried that her son had inherited some of Lev's weasel DNA. As Matty had grown up, he was learning to dodge her questions, just like his father, who was practically a *Jeopardy!* champion in his skill at phrasing every answer in the form of a question. When she asked Lev about getting married, he replied with, "Cool! When do you want to do it?" If she expressed doubt about his commitment, he'd bounce back with, "Hey, babe, don't you know I'm your guy?" Then later, he'd touch her belly and say, "Aren't you psyched about this baby?"

She didn't know if she'd subconsciously taught Lev to speak to her like this, or if he'd known instinctively that it was the best method of slipping under her radar. Either way, his fluency in this mirror dialect made him the only boyfriend she could tolerate, and for a while, the only man she trusted. Maybe she was led astray by the few times he'd expressed his feelings directly, in the early days of their relationship.

Only when they were making love did he allow himself to be swept away by declaratives. "I want you," he said to her, his hand slipping up her shirt. "I need you." And then, when he was about to come: "I love you."

Irene's power gave her no access to absolute truth; she could only know whether or not the speaker believed what he was saying. In that moment, Lev was telling the truth. And that allowed Irene to lie to herself.

Her fourth night behind the screen, she was asked to join her first private chat.

She wasn't in the Romance room when it happened, thank God. That's where she'd started on her second night. In minutes, two different people had asked her, "A/S/L?" She had no idea what that meant; American Sign Language? The next day, after work, she stopped at the Waldenbooks and thumbed through *America Online for Dummies*, looking for definitions, and realized they were asking for Age/Sex/Location. It seemed incredibly rude, until she realized that if she were at a bar, a man would instantly know her Location, and could make reasonable guesses about her Age and Sex. Likewise, she'd be able to tell if she was talking to a man or a twelve-year-old wearing a trench coat and a fake mustache. That second night in the Romance chat room, she was having a perfectly nice, if erratically spelled, conversation with RICHARD LONG when he typed, "SO NOW YOU WAN TO SUCK MY DICK?????"

She didn't go back to the Romance chat room.

Eventually she found an area for single parents that seemed to be inhabited by real adults, because they talked about things no teenager would find interesting: divorce settlements; insurance premiums; whether grounding a child was more punishing for the parent; insomnia. Yet after her experiences in other chat rooms, she kept waiting for, say, BUCKEYEFAN21 to ask her to touch her nipples.

For the first time in her life, she was unable to tell if someone was intentionally lying to her. In this 2-D world of text, these "people connections" were little more than paper dolls with screen names scrawled on their faces.

Yet. As much as she tried not to be drawn in by the creatures of Flatland, after just a few days it was hard not to think of a select few of them as flesh and blood. LAST DAD STANDING, for example, sounded convincingly like a divorced, slightly lonely man who worked at some kind of white-collar job and took care of a grade-school-age daughter. He lived in the Mountain Time Zone, and so usually came online around the same time of night as she did. She looked forward to him showing up, because he was one of the few people who both typed in complete sentences and got her jokes. It was such a relief to not have to type ":)" after every jab of sarcasm—and she liked to jab a lot.

Then tonight, after she'd mentioned that she was feeling stressed, he suggested they start a private chat. It was a bit like being asked to sneak behind the bleachers. Was she the kind of girl who had private chats? How did one even begin such a thing? Literally, how did one start a private chat?

> IRENE T: You'll have to tell me what to do. I've never done that
> before.
> LAST DAD STANDING: I'll be gentle.

No smiley faces—yet she understood that he was joking. Only joking.

In a few clicks, nothing had changed except the title of the chat window, but she was surprised to find that the basement felt cozier, like a private booth in a crowded restaurant. America was online all around them, but Irene and her new friend were huddled together, talking in low voices.

She decided to tell him about the wreck she'd made of her life in Pittsburgh.

> LAST DAD STANDING: Yes, but what KIND of clusterfuck?
> IRENE T: Like all the great ones, it begins with "It was all going
> great, and then . . ."
> LAST DAD STANDING: Ha! I know that story.
> IRENE T: I had a pretty good job. Better money than I'd ever
> had.
> LAST DAD STANDING: Doing what?
> IRENE T: I worked for a financial services company.
> LAST DAD STANDING: I'm guessing that's a company that provides
> financial services.

IRENE: Change the word "services" to "screwing" and you've
　　got it.
LAST DAD STANDING: Oh. That's . . . what's the word I'm looking
　　for? "Bad."

She laughed. Out loud. Did that mean she should type "LOL"?
Some kind of punctuation smiley face?

IRENE T: So, so bad. I didn't realize it, though, because every-
　　where else I'd worked was worse.

When her son was born, she'd been trapped in her father's house,
working jobs that barely covered the cost of child care. Burger King
assistant manager. Shift manager at Hot Topic. Night manager/cashier
at the Dollar General. Lev had long since bolted, so no help there. It
wasn't until Matty was about to enter first grade that she glimpsed daylight and made her escape. Pittsburgh became her destination solely
because a friend of a friend was willing to sublet a room to her. She
took a series of low-level jobs. She was good with money, as every boss
she worked for eventually figured out. She learned how to keep a ledger and, when PCs entered the picture, picked up Lotus 1-2-3 and
databases like Paradox.

She liked the honesty of numbers. The zeroing out of debits and
credits, the black-and-white judgment of reconciliation. A balanced
ledger was a thing of beauty.

Matty turned twelve the year she finally wedged a foot into a
white-collar door. At Haven Financial Planning she became a receptionist with "light bookkeeping duties." It was a tiny firm on the edge
of the city, and when she signed on as employee number five she didn't
know anything about finance, or about any of the instruments by which
money could be hidden, put to work, shielded, and redirected. By the
time Haven fired her and initiated legal action against her, she knew
not only how those instruments could be wielded, but exactly how the
company used them to separate clients from their cash.

It was the lying, of course, that tipped her off and tripped her up.
Not the casual fibs; she wasn't surprised at the way the company's partners, Jim and Jack, told aging clients how wonderful they looked, complimented ugly women on their hair, flattered fools on their business

acumen. It was the deeper, down-to-the-money lies that got to her. One of Irene's jobs was to help with signings, managing the stack of documents with their dozens of yellow SIGN HERE stickies. While the clients signed, the partners ushered them along on a wave of encouragement, talk of future returns, confident-sounding advice. And it was clear to Irene that Jim and Jack were lying their asses off.

LAST DAD STANDING: How did you know they were lying?

IRENE T: Women's intuition.

LAST DAD STANDING: Heh. Did the numbers not add up or something?

IRENE T: I didn't know enough to know what the numbers were supposed to be. So I started studying the paperwork.

That limited power of attorney, for example. Jim and Jack always made it sound like a formality, but in actuality it was the key to the kingdom, because it allowed Haven to put clients' money into "special situation investments." The primary SSI, which could take up to 40 percent of the money, was itself an investment company that funded other corporations, which were usually described as tech companies that were about to "explode" in value. ("Have you heard of the Internet, Mrs. Hanselman? It's huge.") Every time Haven transferred money into the primary SSI, Haven took a portion as a fee. The "technology" firms that SSI invested in were in fact nothing but investment firms, which were also controlled by Haven.

LAST DAD STANDING: So what does that get Haven?

IRENE T: Jim and Jack got another cut every time they moved money from one puppet partnership to another.

LAST DAD STANDING: OH.

IRENE T: It was a vampire machine. Every time they made a transfer, a little more money got siphoned from the client account—until it all evaporated.

LAST DAD STANDING: But how did they explain to the customer when they tried to withdraw their money?

IRENE T: They just told them, Oh, geez, sorry about that, I guess that investment didn't work out. But we have these OTHERS that are still perfectly fine.

LAST DAD STANDING: Which were also puppets?
IRENE T: You catch on quick.
LAST DAD STANDING: Tell me that you told off those jerkwads.
IRENE T: That was my first mistake.

She went to Jack, the marginally more approachable of the two partners, and laid out the documentation on the partnerships and transfers they'd pushed onto their biggest customers. Jack explained to her that *of course* she was confused, this was *complicated stuff*, and gosh, she didn't even have a college degree, did she? The important thing was to not worry, that Haven was *of course* doing the best for its clients.

LAST DAD STANDING: What a dick. He just lied to your face?
IRENE T: You know those Roman fountains, with the face of
    Neptune, and the water gushing out their mouths?
LAST DAD STANDING: Okay . . .
IRENE T: Like that, but with lies.

Irene failed to disguise her disgust, because suddenly Jack's eyes turned flat and glittery. It was a stare she'd seen before in men, in the faces of assistant principals and shift supervisors and tin badges of all types: *Do you really want to call me on this? Are you ready to take me on, bitch?*

She'd replay this moment during the All-Star Tour over and over, and try to get her former self to smile and say, "Thanks for taking the time to explain that, Jack," and keep her well-paying job until she could move on.

LAST DAD STANDING: So what did you say to him?
IRENE T: Something along the lines of Fuck you, you lying piece
    of shit.
LAST DAD STANDING: You are my hero!
IRENE T: I should have stopped there.
LAST DAD STANDING: Wait, there's more?
IRENE T: Well, he called me a cunt, and yadda yadda I slapped him.
LAST DAD STANDING: WOW! That is so freaking cool.
IRENE T: That's where I really should have stopped.
LAST DAD STANDING: There's MORE?

IRENE T: I walked out of his office, went to my desk, and started calling clients. I told them to get a lawyer.

LAST DAD STANDING: Oh.

IRENE T: Yeah. Another big mistake—not getting one myself.

She told him the rest of the story: the first letter from Jack and Jim's lawyer documenting her "assault," the failed attempts to find a competent attorney to defend her, the rapid evaporation of her tiny savings. The day she became homeless.

She detailed every sad, humiliating turn, but there was one detail she was too embarrassed to mention: her last name. She couldn't bear it if he typed back, "Telemachus? That rings a bell. You aren't any relation to that crazy psychic family, are you? Ha ha!"

No. No ringing. No bells. Even the "T" in her screen name made her nervous.

Because she dared not tell him her name, she felt she had no right to ask him his. That felt strangely pure. They were creatures made of words, reaching through the wires to each other, without the distraction of names or faces or bad breath or unfashionable clothes. Without bodies.

IRENE T: I've got to go to bed.

LAST DAD STANDING: Oh God! It's so late there. I'm sorry.

IRENE T: Thanks for listening.

LAST DAD STANDING: Good night, Irene. I'll see you in my dreams.

Oh. Something fluttered in her chest.

Then he exited the chat room, and she was left in the dark, staring at that final message, as cryptic as a fortune cookie's. Had he been flirting with her? Just making a musical reference? What did he intend?

She had no idea. She kept rereading it, looking for clues. The computer, with its much-vaunted Pentium chip, was no help; she'd have had better luck interrogating a carrier pigeon. All her usual tools for managing people, men especially, had been taken from her.

It was exhilarating.

4

Frankie

Where the hell was the sock?

He pulled the dresser drawer all the way open. Ran his hand along the back. The drawer was full of white tube socks and a few colored dress ones, the pairs rolled up into balls. He was looking for a solo white sock tinged pink from a washing machine run-in with the twins' outfits, folded over itself. He kept it right there, in the back right corner. And now it was gone.

He started unrolling socks and tossing them to the carpet.

"What are you doing?"

Loretta, suddenly in the doorway, making him jump.

"I'm looking for socks," he said.

"You're wearing socks." Eyeing him half dressed in his tighty-whities.

"Other socks," he said testily. "Have the kids been in my stuff?"

"Your *stuff*?" Her eyes narrowed. Did she know about the stash? Or was it just Loretta being Loretta? She could do that, go cold. Like she was reconsidering the whole enterprise—marriage, kids, mortgage, everything.

He lifted a hand. "I'm just saying—"

"No one's interested in your underwear," she said. "Your sister's here."

"What?"

"She's in the living room. With Matty?" She stared at him. "First day of the new job?"

"Tell 'em I'll be right there," Frankie said.

"Don't forget your pants," she said.

He pushed the door closed, then yanked the drawer free of the dresser and dumped the contents onto the bed. Finally he spotted the pale pink sock—but it was unfolded. And suspiciously flat.

He pulled open the neck and fished out the bills. Mostly twenties, but a handful of fifties, and a couple of hundreds. Quickly he counted the stash, and came up a hundred bucks short of the three thousand he'd hidden there. Frantically he started counting again.

From the living room Loretta yelled, "Frankie! You coming?"

"Just a minute!" Now he'd lost count. But did it matter? He was drastically short of what he needed today—another hundred wouldn't have made him any less screwed. He pulled on his yellow work polo and his pants, and then folded the cash and pushed it into a front pocket.

Before he left the bedroom he confronted himself in the full-length mirror hanging on the door. Mirror Frank was a mess. Sweat dotted his forehead.

"Embrace life," he said to his reflection. He tried to say this every day. "Embrace the UltraLife."

In the living room, the twins were bouncing around, competing for Matty's attention. Loretta and Irene conspired in the corner. Frankie shook Matty's hand, making sure Irene saw that. "You ready to work?" he asked the boy.

"I guess," Matty said. "I mean, yes, I am."

"You sure this is okay?" Irene asked Frankie. That skeptical tone. "You checked with your supervisor?"

"I say who rides in my truck," Frankie said.

"Because if he's not allowed—"

"I said it's fine, Irene." He put a hand on Matty's shoulder. "And if you work hard, I can see about keeping you on part-time through the year."

"Really?" Matty asked. Loretta and Irene were looking at him with two flavors of disbelief.

Frankie considered backpedaling, then thought: Why not? Frankie would pay the kid out of his own pocket if need be. It sure as hell would do Matty some good. The kid needed a man in his life. A male role model.

"If you work hard," Frankie said. "I guarantee it." The twins hung on Matty's arms, trying to *tell him things*. Frankie knelt and pulled the girls in to him.

"Cassie, Polly. Look at me." Jesus they were adorable. "You're going to be careful today, right?"

"You always say this," Polly said.

"'Cause if you're not careful, Mom's going to separate you, right? We don't want what happened last time to happen again, right?"

"Why don't you take *us* to work?" Cassie said.

"When you're older," he said. Thinking, Holy shit, what a disaster that would be. He kissed them on their cheeks and told them again to be careful. "You ready, Matthias?"

Matty was looking in the other direction, eyes wide. The basement door had opened, and there was Mary Alice, half asleep, wearing nothing but a long black T-shirt and a scowl. Her mother's daughter, all right.

"Vampirella awakes," Frankie said.

"Hi, Malice," Matty said.

She clumped down the hall toward the bathroom without a word.

"Malice?" Frankie said to Matty. "Now she's got you doing it." Matty's mouth was hanging open. "Snap out of it, kid. We gotta carpe the diem." He kissed Loretta goodbye, and made Matty kiss Irene. "Always kiss your women," he said. "In case you don't come back."

"A little dark," Irene said.

The van was not exactly tidy. Frankie had the kid clear off the passenger seat: a roll of Cat 5 cable; a trio of Toshiba phones, their cords tangled like a rat king; an administration manual; half a dozen boxes of UltraLife Goji Go! powdered goji berry juice. "Just throw that shit behind you." The back of the van was crowded with UltraLife boxes. Loretta didn't know how many he had in there. He hoped.

The job site was out in Downers Grove, in the western suburbs. They headed south on Route 83, and Frankie rolled down the window and lit up a cigarette. His stomach was in knots. The wad of cash in his front pocket burned like a radioactive payload. It was going to be a hell of a day, but he'd have to keep up appearances for Matty.

After a while, the kid said, "Uncle Frankie? When did you start—?"

Didn't finish the question. Frankie glanced over. The kid wore an anxious expression. "When did I start what?" Frankie asked.

Matty swallowed. "Nothing."

"Look, this is the way this has to work. When you're riding in my truck, that means you're more than family, you're my partner. Partners can tell each other anything. I'm not going to run to your mother about it. It'll all be between us. Now, out with it. When did I start . . . start . . ."

"The phone business?" Matty said finally.

"The phone business," Frankie repeated. Fine, if the kid wanted to play it that way. Let him warm up. "You know I used to run my own installation company, right? Bellerophonics, Inc. Get it? Bell, phones, and the Greek angle."

"Uh . . ."

"Bellerophon? Greatest of the Greek heroes? Rode *Pegasus*?"

"Sure, sure."

"I had two guys under me, they didn't get it. But you and me, Mat thias, we're descended from heroes. Heroes and demigods."

"So what happened?" Matty asked. "To Bellerophonics?"

"I sank everything I had into that business, and a little more besides. Okay, a lot more. Then, my friend, the business sank me. Had to go to work with these fuckers at Bumblebee. Oh, it's okay. A steady paycheck. You gotta bring home the bacon, and keep your family safe from the wolves."

"Because they can smell the bacon," Matty said.

"You bet they can," Frankie said. "Especially when you owe the wolves a shit-ton of bacon." The kid's eyebrows lifted, and Frankie realized he'd said too much. Change of topic, then. "You know what a PBX is?" Of course he didn't. Frankie told him about the system they'd be working on today: a hundred and twenty handsets plus a dedicated voice mail system. Tried to get across what a great opportunity this was. "God if I'd been exposed to this stuff when *I* was thirteen."

"Fourteen."

"You pay attention, learn the tech, you'll be in high demand," Frankie said. "A stable career waiting for you." Frankie saw the look on the kid's face.

Matty let a half smile escape. "It's not show business."

Frankie laughed. "Is that what this is about?"

"Grandpa Teddy—"

"Grandpa Teddy never held a straight job in his life."

"I know!" Matty said. "Isn't that great?"

"Let me tell you a story about your grandfather. Before he was married, before the arthritis, he conquered every poker table he sat down at. How do you hide your cards from Teddy Fucking Telemachus? You don't, that's how. But it's not always enough, right? Like this one time, this is in Cincinnati, I think, or Cleveland, one of the 'C' cities. Grandpa Teddy's in this deep, weekend-long Texas hold 'em tournament with a bunch of sharks and one whale."

The kid nodded, but he had no idea.

"Whale," Frankie said. "That's a mark with too much money and not enough sense to get out of the water. Anyway, Teddy's doing the usual, taking their money but not too much of it. Don't want to scare the fishes. But after like thirty hours of playing, the whale's cashed out, and the sharks start eyeing each other. You gotta understand, all these guys left, they're not nice guys, right? Mobbed up. Teddy's supposed to be just this mook who's new in town, they don't know who he is, but still. Your grandpa had balls of steel. Clanked when he walked.

"Now, Teddy knows that all this time two of the guys at the table have been cheating their asses off. They're working as a team, wiring the cards to each other, practically writing love notes. Teddy was making his money, but still letting these guys think they're running the show. And up till now it's all been about the whale, right? But now they think *Teddy's* the whale. He's the fucking tourist, he's not one of them, so they start gunning for him. And Teddy, being Teddy, can see them using every trick in the book, dealing off the bottom—these guys couldn't even deal seconds, they weren't mechanics like Teddy—and they're taking obvious peeks. Fucking with him. But what can he do? Like I said, these are not nice guys. They're not going to let him get up and walk away with their money."

He glanced over at Matty. The kid was eating it up.

"Picture it," Frankie said. "The tension in the room. Because these three guys that are left with Teddy, they're not all friends. I mean, they're all connected in one way or another, but—you know what I mean by connected? Never mind. There's bad blood. The guy who's not on the team, the guy working solo, he fucking hates those other two guys. Teddy knows this. But Teddy's still pretending to be the mark, and the only thing all three of those other guys agree on is sucking Teddy dry first. So he stays in, looking for an opening, but he's getting poleaxed, like, every hand."

"But he can read their cards," Matty said.

"Of course he can. Read their hands like they're holding up cue cards. But these fuckers, the two guys working the team? They're dealing themselves unstoppable hands. Not the same guy every time, they don't want to tip off their third guy, but they're having their way with the table. Now, Teddy could just give it all back. He could lose the hands, and get out of there with his life. But this is Teddy Telemachus."

"Never give back the money," Matty said.

"Damn straight. So Teddy figures, the only way to get out of this alive and with his hard-earned cash, too, is be the last man standing. He's gotta turn these guys against each other. Let the tag team fuck up so badly, and screw the third guy so obviously, that they go for each other's throats. Soon as the shit hits the fan, Teddy can grab his cash and go.

"He can't rig the hands while he's dealing, that's too obvious. So he waits, and he waits, and finally he gets his moment. One of the tag-teamers is dealing, and suddenly this guy's got two aces in his hand. And his partner, across the table? He gets a pair of aces, too. They can't fucking believe it. They start running up the pot. By the time you get to the flop, there's ten grand in the pot. Ten thousand dollars, Matty. And when they turn over their cards, and the tag-teamers show their aces, guess what?"

The kid could not guess what.

Frankie smiled big. "Each of 'em has a fucking ace of spades."

Matty laughing now, into it.

"Two aces of spades!" Frankie said. "The guy not on the team went batshit! And he can't blame Teddy, because he wasn't even dealing! Boom, the other guys go at it, and Teddy hits the streets, the bills practically falling out of his pockets."

"So how did he do it?" Matty asked. "How did he rig the hand without dealing?"

"He's Teddy Fucking Telemachus, that's how."

"Was it telepathy?" Matty asked.

"What?"

"Like, he made them see an ace of spades, but it was really, I don't know, the ace of clubs?"

"What the fuck are you talking about?"

"Teleportation?"

"Jesus, Matty, no. He did it in the cut. They asked him to cut the cards, and that's when he—why are you making that face?"

"He does have . . . powers, right?"

Oh Jesus. The kid looked like he'd just swallowed something with legs.

"Of course he does!" Frankie said. "But he's a reader. That's his thing. He can't just teleport shit, or cloud men's minds. Everybody's got their own talent."

"Like your psychokinesis," Matty said.

"Right, right."

"And Mom's thing. And Uncle Buddy's—"

"Don't get me started on Buddy, whatever talent that shithead used to have—never mind. The point of this story . . ."

What was the point? Somewhere along the way Frankie had lost track of what he was trying to prove to the kid. Something about paychecks. But fuck, what had a steady check done for Frankie, except sap his soul? After Bellerophonics went down and he got in deep with the wolves, he'd had one more shot to make it all back. A brass ring moment. And fucking Buddy had ruined it. Now, with all the interest, he was so far in the hole that the steadiest paycheck in the world wasn't going to save him.

"Uncle Frankie? You okay?"

"What, me? Of course." He was sweating again, his stomach burning like a furnace, and the cash in his pocket throwing off its own heat. Two months of mortgage there. "Just thinking about the day, Matty. It's going to be a busy one." He glanced over at the kid. That look on his face again. "What is it, partner?"

Matty took a breath. "It's still *real*, right? You can move stuff with your mind?"

"I'm insulted you even ask," Frankie said.

○

Once, he'd been a pinball wizard. The White Elm Skating Rink on Roosevelt Road, that's where he rolled and ruled. Camped out for hours in a coatroom turned arcade. There was space for only three games, two pinball machines and a brand-new Asteroids cabinet. Most of the kids wanted to play Asteroids, couldn't get enough of it. Not Frankie. At sixteen he already considered himself an arcade purist. Video games weren't *real*. They were TVs, every game the same no matter where you played it.

Pinball machines, though, were alive. Individuals. The same game could be totally different from arcade to arcade; the paddles hard or spongy, springs tilt-happy or sluggish. A single table could change its mood, cranky one day and sweet the next.

Of the two pinball games at the rink, All-Star Basketball was a bore, with dead bumpers and a theme that left him cold. He had no rapport with it at all. But the Royal Flush, that was his baby. Near the top of the playing field stood a diagonal line of card targets—ace of hearts, a pair of kings, three queens, a pair of jacks, and a ten of hearts—that he could knock down with ease, racking up full houses and three of a kinds and sometimes, when he was in the groove, the high-point combo that gave the game its name.

Lonnie, the manager, liked to hassle him. "I oughta kick you the fuck out of here. You put one quarter in the machine and you hog that thing all day."

It was true. Some days it was like the Force was with him, and he could keep the ball in play for long stretches, the steel bearing running smooth and warm as a dollop of mercury. The flippers batted the ball wherever he wanted, knocking down the cards for him—ace, king, queen—the numbers on the scoreboard rattling up and up. Even on a bad day he was pretty damn good. After school and all afternoon in the summers, Frankie would work the Flush, while Buddy, his permanent babysitting assignment, perched in the corner, watching him play.

By junior year, school had become a tedious nightmare. So in late October, on one of the last warm days of fall, he granted himself a vacation day. He biked halfway to the high school, circled back to the rink, then smoked the nub of a joint out back while he waited for the rink to open.

Lonnie met him at the door at noon, grimacing to find a pinball rat and not a paying customer. The man was an alcoholic, face like a bad road, with a mood as unpredictable as Chicago weather. He let Frankie in with a grunt.

The machines were plugged in and humming, Asteroids running through its demo. Frankie ran his fingertips across the scuffed glass of the Royal Flush, tested the plunger. Slid a quarter into the slot.

After thirty minutes he was still on the first ball. He reached into his jacket for his cigarettes and Bic, then lit up.

"What the hell?" Lonnie said. The manager was standing behind him, looking at the table.

The left flipper had just knocked the ball to the top of the playing field, up and around to the joker chutes. Both Frankie's hands, however, had been occupied with cigarette and lighter.

"Did you break it?" Lonnie demanded. "What did you do?"

"I didn't do anything!" Frankie said. Behind him the ball dropped into the drain with a clunk, ending his magic run.

"You rigged it, didn't you?"

"I don't know what you're talking about," Frankie said.

"Get the hell out," Lonnie said. "You're banned."

"What?"

"Out! Now!"

"You can't do that."

Lonnie loomed over him. He was skinny, but tall, a foot taller than Frankie.

Frankie refused to run. He walked out, back straight, neck cold, like a man who knows there's a gun aimed at his head. Got onto his bike and rode away. When he got home, he put his forehead to the wall of the house. He felt nauseated, naked. He'd never let anyone see him move things. Not since Mom died.

○

The job site was a three-story building just north of Sixty-Third Street, a medical research company. Two other Bumblebee vans in the parking lot. "Wait till I show you the cow," Frankie said.

"There's a cow?" Matty said.

"You won't fucking believe it."

Frankie picked up his tool bag, gave the kid a stack of Goji Go! boxes to carry. The receptionist buzzed the door behind her to let him into the building proper, but he ignored it.

Embrace life, he told himself. He launched toward her desk with a smile. "Lois, this is my nephew, Matthias. He's helping me out today. Matty, put the boxes down a sec." Frankie opened one of the boxes, took out two sixty-four-ounce canisters. "This is the stuff I was telling you about."

"Oh, that's okay," Lois said. "You don't have to—oh." He pushed the canisters in front of her. She was in her fifties, friendly and round-faced.

"I drink this stuff every morning, Lois. One scoop for every eight ounces of water. The scoop's right inside the bottle. Some people are addicted to coffee, but goji berries are a super-fruit, loaded with anti-oxidants. Did I tell you about Li Qing Yuen?"

"The one who lived so long," Lois said.

"Two hundred and fifty-six, Lois. He holds the record, it's documented. Lived off of goji berries, ate nothing but. You can't believe what it does for your skin."

"I don't know, I don't really—"

"Usually these are thirty dollars per canister. That sounds like a lot, but you can make a hundred and twenty shakes out of one canister. Did I mention you can mix this with milk, too?"

"I don't have cash," she said.

He suppressed a grimace. "Not a problem," he said. "I trust you. Just make the check out to me. You spell Telemachus like 'telephone,' then 'm-a-c-h-u-s.'"

All this work for thirty fucking bucks. Jesus Christ.

Finally he led Matty downstairs to the phone room. Dave, his boss, crouched in front of the patch panel, punching down new cable. The cutover was tomorrow, and they were behind.

"Where you been?" Dave asked him, already cranky.

"Come on, you know you just started," Frankie said. "Matty, stack those boxes in the corner. Dave, this is my nephew, Matty. He's my apprentice for the summer."

"You poor kid," Dave said, but with a smile. Shook Matty's hand. He was a decent guy that way. "How old are you, Matty?"

"He's thirteen," Frankie said. "But really mature for his age."

"Fourteen," Matty said.

"You want me to do the CPU stuff?" Frankie asked.

"I got it," Dave said. "Hugo and Tim are on the first floor. You can help them."

Typical. Dave wouldn't surrender his position in the phone room to wire jacks. On their way upstairs, the kid said, "Could you call me Matt?"

"What?" Geez, he looked so serious. "Okay. Matt it is. But you have to call me Frank. Not Uncle Frankie. Deal?"

Frankie found the guys wiring up a big conference room. "Boys, this is my nephew, *Matt*. Matt, this ugly fucker here is Tim. The Mexican is Hugo. Don't lend him any money."

Matty looked like he was in shock. Hugo held out his hand to the kid. "This son of a bitch is your uncle? I hope to God you're adopted."

"Seriously, we need to talk," Tim said to Matty. "Genes like those . . ."

"Fuck you," Frankie said to both of them. They turned away, laughing.

Frankie led the boy to the other side of the room. Matty whispered, "Is everything okay?"

"What, those guys? They're fine. You're on the job now. They give you shit, you gotta give it right back. Now take a look at this." Two cables jutted through the access hole, their open ends sprouting colored wire. "The white cable's voice, blue's data." He picked up the end of the white cable. "See how there's four pairs of wires inside? Analog used to use three or four pair, but these new digital phones only use two. We run 'em all, though, in case you want to add more jacks, you don't have to run more cable."

The kid nodded. Frankie was pretty sure this made no sense to him. Then Matty said, "But isn't it all data?"

"What?"

"You said they were digital phones, so the voice is digital, too, right?"

"Smart boy! You got it." Frankie handed him a screwdriver. "Okay, you wire up this RJ11 jack."

The kid gripped the screwdriver like an ice pick. Poor kid. He'd probably grown up without a single tool in the house. See what came of not having a father figure?

"Uh-oh," Hugo said. He stood up and looked at the end of his white cable, frowning.

"What's the matter?" Tim asked in a totally fake voice.

"I'm out of dial tone," Hugo said. "Matt, could you help me out?"

Frankie gave Hugo a hard look.

Hugo handed Matty a set of keys and said, "Run out to my van—it's the one closest to the door—and bring me back a box of dial tone."

"What's it look like?" Matty asked.

"It's on the shelf in the back of the van. You'll know it when you see it."

The kid scampered off. Hugo and Tim held their laughter until he was out of the room. "Dial tone," Tim said. "Never gets old."

"Guys," Frankie said. "He's a kid."

Hugo said, "Come on, Frankie—is he on the crew or not? You gotta break him in."

Matty came back in a few minutes later, looking flustered. Hugo and Tim had their serious faces on. "I'm sorry," Matty said. "I just can't find it."

"It's in a cardboard box about yay big," Hugo said.

Tim nearly lost it. Matty glanced at him, frowned.

"Let's drop it," Frankie said.

"No," Matty said. "Let me check again." He ran out before Frankie could stop him.

"At least he's determined," Hugo said.

Matty came back two minutes later. "I think I found it." He was holding a little cardboard box, one hand on the bottom. He walked over to Hugo and said, "Is this it?" Tilted the box toward him.

Hugo spared a look at Frankie, not quite winking, then opened the box flaps. "Let me see if—" He burst into laughter. Tim came over, looked in, and then he cracked up, too.

"All right, all right," Frankie said. "What is it?"

Matty walked over, his face still serious. Frankie leaned over the box. It was empty except for Matty's hand, which he'd poked up through the bottom. His middle finger was extended. Frankie laughed, and Matty's face relaxed into a grin.

"I like this kid!" Hugo said.

"See?" Frankie said. "You can't fuck with a Telemachus."

○

After Lonnie banned him, Frankie stayed out of the rink, but not exactly away from it. He started riding by, watching for Lonnie's Chevy Monza in the parking lot. Finally an afternoon came when Lonnie's car wasn't there. Frankie was supposed to be home babysitting Buddy, but he parked his bike at the side of the building—not chained to the rack, in case he needed to get away quick—and went inside. The usual guys were huddled in the coatroom.

Then he saw it. The Royal Flush was gone.

Frank pointed to the video game cabinet in its place. Some new game he'd never seen. "Where's the Royal Flush?"

Nobody spoke.

"I *said*, where the fuck is the Royal Flush?"

A freshman in glasses said, "Lonnie said it was broken."

Frankie wheeled on him. The kid put up his hands. "He said you broke it. Sent back the All-Star, too."

Frankie was speechless.

He pushed through the throng of boys to the new video game. Shoved aside the kid playing. He stared at the screen—the *color* screen—and the stupid fucking joystick.

"What the *fuck* is a Pac-Man?"

Frankie wanted to punch the screen. He wanted to shake it apart with pure psychokinetic hate. (Not that it would have worked. Nothing happened when he was this flustered. Plus, he couldn't do anything in front of these morons.)

Frankie shoved his way out of the coatroom and headed for the door of the rink. He reached the parking lot just as Lonnie was climbing out of his car.

"You *took* it," Frankie said. His voice strangled.

"What?" Lonnie said, confused. Then he got it. "The pinball machine?"

Frankie took three steps toward him, his fists clenched.

Lonnie kept his hand on the door. Standing behind it like a shield. "It was broken."

"You shouldn't have done that," Frankie said. A dozen feet still between them.

"Fuck you, you little punk," Lonnie said. "You shouldn't have broke it! You want to fucking *fight* me now?" He slammed the door shut and strode toward Frankie.

In a year Frankie would get his growth spurt and add three inches. Later, in his twenties, he'd gain almost fifty pounds and turn burly. A couple of times strangers in bars would ask him if he used to wrestle, and he'd shrug and lie, "I did all right. Went to states." But at that moment he was just a kid, a skinny-armed teenager.

Lonnie stopped when he was a foot away. "You can't damage the equipment and just walk back in here." His breath fruity with alcohol. He shoved Frankie with both hands, sent him stumbling back. "You're fucking *banned*."

Frankie yearned to take a swing. But he was terrified of what would happen a half second later. He could already feel the man's fist hitting his jaw.

Lonnie shoved him backward again, and Frankie put up his hands, turned his head to the side. "What's the matter with you?" Lonnie shoved him again. Frankie bounced off the brick wall and Lonnie grabbed him by the collar of his jacket. "You fucking cheater."

Lonnie's voice seemed to be coming from far away, the syllables lost in a general roar. Frankie felt his body getting ready to do something, but he didn't know what it was. Something terrible. He could feel it in his hands, like warm steel about to roll.

Lonnie grunted in pain, stepped back. "What the fuck?" His voice garbled. He wiped at his mouth, and the back of his hand came away bloody. He stared at Frankie, frightened now. Frankie hadn't moved his hands.

A new voice yelled, "Get the hell away from him!"

Irene, in her Burger King uniform, and behind her, twelve-year-old Buddy, face screwed up in an expression that looked to strangers like concentration but was actually intense worry. Frankie hadn't seen the car pull up, hadn't heard it.

Irene stepped between Lonnie and Frankie. "What did you do?" Irene said to Frankie. Mad at *him*.

"I'm calling the cops," Lonnie said. Blood in the corner of his mouth.

Irene wheeled on him. "No you're not."

Lonnie straightened. "I'm calling 'em right now."

"You're drunk," Irene said.

"No I'm not."

Frankie thought, You should never try to lie to Irene.

She said, "It's the middle of the day, you're drunk, and you're beating on a little kid. You just drove here, didn't you?"

Lonnie glanced back at his Monza. Confused now.

"You want a DUI?" Irene said. "You fucking watch yourself." She pointed at Frankie. "Get in the car. I'm late for work."

"Just go," Frankie said quietly. Mortified. He knew without looking that all the guys were watching from the rink entrance. "I've got my bike."

"Get in the God damn car," Irene said, sounding like Dad. "I told you you had to watch Buddy. I don't know what the hell you're doing out here."

She stalked back to the car, a big green Ford LTD with rusting door panels. She'd left the engine running. Frankie made for the passenger seat, but Buddy slipped in before him, so then it was three of them in the front seat.

"How'd you find me?" he asked.

"Buddy said you were here," she said. Her voice softened. "He said you were about to do something terrible."

Buddy seemed not to hear. He stared out through the windshield. Twelve years old, all elbows and knees. Then he leaned against Frankie's arm, his cheek hot.

〇

During the second afternoon break, Frankie smoked a cigarette to settle his nerves while Matty watched. The cash simmered in his pocket. He'd told Mitzi that he'd deliver it at lunch. Instead he'd taken the kid to Steak-and-Shake.

"You're really fast," Matty said. "Wiring jacks."

"I've been doing it awhile," Frankie said. "You'll learn."

"No, I mean compared to Hugo and Tim. They've done like three offices together, and you did four on your own. Even with the smoke breaks."

"Not alone. I had you, didn't I?"

The kid wasn't buying it. They walked back toward the building and Matty said, "So is there really a cow?"

"The cow! Right!" He took the kid down to the basement.

One of the scientists sat back there, typing at a computer. She glanced up and said, "I told you, I'm not interested in goji berries."

"You're making a mistake about that. Reputable studies have proven—" Suddenly he lost energy for the sale. "Never mind. Okay if I show my nephew her highness?"

She eyed Matty. Seemed to decide he wasn't a wild child. "Don't touch. But you can look."

Frankie led the boy through a set of doors, down a ramp, and into a room that had probably been slated for a garage before someone decided what they really needed was a windowless, industrial barn: cement floors, big drains, and four steel-railed cattle stalls. The sole occupant, in the nearest stall, was two thousand pounds of Barzona cow named Princess Pauline.

"Is she sick?" Matty asked. Wires connected her to a blue metal switchbox.

"Naw, come closer." Set into Princess Pauline's side, near the front legs, was a foot-wide section of Plexiglas. Inside, meat throbbed. "See through that hole? That's her heart."

"Holy cow."

"I know, it's—hey! Funny."

Matty bent to get a better look between the slats. "Why did they do this?"

"There's an artificial heart in there. That's what they build here."

"And they just want to . . . watch it?" The kid wasn't grossed out, he was fascinated.

Frankie put a hand on his shoulder. "Science, huh?"

They spent a moment contemplating this miracle of animal experimentation. Princess Pauline paid them no mind.

"Something happened to me," Matty said in a small voice. "A couple weeks ago." He squinted as if in pain. Frankie had seen that same worried look on Irene's face all his life.

"We're partners," Frankie said. "You can tell me anything."

"I know, but . . ."

"Is it about girls?"

The kid flushed—then seemed to get mad at himself for being embarrassed. "It's girl *related*," Matty said. "A couple weeks ago, I was . . ." That pained expression again.

"Out with it."

"I was thinking about a girl. Not anyone you know. And something happened."

Behind the kid, the double doors swung open, and there was Dave, looking pissed. "Frank! I need you downstairs!"

Frankie wanted to say, *Shut up, Dave, this is important*. But he needed this job.

Down in the phone room, everybody had gathered around the Toshiba CPU. The laptop was wired to the diagnostics port. "What's the matter?" Frankie asked.

"Half the phones on the first floor are dead," Hugo said. "The laptop won't tell us what's wrong."

"Maybe you need more dial tone," Matty said.

Dave looked at him. "What?"

"Nothing," Frankie said. "Did you check the cards?"

"The laptop says they're all working. Could you just do your thing?"

The crew was all looking at him. "Fine." He popped the lid off the CPU. He started checking the cards, making sure they were seated properly. All the indicator lights were on, but all that meant was that they were getting power; the circuit boards could still be malfunctioning.

The first half a dozen cards he checked seemed okay. Then his fingertips brushed the edge of one of the cards at the bottom.

He pulled the card from its slot. "This one," he said.

The guys knew better than to doubt him.

By then it was time to wrap up. Frankie packed up his tools and he walked with Matty out to the parking lot. Before they reached the van, he gripped the boy by the shoulder.

"So. This thing," Frankie said, picking up their conversation from the cow room. He'd been rehearsing what to say. As a man marooned on an island of daughters, he wasn't quite ready for this moment, but who else could Matty turn to? "The first thing you gotta know, it's totally normal. The same thing happened to me when I was thirteen."

Matty opened his mouth to say something, then closed it.

"This isn't something to worry about," Frankie said. "This is something to celebrate. And I know just the place to go." As if he just thought of it. As if he had any choice.

Mitzi's Tavern was starting to fill up with the after-work crowd, if you could use the word "crowd" to describe the dozen wretches who huddled here for a beer and a bump before facing the wife. The décor was Late-Period Dump: ripped-vinyl booths, neon Old Style signs, veneer tabletops, black-speckled linoleum in which 80 percent of the specks weren't. The kind of place that was vastly improved by dim lighting and alcoholic impairment. Frankie loved it.

"Your grandpa used to bring me here," Frankie said to Matty. "This is where real men drink. You ever start sitting around the bar at a Ruby Tuesday's, I will kick your ass." He pointed to an empty stool. Matty put the UltraLife box on the bar and hopped up.

"No kids," Barney said. He'd been the bartender since forever—came installed with the building. Frankie had never liked him. He was a big mother, over six feet tall. His head was 90 percent jowl, a face like a mudslide.

"We're only going to be here a minute," Frankie said. "Barney, this is my nephew, Matthias. Can you get him a pop? It's his birthday."

"How old are you?" Barney asked the kid.

"Depends who you ask," Matty said quietly.

"Mitzi in the office?" Frankie asked. He scooped up the box from the bar and headed for the back of the room.

"Knock first," Barney called.

Knock first. Jesus. How many years had he been coming here? Frankie rattled the knob of the office door. "Knock knock," Frankie said.

There was no answer, so he opened the door. Mitzi sat behind her desk, on the phone. She shook her head at him, but didn't object when he sat down. He started unpacking the box.

"You know the deal," Mitzi said into the phone. "Friday, no ifs ands or buts." She frowned at the growing number of white plastic bottles lining the front of her desk. Mitzi was older than Barney, but where the bartender seemed to ooze excess flesh from his forehead down, Mitzi was shrinking every year, drying out and hardening like beef jerky.

Then to the phone: "Don't disappoint me, Jimmy." She hung up. "What's all this?"

Frankie smiled. "Last week you mentioned you had an upset stomach. This is the UltraLife Digestive Health Program. This one—" He picked up the tallest bottle. "This is aloe concentrate, original goji berry flavor, plus other natural additives. You just mix it with water, or Pepsi, whatever, it soothes your stomach. This is Ultra Philofiber, a mix of fiber and acidophilus, perfect for diarrhea or constipation."

"Both?" Mitzi said.

"It works on the bacteria in your gut, so it straightens you both ways. And this—"

"I'm not buying, Frankie."

"I'm not selling. This is a gift."

"Oh, Frankie, I don't need gifts—I just need what you owe. Where you been? You said you'd be by at lunch."

"Sorry about that. My boss is an S.O.B."

"Are you going to make good on what you owed me Friday?"

It was highly unusual to allow a client to get an extra weekend. Letting Frankie come in on Monday was a favor, and he knew it. He set the cash on the desk. "I gotta tell you up front—it's light."

Mitzi didn't change expression. She picked up the money, dropped it into a desk drawer, and closed it. Behind her, on the floor, sat a black safe the size of a mini-fridge. After he was gone, she'd move the deposits there. She'd never opened it in his presence, but he spent a lot of time thinking about that safe.

"You're kinda falling behind here, Frankie."

"I know, I know."

"I don't think you do. Counting today's payment—which is how much?"

"Two thousand nine hundred," he said.

"Puts you at thirty-eight thousand, five hundred seventy-five." No hesitation, the number right there in her head. Every visit she gave him the new total, every week he fell a little further behind.

"It's about to turn around," he said. "My UltraLife distributorship is bringing in a lot of income."

"Distributorship," Mitzi said evenly. She shook her head. "I don't want you to get in trouble, Frankie."

"I'm not. I won't."

But of course he already was. He was in debt to the Outfit. Mitzi's brother ran the northwest suburbs. There really wasn't much worse it could get.

"It would kill your dad," she said. "How is he?"

He forced a smile. "Not dead yet. Though he's dressed for the funeral."

She laughed, a sound like wind through dry leaves. "God he had style. Nothing like the Cro-Magnons I grew up with. You give him my regards."

Frankie stood up. He felt shaky, like he'd been clocked in the head. Maybe that's what relief felt like. He should have been happy. Another payment down, another week to turn this ship around.

"Oh, Frank?"

The back of his neck went cold. He turned.

"Which one do I take first?"

"What? Oh." He gestured at the big bottle. "Take the aloe every day, just squirt it into your water. The Philofiber and the Morning Formula you take every morning. Then there's the Evening Formula, which you take, uh . . ."

"Every night?"

"You got it. Straighten you out in no time."

Matty was sipping from a narrow glass, watching the silent TV that hung in the corner. Frankie had planned on sitting with the kid and downing an Old Style or two, but now he wasn't in the mood.

"Let's go, Matty. Gotta get you home."

"Oh, okay." Disappointed. He put down the glass and wiped at his mouth. Barney gave Frankie a hard look. Next time he should bring in something for the man. Maybe a tin of the replenishing face cream. Maybe a bucket of the replenishing face cream.

They were only a couple of miles from home—Teddy and Buddy's home, and now Irene and Matty's. At least Frankie had his own house. Paid his own bills. Kept the ball in play. Were there setbacks? Of course. Ninety percent of small businesses go under. Banks turn their backs on you. The table fucking turns. Game over. But what do you do? You find another fucking quarter, or borrow one, or steal one, and live to play another day.

"Uncle Frankie?"

They were almost home. He'd been driving on autopilot. He made the turn into the neighborhood, and Matty said, "I want to tell you something. It's important."

Frankie eased up to the stop sign and, since no one was at the intersection, put the van in park. "You don't have to thank me. You did a good job today. Consider yourself hired for the summer."

"Thank you," Matty said. "We could use the money."

That was the truth. Irene was broke-ass broke. "So why you still have that look on your face?"

"Something happened to me a couple weeks ago."

"I told you, kid, it's perfectly—"

"No, not that," Matty said firmly. "It was something amazing."

The kid told him what had happened, and how later he'd made it happen several more times. Cars came up behind them and Frankie waved them through, not wanting to interrupt.

Then finally Frankie said, "So you lie there in this meditative state—"

"Right," Matty said. "Definitely meditating."

"And then it happens. You start floating around, seeing into other rooms."

"Uh-huh."

Frankie was getting an idea—or rather, the warm glow that indicated that an idea was about to poke its head above the horizon. Finally he asked, "Does your mom know about this?"

"Not really," Matty said. "I mean, no. She caught me meditating, but that's it. You're the first person I've told."

"That's good," Frankie said. "Let's keep this between you and me."

JULY

5

Buddy

$$\boxed{+}$$

The clock says 7:10 a.m., but this is not nearly enough information. The air is sticky and the sheets are damp from humidity, so it's probably summer. But what year? This is a mystery that cannot be solved from the bed.

He pads downstairs to the kitchen, and there's teenage Matty, cramming a piece of buttered toast into his mouth. That's a major clue. This is probably the year that Matty and Irene moved back home. The year he did all the work on the house. The year of the Zap.

He says to himself: I am twenty-seven years old and Maureen Telemachus has been dead for twenty-one years.

Matty turns when he walks in, then coughs, choking on the toast, as if he's surprised to see him. "Morning, Uncle Buddy," he says finally. He looks quickly away, embarrassed. But by what?

The boy busies himself by pouring a tall mug of coffee. Buddy can't remember why Matty would be up so early and already dressed, but then he notices that he's wearing a yellow Bumblebee polo, and remembers that his nephew is working for Frankie this summer. At least the first part of the summer.

Matty glances at him, sees his frown, and says, "Oh, this isn't for me. It's for Frank." Then: "I'm supposed to call him Frank when we're working together."

Buddy nods. Matty is having trouble keeping eye contact.

"Hey, that's the van. Gotta go." Matty pauses at the front door. Without quite looking at him, Matty says, "Thanks again for letting me use the computer. That's really nice of you."

Buddy thinks, I didn't do it for you. But then, it doesn't seem to hurt any of his plans to have the boy use it.

He goes to the calendar and checks the date. July eighth. All the days are marked off in Xs that are a particular shade of purplish pink. For a long moment he can't remember the July Fourth picnic, then an image of fireworks comes to him, the crackle and boom. They went to Arlington Racecourse to see them. That was this year, he's pretty sure. God knows it can't be next year. He marks an X on today's date. Then, as is his habit, he flips ahead through the months, to the end of the summer. Labor Day is circled in that same shade of pink. It drives a spike of fear into his heart every time he sees it.

September 4, 1995, 12:06 p.m. The moment the future ends. The day it all goes black.

Zap.

He only became aware of the date a few months ago. He woke up to realize that the future had disappeared. For years he'd been plowing through the days, hands over eyes, figuring that eventually a runaway truck or pulmonary embolism would catapult him out of the world.

But this, this ugly stump, so full of complicated doom. He never expected it would end like *that*. Gangsters and G-men. Bullets and burning cars. The gun against his head. It's all terribly dramatic.

Yet if it were only his own demise waiting for him (no matter how outlandish and lurid), he'd close his eyes again and let Time carry him along. But there are other people to consider.

"For God's sake, Buddy!" Irene says angrily.

He turns, confused.

"Put some clothes on!"

Ah. Irene doesn't like it when he walks around naked. This doesn't strike him as fair, since he's the permanent resident and she's just here temporarily. Plus, she's not wearing much more than him, just running shorts and a T-shirt from a bank in Pennsylvania.

"What?" she asks. "You want to say something, say it."

But he doesn't know what to say. That's the problem with a lot of future memories. If he doesn't remember what he said, then he doesn't know what he's supposed to say. Like being shoved onstage without a script. Better to say nothing than risk changing everything.

Irene scowls at him and puts up a hand to shield her eyes. "I'm going for a run," she says.

That's new, he's pretty sure. Irene's never been an exerciser. Though it's probably a good idea. She's looking older. True, he spends a lot of time remembering the young Irene, so these age changes can take him by surprise. But he also wonders if all the nights she's been staying up late, typing in secret, are taking a toll.

He lets the calendar pages fall into place and goes upstairs to his room. In the top dresser drawer, hidden in a nest of Fruit of the Loom underwear, is a colorful women's scarf. He unwraps it, revealing the gold medal. Well, stainless steel painted gold, but it's precious to him all the same. It says THE WORLD'S MOST POWERFUL PSYCHIC. The woman who hung it around his neck was the former owner of the title. She made no demands of him, extracted no vows, but he felt the weight of responsibility all the same.

Come to think of it (but he was always thinking of it, the date hovering, omnipresent), she died on September 4. Is it ironic that the day the future ends is the anniversary of her death? Or is it mere coincidence? Is there any such thing as coincidence?

After she was gone, he told himself that he would take on her duties with bravery, reverence, and fortitude. And for a time, he did. But then, after he met and then lost the love of his life, he gave up. Stopped watching the horizon for fire. And what a mistake that was. This terminal event, the Zap, will burn deeply. He doesn't have to *see* what follows to know what would come for his family: decades of damage; a torrent of tears.

He rubs a hand over his unshaven jaw, trying to focus. There's so much he has to do if he's going to save them. But what to do first?

Oh, right. Put on clothes.

+

He's four years old and Maureen Telemachus is alive, so he's not the World's Most Powerful Psychic yet, just Buddy. He's lying on his stomach in the living room, building a combination Tinkertoy/Lincoln Log trap for Frankie's GI Joe. Joe is standing on a four-inch-high platform. Buddy pushes on a support log, and Joe falls over before the trapdoor opens. The action figure is so hard to balance.

"Are you even watching this?" Dad says, irritated. He's only letting him stay up because Buddy pleaded to see the game. Dad's stretched out in the recliner behind him, looking at the TV between his feet and over Buddy and his construction project. "Three up, three God damn down," Dad says.

"Sorry," Buddy says.

"Don't be sorry," Dad says. "You know why I'm raising you kids to be Cubs fans?"

Buddy shakes his head.

"Any mook can be a fan of a winning team," Dad says. "It takes character to root for the doomed. You show up, you watch your boys take their swings, and you watch 'em go down in flames—every damn day. You think Jack Brickhouse is an *optimist*? No-siree. He may sound happy, but he's dying inside. There's no seat in Wrigley Field for a God damn Pollyanna. You root-root-root for the home team, and they lose anyway. It teaches you how the world works, kid. Sure, start every spring with your hopes and dreams, but in the universe in which we live, you *will* be mathematically eliminated by Labor Day. Count on it."

Buddy tries to think of something to say to make his father feel better, but in that moment all he can remember is that the Cubs once beat the Braves, a team that Dad hates, by a huge score. "Eleven-zip," Buddy says.

"Lie down," Dad says. "You're blocking the set."

"A massacre," Buddy says.

"Okay, how about this—run in the kitchen and get me a beer."

Buddy hops up, runs into the kitchen, and there she is, the World's Most Powerful Psychic. Alive. He can't help but hug her legs in gratitude. Mom already has the can of Old Style open. "Here you go," she says. "Keep the king happy. Then off to bed."

Two nights later, Buddy's construction project is a little more elaborate. There are Legos involved now, and some spare wood from the garage. GI Joe has been joined by one of Reenie's Barbies. Dad squats down beside him. "Hey, Buddy. Whatcha working on?"

Buddy's thrilled to explain. He shows him the first part of the trap,

Joe and Barbie falling together into the box, and Dad lets him go on for a bit before he stops him and says, "That's pretty great, kiddo. I need to ask you about something else, though." Buddy sees he's holding a newspaper. "Guess what the Cubs did today?"

Buddy has no idea.

"They beat the Atlanta Braves. Eleven to nothing. Eleven-zip." Dad shows him the one-word newspaper headline. "Massacre."

Buddy remembers this moment, seeing that long word on the page. He doesn't know how to read that word, but he remembers knowing it, and that's almost like reading it.

"You got it, Buddy." His father is still squatting on the floor beside him. He never does this. "I want you to think real hard. Do you know any other baseball scores?"

Buddy nods excitedly. There's nothing he wants more than to tell Dad all the things that will make him happy.

"So . . ." Dad says.

Buddy tries to remember some baseball scores, but nothing comes.

"Don't try to think too hard," his father says. "Whatever comes to mind."

He tries to think of a number. "One to zero?" Buddy asks.

"Okay, good! Who's playing, Buddy?"

"The Reds," Buddy said. "And the Cubs. Cubs win."

Dad sighs. "That's the score of the game we were watching the other night," Dad says. "Try to think of one that——" He stops himself. Mom is in the room now, looking at the two of them on the floor.

"What's going on?" she asks.

"Nothing," Teddy says. "Buddy's showing me what he's building."

+

Buddy's bolting a slab of steel to the basement wall when he remembers something. That memory—nothing but an image, a mental snapshot from the Zap Day—means that everything he's done for several days will have to be redone. The three huge rectangles of steel he's cut are now the wrong size, and will have to be trimmed or thrown out.

The original size of the rectangles came from his memory of the slabs covering the basement windows on Zap Day, and he'd cut them so that he could bolt them to the walls. But just now he's remembered that the window was uncovered earlier in the day. Which means that the steel has to go up and down, like one of those grates that cover shop windows downtown. That's way more complicated.

He wants to scream. But he doesn't.

His curse, and blessing, is that his memory is full of holes. Everything that he does remember is a fact. Unalterable. The future, he learned when he was six years old, is no more mutable than the past. But there's a loophole. If some future event *seems* awful, perhaps there's something he does *not* recall that would change his understanding of what happened.

Say that he remembers a man in a bloodstained shirt. But does it have to be blood? Perhaps it's only a terrible ketchup stain! Armed with this gap in his knowledge, it's Buddy's duty to fill a bowl with ketchup and throw it at the man. So what if he doesn't remember throwing the ketchup? If he doesn't remember *not* throwing the ketchup, then he is free to act.

His job is to make up stories. To suss out the best possible interpretation for the facts as he remembers them, and then guide events to a happy ending—or, failing that, the least tragic one.

But what if he fails to remember something important? What if throwing the ketchup so startles the man that he has a heart attack? The unknowns pile up around every remembered moment. If he acts, or doesn't act, he may destroy everything. Each hole in his memory may be a deadly tiger pit or a sheltering foxhole.

When he does recall something new, it changes the meaning of what he (thought he) already knew. One stray image bubbling up into his consciousness adds a link to a chain, and seemingly unrelated events suddenly develop cause-and-effect relationships. He can rule out nothing. Everything may be important, everything may be connected to Zap Day. Worse, he is part of the equation. Every word he utters, every action he takes, may pervert the happy ending, or make it possible.

He once found a science book called *Chaos* that came very close to describing what it was like to work and live under these conditions. He asked Frankie to read it, hoping his brother would understand more about Buddy's condition, but Frankie thought that Buddy wanted it explained to *him*. Frankie didn't comprehend the ramifications of chaos theory, and so didn't understand the question that haunted Buddy: How could anyone take meaningful action, when the results of that action could spin out of control and cause irreparable harm?

The World's Most Powerful Psychic, however, cannot afford to lose hope. Yes, his memories are incomplete, a terrible foundation to build upon. Yes, his only blueprints are made of fog. But when he was awarded his medal, there was no guarantee that the job would be easy. So what if he has to move the metal sheet? So what if he has to move it again tomorrow? He has to make do with the information available.

He begins loosening the top lag bolts, regretting now that he made them so tight, then regretting his regret. That's a death spiral if there ever was one. Just keep your mind on your job, he thinks. Both jobs: the one in front of him, and his larger responsibility to the family. But there's so much he hasn't done, and now there's so little time. He always thought he'd go back to Alton. He'd walk into the hotel lobby and she'd be sitting at the bar like the first time he saw her, reading a magazine, legs crossed, one high-heeled shoe dangling from her foot, jiggling like bait on a line. She'd look up at him and smile, and say, "About time you got here."

He yanks the bolt from the wood with a squeal. Mad at himself. He knows the difference between fantasy and memory. He knows this will never happen. September 4 is coming, and he's never going to see his true love again.

+

Buddy is twenty-three years old when he tells Frankie that they need to visit a riverboat.

"You fucker," Frankie says.

"What?" He didn't foresee this reaction.

"You don't talk to me forever, giving me the silent treatment, and the first thing you tell me is you want to go on a fucking boat?"

"It's not just a boat," Buddy says. "It's a casino."

This gets Frankie's attention. "Where?"

"It's opening in six months. On the Mississippi."

Frankie tilts his head. His arms are crossed, because it's cold in the garage. And maybe they stay crossed because he's suspicious. "What did you see, Buddy?"

Buddy tells him about the *Alton Belle*, the first riverboat casino allowed in Illinois. Full of slot machines and table games, just like in Las Vegas.

"Table games?" Frankie says.

"Roulette," Buddy says.

The word hangs in the air. Finally Frankie shakes his head, says, "No. No! You know I can't do that shit anymore." When Frankie gets nervous, nothing works. It's only when he forgets himself that he remembers who he is.

"I saw chips," Buddy says.

"Chips?"

"A pile of chips."

"In front of *me*?"

"Stacks," Buddy says.

Now Frankie's pacing, though there's not much space to move with all the junk and machinery: a snowblower (defunct) and lawn mower; a pile of lumber for a never-assembled shed; a band saw; a chest freezer; sleds and bikes and garbage cans and Mom's old gardening supplies. Frankie's come over because Buddy can't drive to Frankie's house (or anywhere). And they're out in the garage because Buddy didn't want Dad to overhear them.

Even though it's cold in here, Frankie's sweating just thinking about it. He's broke, his business is failing, and lately cash has been evaporating at his touch. "When did you start seeing stuff again? I thought that was gone."

Buddy shrugs.

"Jesus Christ," Frankie says. He sits down on a cooler. Stands up again. Makes Buddy go through everything he saw.

Buddy fills in details, getting quickly back to that stack of chips. "They think it's a lucky streak," he says. "But it's you."

"Me," Frankie says.

"All you."

"Fuck," Frankie says. Pacing again. "I don't think I can do this. I'm rusty, man. Way out of practice."

"So practice. We leave in six months."

"I'm going to need a lot more information," Frankie says. "Everything you've got."

"Don't worry," Buddy says. "I'm coming with you."

"You're leaving the house," Frankie says skeptically. "To go to a casino full of people."

"I need to be in Alton," Buddy says, and that's the truth. For that's where he will meet his true love.

+

Teddy is watching with an exasperated expression as Buddy sweeps up the sawdust. "Jesus Christ, you making a bomb shelter?" One of the windows is in place, attached to a heavy-duty hinge. Soon he'll install a lever that will allow him to flip the steel shades up and out of the way.

"Can you just tell me why?" Teddy asks.

Buddy shrugs.

"No, God damn it. You do not get to just look at me with that dumb look. What the hell are you doing?"

Buddy makes a sound deep in his throat, a smothered moan.

"I can't take it, Buddy. I can, not, take it. This house used to be fit for human beings." Teddy starts listing the damage, the rooms his son has torn apart and left unfinished. And what about the huge hole in the backyard! What the hell was that for?

There's nothing to do but wait for his father to tire. They both know how this will end: Teddy will storm out, and Buddy will go back to work. It's a mystery why Dad hasn't put a stop to the project. In all his memories, there's nothing to tell him why his father hasn't thrown him out of the house or threatened him with violence.

"Okay, how about this," Teddy says. "Just tell me when it's going to end. Can you do that? Look at me, Buddy. Look at me. When are you going to stop?"

Buddy's lungs cramp in his chest. He opens his mouth to speak and quickly closes it. How can he explain?

After ten seconds of painful silence, Teddy growls and leaves in the usual way.

Buddy sits on the closed toilet, pondering. He hates to make anyone angry, even if it's for their own good. For a couple of years, before Mom died, Buddy had given his father every Cubs box score he could remember. Once he wrote, in crayon, all the digits to a future Illinois lottery ticket, though he wrote a 6 instead of a 9 and his father won nothing. (Or perhaps, he realized later, Buddy remembered the way he'd written the numbers in the future, and so the memory was an accurate re-creation of his mistake. These things were so difficult to untangle.)

Somehow Mom found out about the lottery. She got so mad that his father stopped asking him for predictions. Young Buddy was mystified by the ban, especially because he was still allowed to work the Wonder Wheel onstage. But it wasn't until *The Mike Douglas Show* that he understood how dangerous the future could be.

+

Buddy is five years old and Mom is alive. There she is, so tall, holding his hand, looking down at him with blue eyes. Her silver dress sparkles in the stage lights like magic. "We're on TV, Buddy," she says. But it doesn't seem like TV at all. It's just like being onstage at all the theaters they've been performing at. There's even an audience. There shouldn't be an audience for TV, should there?

Mom says, "When Mr. Douglas comes over, you can do your spinner trick." The Wonder Wheel has spokes that make a clackety sound, and on each wedge of the wheel is a different picture: duck, clown, fire truck. People applaud every time it stops on the picture he's predicted, and that's almost every time. His favorite part is starting the wheel spinning, not saying where it will land.

He's getting ready to spin the wheel when a memory hits him like a slap to his head. He remembers his sister holding his hand while they stand at the edge of a grave, looking at a coffin. Their mother's coffin. Suddenly the gleaming box drops into the hole, too fast, and people shout. There in the TV studio, Buddy cries out with them, a wordless shout of fear.

Mom says, "Buddy! Buddy!" She crouches down, and tells him not to be scared. But of course he's scared, because all the memories are coming now, in a rolling wave: Astounding Archibald walking out onstage, calling them fakes. But Mom isn't there to perform the show-stopper trick, and because of that she ends up in a coffin.

Mom, alive, says, "Can you put away your tears?"

He can't, because the memories are still coming, and now he's remembering the night, months from now, when Mom falls in the kitchen and hurts her head. He remembers the medal she hangs around his neck. And he remembers dressing up to go see her in the hospital, and then the coffin falling, and Irene squeezing his hand.

The memories come that fast, bam bam bam, from Astounding Archibald's dramatic entrance to the casket disappearing into the dark. If one thing happens they all happen.

Five-year-old Buddy doesn't know how to make his mother's death not be true. What can he do at this size, at this age? He has memories of being big, tall enough to look down on Frankie, to loom over his father, and he wants to be that huge man right now. He could stop crying, and the future could be different.

"Jesus Christ," Teddy hisses. They're in commercial. Dad doesn't know it, but Astounding Archibald is about to walk onstage, and Mom is going to die. Buddy collapses onto the floor, and the man wearing a headset steps back in surprise. "Get him out of here," Dad says.

Buddy's worked himself into a blubbery, boneless state. He can only think of the hole in the ground, swallowing his mother. She carries Buddy out on her hip, and he doesn't release her even after they reach the greenroom. He's still crying, unable to stop.

He hasn't learned to invent stories yet. If he were older, if he were smarter, he could find some clever way to explain the coffin and keep his mother alive. But he's too afraid, and his body is not in his control. He's failed.

+

Buddy's twenty-seven years old but he feels older. Much older. Or maybe he's just hungry.

He makes a baloney sandwich and eats it standing up at the sink, then washes it down with a tall glass of Carnation Instant Breakfast. He loves that chalky residue in his throat. A whole meal in a glass! Perfect for the precog who has to keep up his strength.

He likes it when the house is empty like this, Irene at work and Matty out with Frankie, and Dad—well, not even the World's Most Powerful Psychic knows what Dad does with his time. He only remembers what he's around for. Not like Mom, who seemed to know everything, everywhere. There was a reason she was the titleholder for so long. Yes, he feels like a fraud some days, or a next-best-thing champion, like Scottie Pippen after Michael Jordan retired, or Timothy Dalton. He does what he can with the talent he possesses.

Sometimes, though, it's as if the talent possesses *him*. For example, he's just remembered taking a walk around the neighborhood with Miss Poppins, a walk that was to start in five minutes. Theoretically he could try to ignore the memory and stay home, but he can't risk it. Everything may be connected to the Zap, even walking a dog. Or stealing a newspaper. The other day he suddenly remembered stealing a *Chicago Tribune* from a neighbor's porch. Not only that, but he had a distinct memory of circling a headline in black marker and then placing the newspaper where his father would see it. Why a *Tribune*? Why that article? He still doesn't know. Soldiers do not have to understand their orders.

Besides, he sometimes likes what destiny has ordered him to do. He certainly likes walking with Miss Poppins. Staying home would be cutting off his nose to spite his future face. And why? To preserve some illusion of free will? Nonsense. Duty eats free will for breakfast.

Outside, the air is still humid, but he has to admit that it's lovely out. Frankie routinely needles him for never leaving the house, but of course that isn't true. He goes out all the time, when he remembers he's supposed to. And he loves his little neighborhood, in all its various phases: the times when there are as many empty lots as houses and the grasses run with garter snakes; the other times when the mini-mansions start to pop up in place of the run-down ranch homes; the long, stable times in between. He feels a kinship with the trees of his street: the Benevolent Brotherhood of Patient Sentinels. They take the long view.

Two doors down, he knocks at the front screen door and calls out, "It's me." Inside, Miss Poppins barks excitedly, tiny electric yips, and then the little puff ball is there at the door, paws against the screen.

"I was wondering if our little old lady would like to go out," he says.

He feels safe talking to Mrs. Klauser. Her days are so regular, and their conversations so circumscribed, that there's little danger of causing side effects. She calls him in, and he edges through the door to keep the dog inside.

Mrs. Klauser is in her usual chair, the TV on. "How's your project?" she asks. "I could hear the band saw from here."

"All's good," he says, and hooks the leash to the dog.

"And your father's doing well?" Mrs. Klauser is frail currently, and that frailty makes her more tentative. Other times she's energetic and forthright. During the year following his mother's death, Mrs. Klauser made the Telemachus family meals two times a week. No one asked her to do this. She saw a need and did something.

"Just fine," Buddy says. "Back in a bit."

Miss Poppins quiets as soon as they get outside and trots eagerly ahead. Within minutes she squats and delivers a polite poop, which he nabs in the plastic bag he's brought with him. They resume their walk, both of them perfectly in sync. The dog knows their usual route through the neighborhood. Today, though, halfway through their walk, Buddy surprises her by cutting between two houses, a shortcut back to their block. It's a surprise to him, too. He didn't remember he'd do that until he was almost about to make the turn.

Miss Poppins adjusts to this detour with aplomb. Dogs live in the moment. Sometimes he wishes he were a dog.

A silver van is parked a few doors down from his house. He remembers this van. A month from now, he will briefly talk to the van driver, a black man whom Buddy recognizes from his childhood. Weeks after that, on Zap Day, the driver will walk into the house. Is it the same driver who is behind the wheel now? Buddy doesn't look through the windshield to check, because that's not something he remembers doing. It's *possible* to walk up to the van and yank open the doors and demand to know what the men are doing there, but not advisable. The consequences could be catastrophic. He walks past the vehicle, past his own house, and up to Mrs. Klauser's door.

"She was a good girl," he tells her.

"Did she poop?"

"Oh yes," he says. Then he remembers something. Something vital. "You should think about getting a puppy," he says.

"Oh no, Miss Poppins is enough for me."

"Think about it," Buddy says. "She'd probably like the company."

He walks back home without once looking at the van.

6

Matty

"This one's Bones," Polly said. Or maybe it was Cassie who'd spoken. He'd never been able to tell the twins apart. "And this one's Speedy."

"Which is ironic, because he's a turtle," Matty said. The twins weren't interested in irony, or commentary. They just wanted him to sit on the Pepto-Bismol-colored carpet in their bedroom while they dumped small stuffed animals onto his lap.

The other girl—Cassie or Polly—hauled more creatures from the long drawer set into the base of the bunk beds. "This is Zip the Cat, and Quackers, and Valentino"—she pronounced it "tine-o"—"and Pincher, and . . . Squealer."

She placed this last one, a beanbag pig, in his palm. The heart-shaped tag attached to it listed its name (Squealer the Pig) and birth date (April 23, 1993). Keeping the tags intact—most of which, like the pig's, were clipped to the ear, pirate-style—was evidently part of the deal, in the same way that hard-core nerds kept their *Star Wars* action figures in their original packaging. "Squealer the Pig is a little obvious," he said.

"This is Inky," the first twin said, dropping a plush octopus in his lap. "And this is Goldie, Snort, Nip, and . . . Ally the Alligator."

"Ally the Alligator? That's not even trying," he said. "Plus, he's clearly dead."

"He's not dead!" one of them said angrily.

"Sure he is—they put his tag on his toe." They stared at him. He said, "Someday you're going to get that joke and just *la-a-a-ugh*."

That was one of Grandpa Teddy's most common lines, but these girls weren't laughing. The twins looked at each other, brows furrowed, and one of them said to Matty, "It was an *accident*."

"They were on top of the TV," the other one said.

"What now?" Matty asked.

A voice said, "A bunch of those things burned up when the TV blew." Malice had appeared in the doorway of the twins' bedroom. She wore cutoff jeans and a white T-shirt that said BOWIE NOW in hand-painted letters. "It was a tragedy. Do you know when they burn they just bleed plastic? It's not even stuffing."

"Shut up, Mary Alice!" one of them yelled, and the other said at the same time, "Get out, Mary Alice!"

"They don't like to speak of the Great Beanie Fire of Ninety-Four," Malice said.

"We're telling Mom!" one of them said, and the twins rushed out. Malice looked back at Matty and caught him looking at her legs—specifically at the white pocket flaps that peeked from the bottom of her shorts. Those flashes of white cloth were inexplicably, unbearably, sexy.

Commandment #1 (*Don't look down her shirt, it's creepy*) required an amendment: *Don't look at her legs, either.*

"So you're staying the night," Malice said.

"Yeah." He got to his feet, sending little toy bodies tumbling.

"Why?" Malice asked.

"Why?" This was a question not even his mother had asked. And why hadn't she? Matty had no good reason to spend the night at Uncle Frankie's—none that he could talk about anyway. When Frankie asked her if he could sleep over, she'd let him go without an interrogation. Now that he thought about it, that was deeply weird.

"Your dad thought it would be fun," Matty said finally.

"Fun," she said skeptically. "To hang out with *us*."

"He said we'd order Chinese."

"Ooh, I take it back, then. Ordering Chinese is a regular cocaine orgy."

He laughed—too loud—and tried to blank the images flashing in his head. "Yeah, well. Have you spent a night watching TV with Uncle Buddy?"

"Good point," she said. "See you round the chow mein."

She walked away. In blatant violation of all rules and amendments, he watched her go.

Compared with Grandpa Teddy's house, Frankie's house was *loud*. Not so much in actual decibels (Uncle Buddy's construction projects made plenty of racket), but in emotional volume. Aunt Loretta yelled at the twins; Uncle Frankie yelled at Malice; the twins yelled for the sake of yelling. Bottled up as they were in this two-bedroom ranch, there was nowhere for their shouts to dissipate and nowhere for him to hide. After years of living alone with Mom, and another six months of living in a house where hardly anyone spoke, Matty found the din to be nerve wracking. He felt like the new recruit in a war movie, the one who jumped at every boom of the artillery.

Only Malice was quiet, though her scowl could blast everyone but the twins into silence. Before the rest of the family finished dinner, Malice disappeared into her basement lair. Everyone else decamped to the living room, where the TV was cranked up to a volume that turned the canned sitcom laughter menacing. Cassie and Polly, excited that Matty had been assigned their room, were building a blanket fort between the couch and Uncle Frankie's recliner where they could spend the night.

Aunt Loretta left the room at regular intervals to have a smoke on the back porch. During one of these absences, Frankie looked over at him and said, "So. You think you're ready?"

"I'm going to try," Matty said.

At ten, after a laugh-injected episode of *Hangin' with Mr. Cooper*, Uncle Frankie clapped his hands and said, "Bedtime, ladies!" They protested, but Aunt Loretta herded the girls to the bathroom and back. Uncle Frankie walked Matty to the girls' room. The beanbag menagerie had not been put away.

"Let's get you some fresh air," Uncle Frankie said. He undid the latch on the sole window in the room and tried to lift the sash, but it didn't budge. "Usually we—ugh, little stiff—we keep 'em closed, because it's the ground floor, and rapists." He slammed the heel of his palm upward and the window shrieked up a few inches. "There we go. But you'll be all right, right?"

"I guess so," Matty said.

Uncle Frankie leaned in close. "I put a sign in the garage," he said in a low voice. "I even left the light on."

Matty nodded.

"A simple three-word phrase," Uncle Frankie said.

"Don't give me any clues," Matty said.

"Right. Good thinking. Got to make this a real test." Frankie looked him in the eye, said, "Good luck, Matty," and closed the door.

"Matt," he said quietly.

He opened his backpack and quickly changed into the gym shorts and T-shirt he'd brought—no way was he going to sleep in just his underwear. He turned out the lights and crawled under the pink covers of the lower bunk. His feet touched the footboard. The upper bunk was alarmingly close to his face.

He turned to look at the room, which was surprisingly well lit. There were two night-lights, and the ceiling revealed itself to be spangled with glow-in-the-dark stickers of stars, planets, and comets. The herd of boneless pets seemed to be sprawled across a miniature savannah. The room was getting warmer. The barely open window was a mail slot for the delivery of humidity.

He closed his eyes. Took a breath.

Concentrate, Matt.

He clenched his fists, released them.

He knew he could slip outside his body. The hard part—which he'd been working on for a month with limited success—was to do so without touching himself. He'd never be able to go onstage if the only way to use his power was to jack off in front of the audience. Uncle Frankie had told him they could make real money with his abilities if he practiced, and Matty had been imagining the return of the Amazing Telemachus Family, starring Matthias Telemachus, Astral Projector. They'd first bring the act to small theaters, building buzz, until they made a groundbreaking performance on live television. All he had to do was astral project. And not think of his cousin. And those cutoffs.

Commandment #2. Do not have lustful thoughts about your cousin.

"Damn it," he said aloud. He tried to think of someone else, anyone else. How about Elle Macpherson?

But suddenly he couldn't summon a clear picture of the supermodel. Why hadn't he packed his *Sports Illustrated* swimsuit issue? (Not actually the whole issue. He'd pulled a few of the good pages from the 1994 edition at the Waldenbooks in the Monroeville Mall in Pittsburgh, which was the most larcenous thing he'd ever done in his life, and guarded them carefully ever since.)

After a half hour, he was still rooted to his body. The air was too close, and the bunk bed a coffin. He threw off the covers and crawled out onto the crinkly carpet, nudging aside plush toys. He rolled onto his back under the open window, spread his arms and legs to the artificial stars, and waited for moving molecules of air to touch his skin.

Nothing. And why was the carpet so stiff? Had the girls spilled Kool-Aid or something? And why hadn't they arranged the stars into real constellations? At least that would have been educational.

Shut up, he said to his brain. Think of Elle Macpherson. But all he could visualize were those rectangles of pocket cloth, white against Malice's brown thighs. Which was crazy. It was just cloth. Cloth that normally was not seen, sure, but it wasn't *lingerie*. There was no reason a couple of inches of cotton should stop his heart.

He pushed his hands away from himself and clutched the carpet.

Commandment #3. Under no circumstances should you touch yourself while having lustful thoughts about your cousin.

The rule would be easier to keep if it wasn't such a reliable ticket to an OBE. (Which stood for out-of-body experience, aka astral projection, which was sort of like clairvoyance and remote viewing, but with a body attached. He'd been reading up.) Over the past few weeks, he'd been able to jump out of his skin half a dozen times. Mostly he barely got to his own ceiling, but twice now, fueled by a fantasy of being forced to sleep in the same bed as Mary Alice because of some unspecified family emergency, he'd pushed his consciousness up and out of the house, so that he was able to hover, kitelike, above the roof.

He'd reported all his successes to Uncle Frankie, without explaining Malice's part in them, and didn't bring up the failures at all. Frankie was especially anxious to confirm that Matty was not just imagining the travels—after all, a roof was a roof. And so this test. All Matty had to do was breathe, relax, and not think of white cotton.

A dozen glassy-eyed animals watched him suspiciously. God it was hot.

Somewhere an air conditioner rumbled. Probably in Frankie and Loretta's room. No wonder Malice slept in the basement. He could almost picture her down there, on the old hideaway bed. One leg poking out of the sheets, an arm thrown over her eyes. He imagined her surrounded by darkness but caught like a girl onstage by the spotlight of the unshaded lamp that sat on the milk crate that served as her bedside table. Her arm moved away from her face, and surprise, her eyes were wide open, more than awake, because it was clear she hadn't fallen asleep tonight; no, she'd been *waiting*. She turned toward the milk crate, checked a small digital clock there, and rolled out of bed. She was still wearing that white Bowie T-shirt, but the cutoffs had been replaced by a pair of black jeans. She picked up a red flannel shirt from the floor and pulled it on without buttoning it, then stooped to tug on a pair of high-tops. She hustled toward the door that led to the back stairs, turned the lock, and vanished. She was sneaking out!

He opened his eyes. He'd been asleep, and now his heart thudded with dream excitement. But maybe he wasn't dreaming. He jumped up and lurched to the window.

There was Mary Alice, walking quickly across the lawn, heading to the street. Dressed in red flannel and black jeans.

"Mary Alice," he hissed. She didn't hear him. Louder, he said, *"Malice."*

She whirled as if shot.

"It's me," he said in a stage whisper.

She froze for a moment, then walked closer to the window and looked up at him. "I know it's you," she said, also whispering. "What do you want?"

He pushed up on the window, and managed to shove it a few inches higher. "Where are you going?"

"Go to bed, Matty."

Matt, he thought. "Wait there. I'm coming out."

"No! Just—"

But he'd already ducked away from the window. He yanked off his shorts and pulled on his jeans, a maneuver that required much hopping and teetering. Then he grabbed his gym shoes and eased open the bedroom door. A few feet away, Frankie and Loretta's door was shut. The air conditioner groaned obliviously. Matty crept down the hallway, holding his shoes.

In the living room, the blanket fort had collapsed and the twins lay in the polyester wreckage, unconscious. He stepped over their bodies and unlocked the front door.

Malice was gone.

He crossed the lawn, the grass slicking his bare feet, and looked down the street in both directions. Nothing.

He couldn't believe it. She'd ditched him.

Yet—he'd had an OBE! Without touching himself! Though once again he'd been thinking of Malice, so that was a problem.

Another problem? Getting back into the twins' bedroom.

He moved quietly around the side of the house, carrying his shoes in each hand like weapons. He could hear nothing but the moan and rattle of the air conditioner jutting from Frankie and Loretta's bedroom window. He reached the rear of the house, where the light from the garage window cast a yellow light across the backyard. The twins' swing set crouched in the half shadows like a huge spider.

He sat at the top of the basement stairs and pulled on his shoes. Malice had closed the door behind her, of course, but if it wasn't locked he could get back into the house that way. But now he didn't want to go back inside. Why couldn't Malice have waited for him? No doubt *she* was having fun, joyriding across the northern suburbs. He was wide awake with nowhere to go. He could take a walk, but Uncle Frankie's neighborhood was sketchier than Grandpa Teddy's. The cars were older and rustier, the beige-brick houses narrower and closer together. Chain-link fences were a recurring landscaping motif. This block was probably safer than the one he'd left in Pittsburgh, but back there he knew which people were the bad people, which ones looked like bad people but weren't, and which people looked like nice people but were assholes.

Then he remembered what was in the garage. He went to the side door and pushed inside. It took him only a few seconds to find the white poster board, set out on the hood of Loretta's Toyota Corolla. In black capital letters it said, SEIZE THE DAY.

That was hardly a random phrase. Frankie said "Carpe diem," like, three times a day. But what about the night? What was a fourteen-year-old supposed to do with the night?

He woke to cartoons blaring from the living room. His bladder was full and he was desperate to get to the toilet. He looked both ways down the hallway and, seeing the coast was clear, scampered across to the tiny bathroom. It was like a closet-sized version of a dollar store, crammed with shampoo bottles and bath toys and scented candles. When he lifted the toilet lid, he rattled the row of UltraLife bath products balanced on the back of the commode. How did five people—six, counting himself—share one tiny bathroom?

When he got to the living room, the twins for once didn't mob him; the television claimed their complete attention. In the kitchen Uncle Frankie sat at the table reading the *Sun-Times*, a plate smeared with dried egg yolk in front of him. In the center of the table was a mound of cigarette stubs in a plastic ashtray, but Aunt Loretta was nowhere in sight. Neither was Malice. He imagined that she'd slunk back to her underground lair before dawn.

"You look like a man who needs a cup of joe," Uncle Frankie said. He was inordinately proud of Matty's new addiction to coffee. It was an inevitable consequence of working with the crew, as it was practically the only thing they drank. Matty had started with a training-wheels concoction that could have been marketed as *Sugared Milk—now with slight coffee flavor!* and then gradually darkened the mix. In six or seven years he'd be able to take it black.

Uncle Frankie waited (impatiently, Matty thought) while he mixed his drink. "So?" Frankie asked. He raised a significant eyebrow. "Anything?"

"Yeah," Matty said. "I'm pretty sure."

"Pretty sure?"

Matty felt embarrassed. "I mean, yeah, but . . ." He took a delaying sip from the mug. "Sometimes it's hard to tell whether I'm imagining what I'm seeing, or I'm really seeing it."

His uncle frowned, and Matty hurried to explain. "Like, I traveled last night, definitely traveled, but—"

"Holy shit! Where to? How far'd you go?"

"Uh, just around the house. But I was also kinda sleepy, so I was thinking, well, what if I just dreamed some of it?"

"You can't think like that! There are always two explanations for what happens, the one that skeptical people fall back on, and the real one, the one you know in your heart. The doubters are going to say, Oh, you moved it with your foot, oh, you peeked at the cards, you *imagined* it. You can't let them get to you. You have to believe in your talent, Matty, and then you go out there and . . . and . . ."

"Seize the day?"

Frankie looked stunned. "What did you say?" Then he roared with laughter. "What the *fuck* did you say?" Now Matty was laughing, too. Frankie wiped a tear from his eye. "You bastard. Just slip it in there like that! You got a hell of a poker face, kid!"

Matty was too embarrassed to correct him. And after all, he did astrally project last night. The fact that he tried to follow Malice was beside the point.

"I didn't think you'd be ready for the next step so quickly," Frankie said. "Do you need to get back home today?"

"Well, I should probably—"

"Because I think you need to stay another night."

"Okay," Matty said quickly.

"Finish your coffee," Frankie said. "Then we move on to phase two."

Phase two evidently involved visiting every pawnshop in the suburbs— for what, Frankie wouldn't say. He'd leave Matty in the Bumblebee van, go inside the shop, and come out minutes later, annoyed that he hadn't found what he was looking for. Then they were off again, across the unbroken sprawl of Chicagoland, a single city made up of interlocking strip malls, decorated at random intervals by WELCOME TO signs with defiantly rural names—River Forest, Forest Glen, Glenview—and enough dales and groves and elms and oaks to populate Middle Earth. The flatlanders had been especially determined to tag every bump of land with a "Heights" or "Ridge." Pity the poor hobbit trying to find anything to climb in the town of Mount Prospect.

In the van, Uncle Frankie always talked to Matty as if he were an adult—or, more accurately, as if Frankie had forgotten he was a kid. It was during the trips to and from work that Matty learned about the phone business, city driving ("never signal on a lane change, it just warns them"), multilevel marketing, Greek mythology, and politics. Frankie delivered monologues on such topics as how Mayor Bilandic had lost the '79 election not because he failed to clean up the snow after those storms, but because he looked like a wimp apologizing for it, while Jane Byrne was clearly the toughest, most unapologetic woman in Chicago. ("You know how sometimes it gets too cold to snow? That was Jane Byrne's face.")

There were some topics, however, that Matty would have been fine skipping. He could not unhear that Frankie's first night with Aunt Loretta was "the craziest sex of my life. A whole 'nother level, like I'd been playing Little League and she was throwing ninety-mile-an-hour fastballs." He couldn't imagine what a fastball might mean in this metaphor.

The best was when Matty could get him to talk about what life had been like when Teddy Telemachus and His Amazing Family were on the road. But a lot of Frankie's stories about their showbiz career were short on details, and those details started to repeat. That made some sense, since Frankie was a little kid at the time, but it was unsatisfying. Even more disappointing was Matty's gradual realization that this glorious, colorful era, which loomed so large in his imagination, turned out, when he did the math, to have lasted less than a year.

Today, though, his uncle wanted to talk about Matty. He couldn't stop brainstorming on the possibilities of Matty's power, and describing the feats accomplished by Grandma Mo. His uncle was jittery with nervous energy, and seemed to grow more twitchy with each stop. "It's not just about viewing things far away, Matty. It's about being specific. It's about *focus*. Like the telephone trick—did I ever tell you about the telephone trick?"

Frankie had, but Matty never tired of hearing about it. "It was usually the climax of the show, right? Mom would be backstage, and Dad would call up somebody from the audience, and tell them to write down details about their house, what was in their refrigerator, all kinds of shit. Put it all in envelopes. Then Mom would come out, sit down next to the person, and start talking. These people were amazed, Matty. She could tell them all about their lives, things only they would know. She didn't even have to touch 'em!"

"What about the telephone?" Matty said, encouraging him.

"Okay, so sometimes—and I never knew why she did it sometimes and not others—she'd say, I see you left somebody home tonight. They're at home watching television. It's a man, yes? A man with reddish hair—or a blonde woman, whatever. And then Dad would bring out the telephone, and they'd run the sound through the speakers so everyone could hear, and Mom would say, Why don't I call home for you? And *bam*, she'd dial the number without even asking 'em." Frankie shook his head in remembered amazement. He was sweating even though the van's air conditioner was blasting. "Brought down the house, Matty. When that guy or gal answered, just like she said they would? People went nuts. If she'd done that on TV, the Astounding Archibald would have looked like an idiot, and we'd have been world famous."

"Mike Douglas!" Matty said.

"The same. Fucker played into Archibald's hands."

Finally, somebody had mentioned the television show. After the tape disappeared, Matty was afraid that he'd imagined the whole thing. "But why didn't she come back out?" he asked.

"Blame Buddy. He kept her from coming out, and he ended the act forever. Nobody found out how great she was. How great we were."

"But the government knew, right?" Matty asked. "She worked for them?"

"Who told you about the government?" Frankie was driving fast, changing lanes without even checking the side mirrors. "That's top secret."

"You've brought it up a couple times."

"Right. Listen carefully, Matthias. Your grandmother, Maureen McKinnon Telemachus . . ."

"Uh-huh?"

"She was a spy. Maybe the greatest spy ever." He glanced at Matty. "Oh, do not laugh, my friend."

"I'm not laughing," Matty said. And he wasn't. But Mom said her brother was a bullshitter, and sometimes he worried that Frankie was more interested in a good story than in total accuracy. Then again, Mom was more interested in total accuracy than a good anything. "So," Matty said. "Did she have, like, a gun?"

"What? No. She was a *psychic* spy."

"Okay . . ."

"*Remote viewing*," Frankie said. "We're talking long-distance, highly targeted clairvoyance. Top psychics from around the country were recruited to locate and detect Soviet assets, stuff the satellites couldn't find. Missile silos, nuclear submarines, science bunkers, all kinds of shit."

Science bunkers? Matty thought.

"The Commies did it, too," Frankie said. He wiped his palm on his pants, then switched hands on the steering wheel and wiped the other one. "They had their own psychics, working to jam ours. Classic Cold War, Matty. High-stakes ops."

"Wow," Matty said.

"But all that's over," Frankie said. "The wall's down, and we won. New World Order. And the way I see it, it's time for some peacetime dividends. Shit." He almost missed the off-ramp, and jerked the van over. Matty grabbed the dash. Behind them a car honked, and Frankie flipped them the bird even though the driver couldn't possibly see it. "The question you have to ask yourself is this," Frankie said. "What's the *market value* of your abilities?"

"Right. Sure."

"You said you wanted to help your mom, right?" He'd confessed to Frankie that he was worried about her. "Then this is your chance. You being my apprentice, that's great and all, a little cash, every little bit helps. But it's not a *game changer*. It doesn't get your mom out of that shit-hole job, and it doesn't get you to college. You want to go to college, don't you?"

"I guess." He supposed he could go if showbiz didn't work out.

"The thing is, you can't go off unprepared. You can't take your big shot unless you're absolutely ready. I had my shot once. Your uncle

Buddy—well, let me just say, your uncle hung me out to dry. But I have myself to blame for that. I got cocky, believed everything he told me. Thought it was all in the bag, a sure thing, and that makes a man sloppy. I didn't practice enough. We're not going to make the same mistake with you."

Frankie pulled up to a shop called Aces of Pawn and parked in front of a fire hydrant. "If a cop comes, move the car."

"But—"

Frankie hopped out. "Two minutes, tops!"

Matty turned on the radio to WXRT, but his mind was on what Frankie had been saying about his "big shot." He pictured himself walking into his mom's room, putting a bundle of cash in her hand, and saying, "Pack your bags. We're moving out of here." Seeing that relief in her face. After she lost her job in Pittsburgh, she'd started hiding her desperation from him. Not that she was cheery, exactly—she'd never been one of those *Brady Bunch* moms—but she deflected any of his questions about jobs or money with an air of boredom, as if explaining why the electricity had been turned off was a story too tedious to go into. Moving back into Grandpa Teddy's house hadn't made the anxiety go away, and for a while it was worse. It was only in the past couple of weeks that the cloud had lifted a bit. Twice now he'd come down for breakfast and caught her whistling. *Whistling.*

Still, they were broke, and he knew it. His job as telephone installation apprentice wasn't enough. Frankie was right. He had to score. Score big.

Fifteen or so minutes later, Frankie banged on the back door of the van, and Matty scrambled out. Frankie held a dolly, upon which was a black cube about a foot and a half on each side—a safe. Matty opened the van door. Somehow Frankie managed to lift the thing into the back of the vehicle. Sweat poured off him.

"I need a safe for my training?" Matty asked.

Frankie grinned. "Practice for the real thing. You're going to love the next part."

They drove a few miles, to the bar they'd visited that first day of work—Mitzi's Tavern. Frankie backed into a parking space. Matty started to get out and Frankie said, "Hold up. We're just looking."

"At what?"

"Your target."

Matty suddenly realized what Frankie had in mind. "You want me to, uh, look inside their safe?"

"No! What good would that do? I want you to get the *combination* of their safe."

"But how—"

"You're getting ahead of yourself. I'll teach you. I have the plan all worked out."

"I can't just rob a bar!"

"You're not robbing anything—I am. And that, Matty, is not just a bar. That place is the headquarters of Bad Shit Incorporated. In the back room, Mitzi's got a safe full of money she's taken from a lot of hardworking folks. You know what street tax is?"

Matty was too shocked to even pretend to know.

"Protection money. Protection from her, and her brother. Every bar, brothel, and bodega has to pay up. If you don't, they make your life difficult. Even shut you down. Trust me, when I ran Bellerophonics, they took a slice, right off the top."

"Why don't the cops arrest them?"

"You're adorable."

"I was just asking."

"It's Chicago, Matty."

"That doesn't explain anything."

"It's a quote. Or a paraphrase. Don't you watch movies?" He took a breath. "Mitzi's brother, Nick Senior, runs the biggest crew in the Outfit. Organized crime. They tell people, if you don't pay us, then the *disorganized* criminals will have their way with you. They tell you, we're the dogs that keep away the wolves. And do you know why people pay up, and don't squeal? Because it *works*. Any two-bit thug knocks over a protected place, Nick Pusateri Senior will take them the fuck out."

"So they're not *all* bad," Matty said.

Frankie blinked, then doubled back. "That's not all they do. They're also loan sharks. They loan money to people at high interest rates, and then if you don't pay—"

"Why don't these people go to a bank?"

"Because a bank won't talk to them. Loan sharks lend money to people that no bank would. For example, entrepreneurs who, despite having a dynamite business plan and a clear vision of the industry's future, are nevertheless turned down on a technicality, like, say, a bad credit history, or no collateral."

"So loan sharks are a good thing, right?" Matty asked. "Otherwise they couldn't get a loan at all."

"Right, except—look. These people are sociopaths. You know what a sociopath is? No conscience. They'd strangle a kitten if it owed 'em two bucks. All they care about is one thing—their money. They don't care if you get sick or if your business goes bankrupt and you have no way to repay them, they just demand their money." Frankie nodded toward the tavern. "Now pay attention."

A tall, bulky man was unlocking the front door. It was the bartender who'd poured Matty a soda. "Ten o'clock, prompt as hell. That's Barney. Pretty much works from open to close. First thing he does is walk to a keypad a few feet inside the entrance and turn off the alarm. There's another keypad at the back door."

"You want me to find out that number, too?"

"You're learning. I'd also like you to peek behind the bar. I know he's got a fungo bat behind there, and maybe a—well, just take a look if you get a chance."

"You think he's got a gun?"

"Not that you have to worry about. Come on, what's that look for?"

Matty realized he was thinking of kittens. "Isn't there somebody else we could steal from?"

"That wouldn't be ethical," Frankie said.

Barney went inside and closed the door. "They won't be open for another hour," Frankie said. "Mitzi comes in the afternoon, knocks off around ten or eleven." He started drawing the layout of the interior on the back of a Tastee Freez bag, starting with the public area Matty remembered from his visit. Then there was Mitzi's office, a tiny kitchen and supply room, and a cleaning closet. Past the two restrooms was a fire exit that let out to an alley.

"That's where the second keypad is. And that—" He drew an X on the back wall of the office. "That's where the safe is, right behind her desk. You just got to watch her, as much as possible, and find out what that combination is."

"And then what?" Matty asked.

"Then you leave the rest to me."

. . .

That afternoon, Matty left Frankie's garage, closed the side door behind him—and stopped. Malice sat on the back stoop of the house. She'd looked up from her book and frowned at him.

"Do I even want to know what you and Frank are up to?" she asked.

"It's nothing, we're just . . . you know . . ." He felt his face heat. "Garage stuff." She looked impossibly cool in a black tank top and black jeans—maybe a different pair than last night. He was suddenly aware that he didn't own a single pair of black jeans, and might never.

God, now she was staring at him like he was a dork. Get ahold of yourself, Matty. *You have no idea what you can do yet.*

"So what were *you* up to?" he said, summoning testosterone. "In the middle of the night."

"Did you tell Frank?" she asked.

"Of course not!"

She thought this over.

"You're welcome," he said finally.

"You're mad at me."

"You could have waited, like, two seconds."

"You weren't invited."

"So invite me." This was, by far, the bravest thing he'd ever said to a girl. And then he immediately chastised himself: She's not a girl, she's your cousin.

Not a blood relative, he replied.

Shut up.

"Maybe next time," Malice said.

"I'm staying over again tonight," he said, putting half a question mark at the end.

"What? Why?"

He opened his mouth, shut it.

She laughed and raised a hand. "Oh, right. *Garage stuff.*"

"So tonight?" he asked, thinking: Second bravest girl/cousin statement ever. A new list.

She glanced behind him at the garage. "You won't tell Frank?"

"I'm insulted you would ask," he said.

. . .

Matty hadn't counted on the difficulty of escaping the bedroom a second time. It had been so easy last night, but tonight it seemed as if no one would go to sleep. The twins got into a squawking slap fight, which forced Loretta to get up and separate them, and then fifteen minutes later Uncle Frankie clomped to the bathroom and back. Matty listened to all this from the lower bunk, with the covers pulled up to hide the fact that he was fully dressed—just in case someone decided to burst in and check on him.

Malice had told him to be ready by eleven. But at ten till, the twins were awake again in the living room, laughing instead of arguing, but still obstacles. The house was so small that they'd hear him even if he tried to go out through the kitchen. The window, then, was his only option.

He got out of bed and stepped up on the toy box. He pushed the sash as high as he could—which was still not all the way up. He'd need something like Uncle Buddy's sledgehammer to manage that. Then he removed the screen and set it on the floor.

Are you doing this, Matty?

Yes, I am. And the name is Matt.

He put his head and shoulders through the window. Outside, the street was deserted, and Malice was nowhere in sight. Above the rooftops, the moon was wrapped in a blanket of clouds. He supposed he should be thankful for the extra dark.

His immediate problem was the six-foot drop to the ground, and the jagged artificial lava rocks that Uncle Frankie used as landscaping. The window was too small for him to get his knees through, so he'd have to Spider-Man it, headfirst.

He leaned out through the window, then reached down and pressed his hands to the brick. He dragged his crotch over the sill, bracing himself with his palms, and slowly brought one thigh through, and wedged his knee against the side of the frame. Then he shifted his weight, brought the other leg forward—

"Come on, already," Malice said.

He pitched forward and crashed into the rocks. In an instant he scrambled upright. Malice had appeared, hands on hips. "I'm good!" he said. "I'm good!"

"Keep your voice down," she said.

She strode away from him and he hurried to catch up. "So where are we going?" he asked. She didn't answer. Up ahead, a car idled at the stop sign. A rear door opened and a girl jumped out, waving her hands at them. *"Chica chica chica!"* the girl said. "Ooh, and her little dog, Matty, too!" Bass throbbed from the open windows.

It was Janelle, the white girl who'd slept over with Malice at Grandpa Teddy's house the night of his first OBE. He considered correcting her about his name, but then Malice was pushing him into the backseat and the girls were climbing in after him and they were off in a blast of static and piano and a rapper yelling, "Watch your step, kid."

He decided to not take this as a warning from the stereo gods.

Two black boys sat in the front, bearing the brunt of the noise. The one driving was tall, his hair smashed against the roof. The one in the passenger seat turned to look over the seatback at them.

"Hey there, little dude!" the one in the passenger seat said, half shouting over the music.

Malice introduced them as the Tarantula Brothers, which made both the guys crack up. Matty laughed, too, because he was nervous, and then got angry at himself for being nervous. He then realized that his failure to say hello—or anything at all—had been transformed into an Awkward Silence.

"He just fell out a window," Malice explained.

They drove across Norridge, or maybe out of it; in the Chicago-land sprawl it was impossible to tell. Malice was looser and happier than he'd ever seen her; she kept falling into Janelle, and the four of them—everyone except Matty—seemed to talk in a language composed entirely of in-jokes, sex slang, and the word "fuck." He gradually caught on to a few things. The driver's real name was Robbie and the passenger's was Lucas; Malice had a crush on Kim Gordon from Sonic Youth; and Robbie was recently grounded by his father (a minister, or maybe a deacon) for listening to the Wu-Tang Clan.

"RZA's from Pittsburgh," Matty said, relieved to have something to add to the conversation.

"You listen to Wu-Tang?" Malice asked. He liked the amazement in her voice.

"They're cool," Matty said, not answering her question. "RZA lives in Pittsburgh" was a Key Fact at his junior high, and it was the sum total of his knowledge about both the rapper and the group.

Eventually they ended up at a Burger King. Malice and Janelle shared an order of fries and, at one point, a single fry.

"Fuck, ladies," Lucas said. "Why don't you just make out for the crowd?"

"Shut the fuck up," Malice said. "Mike's here."

A pickup truck had pulled into the parking lot.

"Why don't you go see your boyfriend, then?" Lucas said.

Malice held up a fry like a cigarette and said, "I think I shall." She sashayed across the cement picnic area to the truck. No one had gotten out of the cab.

"Is that really her boyfriend?" Matty asked Robbie, on the theory that a preacher's son was less threatening.

"Let's just say they see each other on the regular," Robbie said.

"Chronically!" Lucas said, and fell out laughing.

Malice stood at the driver's side of the pickup, leaning into the window, her arms inside it. Then she pulled back and tucked something into the pocket of her shirt. A few more words with the driver, and then she was walking back to them, smiling. "All set," she said.

The five of them got back into Robbie's car and pulled out. "Kmart?" Lucas asked.

"No!" Janelle said. "Priscilla's!"

"Not the fucking swing sets again," Lucas said. "We're going to get busted." But minutes later they were hopping a fence and running across a wide yard to reach a playground in the shadow of a prison-like building: St. Priscilla's Academy. Janelle and Malice ran for the swings, while the boys sat on the rusty merry-go-round.

"Those girls are crazy," Lucas said. He held a cigarette to his mouth and leaned forward. Robbie lit it for him. "Kuh-razy."

"So crazy," Matty said lamely. The girls were now sitting on top of each other, trying to ride on the same swing. He couldn't get over how different Malice was with her friends. She was *happy*. Robbie said, "Are we going to do this or what?"

Do what? Matty thought, but followed the group to the shadows below the walls of the academy. Malice produced a cigarette from her bra. No, not a cigarette.

"You know, you guys could pay every once in a while," Malice said.

"Like it's your money," Lucas said, and they all laughed, even Matty, though he had no idea why.

Matty had smoked once before, in eighth grade, outside a CoGo's, and had not detected any effect except dizziness. This time he inhaled with confidence, and then coughed for an uncomfortably long time. This brought out not laughter, as he'd feared, but concern, sympathy, and much coaching about technique. They kept handing the joint to him for another try. "Hold it in your lungs," Janelle said. "That's it."

Malice patted him on the back after he managed to exhale smoothly.

"How do you feel?" Robbie said.

"Fine," Matty said. "This is good stuff." They all cracked up—but now he felt that they were laughing with him. He lay back on the cool cement and stared up at the sheer wall of the school and the black sky beyond. The clouds had pulled back, revealing bright stars.

He had no idea if this was good stuff, because he couldn't feel any effect. Maybe he was immune. Maybe he was part of a special subset of the population with an innate resistance to the effects of marijuana. A mutant. A sober mutant. A sober, chubby, white, boring mutant. Captain Beige.

God he hated his body. It was kuh-razy that he had to carry this thing around with him all the time. What was the point of being a mind anchored to this dead weight—or *dying* weight, that was it, a blobby mass already becoming old, bubbling with latent cancers, each cell wall ready to rupture like a cheap sandwich bag and spill its chemicals back into the soil. If people had to be trapped inside something, why not a robot body made of something dependable, something solid, like that brick wall? God, the *wallness* of it, looming over him, holding up the night sky, a black ceiling decorated with star stickers. If he weren't trapped like this he could climb that wall with his ghost fingers, so easy, like pulling himself, weightless, along the bottom of the pool, and then, at the top of the wall, look down at the school yard that had become as small as a child's bedroom, the grass as luscious as carpet.

His body lay there, fat and unmoving as a Beanie Baby, but Malice and her friends were dancing, laughing, *alive*. Malice and Janelle swung each other around with half-assed square dance moves while Robbie and Lucas sang "You-ooh-ooh, why you wanna give me a runaround." But there was so much more, beyond this yard. The sky lifted up and up like a box lid, teasing him, and he followed it up. Below him, the suburban landscape unspooled in all directions, porch lights and streetlamps as small as fireflies, and the highways winding through them, twin rivers of lights, white on one side, red on the other, flowing between the city and the suburban lowlands. He laughed to himself, surprised to find that he was happy, very happy, the happiest he'd been since moving back to Illinois. In the distance, the towers of Chicago waited for him like women in sequined gowns, all of them gazing up at their queen, the Sears Tower. Hello, ladies! How y'all doing tonight? Maybe he should—

Suddenly he felt himself yanked through the air. The world around him blurred—and then Malice appeared in front of his face.

"Get ahold of yourself," she said, laughing. "You keep yelling like that you're going to get us all arrested!"

Then she let go of him and he fell back against the lawn, giggling. He was back inside his big, blobby body. But that was okay. He'd found another way out of it.

7

Teddy

Love makes a man desperate. After he'd exhausted his scant resources—two phone books; a suspicious operator; a useless, fruitless, but cinematically romantic drive around Oak Brook—he was forced, at long last, to ask for help from Destin Smalls.

The previous time they'd talked it was the agent who'd called, pestering Teddy about the psychic activity among his descendants. Teddy *may* have implied that Smalls was a nosy, paranoid drama queen. Now it was Teddy calling, and the foot was in the other mouth.

"You've gone off your rocker," Smalls told him.

"It's a small favor," Teddy said to him. "Hardly anything for a man with your connections."

"What in the world do you want it for?" Smalls asked.

"Can you get it or not?" And within hours, Smalls arrived at his front door—but with company.

"Jesus Christ," Teddy said. "You brought *him*?"

G. Randall Archibald—tinier, balder, and more mustachioed than ever—held out his hand. "A pleasure to see you again, Teddy."

"The Annoying Archibald. My God, you look like the guy on the Pringles can, but with less hair."

"And you still dress like an extra in an Al Capone movie."

"Says the cue ball with Kaiser Wilhelm's mustache." To Smalls he said, "Did you bring it?"

The agent held up a slip of paper. "I want to talk first."

"Of course you do," Teddy said with a sigh. He led them to the back patio. The men settled awkwardly into their folding chairs. Archibald eyed the hole in the yard and said, "Burying a body?"

Teddy ignored him and nodded at the paper still in Smalls's hands. "So?"

"Tell me what you want with it, first," Smalls said.

"You scared the lady away before we could finish our conversation."

"Then why don't you just call her? I can give you her phone number."

"I'll take that, too. But I'd prefer to mail her a card. It's more gentlemanly." Teddy reached into the ceramic flowerpot that sat under the window, and came out with the plastic baggie that held his secret stash: a box of Marlboros and a Bic lighter.

"She's married, Teddy."

"I'm aware of that." He lit the cigarette and inhaled gratefully. "You want one?"

Smalls didn't pretend the offer was sincere.

"Archibald?"

"No thanks. Had a touch of the cancer a few years ago."

"What kind?"

"Prostate."

"I'm not asking you to smoke it in your ass."

"There's quite enough emanating from yours," Archibald said.

"Can we please stay on topic?" Smalls said. "This woman's husband is on trial for murder."

"Innocent until proven guilty," Teddy said. "I just want to help her out."

Smalls leaned forward, the piece of paper in his hand like bait. "Two conditions. One, I never gave this to you."

"And?"

"I want you to be straight with me."

"You want to know about the kids."

"No, I—has something happened?"

"I told you twice now, none of the grandkids are doing anything. Zip, nil, null."

"What about the boy?" Archibald asked.

"Matty?" Fortunately, the kid was out of the house, working with Frankie. "Not a chance. His daddy was a no-talent Polack. It would take a lot to overcome those genes."

"Not like your sturdy Greek genes," Smalls said.

"What the hell, Smalls." Teddy glanced at the door, making sure Buddy wasn't standing there.

The agent raised his eyebrows. "They still don't know?"

"Jesus Christ. It's none of your business."

"All right, let's set aside the children for now," Smalls said. "I have a different question."

"You know, we could have had this entire conversation on the phone, and you wouldn't have had to drive all the way over here with this pint-size William Howard Taft."

"This is important," Smalls said. "I want you to—"

"And how'd you get here so fast?" Teddy asked. "You two bunking at the Hinsdale Oasis or something?"

"Would you stop interrupting for one gosh darn second?"

"There's no call for *language*," Teddy said. Archibald chuckled.

Smalls took a breath. Then, in a quieter voice, he said, "I told you Star Gate was closing down."

"And I bet Archibald's wallet is still in mourning."

"There's only a couple agents left," Smalls said. "You remember Clifford Turner? He's detected an enormous spike of psychic energy in this area."

Teddy laughed. "Cliff? He's sweet, but he couldn't detect an armchair if he was sitting on it."

"Teddy, this is important. We're trying to help you."

"Help *me*?"

"Your children, at least. What if the Russians picked up that spike? What if, at this very moment, they're homing in on this area?"

"Looking for my children?"

"No," the agent said. "The next Maureen."

Teddy laughed.

"Just because the Cold War's over doesn't mean the world's any safer," Smalls said. "In fact, with all this instability, threats can come from—"

"Destin. Please."

"What?"

"Has it crossed your mind that you're inventing all this spy drama because you're terrified of retirement?"

"*Inventing* it?"

"Archibald's in it for the money. But you, you need this for different reasons. You've been put out to pasteurize, you've lost the love of your life, your dreams have died—"

"You're talking about me now?"

"So your life didn't turn out the way you thought. So you didn't change the world. So what? It was a pretty good run. And now you've got only one choice."

Smalls raised an eyebrow.

"Embrace mediocrity," Teddy said. "That's my advice to you, my friend. Lower the bar. Accept the C-minus. Give up on the rib eye and order the hamburger."

Smalls stared at him for a long moment, annoyed now but putting a lid on it. God *damn*, it was fun to wind the ol' G-man up. Just like the old days. Having Archibald as an audience was the bonus.

Finally Smalls said, "I wish I was making all this up, Teddy. The world's getting more dangerous by the day. Our enemies aren't in submarines and bomber jets anymore. It's not about missile silos, though God help me, the idea of a fragmented Soviet Union keeps me awake at night. No, our enemies are fanatics with fertilizer bombs. How can we protect ourselves against another Oklahoma City? How can ordinary intelligence suss out two men in a truck?"

Oh, speeches. Square-jawed Smalls was hell on speeches.

"Are you going to give me that address or not?" Teddy asked.

Smalls handed him the folded slip of paper. Teddy studied it without opening it. He thought Archibald would appreciate the move.

"So she does live in Oak Brook," Teddy said.

Smalls seemed surprised.

"Educated guess," Archibald said.

Smalls stood up. "I'm serious, Teddy," Smalls said. "The stakes are high."

Archibald said, "Another Maureen could make all the difference."

"There is no other Maureen," Teddy said, tucking the paper away. "And no next Maureen, just like there was no one before her. She was one of a kind. The Ace of Roses."

□

He'd never seen a smoother operator, and the topper was the photograph gag Maureen pulled on that last day in Dr. Eldon's lab. This was the third or fourth week in October 1962. The campus trees were ablaze, and the air had taken on that amber shimmer of a fall afternoon. Or perhaps it was only the stage lighting of faulty memory. It could have been gray and overcast, and his mind would have cast a golden haze over that last episode of unbridled play before Dr. Eldon's program was yanked out from under him and everything got serious.

And it *was* play. A few months into the experiments, the subject pool was down to just Clifford, Teddy, and Maureen, and protocol had broken down completely. They still performed in a "controlled environment," an observation room with a one-way mirror, behind which an assistant filmed them. But within the observation room it was anything but controlled. Teddy had nudged Dr. Eldon into abandoning his original test plans in favor of an "improvisational approach." Cliff still did solo sessions, but Maureen and Teddy would come into the room together (another protocol breakdown that Teddy had encouraged, noting that psychic activity seemed to be stronger when they were in the same room), and do whatever popped into their heads. "What do you feel like doing today?" Dr. Eldon would ask them, and then Teddy (most often it was Teddy) would propose some new experiment, which of course he'd prepared for.

In short, the inmates had taken over the asylum.

A newcomer to the scam biz might suppose that scientists were the hardest to fool, but the opposite was true. Each letter after a name imparted a dose of misapplied confidence. PhDs believed that expertise in one field—say, neuroscience—made them generally smarter in all fields. Belief that one was hard to fool was the one quality shared by all suckers. And if the suckers *wanted* the results you were giving 'em—if they were already imagining the publications and fame that would come from proving psychic abilities were true? Everything would have been different if Eldon's career depended on debunking Teddy and Maureen instead of confirming them. Hell, all the man had to do was hire a stage magician to watch them work and the psychics would be sunk.

Well, Teddy would be. Maureen he wasn't so sure. What amazed him was how she could outperform him, even when he set up the scams. He'd practice pencil reading all week, come in with prepared envelopes, his pockets crammed with blanks and dummy cards—and Maureen would toss off some feat of casual clairvoyance that would knock his socks off.

"You're killing me," he told her. "Absolutely killing me."

She laughed. Oh, he liked that laugh. They were strolling around that improbably sunny courtyard, on break after spending a couple of hours fascinating Dr. Eldon and the invisible assistant.

"You're the one who's killing them," Maureen said. "You saw Dr. Eldon's face when you guessed all three wishes."

This morning it had been mostly Teddy's show. He'd started with some matchstick divination, followed up with his go-to shtick with the hat and paper. The doc *had* been suitably impressed.

"Oh, that?" he said. "That's just billet reading."

"Is that what you call it?"

"One of the first tricks I learned. There was a kid in my neighborhood who did nothing but read magic books all day and get beat up on the weekends. Tiny little guy. I kept him from getting his noggin caved in, and he showed me the ropes."

"So how's it done?" she asked. "The billet reading?"

"The hardest part is palming the first slip. The rest of it's just reading ahead."

"I didn't see you palm anything," she said. "You never even touched the papers except when you held them to your forehead. Unless . . ."

"It was when I—"

"Shush, let me think," she said. "It wasn't when Dr. Eldon folded the squares and dropped them into the hat—he did that on his own. And when you dumped the messages onto the table, you were holding just the brim of the hat. Your fingers didn't go near the table."

"Do you want me to explain?"

"Hold on, bucko. Now, when the squares were on the table, Eldon touched them—you asked him to arrange them into a triangle—but you never did. No, the only time you touched them was when you held them to your forehead—and you couldn't have read them like that."

"Oh, my dear Irish rose, I've spent my nights at the gaming tables, and I can't tell when you're bluffing. I know you've got moves much more complex than what I've shown the old man."

"Mr. Telemachus," Maureen said in that mock-prim voice that made his skin tingle. "It's your moves that are under inspection here. The folding business—that's quite suspicious. Why the little squares?"

He started to answer and she held up a hand. "You do know what a rhetorical question is, don't you? Try to be quiet for a single minute."

They walked in silence. The people they passed were mostly students, much younger than Teddy, and most were men. He watched them steal glances at Maureen, and he thought, Yep, boys, the girl's with me. If only she'd let him say so out loud! When in public, she wouldn't allow him to hold her hand, or put his arm around her waist. Her mother, she claimed, would be scandalized, as if her mother had eyes everywhere in the city. Maureen had only allowed him to kiss her (and yes, a bit more) twice, and both times it was in the pitch dark of the building's supply closet.

"The shaking of the hat," Maureen said finally.

He laughed.

"I'm right!" she said. "That's the only time I saw your fingers inside the hat at the same time as the papers."

"Caught at the scene of the crime," he admitted.

"And that's when you nab one of the squares," she said.

"And substitute one of my own, yes."

"Where did yours come from? When did you fold it?"

He opened his hand. "Right here." A folded square of paper rested in his palm. "I always keep a couple around."

"All the time? You just walk around with paper in your pants—I mean, your pockets?"

"And a few other things. It only works if the trick's over before the audience knows it's started. It's all about preparation."

"That sounds exhausting."

"And you just, what? Improvise?" In all their time alone together—which wasn't much, only the minutes stolen during breaks and the few more after the day's experiments were over—she'd never once given him a hint of her technique. It was a level of secrecy that he'd previously found only in paranoid, embittered cardsharks.

"How do you know what to write on your square?" she asked, refusing to be distracted.

"There's nothing on mine. It's blank."

"But why would—?"

"Wait for it. When I dump the squares onto the table, two of those are the mark's, and one's mine."

"I don't like you calling Dr. Eldon a mark."

"Shush," he said, in the same tone she'd used with him. "I know which billet is mine because I put a little top crease in it. Barely noticeable unless you're looking for it."

"That's why you have the squares—so your little imposter can sneak in."

"And so the mark—excuse me, the honorable victim—can't accidentally see that one's blank."

"But why the triangle business?"

"Because while everybody's looking at him push the squares around, I've got one hand unfolding the first billet. It takes just a glance to read it—that's why I only have him put two words down. And now the moment that *seems* to be the meat of the trick, from the audience's point of view."

He stopped talking. He was following a piece of advice given to him by his first magic teacher: whether it's an audience or a woman, you have to make them ask for it.

But of course that didn't work with Maureen. "That's the read-ahead," she said. "You've got one on your forehead, but you're just pretending to read it—you're telling us the one you've already read."

"You've got it," Teddy said, only slightly disappointed that he couldn't do the reveal himself. "Then, after they confirm I got it right, I open the paper, nod knowingly, crumple it nonchalantly, and toss it in the hat."

"By which point you've just read what the next wish is."

"Always stay one step ahead of the audience," Teddy said.

"And the last square on the table is the blank," she said. "That's very clever." She looped her arm through his, and his blood whooshed like hot water in a Kenmore. They resumed their stroll.

"What if they look at the messages afterward?" Maureen asked. He could barely hear her over the roar in his ears. "They'll notice the blank."

"Oh, I never throw that last one in. I throw in the first message, suitably crumpled, and palm the blank."

"You've got quick hands, Mr. Telemachus."

If there is one thing more glorious than to walk arm in arm with a beautiful woman, it is doing so with one who's flirting with you. He thought of the professor's three wishes: "repaired furnace," "grant approval," and "publication permission." So boring! God he hoped he never lived a life as small as Dr. Eldon's.

"Now tell me your secret, Miss McKinnon," he said. "How'd you do the photograph?"

Just before the break, Dr. Eldon had handed them a small photograph of a man sitting on a park bench. The picture had been taken from some distance away, but his short, triangular beard and slashing dark eyebrows made him as vivid as a Dick Tracy villain.

"I'd like you to concentrate on this man," the professor had said. He was leaning over his desk, notepad and pen at the ready.

"Who is it?" Teddy had asked.

"I can't tell you," Dr. Eldon said. "That's part of the test."

Which was unusual. The professor hadn't given them a test of his own devising in weeks. "What I need you to do is try to picture where this man is now."

Teddy studied the photograph for half a minute, and then passed it to Maureen.

"Hmm," Teddy said. "I'm sensing . . . a large building. An apartment? Or an office building?" Whenever Teddy was forced to do a cold reading, he just kept throwing out words until the mark gave something away. This time, though, the professor seemed to not know himself. Everything Teddy said he jotted down on the notepad.

"It seems to be an eastern city," Teddy said. "Or southeastern? I can picture the sun coming up—"

"He's on a submarine," Maureen said.

Dr. Eldon looked up. "Pardon?"

Maureen's eyes were closed. "Right now. He's on a submarine, deep underwater. Near the Arctic Circle."

The professor glanced toward the one-way mirror, then addressed Maureen more formally. "Perhaps you'd like to concentrate a bit more. Teddy, do you sense anything else?"

Her eyes snapped open. "I told you where he is," she said before he could answer. The doc sighed, and started scribbling in his notebook. "Small room, curving metal walls. And above him, an expanse of snow and ice, which is why I said the Arctic. Though I suppose it could be the Antarctic."

"Fine," Dr. Eldon said. He wrote all this down reluctantly, like a man signing a confession. "Arctic or Antarctic. Anything else?"

Maureen closed her eyes, then opened them again. "He's gone now. I think I scared him."

"*What?*"

"He saw me. I think that's why I honed in on him so easily. Are you looking for another psychic?"

"No, I'm not—at least I don't think so. Can we please get back on track?" He should have been more excited, but instead he seemed shook up. Nervous. "Teddy, what did you see?"

"It was a metal room I saw, too," Teddy said. "And I sensed the difference between the surface. I thought he was up high, in a skyscraper or something, but down low would make sense, too."

Teddy did not dare glance at Maureen, afraid that she was glaring at him.

Dr. Eldon ran a hand through his thatch of hair and told them to take a recess. He said they'd resume in twenty or thirty minutes.

"Submarine?" Teddy said, as they walked arm in arm. "*Submarine?*" She suppressed a smile.

"You have to admit, that's a ridiculous answer," he said.

"You certainly hopped on the bandwagon," she said calmly.

"You gave me no choice! Next time, don't say crazy stuff like that. Like that business about him being another psychic! Say probable things, likely things, and, most important, *vague* things. You don't tell somebody their grandmother's missing locket is, I don't know, on top of Mount Kilimanjaro, being held by Winston Churchill."

"Oh, Mr. Telemachus," she said. "Why don't you trust your own gift?"

"I do trust my gift. Which includes knowing when to let the mark fill in the details."

She shook her head. "You just insist on doing everything the hard way."

When they returned to the observation room, Dr. Eldon was gone. Standing in front of the desk, arms straight at his sides, was a man in a black suit. His face seemed to consist entirely of a square jaw and a high-top haircut.

Cop, Teddy thought. Pure cop.

"Where'd the doc go?" Teddy asked.

"Please, have a seat," the man said.

"And you are?" Teddy asked. He was not about to sit, and neither was Maureen.

"I'm your new supervisor," he said.

"Excuse me?" Maureen asked.

"Four weeks ago, the man in that picture boarded K-159, a nuclear submarine of the Soviet North Fleet. The boat is on a three-month tour that we believe will cross under the polar ice cap."

"Who the hell is *we*?" Teddy said, though he was getting a pretty good idea. His stomach had gone cold. Scamming an egghead professor out of his grant money was one thing, but this? These people could look up his records.

"The man's presence on the submarine was top secret, known only to a handful of people. Well, a handful of people outside Russia."

"There's something I need to explain," Teddy said.

"Shut up," Maureen said quietly.

"We have important work for you to do," the stranger said.

"Sure, sure," Teddy said. He patted Maureen's arm and turned to go. "You'll do swell, kid."

"Both of you." He held out his hand. "My name is Destin Smalls, and your government needs you."

□

The problem with getting old was that each day had to compete with the thousands of others gone by. How wonderful would a day have to be to win such a beauty contest? To even make it into the finals? Never mind that memory rigged the game, airbrushed the flaws from its contestants, while the present had to shuffle into the spotlight unaided, all pockmarked with mundanities and baggy with annoyances: traffic fumes and blaring radios and fast-food containers tumbling along the sidewalk. Even an afternoon such as this, spent cooling his heels in a well-appointed park, under a sky as clear as a nun's conscience, was chock-full of imperfections that disqualified it from top ten status. Why were the children on the soccer field so fat? Why couldn't people keep their dogs on leash? Why did these moms insist on yelling so much?

Waiting made his fingers itch for cards. Before the accident he never went anywhere without a couple of decks in his pockets. He spent endless hours at diners and bars running through his repertoire—the second strike, the bottom deal, the Greek deal, the family of false cuts and false shuffles. The trick was not to make them look like tricks. Do anything that looked like a "move" and you were asking for a beating.

These days he was lucky he could still button his shirt. His hands had turned to claws. There'd been a few good years after the accident when he thought he was getting it all back, full recovery of motion, but then the arthritis kicked in, and his fingers developed a stutter that made him afraid to sit down at a poker table. Started popping Advil to keep the pain and swelling down. One morning a couple of years ago, he woke up and his right hand was frozen, as if it didn't belong to him at all. He massaged it back to life before breakfast, but the freeze-outs became more common, then started creeping into the other hand. Post-traumatic arthritis, the doctor called it. Someday, maybe soon, he'd wake up with both hands turned to sticks like a God damn snowman.

And yet, and yet, the day might still become a runner-up. Because at this moment, the woman he was waiting for stepped out of her Mercedes E-Class wagon. Her youngest son had already jumped out of the backseat and was running for the field. She called him back (Adrian, that was his name), put a water bottle in his hand, and sent him off again.

Teddy took a breath, feeling as nervous as the first time he'd asked Maureen for a date. Then he rose from the picnic table and removed his hat. The motion, as he anticipated, was enough to get her to glance at him.

She looked away, then turned toward him again, squinting.

"Hello, Graciella," he said.

She didn't answer. It wasn't possible that she didn't remember him, was it? He started toward her, and was relieved when she didn't jump into her car and floor it.

"Do you have a grandchild playing?" she finally asked.

"I have to come clean, my dear. I came here only to see you. I thought we should talk."

"How did you—have you *followed* me here?"

"When you say it like that, it doesn't sound entirely respectable," he said.

"I'm going to watch the game," she said. She opened the back of the wagon and reached in for something. "You have a good day, Teddy." Clearly dismissing him, but all he could think was: She remembered my name!

"It's about Nick," Teddy said.

She went still, like a woman who'd drawn a spade that sabotaged her diamond flush, but was determined to play it out. He felt terrible for disappointing her. If there was any doubt that he knew about Nick Junior and his murder trial, he'd just removed it.

She straightened. "I'm not talking about my husband. Not to you, not—"

"Nick Senior," Teddy said.

"What?"

"There are some things about your father-in-law you should know."

Several emotions moved across her face, fast as wind whipping across wave tops. Just as quickly she mastered herself, looked at him down that strong Roman nose.

"Such as?" she asked.

"I can explain. You mind if I watch the game with you?" he asked.

She studied his face for a long moment. Then she shook her head, not so much agreeing to his request as resigning herself to it.

Eight-year-olds playing soccer, Teddy decided, was a lot like a pack of border collies chasing a single sheep, except that the dogs would've used more teamwork. Graciella's son was somewhere in the red-shirted faction of the mob. All the boy-tykes looked alike, however, and all the ponytailed girl-tykes looked alike, so the best he could do was sort the mass into subsets of indistinguishables.

"Good job, Adrian!" Graciella yelled. Teddy couldn't tell what that job might have been. But he did notice that none of the other parents had come over to talk to her. They formed their own clumps, talking among themselves, or else exhibiting a laser-like focus on the game that prevented them from even making eye contact with Graciella and, by extension, him.

"So you've got a lot of friends here," Teddy said.

Graciella spared him a glance. "These people aren't my friends."

"Afraid of the mobster's wife, eh?"

"As far as they're concerned, Nick's already convicted."

"But you've got hope."

If she'd been a pale woman she would have blushed, he was certain of it. "I shouldn't have written that down," she said. Meaning her third wish: NOT GUILTY. "I don't know what I was thinking, talking about that stuff with strangers."

"Strangers? I'm a harmless old man."

"I'm not so sure about that," she said. "The harmless ones don't try so hard to pick up women at the grocery store."

He laughed. "True enough, true enough."

"You knew who I was, didn't you? Before you even walked up."

"No! Hand to God, I had no idea. It wasn't until I saw a story about the trial that I put two and two together."

She wasn't ready to believe him. He started to explain, and then several nearby parents shouted at once; exciting things were happening on the field, evidently. Graciella stood up and he sat back, content to watch her watch the kids. He used to do the same thing with Maureen. When the act was on the road, they'd be at some hotel pool, and she'd be on alert, keeping them (well, Buddy mostly) from drowning, and he'd be watching her. God she'd been beautiful.

"So how do you know Nick Senior?" Graciella said finally.

"I used to play cards with him," Teddy said, which was not a lie. "And some nights I'd bring his pizza home to the kids."

"I've heard about that pizza," she said. "Nick Junior said his dad wouldn't let him or his sisters eat in the restaurant, but sometimes he'd bring home leftovers."

"That sounds like him," Teddy said. "I used to see how he treated little Nick. Back in the day, it was fine to spank your kids. Beat them even. But sometimes Nick Senior—well, I wouldn't be surprised if your husband grew up hating him."

"He doesn't hate his father," Graciella said. She put a spin on the word "hate" that made it seem as if several other options were available.

"That's good, that's good," Teddy said. "Fathers and sons, that's tricky business." He considered what he wanted to say. He was glad they were having this conversation with lots of noise to cover it and no one too close, yet in sight of lots of people, so that she'd be reluctant to slap his face. Finally he said, "I saw in the papers that your Nick's going to take the stand. Testify in his own defense."

"Maybe. According to his lawyer."

"So he's not?"

"I'm not talking about this with you, Teddy."

"Because I'd be awfully relieved if he didn't."

This made her raise an eyebrow.

"You know what everybody's saying," Teddy said. "A lot of speculation about what he's going to say, and who he's going to say it about."

"My husband's going to say whatever he wants to say to defend himself."

"Of course he will, of course he will, that's perfectly—"

"Why the hell do you care what he says?"

Damn. He'd made her angry. "Graciella, please. I don't want to step out of line. But I wanted to offer some advice."

"You want to offer advice," she said icily. "To me. About my family."

He forged ahead. "Tell your husband not to do it." She opened her mouth to object and he said, "Please, trust me. Your husband may not want to go to jail, but if he does this thing, I'm afraid of what Nick Senior will do."

"He won't be doing anything," she said. "The police have a lot of security around my husband."

"I mean to you, Graciella."

She stared at him, and he couldn't read her expression. Fear? Anger? Some cocktail of them both? He pressed on.

"The police can't help you. Witness protection won't help you. Read the papers. Reggie Dumas, the last guy who testified against the Outfit in the eighties? He was in WITSEC. Two years later, they found his body in his backyard—in Phoenix. It took them years, but they got him, all the way out in the desert."

"I'm such an idiot," she said, almost under her breath.

"Don't be hard on yourself," he said. "Not everyone—"

"You work for him, don't you?"

"Pardon?"

Looking at him now, her mouth a hard line. That cocktail was at two parts anger, one part fear. "Is this about the fucking teeth?"

"*Teeth?* What teeth?"

She stared at him.

"Graciella, please. I just wanted to warn you. I don't think you understand what Nick Senior's capable of."

"Oh, I know he has a temper," she said.

"A temper? The things I've seen him do. Do you know what degloving is?" He raised a hand. "Never mind. I shouldn't have brought that up. The point is, your father-in-law's a sick S.O.B."

"Are you done talking about my family?"

"It's your family *now*. But if your husband sells out his father on the witness stand, you're not the family anymore, not as far as Nick Senior is concerned."

Graciella stood up. "Get out of here," she said.

He pulled himself out of the chair. "Please, I only came because—"

"Get *out*."

Now the parents were looking at her—and, by extension, him. He straightened the Borsalino and lowered his voice.

"You have no reason to believe me," he said. "I'm a cheat and a storyteller. I used to make my living conning people out of their cash. But I promise you, I'm telling the truth. I don't work for Nick Senior. I'm just here to help."

He held out a playing card. "I've written my number on this. If you need me, call."

She refused to take it from him. He placed it on the lawn chair, tipped his hat, and walked toward his car. Behind him, a shout went up on the field, and red-shirted children celebrated and green-shirted children despaired, or vice versa.

◻

In the months after he and Maureen were recruited and packed off to Maryland, their romance accelerated on its own, like a bike going downhill. It wasn't only that they spent so much time together—working side by side every day at Fort Meade, taking the same bus back to Odenton, going home to neighboring apartments. The move itself had changed Maureen. Finally outside her mother's influence, as she said, she'd blossomed. She laughed more easily, seemed less careful about every sentence she uttered, no longer seemed to worry what strangers on the street might think of them holding hands. And at night, Mo lit up like a kerosene torch. By spring they were making love with the lights on.

He wouldn't have traded these months for anything, but he had to admit that the daily routine bored him, made him feel like he was working a straight job, something he'd vowed never to do. He also had to admit that for a straight job, it was pretty bent. Most days the work consisted of lying on couches talking aloud, while a fellow psychic recorded his "observations." Later, Smalls would evaluate the observations for "hits." Maureen and Teddy, the two stars of the show, had scores that were about the same but for opposite reasons. Maureen's observations were highly specific, so that when she hit, her concrete statements came off as undeniable facts. Teddy's answers, however, were artfully vague, so that it was near impossible for him to be *completely* wrong.

For some reason, Smalls had not recruited Clifford Turner, who had demonstrated some actual psychic ability—and that reason was that Turner was black. Smalls had let his prejudice do his thinking for him and had hired instead two white men who were self-deluded yahoos. Bob Nickles was a retired electrician who claimed to be an electricity douser; Jonathan Jones was a young man who'd been "discovered" by two Stanford professors after scoring high in a series of guessing games. Their primary qualifications seemed to be (a) luck, now run out; and (b) their golden-retriever-like enthusiasm. Nickles and Jones would babble on about whatever came to mind, often subconsciously riffing on whatever cues Smalls had let slip about the assignment. A stray mention of "sand" was enough to send them conjuring camels and Arabs all afternoon. What bothered Teddy was not that these two nimrods honestly thought they were having psychic experiences, but that Smalls did, too. Some days the G-man rated their results higher than Teddy's or Maureen's.

The rampant gullibility seemed to permeate all levels of government, fueled by fear of the Russians. The Soviets were pouring money into psi research, and the U.S., Smalls explained, had no choice but to respond in kind. All the intelligence organizations and every branch of the military were financing parallel secret programs. Some of them were focused on mind control, others on mind reading. Smalls's team was in charge of remote viewing. He'd been given a dusty barracks building at the fort, enough money for a secretary, a junior agent, and four psychics, and all the office equipment he could scavenge from

INSCOM and other army detachments. The program had no name, so everyone just called it "the program."

The infuriating thing was that with all this government money flying around, so little of it was going to the ones doing the work—the psychic operatives. They were paying Maureen and Teddy peanuts. When Teddy pointed this out to Smalls, the man went into a speech about duty, protecting the country, and the threat to democracy itself. Asking you to forgo your fair share for the good of the nation, the company, or the church was a common enough scam, but telling you to go broke for the sake of an abstract philosophy? That took balls.

The real money, Teddy quickly figured out, was going to consultants and third-party contractors. Case in point: The morning before the night Teddy proposed to Maureen, they arrived at the barracks to find several workmen in orange coveralls setting up stacks of electrical equipment. Smalls called the seven members of the staff into his office. "I've got some good news," he told them. "Management is very excited about the results that we've achieved so far. We've been given our own funding line, and an official code name. As of today, we are Aqueduct Anvil."

"Wow!" Jones said. "What does it mean?"

"It doesn't mean anything," Smalls said. "It was next in the book."

"What book?"

"The book of available code names."

"You have a book of pre-generated code names?" Teddy asked.

"If you don't, then everybody picks names like 'Thunder Strike.' In other news—"

Teddy raised his hand. "Can I tell people I'm in AA?" he asked innocently.

"Don't tell people you're in anything," Smalls said.

"Can we still call it 'the program'?" Bob Nickles asked.

"Then they'll know we're in AA," Teddy said. Only Maureen and the secretary laughed.

"*In other news,*" Smalls repeated, desperately trying to regain control of the meeting. He never laughed at Teddy's jokes. Any sense of humor in the man was short-circuited in Teddy's presence by his jealousy. The poor lug was sweet on Maureen, but couldn't admit these unclean thoughts to himself, and so had to take out his frustrations on her charming, loudmouthed beau. It didn't matter that Teddy and Maureen's relationship had been classified top secret by the woman herself; Smalls could sense it.

"Management also approved an expansion of the program," Smalls said. "We're going on a hiring spree."

Smalls had gotten permission to test army personnel and read them into the program if their scores matched the desired "psychological profile." Teddy assumed that meant gullibility.

"Test them how?" Maureen asked.

"That's an excellent question," Smalls said. "Thank you, Maureen."

God help us, Teddy thought.

Smalls gestured toward the door. "Here is the man who can answer your questions." Standing there, hands clasped behind his back, was a short man in a black suit. His hair was wispy on top, but his mustache was as thick, oiled, and pointy as a silent film villain's.

"This is G. Randall Archibald," Smalls said. "And he has a device that will revolutionize psi research."

"You don't say," Teddy said.

The mustachioed man surveyed the room. "My torsion field detector can measure psi ability with ninety-five percent accuracy."

"Ninety-five point six," Smalls said. "How about we begin with you, Teddy?"

"Say what?" Teddy asked. He glanced at Maureen. She suddenly took an interest in her shoes.

"You of all people have nothing to be afraid of," Archibald said with the tone of a physician hiding a large syringe behind his back. "Not a talent as powerful as yourself."

◻

Coming home did nothing to improve Teddy's mood. Buddy was crouched in the living room, sweaty and distressed, trying to rewire a lamp. (Why? Was it broken? If it hadn't been it was now.) Frankie sat at the kitchen table, three empty beer bottles in front of him, sucking down his fourth.

"What are you doing here, and what have you done with my beer?" Teddy asked.

"I dropped off Matty. He's a hell of a young man. Good worker, enthusiastic, and ready to push himself. Not like most kids."

"Right," Teddy said. "Not like the kind who hang around your house, expecting a handout."

"Exactly." Frankie finished his beer, got up to pull another one from the fridge. "A real go-getter." Under the table sat a cardboard box.

"What the hell is that?" Teddy asked, knowing full well what the box was.

"I brought you a refill," Frankie said.

"No." Teddy shook his head. "No no no no."

"You know this stuff is good for you. It's got—"

"Antioxidants! Jesus Christ, I know. Take it out of here, Frankie. I got enough God damn antioxidants to drown a steer."

"If you become one of my down-line distributors, the price gets even cheaper."

"We've talked about this. That's your scam, not mine."

"All I'm asking is for once in your life you show a little support."

"Once in my—is that what you said? *Once?*"

"I don't mooch off you," Frankie said, in denial of all historical records. "We all know you're loaded—"

"I'm not loaded."

"—but at least I don't squat here, eat your food, expect you to take care of me."

Teddy opened the high cabinet and brought down the Hendrick's bottle. "So what you're telling me," he said, pouring three fingers into a thick-bottomed glass, "I buy one more box from you, that's it, you'll never ask for anything again?"

Frankie frowned. "What's the matter with you?" He wasn't used to sarcasm from Teddy, whose habit in these post-work sessions was to listen quietly. Two or three times a week Frankie would do this, come in after work, start holding forth on herbal supplements or real estate taxes or whatever had gotten into his brain or under his skin, and consume all Teddy's Heinekens and Ritz crackers. He was in no rush to go home to Loretta, probably because he didn't want to get stuck watching the twins or taking them to gymnastics practice. He'd keep talking until the beer or Teddy's patience ran out. Then Teddy would clap his son on the arm, agree with whatever his last point was, and head upstairs for a nap. (Though it wasn't so much a nap as a retreat.) He'd decided years ago there was no profit in arguing with the boy, and no way to stop his yammering any more than he could start Buddy talking. Theoretically, Buddy would be the perfect sound-absorbing device for Frankie's verbiage, but ever since the riverboat the brothers could barely look at each other.

"I'm fine," Teddy said. "Just fine." He handed Frankie his gin glass and nodded at the fridge. "You're closest, drop some ice in there."

Frankie did as he was told. He popped the last three cubes from a tray and slid the empty container back into the freezer.

Jesus Christ, Teddy thought, I've raised a family of Visigoths.

"So you're going to buy the box?" Frankie asked.

Teddy leaned forward. "Let me tell you a story."

"Ugh."

"That's right, it's my turn. You know what everybody told me when your mother died?"

Frankie all but rolled his eyes. "That you should give us all away."

"Damn straight! Pack you all off to social services."

"Or Mom's family."

"You'da liked that. Raised by a bunch of mick alcoholics." Frankie made a face and Teddy said, "That don't make me racist. Some Irish do drink like God damn fish. Your mom's ma, God rest her soul, was a teetotaler, but her pa? Hard-core alkie. And her brother was a fall-down drunk."

"I thought Mom's brother died in high school—"

"Sure did."

"—of leukemia."

"Alcohol-related leukemia," Teddy said. "That's your genes, there, Frankie boy. Better watch yourself."

Suddenly Buddy charged into the kitchen, looked around wildly, and then lunged for the phone. It rang just as he picked it up. He stared at it a second, then held it out toward Teddy.

"Hello?" Teddy asked.

"So your calling card is a *two*?"

"Graciella," he said. Couldn't help smiling.

"I would have thought you'd pick an ace at least," she said.

Teddy ignored Frankie's questioning look, then walked outside with the phone. God damn he needed a cordless in this house full of people. "See, if I give you an ace, you'd think I was bragging," he said. "I could go down to a face card, but then there's no room to write. But the deuce, well, it may not look like much, but it's wild."

"So," Graciella said. "Degloving."

"Ah. As I said, I shouldn't have brought that up."

"Tell me the story, Teddy."

"Not over the phone. How about the diner by Dominick's?" *Where we first met*, he didn't add.

"They don't have a bar. I'm going to need a drink."

"I know a place," he said.

"I've already called the babysitter," she said.

He went back inside, resumed his seat. Took a long, bittersweet sip of the Hendrick's. Leaned back.

Frankie was looking at him with an odd expression. "What just happened?" he asked.

"Nothing, my boy. Nothing."

"You're smiling at *something*."

Teddy swirled his glass, thinking.

Frankie nodded slowly. "So . . ."

"All right, all right," Teddy said with an artificial sigh. "One box."

□

On the bus ride home from Fort Meade, Maureen was silent, her expression distracted.

"Don't you worry," Teddy told her. "That machine don't mean a thing." She didn't answer. Because of course it did mean something, because Smalls believed in it. And how could he not? The results corresponded with all his biases.

G. Randall Archibald had tested each of them. They didn't start with Teddy, because Jonathan Jones was so anxious to go first. Archibald fastened electrodes to the boy's arms and temples, then plugged him into the stack of electronic devices—which in aggregate evidently formed this torsion field detector. The boxes hummed and whirred and emitted a smell of hot rubber. Archibald asked Jones to go through a remote-viewing exercise, and the staff watched tensely as the dials of the machine twitched and swung. Afterward, Archibald wrote down numbers on a pad, harrumphed to himself, and then called up Bob Nickles. The retiree performed about the same as Jones.

Then came Maureen. As soon as she closed her eyes to concentrate on a target on Russian soil, the gauges slammed to the right like Barney Oldfield's speedometer.

Archibald seemed shocked, and mumbled something about recalibrating the device, but Smalls reassured him. As far as he was concerned, the detector was right on the money.

Teddy went last. Archibald taped the electrodes to Teddy's skin, turned on the machine . . . and waited. The gauges didn't move. Teddy made a joke about Maureen burning them out, and no one laughed, not even Maureen. A second round of testing with the group returned similar results: Jones and Nickles were active but feeble, Maureen was a powerhouse, and Teddy was a dud.

"It's the oldest scam in the book," Teddy said to Maureen, still trying to cheer her up as the bus rumbled toward Odenton. "That guy, Archibald? He's going to make a mint ripping off the government. It's a better deal than being a psychic, that's for sure. He's taking Smalls for a ride. There's no better sucker than a man with signing approval on a governmental line item."

Still Maureen didn't speak.

"Okay, does it work?" Teddy asked rhetorically. "Maybe." That was a lie, but for her own good. "It sure was right about you, though."

Maureen finally looked at him, and he was shocked to see that her eyes were gleaming. It tore him up to see her holding back tears. Worse than full-fledged crying. She said, "You believe in me now?"

"Babe, you're asking a born second-deal man whether he believes in psychic powers. I know every trick in the book, and the ones that aren't in the book? Well, I know enough to watch the left hand when the right one's waving around. And kid, I've been watching every move you've made since last summer."

He sighed. "But God damn if I could catch you. Every day in Dr. Eldon's lab you had me turned around, mystified, and befuddled. And then we got out here, and I thought, at last, I'll be able to watch her every day, there's no way she could fool me every minute. Smalls maybe, but not Teddy Telemachus. And you know what? I was right."

"What? I never—"

"You didn't fool me, Maureen McKinnon, because you weren't trying to. You're the real thing. It took me long enough to believe it—it's against my nature. I'd be damned if some blue-eyed Chicago beauty was going to make a mark out of me. But you, you've got the goods. You're an honest-to-God psychic. And I'm in love with you."

She sat back in the vinyl seat, and now a tear had escaped to track down her cheek. He was mystified again. Was she happy or upset? He decided to go with happy, because the alternative would crush him.

"And what about you?" she asked finally. "Is the machine right about you?"

"You already know," he said. "I've told you every trick I've used." All but two, he thought. The one he pulled this morning, and the one he was about to perform. He was going to do it later, over dinner, but she needed a little magic right now, on this bus crammed with soldiers and secretaries.

"Regard this ordinary chapeau," he said, and doffed his fedora. "Absolutely nothing inside."

She dabbed at her eyes with the knuckles of one hand. "Not now, Teddy."

He reached inside. "And yet, something appears out of nothing." He lifted his hand and showed her the black velvet ring box in his fingers.

"What are you doing?" she asked.

"It's a little cramped, but I'll try to get on my knees."

"No. Please." She covered his hand with her own, pushing his fingers against the box. "I have to tell you something."

"As long as it ends in 'yes.'"

"Something's happened." Her face was so serious. "No. Some*one* has happened."

His chest tightened. "Another guy?"

"Or girl," she said. "We won't know for a while."

"Oh," he said. Then: "Oh!" Then: "Oh my God!"

She watched him, still not smiling. Waiting for him to make himself clear. He said, "Are you sure? Have you talked to a doctor?"

"I didn't have to," she said. "I can see it."

"*What?*"

"It's not just *remote* things, Teddy." She touched her belly. "I looked, and it was right there."

"Jesus Christ on a stick," Teddy said. He breathed out, looking at the seatback in front of him without seeing it.

"You can take it back if you want," she said.

"What?" He couldn't seem to catch his breath.

"The ring."

She wasn't making any sense.

"I need to know what you're thinking, Teddy. I can't see inside your brain."

"What do I think?" He turned to her. His tears and the bright bus window behind her had made her face into a blur haloed in sunlight—a stained-glass angel. "I think this kid's going to be the greatest thing in the world!"

◻

"Welcome to the Hala Kahiki Lounge," he said to Graciella. "The finest tiki bar in Chicagoland."

She eyed the room's bamboo paneling, the fringed lamps, the plastic, grimacing gods lining the walls. "I'm guessing it's the only one?"

"Perhaps, perhaps. But don't disparage an establishment merely because it's outlasted its peers." Patti the waitress greeted him with a kiss on the cheek and showed him to his usual table. He ordered a rum they flew in from Barbados. Graciella stuck with bourbon.

"So," she said significantly, midway through her second drink.

"It's really not a story for polite company," he said.

"All day I sit in court listening to terrible stories," she said. "And every night I talk to my divorce lawyer. I haven't been in polite company for a long time."

"You're leaving Nick Junior?" He tried not to sound happy about it.

"If I can without killing him." She waved a hand. "This story of yours. Get cracking."

"Right." He stirred his drink, deciding where to begin. "I told you

I used to play cards with Nick Senior? There were a few of us who got together every week for a regular game at his place."

"The pizza restaurant," she said.

"Nick had a big table in the kitchen. He'd make pies as we played, open up the wine . . ."

Graciella gestured with two fingers: speed it up.

"Well then. One of these guys in the group, let's call him Charlie, he was one of Nick's best friends. They'd known each other for years, and Charlie did some work on the side for Nick. Nothing violent, but not exactly legal. They'd had this deal for years, no problems. Well, we show up for poker night, and there's tension in the air. Seems Charlie has screwed up, and screwed up bad. A job went south, one of Nick's friends got hurt, and Charlie lost a bunch of money that belonged to, well, certain people—"

"I know what the Outfit is," she said.

"Of course you do, of course you do. And you've heard how much they care about their money. So Nick's making a pizza for the group, white flour up to his elbows, and he starts asking Charlie about how he screwed up. Charlie's nervous but he's playing it cool. And Nick keeps talking at him, and the whole time they're talking Nick's running dough through the pizza roller—you know what that is?"

She shook her head.

"A big machine, with two rollers like metal rolling pins, squashes the dough. It gets going pretty fast, too. And suddenly two guys at the table grab Charlie by the arms and bring him up to the machine."

"Oh God," she said. Getting it now.

"Both hands," Teddy said. "Shoved them in there. First thing that happens, the fingers get crushed flat. The rollers jam up on the wrists, but keep pulling. Then the skin rips off, all the way down to the fingertips."

"Like a glove," Graciella said quietly. She swallowed the rest of her drink.

"I'm sorry I had to tell you that," Teddy said. "But when I think of you, and your boys . . ."

"No. It's all right," she said. She looked into the glass as if it was about to magically refill. "My husband didn't kill Rick Mazzione," she said.

"I didn't say he did."

"He's an idiot, and an asshole, and he may have done plenty of other things—but not that one."

She reached into her big purse, pulled out a green bag, a soft-shell, insulated lunch box with cartoon characters on the front. "I'd like to show you something." She unzipped the bag. Inside were a blue plastic freezer pack and a clear plastic sandwich container. She pushed the container over to him.

He opened the lid, and inside were half a dozen gray pebbles. No, not pebbles.

"Rick Mazzione's teeth," she said. "Nick Senior would very much like them."

"*Why?*"

"It's a long story," she said, and called for another bourbon.

8

Irene

☆

She waited fifty feet from Gate C31, half hidden by a column, as the passengers from Flight 1606 disembarked. She felt like a grocery store dog, one of those jittery creatures tied up outside the glass doors, desperately scanning each human face for its master: Are you the one I love? Are you?

Then she thought: Oh God. The word "love" is in my head.

She was not in love. How could you fall in love with an AOL icon, or a few hundred screenfuls of text? The thrill she felt every time a computer informed her that she did, indeed, have mail was as palpable as a lover's touch.

People kept pouring down the Jetway. It was an early morning flight, and many of the passengers were mussed and sluggish, as if they'd woken up to a fire alarm; they reached the main corridor and peered left and right and left again, trying to get their bearings, before lurching off. The business travelers, however, were *all* business, from their business jackets to their business skirts and their shiny business shoes. They sliced through the crowd of civilians like business sharks.

Last Dad Standing—aka Joshua Lee—was one of those business types, a man who traveled across the country all the time in, yes, business class. She was terrified, though, that she wouldn't recognize him. He'd sent a picture of himself standing in the shade of a palm tree, but her black-and-white ink-jet printer had turned it all into a low-contrast smear, so she'd left the printout at home. The harder she tried to keep the picture in mind, however, the more she doubted her memory.

But there was another reason failing to recognize him terrified her. After they'd been talking online for more than a week, they'd had this exchange:

LAST DAD STANDING: I have something I need to tell you. Two
    things, actually.
IRENE T: Sounds serious.
LAST DAD STANDING: First—my daughter is Chinese.
IRENE T: That's great! I didn't know you'd adopted.
LAST DAD STANDING: Not exactly.

And she'd thought: *Not exactly?* What did that mean? They'd stolen her?

LAST DAD STANDING: That brings us to the second thing. Her
    parents are Chinese, too.

She almost typed back, "Of course her parents are Chinese." Then the penny dropped. Joshua *Lee*.

She felt a rush of embarrassment: retroactive, conditional embarrassment. Had she ever said something bad about Chinese people? Or Asians in general? She mentally scrolled back through the messages they'd exchanged. But of course a racist wouldn't even remember if she'd said something off-color.

Then she became doubly embarrassed when she realized he must be waiting for her to respond. And probably laughing. What a jerk, to tell her this way! Quickly she'd typed back:

IRENE T: Have you told your daughter yet that her parents are
    Asians?
LAST DAD STANDING: Heh. We're waiting for the right time to
    break it to her.
IRENE T: And me, too, evidently.
LAST DAD STANDING: Are you mad I waited?
IRENE T: No. I don't care what you are.

LAST DAD STANDING: That's a relief. Because I'm actually an 80 yr
   old grandmother in Flagstaff.
IRENE T: Then stop typing and knit me something.

They exchanged biographical details like trading cards. He was
third-generation Chinese, she was third-generation on the Irish side
and who-knows-how-many generations on the Greek side (Dad was
hazy on his family history). Culturally, the widest gulf between them
was southwestern versus mid-. (They ignored Male versus Female and
White Collar versus Working Poor, and she didn't bring up Sane versus Psionic.)

She tried to tell him his race didn't matter, that he didn't even need
to mention it, but he said of course he did; it would have been the first
thing she noticed if they'd met face-to-face . . .

. . . which was what they were about to do.

The flow of exiting passengers slowed to a trickle, then stopped.
Half a minute later, a pair of flight attendants came out, wheeling their
micro bags behind them. Where was he? Did he slip past without her
noticing? Or was he not on the flight?

"Irene?" a voice said.

She turned, and looked up into Joshua Lee's smiling face. Of course
she recognized him. He was exactly himself.

She lifted her arm as if to shake his hand, then realized that was
ridiculous. She leaned forward and hugged him. His chest was solid.
And his hand against her back, so real. The *thereness* of him shocked
her.

"So this is you," he said.

"It's me," she said.

"It's so good to—"

"No!" she said. "You promised."

"Right," he said. "The rules. No pleasantries."

"And no emotion words." She winced apologetically. "I know it's
weird."

He started to say something, then stopped himself. "Is hunger an
emotion?"

"Edge case," she said.

"Can I ask if you're hungry? Would you like something to eat?"

"I'll allow it," she said.

"Because I've got three and a half hours before my flight, and I want to try that sandwich you were talking about—the combo."

"Oh, you can't handle the combo. Besides, it'll take us a half hour to get to my car, another twenty minutes to drive to the restaurant—"

"That's plenty of time."

They walked toward the exit, her skin inches from his. She'd been so wrong. Hunger was no edge case.

One night in the chat room, he'd mentioned that he frequently came through Chicago on the way to New York and sat through long layovers. She ignored the hint. He brought it up a couple more times, and then finally came out and said that he was flying through O'Hare next week and wanted to see her. She tried to explain that this was impossible, and that led to a long discussion of what he called her "trust issues" and she called her "reality issues."

LAST DAD STANDING: Why are you so afraid I'll lie to you?

IRENE T: Everybody lies. I'm not saying you're a bad person. I lie all the time. I'll lie to you!

LAST DAD STANDING: You can see how I might have trouble with this.

IRENE T: That's why it won't work for us to meet. I just can't take it in person. Not with someone I care about.

LAST DAD STANDING: See? You care about me! I win.

IRENE T: Unless I'm lying. But I'm not. You see how nice it is to believe me?

But he wouldn't give up. He wore her down, and eventually she agreed to meet him at that airport, but only if he followed certain rules.

IRENE T: You can't say, It's so nice to meet you. You can't say, You look nice.

LAST DAD STANDING: What if you DO look nice?

IRENE T: Doesn't matter. If you say it once, then you'd feel you have to say it every time.

LAST DAD STANDING: I don't see the problem if I'm telling the truth. If I'm happy to see you, I want to tell you.

IRENE T: Tell me here, if you have to. But not out there.

LAST DAD STANDING: Where you can see my big lying liar's face?

IRENE T: I'm sorry. I can't do this any other way.

LAST DAD STANDING: Then that's the way we'll do it. I'm happy to
    try total honesty. No lie.

As they drove out to Johnny's Red Hots, trying to fill the silence without tripping over her conversational rules, she realized she'd made a terrible mistake. "Total honesty" was not what she was asking for; that was what they already had, when they were online together, talking in the dark through their keyboards. She was asking for something impossible: earmuffs that filtered out untruths yet let the rest of his voice through.

Johnny's had just opened for lunch. She wasn't hungry, but she ordered fries to be sociable. He ordered the combo and carried it back to the table in wonder.

"I can't believe this is allowed by state law. You can't just put a pile of shaved beef—"

"Italian beef," she said.

"*Italian* beef on top of a sausage—"

"Italian sausage."

"Right, and then they just let you *eat* it?"

"In Chicago," she said, "meat is a condiment."

Food was a safe topic. As were weather, traffic, air travel, and everything else they didn't want to talk about. She wanted to ask him if he'd spent as much time picking out his clothes this morning as she did; if she looked like, sounded like what he expected; if he was as nervous and giddy as she was. But all that was off the table, by her own decree. When Joshua finished the combo (and he did finish it, sopping up the juice with the last of the soggy bun and popping it into his mouth like a born Southsider), she realized that even with the drive back and the walk through security, they had an hour to fill and nothing to fill it with.

"I'm sorry," she said. "I shouldn't have done this."

"What are you talking about? I'm glad—" He stopped himself. No feeling words.

"See?" she said. "I'm a basket case."

He thought for a moment. Then he reached across the table and put his hand over hers.

"No talking, then," he said. "Let's just look at each other. And later—"

"Later we can say everything online," she said.

"Like good online Americans," he said, and she laughed.

"You can keep holding my hand, though," she said.

"I should really go wash off the grease." And that was the truth.

They drove back in a silence that was thoroughly drowned out by the roar of blood rushing through her. There was something she needed to tell him before he went, something that could end the relationship before it started. After shuffling through the metal detectors, they walked hand in hand through the terminal to his next gate.

"I have to tell you about who I am," she said. "About my family."

"I know all about the Amazing Telemachus Family," he said.

She stopped, let go of his hand. "You do?"

"I asked around, and a friend of mine knew all about you. I figured you were waiting for me to look you up. When you finally told me your last name, you made it sound notorious."

"I did not."

He gave her an amused look. "Am I lying?"

He wasn't. She felt a hot dread, nine-year-old Irene stepping before the cameras.

"So what do you think?" she asked.

"Without using feeling words?" His voice was amused, his eyes kind. She couldn't see a hint of the disdain she'd imagined.

"Right," she said. "Rules." She put her arm through his, and they resumed walking.

"I do have a lot of questions, though," he said.

"Let's talk about it later," she said. Everything was easy in front of the screen, their words zipping effortlessly between the satellites. They'd talked about his divorce, her near-marriage to Lev, his stressful job and her mind-numbing one. Mostly they'd talked about their children. He had joint custody of his ten-year-old daughter, Jun, and worried about the effects of the divorce on her. Irene fretted about Matty, master of sulking and secrecy, who was spending an inordinate amount of time alone in his room.

LAST DAD STANDING: You can't worry about it. Kids are like that.

IRENE T: You have a daughter who tells you everything.

LAST DAD STANDING: Matty's a teenage boy. I never told my parents anything, and look how I turned out. Divorced, in therapy . . . Oh wait. You should worry.

IRENE T: You're in therapy?

LAST DAD STANDING: Was. I've kind of slacked off lately.

IRENE T: Maybe I should get Matty a therapist. When I talk to him, I feel like it's a cross-examination.

LAST DAD STANDING: Permission to treat teenager as a hostile witness, your honor.

IRENE T: Exactly!

Her family's history in the psi business had been the only topic she hadn't had the courage to bring up, and now that he'd hauled it into the light she couldn't believe she'd held on to the secret so long. The thing about skeletons was, you never knew how much space they were taking up in the closet until you got rid of them.

Right now she needed to walk without words, arm in arm with a handsome man who was inexplicably willing to put up with her insane demands, who was not freaked out by her history as a pint-size mind reader.

A man who was about to leave her.

She and Joshua stood without speaking, and as the time to board approached she leaned into him. He put his arm around her.

There you are, she thought. The scent of him touched off something in her back brain that made her think of sunlight and wood and salt.

The PA blared. "That's me," he said.

"I know," she said. She did not want to let go of his arm. But she did it. That was the Irene thing to do.

"Thank you for coming out here," he said. "Taking time off."

"I figured the grocery store could get along without me," she said.

"I'm coming back through again on Thursday," he said. "Maybe we could do this again? It'll be in the afternoon, so maybe we could, I don't know, have a drink. Go someplace nice?"

"I'm sorry this was so weird," she said.

"It wasn't weird at all."

The PA called his section again. He looked over his shoulder, and when he turned back he saw the change in her. She couldn't hide it.

"Oh, Irene." He thought she was sorry to see him go. She was, but that wasn't why she was holding back tears.

Then she saw him understand. "Fuck," he said quietly.

The first lie hung in the air between them. It *had* been weird. Crazy weird. And he'd been too afraid to tell the crazy weird woman who'd driven out here to meet him.

"I'm so sorry," he said. "I didn't mean—"

He stopped himself in another lie. Because he did mean it, and he knew that she knew that he meant it. Both lies were too small to worry about. It was that they were the first in an unstoppable cascade of untruths and half-truths and polite lies and outright deceptions that would pile up around her until she couldn't see him anymore. She'd been caught in this avalanche before. She didn't think she could dig her way out a second time.

When she was young, she thought she'd gotten the best talent in the family. No one could take advantage of her. No one could pull the wool over *her* eyes. While everyone else meandered through life as prey for hucksters and con artists and cads, she was fully armed with x-ray specs and a shoulder-mounted bullshit detector. She was the girl who could not be fooled.

God, what a fool she was.

"I have to go," she said.

"Irene, please, I don't want to leave like this."

"It's okay," she lied. "It's okay. I just can't—"

Can't what? she asked herself. Can't do this again. Can't even start this.

"I just can't." And then she walked away before more words, his or hers, could trip her up.

She drove home slowly, for safety reasons. The state of her soul was not fit for Chicago traffic. When she finally pulled into the driveway, she sat for a long time, staring blankly over the steering wheel. Then Buddy stepped out of the front door wearing an apron and oven mitts. He waved for her to come in.

"Well, fuck," she said.

Inside the house, the air was thick with the smell of warm cookies—

white chocolate macadamia nut cookies. A dozen were already on the cooling rack, and Buddy was pulling another pan from the oven.

"I need all of these," she said. He nodded.

Mom had directed her cooking lessons at Irene, but it was Buddy who'd memorized her recipes. He would make them, but only on his schedule. You couldn't ask him to make Mom's pepper steak, or the bean and bacon soup, or the macadamia nut cookies. You had to wait for the whim to strike, then hope you were around to reap the benefits.

Mail sat on the counter. She shuffled through the stack, dreading a bill addressed to her, but the only thing of interest was a fat envelope for Teddy, from ATI Advanced Telemetry Inc. He'd gotten these envelopes for years, on a monthly basis. He never opened them in front of her, and she thought she knew the reason why.

Matty appeared in the kitchen door, still wearing the yellow Bumblebee shirt Frankie had gotten him. "What *is* that?" he asked.

Buddy shut off the oven, grabbed three semi-cooled cookies, and walked out the back door. That was the other thing about his impromptu cooking events: cleanup was on you.

On the table was a note in her father's wobbly scrawl: "Irene— Dinner Wednesday Palmer's. Dress nice."

"What's this about?" Irene asked. Matty shrugged, reached for a cookie. His hair was mussed, and a pair of zits decorated his chin, but his father's bone structure hid beneath the baby fat. The kid had no idea how handsome he was going to be.

"These are pretty incredible," Matty said finally.

"I was about to say, you shoulda tasted Grandma Mo's, but Buddy's may be better."

"So was it a job interview?" he asked.

"What? Oh, the skirt."

"And the makeup."

"I wear makeup."

"Not since Pittsburgh. And, uh, it's all smeared."

She dabbed at the corner of her eye. "It's not been a good day," she said. She put on a smile to reassure him. He didn't look convinced. "So how was your day? Is Frankie behaving?"

"You didn't answer my question," he said.

"Neither did you. How about this—we go one for one. You answer mine, I'll answer yours."

"Like you're really going to answer my questions."

She laughed. "I will!"

He frowned, looking for loopholes in the deal. Teddy would have been proud. "All right," he said. "But there's a three-question limit."

"You strike a hard bargain, Mr. Telemachus. So is that your first question—was I at a job interview?"

"You're just going to say no, then ask me a question. So let's make this short-answer: Where did you go?"

"To see a friend."

"Was it the guy you talk to on the computer?"

"How did you—? And that's two questions."

"I'll use both of them to hear this," he said. "And it wasn't hard to figure out. You're on the computer all the time. I figured it had to be a guy."

"I could be a lesbian," she said.

"Really?"

"His name is Joshua."

"Josh-u-a," he said. "Josh. The Joshinator."

"So how is it working with Frankie?" she asked. She could see that he wanted to bolt from the table.

"It's fine," he said. Then realized that wasn't the truth. "It's . . . intense."

"Intense how?"

"Two questions," he said.

"I also think this answer is worth it."

"It got . . . I don't know. Uncle Frankie expects, like, a lot out of me? I don't think I can do everything he wants me to do."

"Oh God, is he trying to rope you into that UltraLife stuff?"

Matty looked embarrassed.

"Jesus, you're a *kid*. I'm so sorry, Matty. I'll tell him to keep you out of it."

"No! I mean, he's not involving me in that. It's just that working with him is hard, because he's so . . . ."

"Intense?" Irene said. "And grandiose?"

"That's it," he said. "Intensely grandiose."

"I shouldn't have pushed you into working with him," she said. "I just thought you'd like it."

"You didn't push me into it. I want to do it, to make you some money—"

"Make *me* some money?"

He flushed again. "Make *us* some money, I mean." That was the truth as well.

"Honey, that's not your job," she said. "I make the money. You're the kid. I don't want you to go through what I did."

His eyes widened. "You mean like the ESP stuff?"

"No, I mean—" She wished he wasn't so excited by the showbiz history. "I had to become an adult before my time. When Mom died, I was just ten, and suddenly I was the one having to take care of Frankie and Buddy. Even your grandfather."

Matty picked up another cookie, looked at it for a long moment. "Frankie said Grandma Mo was so powerful the Russians had to kill her."

"Frankie's a conspiracy theorist. He also says the Astounding Archibald killed her. Or is Archibald a Russian spy now?"

"I know but . . ."

"But what?"

"She *was* a spy, right? She worked for the CIA?"

She worked for Destin Smalls, Irene thought. "She was employed by the government. I'm not quite sure which agency."

"So did they, like . . . train her?"

"What?"

"I mean, someone like that, they would have taught her how to—"

"They taught her nothing."

Irene's anger came sudden as the bite of glass under a bare foot. There was something she'd forgotten. Something about Destin Smalls. But the memory refused to show itself.

"Mom?" Matty looked concerned.

"She was a natural talent," Irene said. She cleared her throat. "They took advantage of her, and used her, and then she got sick. No big mystery."

Irene remembered that morning, seven months before her mother died, that Irene found her sitting on the edge of the bed, crying. Then she'd wiped away her tears and driven off with Destin Smalls. That memory, at least, was clear and sharp.

"Why are you asking about this stuff?" Irene said.

"No reason," he said. A lie.

"Stop it. There's a reason."

"This isn't fair," Matty said. "You have an advantage. But you lie to me and I'll never know it."

"I've answered all your questions truthfully and to the best of my ability," she said.

He twisted his mouth into his thinking face. Planning his next move. "Okay, so this Joshua guy. Do you love him?"

She wiped her face with her napkin. "I've only met him in person once," she said. "Just this morning."

He laughed. "You are really not answering the question."

"It doesn't matter if I love him," she said.

A memory was unspooling out of the dark: Destin Smalls and her father, standing in the living room, both of them looking at her.

"It's not going to work out," she said. She recognized doomed romance when she saw it.

☆

Destin Smalls picked up her mother every morning, and dropped her off every afternoon. She learned to hate the arrival of his car, a gleaming hulk with a grill as wide as a whale's baleen, and the way her mother hurried out to it. Eager. Laughing sometimes. In the afternoons Irene would watch from the front window as her mother sat in the car with Smalls, talking and talking, delaying her return to the house, her return to her children and husband. Her return to her duties.

Her mother seemed exhausted by whatever she did all day with Destin Smalls. When she was too tired to make dinner, she'd sit in the kitchen with Buddy on her lap, and instruct Irene on how to cook, only getting out of her seat in emergencies. When Dad came up out of the basement for the meal, he'd heap praise on Irene. She was happy to do the work, until the day she told her mother she'd rather play with her friend.

"We're not playing now, we're making dinner," her mother said.

"Marcie's waiting for me," ten-year-old Irene said. "*You* make dinner."

"Just put the ground beef in the pan," her mother said, exhausted.

"First, brown the meat," Buddy said. He was standing beside her chair, arms draped over her shoulders.

"That's right," their mother said.

"This isn't fair," Irene said.

"First brown the meat!" Buddy yelled. He didn't like it when anyone argued with Mom.

As the summer wore on, her mother sometimes wouldn't stay in the kitchen as she cooked. Mom would hand Irene a recipe card and then go up to her bedroom to rest. Irene liked it better that way.

One morning in late July or early August, her mother was still in the bathroom when Destin Smalls pulled up in his shiny huge car. Irene watched him from the living room, his big rectangle face swimming up to the windshield like a pale fish, peering up at the house. After a few minutes, he stepped out of the car. Irene jumped back from the window. His silhouette glided across the curtains. And then he rang the doorbell.

Irene ran up the stairs and knocked at the bathroom door. "Mom?"

There was no answer.

"Mom? Mr. Smalls is here."

"Tell him I'll be down in a minute," Mom said. Her voice was brittle with false cheer.

When Irene returned to the living room, Buddy was opening the door.

"Hi there, Buddy." Smalls reached out to rub the boy's head. Buddy ran into the next room. He hated anyone touching him.

"She's not ready yet." Irene pointed at her mother's chair, even though her father's was closer. "You can sit there."

Mr. Smalls sat on her father's ottoman, facing the stairs that led up to the bathroom—and the stairs that led down to the basement, where her father was sleeping.

"So how's school, Irene?" Mr. Smalls asked.

"It's summer," she said.

"Right, right." He glanced toward the stairs leading to the second floor.

"She'll be down in a minute," Irene said.

"I thought I heard voices," her father said. Teddy stepped into the room. He wore pajama bottoms and an undershirt, and his cheeks were shadowed. "How are you doing, Destin? Business good at the spook shop?"

"Good to see you, Teddy." Destin stood and extended a hand. Her father hesitated, then shook. He'd taken off the bandages a few months earlier.

"I was just talking to Irene here," Mr. Smalls said. "She's turning into a lovely girl." He looked down at Irene and smiled a false smile.

"Are you in love with my mother?" Irene asked.

"What?" Smalls said.

"I said, are you—"

"Of course not!"

Her father was staring at her. He knew exactly what she was doing.

From upstairs came the sound of water running in the sink, and then the door opening. Each sound seemed unusually loud. "Sorry I'm running late," her mother said, and stopped on the stairs. She frowned. Looked at Dad, then at Destin Smalls.

"Mr. Smalls is a liar," Irene said, and walked out of the room.

☆

Later in the week she came home from Aldi's to find Teddy pacing the living room. "Where have you been? We've got to be there by six!"

Oh, right. Wednesday dinner at Palmer's to meet his "sweetie." Somehow, somewhen, Teddy had started dating. She thought she knew why Teddy wanted Irene to meet the woman, and hoped she was wrong.

"Give me a minute, Dad. It's been a long day."

"Just get into the best dress you got. No—second best. She's the star, not you."

Teddy, of course, was already wearing his most expensive suit, a gunmetal-blue number with navy pinstripes, and one of his more diamond-encrusted watches. Teddy Telemachus never took second billing. "Now hurry up!" he said. "I don't want her waiting for us."

Her being the "sweetie." He still hadn't explained why he wanted Irene to come out to a restaurant with them.

"Jesus, all right already. Could you at least put in a Tombstone pizza for Matty?"

"I can't *cook*," Teddy said. "Not in this!"

"I'm pretty sure I can put a pizza in the oven," Matty said.

"Good man," Teddy said. "Just don't eat the whole thing, okay?"

"Damn it, Dad!" Irene said.

Irene went upstairs, but all she could think about was going into the basement and turning on the computer. For the past two days she'd kept edging up to it, warily, as if peeking over the lip of a cliff, only to back away before she lost her footing. But a half hour later she'd approach it again, as if to remind herself that the fall could kill her.

She imagined an inbox filled with confused messages from Joshua. Or worse, an inbox with no messages from Joshua. Logging into the chat room was out of the question. If she did, she'd immediately start talking to him, which would lead to her promising to meet him at the airport on Thursday, and once she was face-to-face with him, the whole process would repeat, from first touch to hormonal tsunami to the sudden apprehension that their relationship was doomed. The only sane thing to do was nip that Wagnerian cycle in the bud. Kill the wabbit.

She put on one of the dresses she used to wear to work, back when she worked in a place that didn't require polyester smocks. Smocks were the official uniform of those hanging on to the bottom rungs of the economic ladder; a parachute that would never open. Joshua said he worried about money, but he was in no danger of plummeting into poverty.

She emerged from the bedroom to find Teddy bouncing on his feet at the bottom of the stairs. "Is this okay?" she asked him.

"It's kinda dowdy," he said. "Perfect choice."

He drove, cursing traffic the whole way. She'd never seen him this nervous. "So how did you meet this woman?" Irene asked. "You hanging out in some senior center you haven't told me about?"

"I'll tell you when we get there. It's a great story, great story. Almost destiny."

They didn't walk into the restaurant until ten after six. Dad scanned the lobby and bar for the mystery woman, and was relieved that she hadn't arrived yet. Irene apologized again for making him late, but he waved it off.

"Six-thirty reservation for Telemachus," Teddy told the hostess.

"Six-*thirty*?" Irene said.

"I knew you'd be late," Teddy said.

Their table was available now. Teddy hung his fedora on the brass hat rack, and Irene wasn't a bit surprised that there were half a dozen hats already there. Palmer's Steakhouse was Teddy's favorite restaurant because the rib eyes were thick, the drinks strong, and the prices cheap. The average age in the dining room stayed north of sixty.

Dad positioned Irene to his left and reserved the chair on his right for his guest. The waitress was pouring water before they'd pushed in their chairs. Teddy had a thing for the waitresses, an all-Ukrainian squad with severe cheekbones, chain-smoker lips, and great legs. They moved the plates on and off the table like it was some kind of Olympic event. Nobody dawdled over the salad at Palmer's. While you were taking your last sip of soup, the bowl would be gone before you put your spoon down.

"G and T?" the waitress asked him.

"You know me too well, Oksana. But I'm going to hold off ordering until my friend arrives."

"*Another* friend, eh?"

"I'm his daughter," Irene said.

The waitress shrugged and walked away. Teddy laughed.

"I don't even know why I'm here," Irene said. "What's this woman's name?"

"There she is now." Teddy stood up and buttoned his coat. He met her halfway across the room and took her arm.

Irene had expected that Dad might go for a younger woman— someone in her sixties, perhaps. This woman looked to be holding tight to her early forties with the assistance of good makeup, Tae Bo classes, and money. That little black dress would have cost the entirety of Irene's little blue paycheck. What the hell was going on here?

Dad escorted her to the table. "Graciella, this is my daughter, Irene."

Graciella. That name seemed familiar. "A pleasure to meet you," Irene said, and shook her hand. Then it was just a matter of waiting for the first lie. Three . . . two . . .

"I'd say that Teddy's told me all about you," Graciella said. "Except that he didn't say a thing."

Honesty, right out of the gate. Whaddya know.

Irene said, "Well, Dad didn't even tell me your name till just now."

"I'm not surprised," Graciella said. "I think he likes to play the mysterious man in the hat."

"I've made a mistake," Dad said jokingly. "Dinner's over. So glad you two met."

The waitress materialized at the table. "Drinks now?"

"Oh yeah," Irene said. "We're going to need a lot of drinks."

The meal proceeded with Palmerian efficiency, propelled by the fast hands of Oksana. The conversation weaved between the flying plates on a river of alcohol. Graciella was a drinker, and Irene was happy to keep pace while she tried to suss out who this woman was and what she was doing with her father. When she fibbed, it seemed to be mostly for politeness; the big lies, Irene suspected, were lies of omission. She mentioned kids, and said they were all fine (kids were never all fine), but the husband was absent from the conversation—despite the wedding ring on her hand and an engagement diamond the size of a meteorite.

Dad had turned courtly and solicitous—to Graciella anyway; Irene was left to order her own drinks. Dad laughed at everything the woman said, kept touching her arm, recommended favorite menu items like he was on staff. After they'd ordered dessert ("The lava cake's stupendous," Teddy announced), Graciella excused herself to the ladies' room.

"So," Teddy said. "Do you like her?"

"What the hell are you doing, Dad?"

"Try to calm down. I know it's difficult for children when their widowed father falls in love, but I was hoping you could—"

"Back the hell up. You're in *love* with her?"

"I am," he said with formality.

"Are you sleeping with her?"

"That is none of your business."

"Dad, she's married."

"Not wisely, and not well. Nick Pusateri doesn't deserve her."

"Who's Nick—?" And then she remembered where she'd heard the name. "Shit. Is Graciella the mobster's wife?"

"Don't be judgmental. It's not attractive."

"You're banging a gangster?!"

"I'm not *banging* her," Teddy said. "Besides, I'm pretty sure she's throwing no carnal thoughts in my direction. I'm"—he made a vague gesture with three fingers—"cute."

"You're also twice her age."

"Don't be ridiculous. I don't fall in love with anyone unless they're at least half my age plus seven. Bare minimum."

"You just *decide* who you fall in love with, huh?"

"You should try it sometime. Walk into a grocery store—not that awful place you work, I recommend Dominick's—and pick out a stranger. Look for the beauty in them. Look at the way they hold a melon. Listen to the way they talk to the clerk. And say to yourself, I love this person."

"You do this a lot?"

"Every day."

"You're going to get arrested."

"It would be worth it," he said.

"Fine. You're an emotional daredevil. All I'm saying, you couldn't try to jump into the pants of somebody who wasn't Lady Macbeth?"

"Lady Macbeth wouldn't wear pants."

"Listen to me, Dad—you can't be trying to screw a gangster's wife. It's suicidal."

"And you're not listening to me." He glanced toward the restrooms to make sure Graciella wasn't on her way back. "It's not about screwing and banging and—where did you get such a filthy mouth? It's not about sex. I haven't used my dick in so long I wouldn't know where to find it. I sent it out for a pack of Camels in 1979 and it never came back."

"I really don't want to be talking to my father about his dick."

"Irene, this is about finding someone. You find someone and you make them the most important person in your life—even if just for a little while. A day! An hour even! Tell me how that's a bad thing."

"The bad thing is when the important person's husband shoots you in the back of the head."

"Fair point," he said. He still had one eye on the entrance to the restrooms.

"What am I doing here, Dad? I'm the last person you should bring along if you want to stay with this woman."

"She's coming back," Dad said. "I just need to know one thing—do you like her?"

Irene sighed. "I kinda do, actually."

"Perfect," he said.

And suddenly Irene realized that she'd been tricked into something. What, she had no idea.

She'd discovered a fact of modern life by standing at a cash register for hours: mindless work could nevertheless fill up your mind, like radio static. If she stayed busy—pushing canned goods down the chute with her left hand while busily ten-keying the prices with her right, making small talk, sorting cash—then she didn't have to think about what day it was, what time certain flights landed, or how she was going to die alone.

"You getting a cold, doll?" Phyllis asked from the next register.

"I'm fine," Irene lied.

Phyllis harrumphed. She was a champion harrumpher.

Irene had stayed off the computer for four days, a new record since the day it arrived. Her father was delusional about choosing to fall in love, but maybe the opposite was true: you could choose not to fall in love. All she had to do was keep totaling the cans of Aldi cola (twenty-two cents apiece), keep boxing the groceries, and send each customer out of the store with a cheery goodbye.

"Kill the wabbit," Irene said.

The customer, a woman who was too old to date her father by twenty years, said, "Pardon?"

"Nothing," Irene said, and presented her the receipt as if it were a winning lottery ticket. "Have a nice day." On to the next customer.

But there was nothing on the conveyor belt. Irene looked up, and the next customer was a man in a business suit.

"Joshua? What are you—?"

He put a finger to his lips.

She stepped around the deck of the aisle, embarrassed by her polyester uniform, her pulled-back hair. She hadn't even put on mascara. "You shouldn't have come here."

Without saying a word he stepped to her. Raised his eyebrows. Waited.

Shit. He was right. No more words.

She pulled his face to hers and kissed him.

9

Frankie

How the hell did coaches stop themselves from killing their star players? Frankie wondered. At first you're in love with everything they can do for you. You start dreaming about glory. You can hear the roar of the crowds. But then you start depending on them. You need them. And eventually, as the training wears on, the star begins to doubt you. They have ideas of their own. And every time they don't do what you ask them to do, you feel like they're taking something away from you. Stealing glory.

"Listen, Matty. All you have to do is watch me open the safe, then come tell me the combination. If you don't practice, it's never going to work. Trust me. I've been through this."

"I am practicing," Matty said. He sat on the safe, arms around his stomach, staring at the garage floor. "Just . . . not in front of you."

"Don't you trust me?"

"It's not you. I can't do it in front of anybody."

"How do you know unless you try? I'm beginning to think you don't have what it takes, Matty."

"I've gone really far, Uncle Frankie. The past couple weeks. All on my own. So I'm ready to try Mitzi's Tavern."

Frankie was stunned. "Right now?"

"Tonight. Or tomorrow night. It depends."

"On what?"

The kid flushed red.

"Jesus, okay," Frankie said. "You do what you do. I believe in you. You're my Walter Payton, Matty. I know you can bring this home for us." He rubbed a hand across his face. He was sweating again. Was he sounding too desperate? "Just let me know if I can help. Or something."

"I just need one thing," Matty said.

Yes!

"Name it," Frankie said.

"I need money," he said. "Fifty bucks."

"What? Why?"

"Please. You can take it out of my cut."

"All right. All right. If my star needs cash, cash he will receive."

○

The summer of 1991, he made the garage into his own private Bellagio. He'd gotten ahold of a real roulette wheel that was used by St. Mary's church for their Vegas Night fund-raiser, as well as a felt cloth layout with all the bet markings on it, and set it up on a table that was the right height. He even borrowed a box of chips from his dad's stash, just for flavor. Then, for hour after hour, he'd spin the wheel, send the "pill" rolling along the track, and then try to push it, just like he pushed the pinball around on the Royal Flush game at the skating rink.

Grabbing the pill, though, was a lot trickier than moving the pin-ball. For one, it was lighter, just an ounce or so, and too much of a nudge sent it flying out of the wheel. But worse, it was plastic. Frankie had always had a better feel for metal.

He couldn't affect the little white ball at all. It would bounce over the frets, fall into a random number . . . and sit there, ignoring him. "Fuck you," he said to it. "Fuck you and your little white ass."

He would have given up immediately if it weren't for Buddy's vision. Loretta was pissed about how much time he was spending in the garage. She had two toddlers in the house, getting wilder by the day. There was no way they could afford twins, not on his salary. Bellerophonics was failing, and he was borrowing from the Pusateris to keep it afloat. He'd told no one this.

He needed a win. He needed those stacks and stacks of chips.

If, according to Buddy, Future Frankie could control a roulette table, that meant Current Frankie just had to learn how, right? But nothing was happening. It wasn't "hard work," because it wasn't working at all. The ball wouldn't even slow down for him in the track. The damn thing wouldn't so much as tremble in his presence.

"Fuck you!" he screamed at it. "Stupid fucking piece of plastic crap!"

He went to Buddy and told him the deal was off. "Your vision's bullshit," he said.

Buddy said nothing. He was on the back patio, doing his newspaper thing, flipping back and forth through the pages, frowning and shaking his head, like an old man who can't believe what the world's come to.

"Buddy, look at me. Hey." Frankie put his hand in front of the page. Buddy swung his big face toward him. "I can't do it," Frankie said.

"You're guaranteed to win," Buddy said.

"If it's guaranteed, why bother to learn to push at all? Maybe I just win by luck."

Buddy shook his head. "No. You drive me to the casino. You play for two hours. You get stacks of chips. The only way that happens is if you control the ball, just like you used to at the rink."

"It's not working," Frankie said. "I can't do it with that stupid fucking plastic thing."

"Be the ball," Buddy said.

"That's fucking *Caddyshack*," Frankie said. Buddy had watched that movie dozens of times.

"Love the ball." Buddy stood, folded the paper.

"Yeah, but what if I choose not to do it?" Frankie said. "Your vision can't make me."

"Shut up," Buddy said.

"But—"

Buddy wheeled on him, jabbed a finger in his chest. "Shut up! Shut up! Shut up!" Three angry jabs. He was near tears.

"Jesus Christ," Frankie said. "Fine. I'll try."

He went back to his garage, listened to the clacking spin of the wheel, the tinkety-tinkety-tink of the pill as it found its home. Nothing he did slowed it down or sped it up or bounced it into the numbers he wanted. "Mother*fucker*!" he screamed.

His problem in the past had always been confidence. Just having somebody looking at him while he worked was enough to make him nervous and lose his touch. And if those people wanted him to fail, if their negative vibes were coming at him like fucking Astounding Archibald's on *The Mike Douglas Show*? Game over.

But maybe this was a different problem.

Love the ball.

Frankie picked up the roulette ball, held it up to his face. Took a breath.

"I would like to apologize for calling you a motherfucker," he said.

He began to carry the pill around with him. He'd roll it around in his palm until he could feel it warming to his blood. He'd clean it with chamois. He talked to it the way he used to talk to the twins when they were in Loretta's belly, telling them the story of Castor and Pollux.

Loretta, speaking from somewhere on the other side of her belly, said, "What did you just call them?"

"Castor and Pollux? The greatest twins in Greek myth?"

"Hell no."

He'd have to win her over. The same with the pill. "Just tell me where *you* want to go," he told the ball. "Or just the neighborhood." Predicting the exact number where it landed paid thirty-five to one, but that level of precision wasn't required, and wasn't even the smartest way to go about robbing the bank. He could bet one of the dozens (say, numbers one through twelve) and that would pay off two to one, and no one would suspect him. Once he got confident he could play a street of three adjacent numbers for an eleven-to-one payout, or a two-number split for seventeen to one.

The problem, of course, was that adjacent numbers were never adjacent on the wheel. The one and the two, for example, were across the wheel from each other. There was one bet, though, that could help him out.

"I have a suggestion," he mentioned to the pill casually, as it contemplated its drop into the wheel. "Why not drop into the basket?" The basket was a special bet that paid off eleven to one on the single-zero, one, or two—and the single-zero and the two were side by side on the wheel.

He watched the pill lose momentum, and then plunk across the frets like a banjo player. Finally it came to rest like an egg on a pillow.

Zero.

After he finished whooping and jumping around, he picked up the pill and kissed it. "Thanks, pal," he said. "Good job."

He sat in his van a half block from Mitzi's Tavern, watching guys walk into the bar sad and exit sadder, like penitents going to confessional and coming out sentenced to a thousand Hail Marys. Fridays were payday—or rather, pay up day. A lot of these guys owed their whole paychecks to the Pusateris and were hoping they'd be allowed to take a slice home.

Frankie was one of those guys. His problem was, he didn't have the dough. Again.

Nick's rule was, Don't make me come looking for you. So even if you couldn't cover your payment, you had to show up to Mitzi's, explain yourself, and take your punishment. First time, you got her I'm-Not-Angry-I'm-Disappointed speech. Second time—he didn't know what happened the second time. But he was about to find out.

He walked across the street like a man with a bomb strapped to his chest.

Inside, it was so dark he could barely make out Barney behind the bar. Frankie took a stool and waited for his eyes to adjust. "Is she free?" he asked. He knew she wasn't. He could hear Mitzi in her office, yelling at the guy ahead of him.

Barney didn't look up. He was squinting at a *Reader's Digest* over the tops of his glasses, which somehow made him look even more like Droopy Dog.

"Bud Light," Frankie said.

Barney turned a page. "You won't be here that long," he said.

Frankie started to object, then figured there was no percentage in pissing the man off. "Good point," he said.

Here was the difference between Frankie and the poor bastard getting chewed out, and all those other bastards who'd gone in before him: Frankie was practically family. Teddy had worked for Mitzi's brother back in the day, and Frankie had been coming in this bar since he was a kid. Mitzi liked him. That fondness, he figured, was credit that could earn him a grace period of at least a week. Even if Teddy had no idea this was happening.

The door to her office opened, and a young guy with tight jeans and an even tighter shirt came out. A big Italian goombah, six-foot-something, with too much gel in his hair. Tears were running down his cheeks. He hurried out to the door and vanished in a flash of daylight.

"You're up," Barney said.

He eased himself off the stool. The room telescoped, and the path to her door became a great distance. His legs walked it against his will.

O

The *Alton Belle* floated in the shallow Mississippi like a star-spangled wedding cake. It was a replica of a nineteenth-century paddle wheel steamer strung with lights and pulsing with disco music, promising some kind of Mark Twain–meets–Vegas grandeur. Frankie was so nervous he felt like throwing up.

Buddy, though, was vibrating with excitement.

"This is how you saw it, right?" Frankie asked. They hadn't left the car yet. Frankie had driven the four and a half hours, of course, because Buddy had never learned to drive.

"Exactly," Buddy said. "This is exactly right."

"Stacks of chips," Frankie said.

"Stacks," Buddy confirmed.

They joined the stream of people walking the gangplank. They had a half hour before the boat left the dock for its first cruise of the night;

by law the casino had to be on a functional, moving ship. Inside, it was incredibly loud, bells jangling as if every God damn player was a winner, just scooping coins from the slots. Even with all the mirrors, the place seemed much smaller than Frankie had pictured it. Every available space was crammed with slot machines, and every slot machine seemed to have an old person leaning on it as if it were life support.

"Where do we go?" Frankie asked. Buddy didn't seem to hear him. "Where is the roulette table?" Frankie said, louder.

Buddy shrugged. "I don't know this part."

"Wait, there are parts you don't know?"

"This way," Buddy said, ignoring Frankie's panic. The big man pushed through the crowd, Frankie following close in his wake. They were aiming for the middle of the boat, but walking in a straight line was impossible; they kept getting diverted by banks of machines, all clanging, beeping, and flashing for their attention. You could almost fool yourself into thinking you were in a tiny Vegas casino, if not for the customers, who were 80 percent midwestern shit-kickers: John Deere caps and St. Louis Cardinals T-shirts, flip-flops and basketball shorts; even guys in overalls. If the taxpayers of Alton, Illinois, were expecting high rollers, they were in for a disappointment. None of these yokels were James Bond.

Buddy checked his watch, then led them up the grand staircase to the A deck, where they found an array of blackjack tables, a long craps table, and two roulette tables. At the chips window Frankie handed over his life savings—two thousand and five hundred dollars—and the woman handed him back a crushingly small stack of chips in a plastic tray. The entirety of his hopes and dreams was smaller than a box of Girl Scout cookies.

"Where's yours?" Frankie asked his brother.

"You don't need any more," Buddy said.

"According to the vision," Frankie said.

"Right," Buddy said.

Chips in hand, they walked up to the tables. "Which one?" Frankie asked.

Buddy frowned at him.

"Which roulette table?" Frankie clarified.

Buddy studied them both, and then pointed to the one on the left.

"Are you sure?" Frankie asked. "Because you don't look too sure."

Buddy said nothing.

They approached the chosen table, Frankie's fingers tight around the tray of chips. Only one other customer stood at the rail. The croupier, a tall black woman, called for bets. Frankie looked at the wheel and froze, his heart pounding. Frankie grabbed his brother's arm and yanked him back into the crowd.

"What the fuck is that?" Frankie demanded. Buddy didn't know what he was talking about. "That wheel! It's too big!"

Buddy shrugged.

"And the ball's bigger, too!" Frankie said. "I don't even know how much it weighs! Why didn't you tell me they came in different sizes?"

"It's all going to work out," Buddy said.

"What fucking use is a fortune-teller who can't tell me how to win the fucking fortune!"

Buddy grabbed him by the shoulders. "Listen to me."

"What?"

"Stacks of chips. Piled high. That's what I saw."

The steam whistle blew, and the floor trembled. The boat was under way for its hour-long cruise.

"Now is the time," Buddy said. "Right now." Buddy was so *intense*. And talkative. He'd barely spoken since Mom died, and now he was issuing orders like General Fucking Patton.

"Okay," Frankie said. He took a breath. "You saw the stacks, though, right?"

"Shut up," Buddy said.

Frankie moved up to the table but did not signal to bet. A couple more players had joined in, a woman in a low-cut tank top and her lower-browed boyfriend. The Cro-Magnon placed a couple of twenty-dollar chips on red, and the croupier called for last bets.

Then the spin. At least the sound was the same as the church set in his garage. Frankie kept his eyes on the white pill racing along the track.

"Be the ball," Buddy said in his ear.

Love the ball, Frankie thought.

Of course the casino wouldn't let him touch the pill. He'd have to befriend it from a distance. "Who's a good boy?" he said under his breath. "You are. Yes you are. Land on black for me, okay? Black, black, black . . ."

The croupier glanced at him, then looked back to the table and called, "Black! Twenty-six!"

The Cro-Magnon grunted. Frankie smiled. "Good boy," he said.

Fifteen minutes later, Frankie and the pill were the best of pals.

O

Mitzi sat behind her desk, hardly anything visible but that wizened face and a pile of hair, like a shrunken head. "What, no gifts?" she asked.

Frankie tried to smile.

"Because I got to tell you, that philo-ultra-magic whatever put me regular as a Swiss clock."

"Really?" He felt an egg-sized warmth high in his chest. Hope, or heartburn, or both. "I'll bring some over next time."

"And what do you got for me *this* time?" she asked.

He opened his mouth, but words failed to arrive. He lifted his hands. They hovered there for a second, and then settled nervously on his knees.

Mitzi didn't seem surprised. She'd probably read the news on his face as soon as he walked in her door.

"You're at forty-four thousand, five hundred and eleven," Mitzi said.

Jesus, the interest was killing him. "I know," he said.

"And seventy-eight cents."

His hands came up again, failed to get any lift, and came down hard. "I know that's serious money." He took a breath. "I was just wondering, maybe you could—"

She cut him off. "I can't do anything for you, kid. You did this. And now it's out of my hands."

"I just thought that maybe, I don't know, since we've known each other so long, you could maybe talk to Nick Senior? Put in a word?"

Mitzi stared at him. "A *word*? What word would that be? 'Abracadabra'?"

"Our families go way back, right? Teddy and Nick Senior—"

"You don't know shit about Teddy and Nick."

"Okay, sure, Dad didn't tell me everything, mum's the word, right?

I don't ask for specifics, and Dad's a pro, he don't tell. I just thought if you ask your brother to let the son of an old friend—"

"No, Frankie. *You're* going to talk to Nick."

"What?"

"And he's not in the mood for this shit. It's a bad time. You read the papers?"

"The trial," Frankie said.

"They say Junior's going to testify against his own father," she said. "Family turning on family. So you really want to appeal to *history*, you go right ahead and try that. But if I were you, I wouldn't show up with your hat in your hand—not unless you got at least ten grand in there."

"Ten?"

"Ten is the minimum to keep Nick from going ballistic. Bring twenty."

"Where am I going to get twenty grand?"

"You'll think of something," Mitzi said.

You bet your ass I'll think of something, Frankie thought.

O

Later, whenever people talked about the best times of their life—a topic that often came up in the bars he frequented, among people whose inventory of great times was pretty thin—and it was Frankie's turn to lie, he'd tell people about the day his twins were born. But the twins' birth was two minutes of mucus-coated awe after eighteen hours of Loretta thrashing and cursing like Linda Blair in *The Exorcist*. No, the *best* time of his life was the first hour he spent at the roulette table in the *Alton Belle* riverboat casino in September 1991.

His first bet was on the basket, the zero-one-two combination. The croupier scooped up his chips and placed a marker there. Buddy stood behind him as the pill circled the track, and when it dropped onto the zero, his brother grunted in satisfaction. Frankie could hardly contain himself. Fist pumping may have been involved. He'd only bet a hundred in chips, but at eleven to one he'd just made back a third of his stake.

"Take your time," Buddy said. Advice that was undercut by the fact that Buddy kept checking his watch.

Frankie decided it would be too risky to keep winning on the same numbers, so he put two hundred down on the first dozen. The numbers one through twelve were scattered around the wheel, and in order to win he needed to get the pill to drop at the right time; one number early or late was no payout. The first time he missed by a digit. He'd *felt* the pill that time, almost like it was rolling in the palm of his hand. The heavier weight, he realized, made it feel a little closer to the pinballs he used to have such rapport with.

"It's good to lose a few," Frankie said to Buddy. His brother nodded, not worried at all.

Frankie put two hundred more down on the dozen, same bet as before, and the next spin came up on the black six. Two-to-one payout, four hundred bucks.

The pill loved him. Wanted to please him. It would slow down or speed up as he desired, happily bound over nonpaying slots and rattle home in his favorite numbers. Frankie kept his bets small, trying not to attract attention, but the urge to push all his chips onto, say, double-zero was nearly irresistible.

An hour in, Frankie was holding fifty-three thousand dollars in chips. The waitresses wouldn't stop bringing him drinks—he was ordering gin and tonics, his dad's drink—and a crowd of other players had gathered around the table, trying to absorb some of his luck. Everybody was trying to play with him, chips all over the layout. Why the hell hadn't he done this before? Frankie thought. He should have moved to fucking Reno ages ago!

"This is a great gift, Buddy," Frankie said. He was tearing up he was so grateful. And maybe a little drunk. "Thank you."

Buddy seemed embarrassed. "It's nothing." He picked up a stack of chips, and started counting them into his hand.

"What are you doing?" Frankie asked.

"I need these," Buddy said. "Exactly one thousand, two hundred and fifty dollars."

"What for? Wait—is this another part of the vision?"

"Definitely," Buddy said.

Far away, the steam whistle blew again; the boat was approaching the dock. The first cruise was over, and the next one would be starting up soon. Frankie didn't want Buddy to leave him—he'd been counting on his brother to keep everything in line with his visions. But Frankie had to admit, he had the roulette portion under control. And if Buddy had a scheme for another part of the boat, slots or Keno or craps, Frankie shouldn't stand in his way. Any game in the casino was vulnerable to his brother. Any jackpot was there for the taking.

"You go do it, Buddy," Frankie said. He handed him another five hundred in chips. "Knock 'em dead."

Buddy looked at the extra chips, then set them back on the table in front of Frankie. "I've got what I need," he said. "Just keep playing. Don't stop."

The croupier sent the ball spinning and called for bets.

"Wait," Frankie said to Buddy. "I'm supposed to go for one more hour, right? Where do I find you after?"

Buddy checked his watch. "I'll find you," he said, and headed into the crowd.

Frankie didn't like it, but he kept his cool. And after a few more spins, it was clear his friendly relationship with the pill was intact. Other players started to copy his bets, and he could feel the crowd's attention on him. It was like being onstage again with the Amazing Telemachus Family, but better. He was the solo act. The closer. The top bill. If only his mother could see him now.

"Twenty-eight," Frankie said. "Straight up." One number, thirty-five-to-one payout.

The croupier gave him the merest glance, and Frankie could read her disapproval. Well, fuck you, lady! he thought. I'm here to win. I know it, the crowd knows it.

Then the pill dropped onto the twenty-eight, and the laughter and applause broke out around the table. Someone clapped him on the back. The woman next to him, a chubby redhead with friendly green eyes, giggled and rested a hand on his forearm.

On the next bet, Frankie said, "Let it ride." The redhead gasped. Very satisfying. Myriad hands pushed chips onto the layout, everybody wanting to get on the party bus. He barely needed to look at the wheel to tell the pill where to drop.

The shouts went up like fireworks.

He suppressed the urge to take a bow. In front of him was more money than he'd ever dreamed of making.

A man in a dark suit and gold name tag had appeared behind the croupier, whispering into her ear. The croupier nodded, then stepped away from the table. The man with the name tag waved another croupier forward, this one a burly white man.

The new croupier called for bets. Frankie took a small stack, just a thousand bucks, and bet on red. It was a double-or-nothing payout, like hardly playing at all, but it gave him time to think. This time he didn't try to control the ball, just let it run around the track, off the leash.

"Red! Thirty-two!" the croupier said. Another win. The floor manager or pit boss or whatever he was had not left the table. He looked at Frankie with a blank expression that could have meant anything.

Shit, Frankie thought. Now even blind luck was fucking him over. He needed to lose, and now. He left the small stack on red, and matched it with another thousand. The crowd seemed disappointed. To go from a straight-up bet to a time-waster?

He couldn't leave the table, though. That would break the vision. And what would happen then?

"Tissue, champ?" It was the redhead.

He'd started to sweat. Nixon-versus-Kennedy sweat. He took the handful of Kleenex and mopped his eyes. The pill was humming along the track, and he was thinking, Black black black black—

"Red!" the new croupier said. "Red seven. Seven red."

"Fuck," Frankie said.

"What's the matter?" asked the redhead.

"Pick a number," Frankie said. Belatedly he put a smile on his face.

"I think you'd better do that," she said.

"Please. Any number."

"Twenty-one," she said.

"Great." Frankie pushed five thousand onto twenty-one, then watched with dread as the croupier replaced the stack with the marker. The pit boss was staring at him. Frankie glanced at his watch. He just needed to last five more minutes. Five minutes! Then he could cash out and get the hell out of here.

The redhead gripped his arm more tightly as the pill slowed. "Come on, twenty-one!" she said.

"Jesus, just shut up," he said under his breath.

"What did you say?" She pulled her arm away.

"Nothing, just—" His eye was on the ball. Months of practice had taught him to judge velocity. And God damn if the pill wasn't heading for the neighborhood of twenty-one: nineteen, thirty-one, eighteen, six . . . and then it dropped. Twenty-one.

"FUCK ME!" Frankie shouted.

Later, he realized that it looked very much like a bomb going off. The roulette wheel jumped ten feet into the air and spun away like a flying saucer. The pill shot into the crowd. Every chip around the table—Frankie's huge stacks, the croupier's supplies, the winnings of every player at the table—exploded ceiling-ward and rained down. Every customer within fifty feet of the table became a shouting, grasping, delirious animal.

The redhead looked at him in shock. "What did you do?" she said.

Firm hands grabbed him under his arms. Two large men in dark suits had seized him. "This way, asshole," one of them said, and they hauled him toward a door.

"It wasn't me!" he shouted. "It wasn't me!"

○

He left Mitzi's Tavern, thinking about big numbers. Big numbers and contingency plans. How the hell was he going to raise twenty grand? There was only one way.

"God damn it!" He'd pulled into the driveway and had banged into a line of big plastic buckets, sending them tumbling. Farther up the driveway sat bags of cement mix, a stack of blond lumber, and a pallet of something covered by a tarp. He backed up and parked in the street.

Buddy squatted by the front door of the house. He was hammering away at a wooden frame that he'd erected around the cement step. Frankie marched down the driveway, heading for the garage and the back of the house, ignoring him.

Buddy put down his hammer and stood up. "He's not there."

"The Buddha speaks," Frankie said. Then: "Who's not there?"

Buddy said nothing.

Frankie walked toward him. It looked like he was building a form to repour the cement step, which had been listing for the past decade.

But why now? Why anything, with Buddy. "Why do you care who I'm looking for?" Frankie asked. "Maybe I'm looking for Irene."

Buddy squinted at him. Then Frankie realized that Irene's car was nowhere in sight.

"Okay, fine," Frankie said. "Where's Dad? And don't you fucking shrug at me."

Buddy stood very still, emphatically not shrugging. After thirty seconds, Buddy said, "It's all going to work out."

"Really? Work *out*?" Frankie stepped close, getting in his space. "Work out like the fucking casino?"

Buddy blinked down at him.

Jesus Christ, all Frankie wanted to do just then was clock him. But he'd never laid a hand on his brother. When they were kids, Buddy was too small to smack, and then, suddenly, he was much too big. At any size, though, there was no point to it. It'd be like punching a golden retriever.

Buddy's gaze went glassy, like a TV show had clicked on in his head.

Frankie snapped his fingers at him. "Hey. Retard."

Buddy focused on Frankie. He frowned.

"Why'd you do it?" Frankie said. "Come on. Just come clean." Buddy had never told him where he'd disappeared to with his stack of chips. Never told him why he'd sent him to the *Alton Belle* in the first place. He was supposed to be rich, damn it. Bellerophonics would have been saved, and he wouldn't be in hock to the fucking Outfit and wondering if the next time he stuck a key in the ignition the van was going to explode.

Buddy said, "It's all going to—"

"Yeah yeah yeah," Frankie said. "Of course it will."

AUGUST

10

Buddy

$$\boxed{+}$$

The World's Most Powerful Psychic has been dead for twenty-one years. Long live the World's Most Powerful Psychic.

Buddy doesn't feel powerful, however. Time's riptide is having its way with him. He's clawing to stay in the present but keeps being dragged over and over into the past. Once, his memory of the future was as lengthy (and full of holes) as his memory of the past. But now, there's so little future left. Everything ends in a month, on September 4, 1995, promptly at 12:06 p.m.

Zap.

Sometimes when he thinks about that day he's terrified. Other times, he's merely sad. He will miss out on so much, but what hurts most of all is that he will never see his true love again.

But still other times, he's grateful. There are undoubtedly many awful things to come after that dead stop, and he doesn't have to watch them over and over. The future will no longer be his responsibility. Someone else will become the World's Most Powerful Psychic, and he'll be able to rest at last.

The small supply of futurity, however, only makes the pull of the past stronger. He knows he can't wallow in history, but sometimes— like *right now*, this very moment of consciousness—he longs to be somewhen else, somewhen cold, snow outside the window. Because in this *now* it's ninety-five degrees and the sweat is running off his naked chest. He's bent over the front step, setting out ceramic tiles in rows and columns, and his underwear is plastered to his ass. It's imperative to lay out the tile, dry, before cementing it in place.

"So is this the way you want it?" a voice asks. Oh, right. Matty—the fourteen-year-old version—is helping him. He's mixing up the thinset in one of the big plastic buckets.

Buddy nods. But then the kid moves on to new questions. Wants to know everything about the Amazing Telemachus Family. Where they performed, what people thought of them. Buddy ignores him. The less Matty knows, the better. At least, Buddy thinks that's true.

Matty keeps talking. He really wants to know about his grandmother. What did she do onstage? Did she really work for the government? "Could Grandma Mo travel outside her body?" he asks.

This question makes Buddy look back at the boy and frown.

"You know," Matty says. "Like, walk through walls?"

Buddy stares at him.

"Because that would be real useful, right? That would make her the perfect spy."

Buddy nods slowly.

"How far do you think she could travel? I mean, all the way into Russia? Frankie said the Russians had psychics, too. Do you think she could go anywhere she wanted?"

Buddy shakes his head. She had no limits, he thinks. Nothing could stop her except for one thing. Time.

+

His mother sits across from him at the kitchen table. There's snow outside the window, and soon his father will come home with pizza for dinner, and his brother and sister will rush in, their jeans soaked, faces red from the wind, after sledding with the big kids. But now, right now, he's in the warm kitchen with his papers and crayons—and Mom. She is doing her own project, reading and rereading a stack of business papers with business numbers on them. She's been crying, but now she's stopped crying, because she sees he's scared.

"Show me what you're drawing," his mother says.

He doesn't want to. It's sad. But she's seen his other sad drawings, so he moves his arm and she leans forward. It's a black rectangle surrounded by green except for a few scribbles of red and yellow. She says, "Are those flowers?"

"I'm not good at them," he says.

"Oh, *I* think you are," she says. "And I like that there will be flowers near me. It's a really nice grave, Buddy."

It's been months since the TV show where everything went wrong. Mom talks about all his sad pictures like they're no big deal. She hardly cries (at least in front of him). She looks through what he's drawn today, and then says, "Why don't you draw me something from when you're, say, twelve years old?"

He tries to remember all the way to twelve. He's sitting in a building. It's summertime, the medal heavy and slick against his chest. He's taken to secretly wearing it under his clothes, like Superman's outfit. Frankie's there in the building, looking tall and skinny and tough. One of his favorite Frankies. Buddy draws another rectangle and Mom says, "That's not another grave, is it?"

He shakes his head. "It's a pinball machine," he says. "Frankie's really good at pinball. Plays it all day."

"Oh," his mother says. "That's nice." She's not crazy about the idea, he can tell, but she has no idea how good Frankie's going to be. "And you're there, too?"

"I just watch," he says. He draws himself next to the pinball machine, and draws a circle where the medal would be.

"Does Dad know about that?" she asks. "That you two are hanging out in a pinball parlor?"

He shrugs. He sees what he sees. He can't read minds.

She takes one of the blank sheets of paper and starts writing on it.

"What are you doing?" he asks.

"I just wrote down, 'When Frankie is sixteen, he gets really good at pinball.'"

"Oh."

"I like to know what you'll all be doing," she says.

"After you're dead," he says.

"It's like a future diary," she says. "You draw, and I write down words, but it's the same thing."

"It doesn't make you sad?"

She thinks about this. "Sometimes." He likes that she doesn't lie to him. "But other times, I'm just happy that you all grow up together, that you take care of one another."

He doesn't like to think about Mom not being there, in the future. But he's known ever since *The Mike Douglas Show* that she'd be leaving them. Just like he knows that Irene is going to have a baby, and the baby's going to be a teenager named Matthias, and someday he and Matthias will put brown tile on the front step.

Suddenly he's dizzy. His body is little and big at the same time. His arm by the window is cold, but he can feel the sun on his back, feel the sweat running down his sides.

"Buddy?" Mom asks. "Buddy, look at me." She comes over to his side of the table and crouches down. She turns his face in her hands. "Stay with me, kiddo."

Yes. There she is. Mom's here. Alive. Alive.

She runs a hand across his damp hair. "You're sweating," she says.

He pushes a palm against an eye. He nods.

"Tell me what this is, Buddy," she says, and points to the drawing of himself.

"It's a medal. I used to wear it all the time, then."

"What medal is that?"

"The one you're about to show me," he says.

Her eyes go wide. Talking about her death didn't make her cry, but this does. Then she smiles, a brilliant, uncontained smile, and says, "Oh, *that* medal."

She leads him upstairs to her room, and opens a drawer. "This was given to me a while ago, but soon it will belong to you." It's wrapped in a scarf that she never wears because it's too fancy, too colorful. Teddy's taste, not hers. She peels back the cloth, and the gold is as bright as her smile.

"You have a wonderful gift," Mom says. "I know it's hard sometimes. I know you get worried. But I know you'll always do the right thing, because you have a good and noble heart." She waits until he looks her in the eye, and then she touches her forehead to his. "Listen to me," she whispers. "It's all going to work out."

+

Irene pulls up with the windows down, and he can hear her singing along with the radio. Even after she turns off the car she keeps singing: "Ba-a-a-nd, on the run. Doot-do-do-do-doo." Buddy loves to hear her. She sings all the time when she's a girl of nine and ten, and hardly at all when she's older. But in the early weeks of August 1995, right before the end, she turns into Maria von Trapp. She sings every time she takes a shower. She hums while she's cooking dinner. And when she's not saying anything at all, she seems to be swaying to music he can't hear.

She sees the newly tiled front step, finished now except for the cleanup, and instead of yelling at him or asking him what the hell he's wasting his time on, she just shakes her head. "Buddy, that's indoor tile."

Matty says, "So?"

"So it's going to be slick as hell in the winter."

"It's not slippery," Matty says. "Try it."

"Wait till it rains," she says.

"Just try it."

Irene abandons her complaints. She steps up with mock seriousness, compliments Buddy and Matty on their handiwork, and goes inside, still humming Paul McCartney.

Matty's looking at him. "It's weird, right?" the boy says. "How good a mood she's in."

Buddy shrugs. It's time to sponge up the dust and excess grout. And he has more work to do before sunset: mail to deliver, people to talk to, a meal to make. What is he forgetting? Not the cold. He remembers the winter. No, *now*: Dad driving home, asking what's for supper. The color of his mother's scarf. *No.* Matty leaving for the gas station to buy milk. And what else? Frankie showing up, looking for Matty. The feel of the medal in his small hand.

"Uncle Buddy?" Matty says. "You okay?"

Buddy holds on to that voice. Fourteen-year-old Matty. They've just finished tiling the front step.

"Did I make you mad?" Matty asks.

He shakes his head. "We need milk."

"Milk?"

"For supper." Buddy walks toward the house. "There's money on the kitchen counter."

"But—"

Buddy raises a hand. He's already said more than he's comfortable with. Words are dangerous. He goes upstairs, and stays there even after he's done with his shower, so that he's safely out of the way when Frankie barrels into the house, looking for Matty. But the boy is gone, so he instead declaims to Teddy in his too-loud voice that he's selling the hell out of UltraLife products. Going through the numbers, talking about the percentages he's making on each sale. He wouldn't try that bullshit with Irene. But she's out of the way, too. As usual, she's in the basement, in front of the computer, online again.

Which leaves only Teddy to absorb the lies. Poor Teddy. And poor Frankie, who's embarrassed because he asked Teddy for a loan last week, and was turned down. Of course he was. Frankie wouldn't say why he needed the money. Now he has to make sure everyone in earshot knows he didn't need the money anyway—he's got big plans, a surefire way to come out on top. Buddy thinks of the day in the casino, the chips stacked in front of his brother, just like he promised, and the roulette ball listening to him the way the pinball used to. Wasn't it enough that he gave Frankie that hour of bliss? True, only an hour, but that's more than most people get. Buddy only got forty-five minutes.

+

He's twenty-three years old when he leaves his brother alone on the *Alton Belle*, walks the half mile to the Days Inn, and sees her, the girl of his dreams. In fact, he's dreamed of her for years.

She's sitting on a bar stool, turned slightly away from the bar, her tanned bare legs crossed at the knee. One hand lazily twirls the swizzle stick in her drink. And oh, those hot pink nails, the same color as her lipstick. The long blonde hair (a wig, but it doesn't matter, not to him) cast into another shade of pink by the neon light of the Budweiser sign. His heart beats a tattoo, sending him to her. Pushing him across the room.

The bar is almost empty. The hotel, though only a few blocks from the *Alton Belle* dock, can offer none of the attractions of a casino, and this early in the night no one's ready to drown their sorrows. Yet she's there, waiting. Almost as if *she* had a vision of this meeting.

He's ready. One pocket is stuffed with cash, a fraction of Frankie's winnings at the roulette table. (Frankie is still on the riverboat, enjoying himself—for now. Buddy already regrets what's going to happen, even though he's powerless to stop it from happening.) The other pocket contains a hotel key card. His mouth radiates cinnamon freshness thanks to the three Altoids he chewed on his walk over from the riverboat.

He sits down, one stool away from her. The bartender is nowhere in sight, and he doesn't know what to do with his hands. He reaches blindly into his pocket and puts a bill on the bar. Sees with surprise that it's a hundred.

The woman says, "Good day at the *Belle*? Or haven't got there yet?"

He smiles. She's thin and tanned and maybe thirty years old. Her eyes are rimmed by black eyeliner.

"I got lucky," he said.

"Or maybe it was your turn to get something nice," she says.

This is what he's been telling himself: Wasn't it his turn? Yet his own words rang hollow. Everything he knows about the whirlpool of past and future tells him that the universe does not owe you anything, and even if it did, it would never pay up. He never convinced himself he was owed this moment, but hearing the words come from someone this beautiful makes him want to believe. It was his turn, tonight, and not Frankie's. Oh God. Poor Frankie doesn't know what's about to happen to him.

"Don't look so worried," she says. "Come sit a little closer."

How can he not obey? He shifts onto the next stool.

"Tell me your name," she says. He likes the huskiness in her voice.

"Buddy."

"Cerise," she says. She puts a hand over his—and leaves it there.

He can feel his heart in his throat. She smiles. "You don't have to be nervous, honey. You're over twenty-one, right?"

He nods, unsure where to look. She's wearing a tight, spangly tank top with spaghetti straps and a black pleather miniskirt that barely reaches the tops of her thighs. He has a future memory of her underwear—a lime-green thong. He really needs to stop thinking of that lime-green thong.

She glances down at his lap. "Oh, you poor man," she says. "I think you need the full treatment."

He reaches into his pocket again and she says, "Not here. You have five hundred dollars?"

"And I have a room here," he says. "Upstairs." A clarification that's probably unnecessary. He doubts they have guest rooms in the basement.

"Then what are we waiting for?" She downs the rest of her drink, then nods at the bill resting on the bar. "A twenty will cover my tab, hon."

He takes out the wad of cash, thumbs through it. Finally he finds a twenty-dollar bill.

Cerise chuckles, leans in close. "You probably don't want to flash your whole roll like that. This ain't East St. Louis, but still."

"You're right," he says. She doesn't know that he's going to give it all to her, in forty-five minutes.

They take the elevator up. She asks for the room number, and he tells her: "Three twenty-one." She leads him there without glancing at the navigation signs, and as they get closer, he's thinking of the room number like a countdown: three . . . two . . .

He lets her inside. She glances at the open closet, peeks into the open bathroom, and says, "You travel light."

He doesn't understand this comment at first, then thinks, Right. No luggage.

She puts her string purse on the dresser next to the TV. When she turns to him, she's surprised. "Honey, you're shaking." Then she understands. He can see it in her face. She steps to him, and touches his cheek. "You have nothing to worry about," she says softly.

But it's what she says next that makes him fall in love with her. The words ring like chimes backward and forward through all the Buddys, across the years: sitting beside a cold window on a winter afternoon;

arguing with his brother in high summer; lying on the grass on the last day of the world.

She smiles and says, "It's all going to work out."

$$+$$

Buddy crouches beside his bed. From underneath he pulls out a metal lockbox closed with a padlock. He dials the combination and slips off the lock. Inside are several white envelopes bound with a red rubber band looped two times around. Once, there were so many envelopes the rubber band could barely go around them. (Though he'd started out with a different rubber band. Then it got old and snapped, and he had to find one that was exactly the same color and thickness.)

All of the envelopes are addressed to Teddy, except one blue one that has Matty's name on it. That one Buddy isn't supposed to deliver until later. He takes the topmost Teddy envelope, and makes sure it has today's date. Only one more letter to his father is left. His mission for Mom is almost over. He carefully puts the lock back in place and hides the box again.

With the envelope hidden in his shirt, he sneaks downstairs, trying to stay out of sight of the kitchen door, where Frankie is still yammering away at Teddy. Buddy slips out the front door.

As he remembers, a van is parked just down the street. A silver one, that will return here on September 4.

He puts the envelope in the mailbox and closes it with a silent sigh. One more secret duty nearing its completion.

Speaking of duty, he thinks, and turns toward the van. The man behind the wheel, a gray-haired black man, watches him approach from behind sunglasses. He probably thinks the glasses are sufficient disguise. After all, they have only met once before, at Maureen's funeral, when Buddy was six years old. Buddy raises a friendly hand, as if greeting a stranger, and then walks up to the driver's-side window. He makes a twirling motion, and the driver rolls down the window. There's a passenger in a rear seat of the van, but Buddy doesn't see his face. He won't, until September 4.

The driver says, "Yes?"

Buddy does have an exact, clear memory of this moment, so it's a relief to not have to worry about what to say. "Have you seen a teenage boy walk by here?"

The driver does not quite glance behind him, at the man in the backseat. Then he shakes his head.

Buddy says, "I sent my nephew, Matty, to the gas station for milk, and he should be home by now. It's only four blocks from here, and I was getting nervous."

The driver says, "We haven't seen him."

"Okay," Buddy says. "Thanks anyway." He turns and walks back toward the house. He's feeling proud of himself, because not only did he deliver the letter, but he got through the conversation with the van driver perfectly, with all the words in the right order.

Behind him, the van starts up. It makes a three-point turn, and drives away.

"It's all going to work out," the World's Most Powerful Psychic says to himself. He just has to keep doing his job—until it's no longer his job.

II

Matty

It took Matty one day to become a criminal, three weeks to become a psionic superspy, and a short walk to the gas station to make him give up astral travel forever.

His life as a criminal began the day he borrowed the fifty dollars from Frankie. Matty carried the money in his fist as he slowly made his way down the basement stairs to Malice's room, softly calling her name. Each step revealed a bit more of the basement. Malice lived in a pigsty. Clothes were not just scattered over the floor, they covered it, a foot-high mulch of flannel, denim, and T-shirt. There wasn't much furniture—a bed, a bookcase, a green armchair, a milk crate that functioned as a bedside table, an old TV—but every flat surface was a Jenga of dirty Tupperware, food boxes, CDs, and cups. So, so many cups.

Finally he reached the bottom of the stairs. She sat on the rollaway bed, facing away from him, headphones on, a notebook balanced on her knees.

"Malice?" he called.

She pulled the headphones down and twisted to face him. "What the fuck?" Her arm knocked into a pile of books, atop which rested a plate with a half-eaten sandwich. The plate tipped and fell facedown into a pile of clothes. Malice made no move to pick it up. "What are you doing here?"

"Sorry! I didn't mean to sneak up on you. I just—wow." He lifted the sandwich by two fingers, instantly regretting it. This was no recent meal. "I just never knew girls could be such slobs."

She climbed out of the bed. "You can leave now." She was wearing a pair of running shorts and a T-shirt that said NO EMPATHY.

"I will." He set the sandwich and plate back atop the stack of books. "I wanted to ask you a favor."

"You can't come out with me again."

"Oh, I don't want to—that's not—" He shook his head. "That wasn't my fault."

"You have zero tolerance, dude. It was like you were on acid. You were totally zoned, and then you started yelling."

"It wasn't my fault!" he said. But of course he hadn't been able to explain what had happened to him while he was high. And up until he came to with everyone looking at him, it had been one of the best nights of his life.

"So," Malice said. "You get scared straight?"

"Not exactly. That's what I wanted to talk to you about."

He looked around for a place to sit, but even the armchair was covered in crap.

"You're not staying," Malice said. "What's the favor?"

"I want to buy more pot."

She laughed. A bit harshly, he thought.

"From you," he said.

"No," she said. "No way."

"I really need it," he said.

"You *need* it? Okay, now I'm really not giving you any. You're thirteen."

"Fourteen."

"I'm not getting my stepcousin addicted to pot. Plus, I don't think you're cut out for it, man. I mean—" She stuck out her arms and shimmied, bug-eyed. "Gaddiga-gaddiga-gaddiga."

"I did not look like that."

"Dude, it was much worse."

He opened his fist, revealed the wad of cash. "Here."

She eyed the bills, but didn't touch them. "Where'd *you* get forty bucks?"

"Fifty." He wasn't about to tell her he'd borrowed it from her father. "You do this for me, and I can get you a lot more money. Later."

Her eyes went wide. "You shit! You think you're going to be a dealer?"

"What? No!"

"Don't fucking lie to me, Matty."

"I would not lie to you. I'm just going to get more money later. And I could pay you."

"How much?"

"I don't know. You tell me."

"No," she said. Then: "How much are you getting later?"

That was a good question. How much money was in Mitzi's safe? How much was his share? Grandpa Teddy would have been ashamed that he hadn't made that clear in advance, family or no family. "I don't know, exactly."

"I want two hundred," she said.

"Two hundred dollars?"

"Connection fee. Like paying a toll. Take it or leave it."

He didn't really have any choice. "Okay," he said. "Two hundred—"

"Three," she said.

"Oh come on!"

"It doesn't matter," Malice said. "I don't believe you anyway."

"Oh, I'm going to get the money."

Her eyes narrowed. "Is this part of the secret project?"

"Secret what now?"

She plucked the bills from his hand. "I'm so tired of this Amazing Telemachus shit," she said. "You're so fucking special, but whenever something goes wrong, you just blame it on some 'psychokinetic acci-dent.'" She tucked the money into the waistband of her shorts, a ges-ture with no sexual overtones—for her. "It's hard enough with Cassie and Polly in the house, but now Frankie's bringing you into it."

"Pardon?" Matty really wasn't following. What was up with the twins?

Malice lifted the head of a ceramic monkey and pulled out a plastic bag. "This is all I have on me, but I can get more. Do you know how to roll a joint?"

He shook his head.

"Consider this lesson part of my fee."

The journey to psionic superspy began that night, in Frankie's garage. It was a lot like Luke Skywalker's training on Dagobah, except that Frankie was no Yoda, and had no idea what his apprentice was up to. The Jedi was going to have to train himself.

"It just has to be out here," Matty told him. They were making a bed on the garage floor out of a pair of crib mattresses—leftovers from the twins—and a couple of blankets. "And I can't be watched."

"So I'm going to tell Loretta that you're sleeping out in our garage?" Frankie asked.

"I know it's weird," Matty said. "But I'm sure she's seen weirder things, right?"

"You have no idea," Frankie said. "What else do you need?" Matty hesitated, and Frankie said, "Out with it."

"There's something I've been meaning to ask you," Matty said.

"Shoot."

"How much is in there?"

"The safe?" Frankie shrugged. "Well, you'll be able to tell me, won't you? You'll just—" He waggled his fingers. "—take a look."

"Oh, right," Matty said. "But, you know, ballpark?"

"Ballpark?" Frankie said. "It's a big fucking park, Matty. A hundred K, easy."

"A hundred—?" His voice squeaked.

Frankie laughed. "We're not doing this for chicken feed. We're going to hit them on payday, Matty. As soon as their customers fork it over, then bam."

Matty suddenly thought: Did that mean they were stealing the victims' money? Maybe the right thing to do was to give it back to them. But then how to figure out who was owed how much? You couldn't do that without a ledger, something with all the names and addresses. And if they gave it all back, then maybe Frankie would get what was owed to him, but Matty would get nothing. Or rather, Mom would get nothing. And he was doing this for Mom, right?

This was all a matter of moral timing. When did the property of innocents transform into the corrupt holdings of criminals—as soon as it entered the safe? Maybe it was like the miracle of transubstantiation, but in reverse. An anti-Communion.

"Hello, Matty?" Frankie said. "You need anything else?"

"Oh. Let me think." He examined his inventory: a Chicago-area map, spread on the floor, with big red arrows marking the way from Frankie's house to Mitzi's Tavern; two cans of Coke in a Styrofoam cooler; a spare pillow in a My Little Pony pillowcase.

"I'm good," he said.

But was he?

"Almost ten o'clock," Frankie said. "Better get crackin'. I'll leave you to . . . whatever it is you do."

Frankie closed the garage's side door behind him. Matty reached into his back pocket for the baggie.

The door popped open. "Good luck," Frankie said.

Matty stood very still.

Frankie started to say something else, seemed to think better of it, and closed the door again.

"Oh my God," Matty said to himself. He waited five minutes before taking another look at the baggie. Finally he slipped out one of the three tidy joints that Malice had rolled for him (he never succeeded in rolling one himself) and flicked the Bic lighter she'd loaned him ("All part of the service," she said).

Ready for liftoff, he thought. Ignition.

Liftoff did not occur. He sat on his baby-mattress launchpad for several minutes, inhaling and coughing, coughing and inhaling, and told himself everything would be fine if he stopped worrying. And he was right. At the same moment he noticed that he'd stopped worrying, he noticed that he was sitting beside himself.

"Hey, good-lookin'," he said. His body giggled. The joint dangled between his fingers.

"Maybe you should put that down," he said.

His body took one last toke, then placed the joint on the cement.

"I'll be back in a bit," he said. He drifted through the wall of the garage and hovered a few inches over the grass. He thought about looking in on Malice, but decided against it. That was one habit he needed to break. He couldn't be a drug addict, a burglar, *and* a perv.

Flying, though, that was a pure good. He coasted over Uncle Frankie's rooftop, and moved slowly up into the trees, then over the streets, gradually gaining altitude, until he could again make out the towers of the city, glittering in the distance. Acres of air hung below his feet, and he was only mildly disturbed by this.

He thought, Probably a good thing I'm high. (High. Heh.)

Moving took no effort at all; he was pulled along by the string of his own attention, reeled in by whatever caught his fancy. That brightly lit water tower next to I-294, painted like a rose. The jets, roaring toward O'Hare. Quick as a flash he was flying alongside the windows of a plane, inches from the face of a bored red-haired woman staring out.

Matty made wings of his arms. "I'm an astral plane," he said. Far away, his body laughed; he could feel the echo of it.

"Focus, Matt," he said. Where was Mitzi's Tavern? He had no idea. And he couldn't see the map of Chicago without zooming back to the garage, or reentering his body.

Speaking of which, where was his body?

Holy shit!

He spun in the air, panicked, lost in the night sky. Below, dots of light fenced dark rectangles of rooftops and yards. Which of those was Frankie's house? The only time he'd gone this far from his body, he'd been sucked back into it by Malice slapping him around.

He began to fly at random, zooming close to street signs, trying to remember the map of Chicago. Why hadn't he studied it more? Why hadn't he arranged for Frankie to come wake him up?

His body was the anchor. He'd gotten this far from it by following whatever drew his attention. Maybe, then, he only had to pay attention to his body.

He tried to think about his arms, his chest. His throat. The tickle of smoke at the top of his lungs. He coughed—and felt his body move. The sound of the cough seemed to come from far away.

"Okay, Matty," he said aloud. His voice came through more clearly, and he began to follow it back across the network of roads and houses. "Here we go."

A minute later, he slipped through the roof of the garage. His body said, "Next time, maybe you should be *less* high."

He didn't make it all the way to Mitzi's Tavern until ten days later. The biggest obstacle was finding a place and time to smoke. He couldn't keep staying at Uncle Frankie's house. Grandpa Teddy's place, though, was crowded and chaotic. The basement was out of the question; Mom had made that her second home, camping out there when she wasn't at work to talk to the Joshinator. Buddy could barge into any room at any time. And the garage was too risky; Grandpa Teddy had a door remote, and the thought of the door sliding up while he was passed out on the floor terrified him.

He eventually settled on a spot behind the garage, between two overgrown bushes. If he sat cross-legged, with his back to the garage wall, he was invisible unless someone walked up right in front of him. He thought of it as his nest. But the only time to slip into it was between the end of work with Frankie and the return of his mother from work.

At least it was easier to travel in the daytime. He memorized the route from Grandpa Teddy's to Mitzi's, and after a few trips he was able to get there in seconds, as long as he didn't let his mind wander—literally. Anything could distract him: sirens and church bells; old ladies and young girls; animals, especially birds, which were *amazing*, and seemed to be everywhere he turned his attention, a nation of tiny, officious observers who could not only see Matty's astral form, but hungrily track it.

That last bit of paranoid insight, he realized later, came courtesy of the marijuana. He was having trouble fine-tuning his cannabis intake. Too much and he never arrived at the tavern, too little and he barely had time to look around before his body snapped out of it.

And time was a problem. Barney the Bartender never went to the door alarms during the day. Finally Matty was able to get there early enough one morning to see him open up the bar and type the disarm code into the alarm console: 4-4-4-2.

Frankie was overjoyed. Then almost immediately he forgot the joy and started worrying about the safe. Days went by without Matty being able to give him the combination. "What's the problem?" he asked one afternoon in the Bumblebee van. "It's just three numbers."

"Most of the time I'm there, she never gets up from the desk," Matty said. "I've only seen her open the safe twice—and the first time she hunched over it, so close I couldn't see the numbers. Practically on top of it. And the next time she went for the safe, I tried to zoom in, but I overdid it. I went straight through the wall, and then—whoosh."

"Whoosh? What's whoosh?"

Matty felt his face grow hot. "I ended up . . . away. Like, really far away."

"Like what, Glenbard?"

"Over the water. Lake Michigan."

"What the fuck!" Frankie had said that too loud, and lowered his voice. "What the fuck?"

"I know! It kinda freaked me out. I panicked. Luckily, the—" He was about to say that the pot wore off, and squelched that. "I came to, and I was back at home."

"Okay, okay, this is good news," Frankie said. "You're getting stronger. You just need control. It's a classic Telemachus problem. *Too much power.*"

Matty liked the sound of that.

"Tell me what you need," Frankie said. "Talk to your coach."

Coach? Matty thought. Aloud he said, "I think I need to spend the night again at your house."

"Why's that?"

Why, indeed. Because (a) he'd smoked half the pot and needed to stock up if he was going to stay on his game; and (b) he wanted an excuse to hang out with Malice. The only reason he could give Frankie, though, was (c): "Mom's getting suspicious of all the time I'm spending alone."

"Right, of course she is," Frankie said. "I'm coming over for dinner in a couple days. I'll ask her then."

"Thanks, Uncle Frankie."

"It's nothing." He clapped Matty on the shoulder. "It's just another obstacle. Like the twelve labors. You know what I'm talking about?"

"Sure. Hercules."

"*Heracles*, Matty. Learn your Greek. That's your heritage. We're sons of gods—demigods at least. We come from *heroes*. Heracles, Bellerophon. Theseus—"

"Okay . . ."

"And what can stop a hero if he sets his mind to it?"

"Nothing?" Matty said.

"Damn straight."

. . .

Then Uncle Buddy asked him to walk to the gas station to buy milk for dinner.

That simple request turned into an attempted kidnapping by a pedophile—at least, that's what it looked like at first. Starting sometime when he was four years old, and repeating at frequent intervals, his mother had described exactly how it would go down: a windowless van would pull up alongside him, and a strange man would lean out and offer to show him something *really neat*. Maybe it would be a puppy. Or a Game Boy. And what was Matty supposed to do? Run, of course. Run away and find Mom.

Now that it was finally happening, though, Matty found himself rooted to the hot sidewalk, the cold milk jug sweating in his hand. The predator, an old black man with white hair, had leaned out of his driver's-side window of a silver van and said, "Hey, Matty. Got a second?"

And what did Matty do? Smile uncertainly and say, "Uh . . ."

"Destin Smalls would like to talk to you."

Smalls? The guy who'd been on the phone with Grandpa Teddy?

"He's a friend of your grandfather's. And your grandmother, Maureen."

No puppy. Just a phenomenally intriguing teaser. Still, a cue to run. Instead, Matty waited as the man stepped out and walked around the front of the silver van. He moved stiffly, as if he had a bad hip. Then he waved for Matty to follow.

Matty obeyed. It seemed rude not to. "I considered her a friend, too," the driver said and held out a hand. "Clifford Turner. It was an honor to serve with her."

Serve with her? Holy cow, Matty thought. The government stuff. It was all real.

Cliff pulled back the van's side door, which had the effect of a magician pulling back a curtain to reveal . . . a huge white man in a blue suit, crammed into the far captain's seat.

"Matt. Pleased to meet you in person. I'm Agent Destin Smalls." His voice was low and confident. And he'd called him Matt. He gestured to the empty seat next to him. "Come on in. It's air-conditioned."

Okay, *that* was straight out of the pedophile playbook. "I have milk," Matty said.

"I see that."

"I mean, my family's waiting for me," Matty said. "They'll come looking for me."

"This won't take a minute. I just wanted to introduce myself."

Matty looked at Cliff. "It'll be fine," the man said. "I promise."

Matty climbed in and set the milk jug on the carpeted floor. Cliff shut the door from the outside, sealing them in.

The back of the van, behind the seats, was mostly dark, but blinked and hummed with electrical equipment. The air-conditioning (which did feel nice) was probably necessary to keep all those machines running.

Smalls saw him looking. "That's high-tech stuff. Advanced telemetry."

"What's it do?"

"It helps us find gifted individuals, Matt. People like . . ."

Matty tried to keep his face from spasming.

". . . your grandmother."

"Oh really?" Matty said. The words came out an octave higher than he intended.

"Indeed. How much has your grandfather told you? Did you know that Maureen Telemachus was the most important operative we had during the Cold War?"

Classic Cold War, Frankie had said. *High-stakes ops.*

"Cuba? Maureen was there," Smalls said. "The Straits of Gibraltar? She told us what happened when the USS *Scorpion* exploded and died. These were tense times. Both sides so terrified of each other, we were in very real danger of the world ending. Our job—your grandmother's job—was to find out where the Russians were keeping their missiles and keep our eyes on them. The worst-case scenario was if the enemy believed they could launch with impunity."

Matty didn't know what to say, so he said, "Wow." He was pretty sure this was the most important conversation of his life and didn't want it to grind to a halt just because he didn't understand most of what Agent Smalls was telling him. He knew about the Cuban Missile Crisis, but the rest of it was a mystery.

"Indeed. And the Communists had their own psi-war program as well. We were constantly on guard against psychic incursion."

"So, Grandma Mo and the Russians, did they, like, fight it out?" Matty asked.

"Fight?"

"Psychically," Matty said. "Like, on the astral plane."

"Where did you get that from? Comic books?"

"No," Matty said defensively. If his mom were here, she'd know he was lying. Psychic duels were straight out of the X-Men.

"You're not far wrong. The gifted can sense each other. In fact, Cliff out there? He's detected spikes of activity in this area."

Matty felt his heart thump in his chest. Cliff *detected* him? Matty lost track of the conversation; his panic deafened him. Did they know what he'd been up to with Uncle Frankie? Would they turn him in to the cops?

Smalls, though, had continued to talk. "You must know your family is special," he said in a confiding tone. "Not just your grandmother. Your uncles, Buddy and Frankie, used to have abilities. Your mother, too."

Matty played dumb. "That was just an act. A stage show. They got debunked."

"Did they?" Smalls asked. "Perhaps. But perhaps they merely stopped performing. The question I have, naturally, is if you've seen any *new* activity. Perhaps among your cousins?"

"Like what?"

"It could be anything," Smalls said. "The ability to move objects. Sense water moving underground. See things from far away."

"I don't know anything about that," Matty said. Thank God Smalls didn't have his mother's ability.

Agent Smalls smiled. "All I'm asking is that you keep your eyes open. Can you do that for me?"

Matty thought, Does he want me to spy on my own family?

"The threat to America didn't end with the Cold War, Matt. Not by a long shot. The Soviet Union is dead, but the Russians still have their own psychics, don't doubt it. How many other governments have their own operatives? How many fringe groups and terrorist organizations? Worse, how many of these bad actors are trying to *recruit* gifted Americans?"

Smalls delivered this line with Old Testament gravity. Or at least Old-Hollywood-Bible-Movie gravity. Matty sat back in his seat, milk forgotten.

"That would be bad," Matty said.

"Not only that, these foreign powers might decide that they can't afford to have us hire these people, either. They might decide to neutralize the psychic."

"You mean, like, *kill*—?"

He shook his head. "I'm sure that won't happen," he said, in a way that suggested that was exactly what could happen. "But there are other ways to neutralize the psychic. There are devices that can simply remove those abilities." He snapped his fingers. "Like turning off a light switch."

Oh God, Matty thought. He'd neutralize *me*.

Smalls reached inside his jacket, and Matty gripped the arms of the chair. The agent's hand came out holding a business card. "I'm on your side, Matt. I want to protect your family. I want to help them. Your grandfather doesn't want me talking to any of you, because he thinks you're too young to understand how important this is. Another Telemachus could step into your grandmother's shoes. The nation would breathe a sigh of relief."

Matty looked at the card, then put it in his jeans pocket.

"If there's anything I can do, reach out to me," Smalls said.

Matty emerged from the van with the feeling that much time had passed, though it had only been minutes. The sun shone at a more oblique angle. The trees whispered together conspiratorially. Even the milk jug seemed heavier, weighted now with hidden significance.

Cliff shook his hand again. "Great to meet you, Matty."

"I . . . yeah."

"Someday I want to tell you about something your grandmother did for me once. She took me along on one of her long-distance journeys, way beyond what I could do on my own. It was one of the most profound experiences of my life."

"That would be great," Matty said. Unless Destin Smalls turns me off like a light switch.

He walked home and into the house. He was sure his family would see all this new knowledge cooking his insides like radiation, but no: Grandpa Teddy barely looked up from the newspaper, while across the table from him, behind a fence of empty beer bottles, Uncle Frankie explained something about the Van Allen belt. "Sure, robots could get past the belt to the moon, but human beings?" Mom was busy at the stove. Only Uncle Buddy, chopping onions and green peppers at the counter, looked him in the eye. Matty, suddenly embarrassed, tucked the milk into the fridge. But before he could escape to his room, Mom told him to set the big table.

He was forced to ferry plates and glasses from the cupboards to the dining room, walking back and forth like a duck in a shooting gallery.

Matty went to his mother and said in a low voice, "Is Uncle Frankie staying for dinner?"

"I don't know. Ask him."

"Can you do it?"

Mom frowned at Matty as if to ask, What's your problem? Then she said over her shoulder, "Frankie, you eating or not?"

"You don't have to make more on my account," Frankie said.

"Jesus, there's enough pasta to go around. Yes or no?"

He sighed elaborately. "Wish I could. But Loretta and the girls are waiting." He stood up, drained the last of his current bottle, and set it on the table.

"You're welcome," Grandpa Teddy said.

Frankie raised a hand in salute. "Hey, Matty, help me get something out of the van."

Matty froze.

"Come on," Frankie said, already in motion. "The rest of you, enjoy your fine repast. It'll probably be mac and cheese at my house."

Matty hesitated, then finally followed his uncle out to the driveway.

"So anything happen today?" Frankie asked.

"Nothing happened," Matty said.

"No trips? No visits to the tavern?" He was so eager. So desperate. "We really need that combination."

"I can't do it," Matty said.

"What? What's the matter? Is your mom getting in the way?"

"No, it's not that, I just don't think—"

"Self-confidence. I knew it." He put his hand on Matty's shoulder and leaned close. "I've been there. I know what it's like to doubt yourself. You just have to push through."

"I mean I can't do it, ever." He struggled to make eye contact with Frankie, and couldn't pull it off. His uncle's right ear became his focus. "I'm out. I quit."

"Quit?" His voice was so loud. "What the fuck are you talking about?"

Matty didn't know what more to say. The government is on to me? They can track me? They can *erase* me? Frankie would argue him out of every point.

"You can't quit," Frankie said. "You're a Telemachus. We don't quit!"

"I know, I know." But wasn't quitting what they were most known for? The Amazing Telemachus Family had walked offstage and into mediocrity. Frankie gave the benediction years ago at the Thanksgiving table: We could have been kings.

"I'm sorry," Matty said. He was tearing up. He didn't want to cry in front of his uncle. "I'm sorry."

Frankie kept talking, cajoling and shaming and pleading in fast-paced combinations, like a bantamweight working the heavy bag. Matty weathered the blows, unable to speak, unable to move. He wanted to disappear. He wanted to fly out of the top of his head and let his body flop onto the driveway like a bag of wet grass. But that was exactly what he could never do again.

12

Teddy

Love was waiting for him in the mailbox, coiled like a rattlesnake. A plain white envelope. He knew what it was even before he saw his name in Maureen's razor-sharp cursive, and in a trice the old, sweet poison raced to his heart.

Oh, my love, he thought. You knock me out, even from the grave.

The letters were coming more frequently now, and he had no idea why. There'd been a flurry after she died, then a tapering off, so that for years at a time he'd thought they'd finally stopped. But this was the second one this summer. Was it a sign of the end-times? He *was* getting old. The obituaries were full of hardier men, younger men, struck down by strokes and prostate cancer and heart attacks. The stress of these letters was enough to do him in. Mo was going to kill him at the mailbox.

"Are you all right?" Irene asked. She was twenty feet away, standing by the car. Too far away to see the handwriting on the envelope.

"Paper bullets," he said. He tucked the envelope into his jacket pocket. There'd be time to look at it later. "Straight to the brain."

"How are you getting mail on a Sunday?"

With anyone else he would claim that it was misdelivered and a neighbor must have put it there—but this was Irene. His only choice was to dodge the question entirely. "Let's go," he said. "Graciella's waiting."

Irene made no move to get in the car. "We have a deal, right? If I go with you, no matter what happens, you're watching Matty for me."

"Yes, yes."

"Four days, next Thursday through Sunday." He'd made the mistake of giving her the keys so she could get the air-conditioning going, and now she was holding them ransom. She stood by the driver's-side door, one hand drumming the roof. He winced to think of her rings scratching the paint. She said, "And you will *watch* him this time."

She would *not* let him forget about the time he babysat Matty when he was two. "He's a teenager now, not a toddler," he said. "This time if he drinks a glass of gin it will be on purpose."

Irene groaned, but surrendered the keys.

She managed to sit in silence until the third stoplight. It was more than he could have hoped for.

"Do you trust this woman?" she asked. Meaning Graciella.

"Do *you*? You're a better judge of character than I am." In fact, that's why he kept bringing Irene along.

"She's using you," she said.

"I *want* her to use me. That's the point of friendship, Irene."

"She's not a friend if she's after your money."

"Money? What money? I'm on social security, for Christ's sake."

"This car's a year old. You get a new one every eighteen months."

"That's just good sense. New cars are dependable. You break down on the skyway, you're likely to get killed."

"And the suits? And the watches?"

He took a breath. How to phrase this, for a woman who can smell a lie? "Just because I don't dress like a hobo doesn't mean I'm rich."

"I know about ATI, Dad."

He pretended to concentrate on the traffic in the side-view mirror. "What's that now?"

"Checks were coming to the house all through high school, and they're still showing up."

"You're going through my mail?"

"Don't have to. I can see the envelopes. Advanced Telemetry Inc.'s a privately held electronics company, but there's suspiciously little on file."

"You investigated me?"

"Them, Dad. Turns out they're some kind of consulting business."

"You're a snoop. It's your greatest failing."

"I'm sure you've got a list. So what is this, Dad? Are you a consultant? Is this a holdover of what you and Mom did?" Her eyebrows rose. "ATI is the front that Destin Smalls uses to pay you, isn't it?"

"Don't be ridiculous."

"I'm just worried, Dad. I don't care about the money, but I don't like that this woman is taking advantage of an—of you."

"Of an old man. Say it."

"Don't have to. It's obvious you've gone senile."

"She doesn't need my money. She's mob royalty."

"So what's her angle, then? You said she wasn't interested in you romantically, so she must want something. Why are you smiling?"

It warmed his heart to hear his eldest child musing about angles. Irene was always the sharpest of his children. She had all of Maureen's intelligence and a good dose of his craftiness. Maureen used to think that Buddy was the genius of the family, but it was little Irene who had a mind like a Ginsu knife. The Human Lie Detector. And that was why, if he was going to help Graciella, he needed Irene at his side.

"I thought you liked her," Teddy said, trying to sound hurt, and failing even to his own ears.

"Liking has nothing to do with it," she said. "This is business."

He laughed until the next stoplight.

"How much is ATI paying you?" Irene asked. Hanging on like a God damn terrier. "In round numbers."

"*They* are not paying me *any* numbers," Teddy said. "Round, square, or rhomboid. *I* am paying myself."

She made a skeptical noise, even though she had to know he wasn't lying.

"I'm half owner," he said. "Stop making that face. It was my idea to start the company. Once I got a glimpse of how government worked, how could I not? It's the craziest damn business. Skinny bakers, top to bottom."

"You're saying that like it's a saying."

"Skinny bakers! 'Never trust a skinny baker.' That's absolutely a saying."

"And what does that have to do with the government?"

"Allow me to expound," he said. "The people *inside* don't get to eat any of the cake, but they compensate by throwing cakes out the window. Barrels of cake. The military industrial complex is made entirely of barrel throwers and cake eaters. In this metaphor, cake equals money."

"Let's just call a moratorium on metaphors."

"A metatorium."

"And coinage."

"The point is, Destin Smalls is the most gullible man on the planet, and yet he could funnel millions into dubious projects. He'd pay G. Randall Archibald outrageous sums for the most transparent flimflammery. Torsion field detectors. Micro-lepton guns that never quite worked, oh, just need another half mil in development—"

"Oh my God," Irene said. "This is about competing with Archibald. Still. Again."

"This is about making money, plain and simple," Teddy said.

"Did Mom know about this?"

He started to answer, then thought better of it.

"Then no," Irene said.

"She knew," he said. "Eventually." Before Irene could ask he said, "Your mother, she was very conservative about money, very conservative. Didn't like anything speculative. The start-up costs were significant, and took a long time to recoup. I was very sad that the company didn't start earning back on our investment until well after her death."

"You can't say 'our' if she didn't agree to it."

Yet she paid all the same, Teddy thought.

"Help me find the address," he said. "One-thirty-one. Look for a real estate sign."

They found it soon enough. NG Group Realty. The parking lot was empty except for Graciella's Mercedes wagon. He eased his car next to hers and Irene put a hand on his arm.

"Answer this: Has Graciella asked you for money?"

"No," he said. The honest truth.

Irene shook her head. "I don't get it, then."

"You're asking the wrong question," he said. "It's not what she's getting from me, it's what I'm getting from her."

"Which is?"

He couldn't lie, not to Irene, but he could choose what true thing to say. He thought of saying, "Revenge," but that sounded melodramatic. He considered "Justice," but that was both melodramatic and out of character.

"I get to be back in the game," he said.

◻

One of the great regrets of his life was that he never told Maureen about ATI. Another one of his great regrets was that she found out on her own.

He remembered the night. He'd driven home through a snowstorm and entered the house like the Great Hunter, bearing the finest pizza in the Chicagoland area. Maureen cleared the papers and crayons from the kitchen table, and the whole family sat together under the warm lights, Frankie excitedly describing fantastic sled crashes, getting them all to laugh, even Buddy. It was when they all huddled together like this that he was most happy. They were coconspirators, happy thieves dividing up the take, laughing it up while the mundane world went on with their dreary lives. It was the next best thing to being onstage together.

After dinner, Teddy lit a cigarette and watched Maureen wash the dishes. He was not by nature a content man, but this came pretty damn close. Then he noticed, on the counter next to his elbow, the stack of pages that Maureen had moved from the table to the counter. They weren't Buddy's coloring pages, as he'd assumed after seeing all the crayons. They were bills and bank documents. He lifted a few pages, and saw the red logo of their mortgage company. It was Teddy's job to handle the money and the house payments. He'd insisted on it.

He replayed the past hour in his mind, knowing that Mo had been looking at those pages before he arrived. Now her laughter seemed a bit forced. Her attention had been elsewhere.

"You want to talk about anything?" he asked.

Maureen didn't turn around. "Is there anything to talk *about*?"

He knew that arid tone.

In retrospect, he was a fool to think she wouldn't find out sooner or later. How could any mortal hide anything from Maureen Telemachus? He'd dipped into the family savings, if you could use the word "dip" for such a thorough excavation, and he'd also taken out a second mortgage.

"Tell me what you did with it," she said. "Are you gambling again?"

She thought he'd gone back to his wicked ways. Ironically, he *had* returned to his wicked ways, but only to make up the money sunk into ATI.

"What I used to do wasn't gambling," Teddy said, unable to keep the indignation from his voice. In those days, he was even more of a peacock than now.

Maureen, without even looking at him, made it clear she was taking none of his bull. Why should she? She'd taken so much of it for years. "Oh, Teddy," Maureen said. "Everything we worked for, you're throwing it away."

"I certainly am not," he said. "I'm *investing* it. There's a big difference."

"Investing in what?"

"I'll tell you," he said. "Just sit down. Please."

She dried her hands and took a seat opposite him at the table, quiet as a hanging judge.

"A business opportunity presented itself," he said. "I had an idea for a company, and a coinvestor to create it with me. This company would create an ongoing revenue stream, but it required some initial capital, just to get things rolling. Short-term start-up costs, long-term returns."

"Ongoing revenue stream," she said.

"That's right!"

"Are you listening to yourself?" she said softly.

"I want *you* to listen to *me*," he said in a reasonable tone. "I'm trying to put food on the table. What choice do I have? Everything else I've tried—"

"The *act*," she said. She shook her head in a way that years later would be echoed by their daughter. "You're still angry. You can't let it go."

"We had a plan, Mo. Everything depended on you coming out, and you didn't do it." Teddy knew Archibald was scheduled to interrupt their act. He deliberately gave the skeptic something easy to expose, the old séance trick with his foot, something the cameras could pick up. The family wasn't *debunked*; their defeat was bunk itself, the setup for the big reversal. Mo would do the telephone gag, flummoxing Archibald. The famous skeptic would admit on national television that they were the real thing, and their fortunes would be made.

"What did you want me to do?" Teddy said, exasperated.

"Get a job," she said. "A real job."

"This is better than a job," he said. "This is a legitimate business venture."

"You come in here with Nick Pusateri's pizza, and you're going to talk to me about legitimate?"

"This has nothing to do with him." Which was the truth. "All I did was buy a pizza." Which was a lie. He'd stopped by Pusateri's to talk about their next job. But he couldn't tell her that, because he'd promised that he'd never work for that man, or the Outfit, again.

"Then tell me what this investment is," she said. "No hemming and hawing. None of your flimflam. Tell me exactly who you're in business with, and what you're doing."

"I can't, Mo. I just can't. You just have to trust that what I'm doing, I'm doing for the family."

"Trust," she said bitterly.

He nodded. "That's all I need. A little trust."

"Yet you can't trust *me*," she said. Her lips were trembling. "Your wife."

"Not until it pays off. Then, I swear, you'll understand why I—"

Frankie burst into the kitchen, followed by Buddy. "Can you make cookies?"

"I'm not one of your marks," Maureen said. She gathered up the bank statements, ignoring the boys, who were clamoring for her attention. He watched her in silence, thinking they were done with the argument, and then she handed him the pile. "That's not true," she said. "I was your first mark."

The next morning, Maureen informed him that she'd accepted Destin Smalls's offer to work for the government in a new program called Project Star Gate. And not long after that, Nick Pusateri ended Teddy's career as a cardshark.

□

Graciella unlocked the door to the offices from the inside and let them in. There were no hugs—she was not that kinda gal—but she shook hands with Irene. "Welcome to NG Group."

"You're the G?" Irene asked.

"The N liked to keep me in the dark, even though I was the owner on paper."

"And now you want to be the owner in fact," Teddy said.

"Now I have to be. I don't know how much of this business is real, and how much of it is a front for the other Pusateri business. I don't even know if I'm the only owner. I wouldn't be surprised to uncover a few silent partners." She led them through an empty cubicle farm—none of the agents had yet come in—to a big glassed-in office. She gestured toward the computer and the large beige monitor. "Nick Junior gave me the password for the accounting software, but I don't know what I'm doing. Your dad said you were good at this."

Irene gave him a look, then said to Graciella, "What are you looking for, exactly?"

"The money," Graciella said, and Teddy laughed.

Irene went to work like some kind of . . . computer person. She got the machine running, and for the next five minutes did nothing but grunt and talk to herself, eyes scanning the screen, while Graciella hovered behind her. He'd have never expected his telepathic daughter to learn accounting, but he had to admit it was a pleasure to have a child with such arcane skills.

Teddy, ensconced in an overstuffed womb chair designed, evidently, to lure clients into childlike trust, watched the women as long as he could before boredom overcame him. He checked the Rolex. They'd been here five minutes. "Tell her about the teeth," Teddy said to Graciella.

"I think she's busy," Graciella said.

Irene looked up. "Did you say teeth?"

"You're distracting her," Graciella said.

"It's pertinent to the situation," Teddy said. "It's why we're here."

"Teeth?" Irene repeated.

"I want her to hear it from you," Teddy said to Graciella. Then to Irene: "They're proof that Nick Junior is an innocent man."

"He's not completely innocent," Graciella said. "But he is the father of my children. I have to think of them."

"Teeth," Irene prompted.

Graciella leaned back against the window ledge, crossed her long legs, and frowned as if deciding where to start. She looked terrific in a tight green skirt and a Creamsicle-orange blouse, a combination that he wouldn't have thought would work but most certainly did. More evidence that women were braver than men.

"This can't leave this room," Graciella said. Irene nodded, waiting for her to continue. Graciella said, "You know Nick Junior is on trial for the murder of Rick Mazzione. And you may have read that Nick Senior owned a piece of Rick Mazzione's business. Took it, really, when Rick fell behind on his loan payments. Rick tried to pay up, but the debt was never settled, and Rick began to complain openly about this. He was perhaps getting angry enough to go to the police. Maybe he already had. So Nick Senior decided to find out."

Irene took in this information like a pro. No girly gasps, no derailing questions. But she was definitely evaluating each sentence. That was why Teddy wanted Graciella to tell the story. If Teddy had done it, Irene would know only that Teddy believed what the woman had told him. With Irene, you always had to be thinking of the secondhand-story problem.

"This is where my husband gets involved," Graciella said. "Nick Senior told him to invite Mazzione to a meeting, and then drive him out to a construction site. They began to . . . ask him questions. Nick Senior didn't like the answers, and got angry. He punched Mazzione in the mouth."

Irene nodded. "Teeth."

"He knocked a few of them loose. Nick's hand started bleeding, which only made him angrier."

"He gets angry easily," Teddy explained to Irene.

"I'm getting that impression," Irene said.

"My husband told me that Nick Senior went a little crazy then. He started pulling Mazzione's teeth out with a pair of pliers. All of his teeth. Except for the molars. He couldn't get the molars."

Irene looked at Teddy. "You were friends with this guy?"

"Work friends," he said. "Not the same thing."

"Then Nick shot him. Not my husband. Nick Senior."

"Your husband *told* you this?"

"You don't believe me?"

"I believe you believe your husband."

Teddy almost laughed. The secondhand-story problem, in action.

"Nick Senior made my husband bury the body on his own," Graciella said. "When they found it, months later, it was missing those teeth, and they weren't at the crime scene. My husband had saved them. He kept them in a cigar box in his sock drawer."

"Because keeping souvenirs of human body parts is a normal thing to do," Irene said.

"Monks keep bones of saints," Teddy said reasonably.

"You don't have to defend him," Graciella said. "My husband's not perfect. And he doesn't always think through his actions. But in this case, it's a good thing."

Irene raised an eyebrow. "Because . . ."

"Nick Senior's blood is on Mazzione's teeth. They put him at the scene of the crime."

"They wouldn't take Junior's word for it?" Irene asked.

"My husband won't testify against his father. He'd never do that. But *I* will absolutely turn the teeth over to the district attorney. I've already hinted to the police that I have proof. That may have been a mistake, though. Nick Senior seems to know I have something."

"You can't get cops to shut up," Teddy said. "Plus, Nick Senior may have bought a few of them."

"Or a lot of them," Graciella said.

"So why haven't you done it?" Irene asked. "Turned them over. Gotten Nick Senior charged."

"Because the charges may not stick, and I want something more than his arrest," Graciella said. "I want independence."

Somehow, when Graciella was melodramatic, it worked, like orange on green. Who knew?

"I want my own life after my husband goes to jail," Graciella said. "I want a clean business with no Outfit connections. And I want my boys to grow up without seeing their grandfather's face ever again. I'll trade the teeth to him for that."

Teddy watched his daughter's face. Her eyes had gone squinty. It was the look Maureen used to give him when he came home with liquor on his breath. Damn it, had Graciella lied to her—lied to them both?

"How many photocopiers are in this building?" Irene asked.

"Three," Graciella said. "One is color."

"I'm going to need copies of all the tax returns, and all the paper ledgers you can find," Irene said. "Oh, and blank floppy disks. A lot of floppy disks."

□

He used to love the feel of cards in his hands. There was no finer pleasure than to sit around a table drinking and smoking and telling lies with a group of well-heeled men, dealing them exactly the cards he wanted them to hold. Of course, those men weren't friends, could never be friends. The *next* best pleasure was to sit around a table drinking and smoking and telling lies with men who knew him well enough never to let him deal a deck of cards, or even cut them.

"Tell 'em about Cleveland," Nick Senior said.

"That's okay," Teddy demurred. He'd only returned from Ohio a couple of nights before.

"No, really. Guys, you will not fucking believe this story." The Guys being Charlie, Teppo, and Bert the German. The regulars. Their usual Tuesday-night routine was to camp out in the back of Nick's restaurant and eat pizza and drink Canadian Mist until dawn. They played, Teddy watched.

"What happened in Cleveland?" Charlie asked. Not the sharpest knife, Charlie. It was a miracle that he could talk and deal at the same time.

"Nothing," Teddy said. He glanced at Nick, who was rolling out pizza dough at a big table. The best part of playing in the kitchen was that Nick kept them fed. The worst part was that every game was on Nick's home turf. "A little trouble with a card game."

"Come on, what'd you do?" Charlie asked. Already laughing. He was the group's official fuckup, a kind of mascot who'd lost Nick almost as much money as he'd made him. He sensed that Nick was mad. They all moved carefully when he was in a mood, for the same reason that you played gently with nitroglycerin.

"Tell 'em," Nick said. His stevedore arms were white to the elbow with flour. He was a big man, and determined to stay as big as he'd been in the fifties. He kept his hair in an oil-black D.A., wore the same shirts and tight pants he'd worn as a teenager, and listened to the oldies channel on the AM. The fixation on his youth was beginning to look ridiculous, but of course nobody was going to point this out to his face. "It was a hell of a setup," Nick said. "I put Teddy in a tough spot."

Teddy shrugged. He was not going to complain to Nick in front of these guys. "Why don't we just play cards?" he asked.

"See, I sent Teddy down to help my cousin Angelo," Nick continued. "He'd gotten himself into a game with a couple New Yorkers, Castellano guys."

"Castellano," Charlie said. "Shit, why?"

"Angelo was forced into being polite," Nick said. "I said, hell, if you're stuck playing with these fuckers, the least we can do is take their money. I said, I'm sending you a guy. I'll bankroll him myself, twenty grand of my own money. I said, this guy's the best fucking mechanic in the business."

The guys looked at Teddy, who offered a self-deprecating smile.

Charlie laughed. "They let *you* be dealer?"

Teddy shook his head. "I was playing the whale."

Nick said, "I told him to wear that fucking Newman Rolie. Flash it around."

Teddy was wearing it now. A 1966 "Paul Newman" Rolex Daytona with a diamond dial. Worth twenty-five grand, and the thing would only gain in value. It was like walking around with a Lakefront condo on his arm. Teddy dropped his hand below the table. "My job was to lose, but mostly to Angelo," Teddy said. "Angelo, though, was struggling to keep up with the New Yorkers."

Nick snorted. "For good reason, it turns out. But to make it worse, the New Yorkers have two backup guys in the next room, hanging out with Angelo's guys. Everybody's armed to the teeth."

"Holy shit!" Charlie exclaimed.

"But tell 'em the real problem," Nick said.

Teddy kept his face still, projecting calm. Good humor.

"Go on," Nick said. A commandment.

"The real problem," Teddy said finally, "was that the New York-ers were tag-teaming us. They were signaling to each other, trying to cheat Angelo and me. One of them even tried bottom-dealing."

"On *you?*" Charlie said. "He's trying to out-mechanic the mechanic?"

"Fat chance," Teppo said. He was five-foot-squat, a hundred and forty pounds, but Teddy had seen him crush the windpipes of men twice his weight. "So what'd you do? Start cheating back?"

"Of course," Teddy said. "But I couldn't make any big moves dur-ing my deals, because I can't tip 'em off that I'm a plant. But I can't let the game keep going, because Angelo's losing money every hand."

Bert the German grunted in appreciation of the conundrum. Bert hardly ever spoke. He was more dangerous than Teppo, and completely loyal to Nick.

"It was eating you, too," Nick said. "Admit it. You didn't like these guys trying to out-cheat you, Teddy Telemachus."

"Of course he was mad!" Charlie said. "Who wouldn't be?"

Shut the hell up, Teddy thought.

"Pride," Nick said. "Pride starts to creep in."

Teddy looked up into Nick's eyes. "Yes," Teddy said. "A little bit of pride."

"So you had to take them down," Nick said.

Teddy nodded.

Teppo and Bert had gone still. They could feel the change in the room. But fucking Charlie was swiveling his head between Nick and Teddy, laughing. "How'd you do it? Teddy? How'd you do it?"

"I'd like to know that myself," Nick said. "Somehow he rigged the next hand, without even dealing it himself. How'd you do that, Teddy?"

Teddy tapped the surface of the table, remembering the last hand of the game. One of the New Yorkers was dealing. He pushed the deck to Teddy for the cut. Teddy made an amateurish cut using both hands and slid the deck back to the dealer.

So much preparation had gone into that simple transaction. Teddy had arrived in Cleveland with all the decks that they'd be using that night. One was clean, but the rest were pegged so that he could read the bumps under his fingers as he dealt. Plus he had two extra decks, one in his jacket pocket, one in a felt pocket stitched to the underside of the table, loaded in two different schemes.

Nobody noticed when he slid the pocket deck free. Nobody noticed when, thirty seconds later, he borrowed a card from the jacket deck and slipped it into the deck in his hand. And nobody noticed that the deck he returned after the cut was not the one he'd been handed.

Nick was waiting for an answer. Teddy shrugged. "Does it matter?"

Nick smiled. "I guess not."

"Okay, so *what* happened?" Charlie asked.

"I only know this secondhand from Angelo," Nick said. "And he was pretty hard to understand through all the bandages. But supposedly? Incredible. See, those two cheating fucks from New York, they find themselves with incredible hands. They start outbidding each other, and Angelo's too stupid to get out of the way. Soon the pot's huge, and everybody's still in. They turn over the cards, and one of the New Yorkers's got a straight, and the other's got four of a kind, all deuces. Amazing, right? But here's the topper: both New Yorkers are holding the two of spades."

Charlie was laughing, confused. "What? Holy shit!" Teppo and Bert weren't laughing, though. Teddy had suspected that the two of them had already heard this story from Nick, and the suspicion was turning his gut to ice.

"You can imagine how pissed off Angelo is," Nick said. "Not the coolest head in the best of times. He starts shouting, and the New Yorkers know that somebody's just fucked with them, and now they're pissed. The goons storm in from the next room, and that's when the shit hits the fan."

Nick is looking at Teddy now. "A gun comes out. Angelo holds up his hand, and the bullet goes through his hand and into his jaw. The docs think the jaw can be fixed, but the hand, well the hand is just fucked. He's going to bat lefty now."

"Holy shit," Charlie said. He was not an imaginative curser.

"I drove him to the hospital," Teddy said. "I apologized to him."

The men mulled the end of the story as if savoring a meal.

Then Nick shrugged. "I'd have preferred you held on to my money."

Teddy felt his heart thump once in his chest. Everyone looked at Nick.

He wasn't even pretending to work with the dough now. He flipped the switch on the pizza roller, and the two big cylinders whined up to speed.

Bert the German put a beefy hand on Teddy's arm, tugged for him to stand up.

But Teddy couldn't stand up. His legs had stopped working. Acid stung the back of his throat.

Teppo and Bert hauled him upright. Charlie said, "What's going on, guys?" He was the only one in the room who didn't know what was about to happen.

"Take off the watch," Nick said.

□

After three hours of poring over files, Irene told him and Graciella that two things were clear: there was too much to copy, and there was definitely something fishy going on with the numbers. Irene, though, was due for her shift at Aldi's.

"Let's pack it up," Graciella said. She no longer trusted for the paperwork to be safe in the office, because she had no idea how many people had keys, and who those people were loyal to. The only solution was to take everything they could get their hands on and move it off-site, where the women would go through it at their leisure. They filled the Buick's trunk and the back of Graciella's station wagon. She followed Teddy and Irene to the house, where they enlisted Buddy and Matty to help them unload.

It was an odd experience for Teddy. He'd been intending to keep Graciella away from the males of the family, so as not to scare her off. But she seemed charmed by Buddy's shyness, and laughed at Matty's hesitant jokes. In retrospect, that made sense: Graciella was raising three boys, and Buddy was as much a kid as any of them. Fortunately, he was a kid with a hobby. In the basement he'd been building deep shelving units out of spare lumber. The file boxes fit perfectly into place, like they were meant to be there.

Graciella said nothing about the metal window shades, but she asked about the large structure taking shape at the other end of the basement.

Buddy ducked his head and went upstairs.

"I think they're bunk beds," Matty said.

"Best not to ask questions," Irene said. She'd pulled on the polyester Aldi's smock. "I've got to go. Graciella, I'll get back to the ledgers tomorrow."

"I can't thank you enough," Graciella said. She went to Irene and took her hand in hers. "I mean it. I can't. But I'll try to make it up to you someday."

Teddy thought: They're having a moment! My girls are having a moment!

Graciella said that she should be going, too, because her mother was probably getting tired of watching the boys. Teddy said, "You can't go, I need your help with something. I have entirely too much gin in the freezer, an oversupply of tonic, and an abundance of cucumbers."

"Not limes?"

"It's Hendrick's, my dear. Cucumber slices, always."

"I suppose I can do my part during this difficult time," she said.

They took their drinks outside, into the August sunlight, and Graciella said, "You have hammocks!"

"We do?" They did. Two Mexican hammocks, slung in the shade between the three oaks. Another Buddy project, Teddy thought, financed by yours truly.

"I love hammocks," Graciella said. She skirted the dirt patch—Buddy had provided as much explanation for filling the hole as he had for digging it—and eased into one of the hammocks, laughing while trying to keep her drink from spilling.

Teddy carried over one of the lawn chairs. "Aw, what are you doing with that?" she asked. "Take the other one."

"I'm not a hammock person," he said. He set up the chair across from her, removed his jacket, and draped it across the back. The white envelope slid out onto the seat of the chair. He'd forgotten about it. He picked it up nonchalantly and slipped it into the jacket side pocket. Graciella noticed but didn't remark on it.

He sat across from her and they sipped their drinks while Graciella said pleasant things about Matty, the house, the yard. Perhaps some were lies but he didn't care. The moment was as fine as any he could remember. A warm day at the end of summer, a beautiful woman in orange and green like a tropical flower blooming in his own backyard, a cold glass in his hand. It made him want to say philosophical things to her. He tried to construct a sentence about old age, bitter gin, and sweet tonic—the sweet tonic of youth!—but then lost concentration when Graciella kicked off one shoe, then the other.

"Did I ever tell you the story about how my act was stolen by the king of late-night?"

She laughed. "I think I would have remembered."

"At last! A fresh audience," he said. "It was 1953, and me, a high school pal who did magic, and L. Ron Hubbard were all sitting in a watering hole in L.A."

"The Scientology guy?"

"The very same. We were discussing how easy it was to separate a mark from his money—especially one who was a true believer. I began to demonstrate my abilities as a billet reader—"

"The three wishes thing?"

"Again, spot-on, my dear. I dazzled the barflies in attendance, and afterward, a kid from Nebraska introduces himself, buys me a drink, and tells me he works on the radio but got his start as a magician. Tough to do magic on the radio, I say. He asks me to show him the billet gag, out of professional courtesy. Now, I'm not one to show some fresh-faced mook how I make my living, but he keeps after me, keeps buying me drinks, so I figure, why not, he's bought himself one trick. I walk him through the gag, and you know what he asks me?"

"I have no idea."

"Why the hat? That's the question. Why the *hat*? I tell him, the hat's the whole act! It's not just that it distracts the audience from looking at your hands; it concentrates attention! The hat is the theater, it's the drama!"

"I have to agree," Graciella said.

"And the kid says, Maybe it could be bigger. I coulda punched him. He walks out of the bar, and ten years later, I turn on the TV, and what do I see? That kid, with his own talk show. And what does he do for laughs? He does my act, wearing a God damn turban!"

"Johnny Carson stole your act?"

"Carnac the Magnificent my ass," he said.

He loved the way she laughed. "How much of that is true?" she asked.

"As much as you'd like," he said. "As much as you'd like."

Graciella began to swing toward him, then away from him. Her toenails were pink.

"Ever hear of a guy named Bert Schmidt?" she asked. "They called him Bert the German."

"I may have heard the name," he said.

"He testified against Nick Junior this week."

"Huh." He never would have thought Bert would turn on any Pusateri.

"He said he heard Nick Junior bragging about killing Rick Mazzione."

"But not Nick Senior?"

"Nope."

Maybe Bert was still loyal to Nick Senior after all. Was the father really setting up his own son? Or had Nick Junior been stupid enough to brag about a murder he didn't commit?

"It's looking like I'll be on my own soon," Graciella said. "I really hope Irene can figure out what's happening with the NG Group."

"I have complete confidence," Teddy said. "She's got a head for numbers. It's a crime that she's not running her own company." He loosened his tie. "But are you sure you *want* to know what's going on?"

Graciella made a questioning noise.

"Say that NG really is a front company," Teddy said. "Would you shut it down on principle, forgo all that income?"

"If Nick Senior is involved, then yes."

"My guess is that Nick Senior is involved up to his God damn neck."

□

He'd never been much of a sleeper. Restless mind, restless fingers. But after the accident (for that was what he called it when he came home from the hospital with his hands in bandages, and that was what Maureen told the kids, even if Maureen didn't believe it herself), neither fingers nor mind were working and he found it nearly impossible to get out of bed.

Or rather, couch. He'd moved down to the basement after coming home, like a wounded dog going to ground. The pain pills made all hours equal, and in the basement he could watch TV or sleep at any time, night or day. The boys accepted the living arrangement without questioning it, though Frankie did ask if he could sleep in the basement, too. Irene repeatedly attempted couch-side interrogations, but even in his pill-fogged state he knew it was better to evade her questions than to try answering them. He'd open his eyes and there she'd be, frowning down at him. She'd ask blunt questions like "Why aren't you sleeping in your bed?" and "Why is Mom crying?" He'd say something like "This is where the TV is," or "Everybody cries." What choice did he have? The truth was off the table. He couldn't tell a ten-year-old, "I lied to your mother, betrayed her, and put our entire family's future at risk." The real reason he'd moved to the basement was so he didn't have to see the expression on Maureen's face when she looked at him. He wanted to stew and sulk in darkness.

He sat in that basement through the winter and into the spring, and slept in a bed only when he was at the hospital for the hand surgeries. Every morning Destin Smalls picked up Maureen and drove her to a government office downtown. (So vital was she to the project that living in D.C. was not a requirement; remote viewing, after all, could be done remotely.) Smalls dropped her off in the afternoons, though not always on time. Sometimes Mo—or her new assistant cook, Irene—didn't get supper on the table until six. Sometimes it was little more than stove-top C rations: macaroni and cheese; bean and bacon soup; or the kids' favorite, Breakfast for Dinner.

Mo tried to talk to him. When that failed, she tried to get him to talk to someone else—friends, his doctor, his hand surgeon, or "anyone who might help"—without using the word "psychiatrist," which she knew would set him off. Men of his generation did not go to shrinks, certainly not men who'd emerged from the war unscathed. Teddy's luck was largely due to the fact that he'd never left the States. He served on the front lines of the bureaucracy, deploying his typewriter with machine-gun speed, while at night embarking on daring raids to local bars and engaging in furious hand-to-hand poker games.

But after the accident, he knew his luck had run out. He began to see his body as an unreliable vehicle, prone to failure and breakdowns, and as protective as cardboard. Was this how Mo thought of herself, when she was out traveling the astral plane? Did she know how fragile this shell was? One day he climbed out of the basement—aka the pit of self-pity—to ask her what it was like.

Mo was washing up after dinner, scrubbing the cheap JCPenney pots she bought after their wedding. It was summer, months after she'd told him the diagnosis. He was alarmed at how exhausted she looked, how pale.

"Where'd you go today?" he asked. He made his voice cheery. "You know. Out there." He'd not asked about her job since she started it.

"You know I can't talk about it," she said flatly. She was too tired to make that sound angry.

"I have a security clearance, too, you know."

"Had." She moved the sponge automatically, as if she wasn't seeing what her hands were doing.

He said, "Agent Smalls must know that he can't keep a wife from talking to her husband."

She looked at him, and her face was so sad. "I was in the ocean," she said.

"*In* the ocean?" Hunting for submarines, he thought. Smalls was obsessed with submarines. "Was it beautiful? How deep did you go?"

"Deep," she said. "It was so beautiful." She dried her hands with a cotton towel. "I need to talk to you about something."

He braced himself. He knew he'd been failing her. But he didn't have the words ready to apologize. Or to tell her what he was going to do different. He had no plan, no scheme. What he had was two useless hands, a couch, and a TV.

She sat down next to him. "It's about the children," she said. Immediately he felt relieved. "I want you to promise that you'll never let them do what I do. Never let them work for the government."

"That's an easy promise," Teddy said. Buddy had stopped being able to predict anything. Frankie couldn't bend a paper clip. And Irene was too honest to work for the government.

"This includes the grandchildren," she said.

"What grandchildren?"

"Someday our children will have children."

"Sure, but—"

"Don't argue with me!" Mo shouted. The anger seemed to erupt from nowhere. Her body looked too worn out to make such a noise, and it had left her even emptier. Her eyes welled with tears.

"I promise," he said. He was good at promises. They came easily to him. "You can depend on me," he said.

□

He was touched when Graciella fell asleep in the hammock. Even after he finished his drink he did not get up to refill it, for fear that he'd awaken her. He watched her for a while, and then pushed back the Borsalino to gaze up at the leaves moving in the breeze. Two squirrels scampered across high limbs. The hat began to slide off his head, and something about touching the crown of the hat reminded him of the letter.

He took it from his jacket pocket and looked again at his name in Maureen's sharp cursive. Then he held the envelope, unopened, to the crown of the hat in the traditional manner, just in case Graciella happened to peek. Then he opened the envelope, the glue so old the flap almost popped free on its own. Inside was a single page of coarse drawing paper. He unfolded it, then grunted in surprise.

Graciella stirred, but did not awaken.

He picked up the envelope and thought, God damn you, Mo. God damn you and Buddy.

The crayon drawing was as crude as you'd expect from a six-year-old. On a field of green, two stick figures lay inside a rectangle. One of the figures wore a triangle on its head.

At the top right, Maureen had written him a message:

My Love. Buddy says that the one with the hat is you, and the one beside you is "Daddy's girlfriend." He doesn't know why you're in a grave, if it is a grave. Be careful, Teddy.

I'm glad you found someone. No, that's not quite true. I want to be glad. I will be glad. As I write this I'm so sad, but I'm trying to take the long view. Buddy's view.

Speaking of our boy, I ask you again—please don't get in his way. Give him his space.

Love,
Maureen

13

Irene

"Not exactly Barbie's Dream House," she said to Graciella. The two women stood on the street outside a 1967 ranch home with foot-high weeds in the yard, a cracked driveway, and a garage buckling under the weight of gravity. The FOR SALE sign leaned against the front door, even though the house had sold two months ago. No one had moved in, and no one probably ever would.

"You're saying NG Group sold this?" Graciella said.

"Yep. Ask me for how much."

Graciella looked at her over the top of her sunglasses.

Irene said, "One point two million."

Graciella looked again at the house. "Is it on top of an oil well?"

Irene laughed. "Nope. Strictly a fixer-upper."

"Then my husband's a real estate genius. Who bought it?"

"That's the interesting part," Irene said. "You did."

"NG Group?"

"Not immediately. But eventually, yeah. It's now back in your portfolio."

"And you're dying to tell me why."

"I am."

"Go on, go on. Don't let me stop you."

"Say you have a million in cash you don't want to explain," Irene said. "You can't just deposit it in the bank—banks have to report big deposits. So you go to a friendly real estate agency and buy a little starter home for a million. But a week or a month later you decide you don't want that crappy house. So you sell it back to the company for the same price, they take their realtor's cut, and they deposit the rest in your bank account."

"And banks don't raise an eyebrow for house sales," Graciella said.

"In practice, you don't buy and sell to the same company," Irene said. "There's a handful of real estate companies that NG works with, and they're all passing cash and properties around to each other like chips in a poker game—it's not real money till someone cashes out."

"You mean when the cash is all clean."

"You got it."

"Well, damn," Graciella said. "I don't own a real estate company. I own a laundry." She looked at Irene. "And you're smiling."

"I'm sorry, it's just that—"

"Don't apologize! You love it. Figuring it all out. How they're fooling people."

"I can't help it," Irene said. "I was raised by a cardshark."

"When I first met Teddy, I was hoping for a miracle. But I think the real miracle is that I found your father at all. And you. It's funny how these things work out, from one chance meeting. That wasn't even a grocery store I go to. An envelope showed up in my mailbox full of coupons and cash gift certificates for that Dominick's. Some little girl must have sent it—my address was written in pink crayon."

"*What?*"

Graciella frowned at Irene's extreme reaction. "You know something about pink crayons?"

"No, no," Irene said. And thought, *Buddy*. "Go on."

"There's not much else. I decided to try out the store. Then I met your father, and it turned out that he knew my husband's family. It's kind of amazing."

"That's the word for it," Irene said. She'd have to talk to Buddy and find out what the hell he was up to. She changed the subject. "I'll be able to get more done on the financials after my trip." She was going to fly out to Phoenix tomorrow morning. She'd been referring to it as "my trip." Not "my trip to Arizona" or "my big job interview" or "my long weekend of hot sex."

"Whenever you can," Graciella said. "I'll make sure you're paid for your time."

"You don't have to do that. Dad asked me to help. It turns out I could be of use, so—"

"Your father, sweet as he is, doesn't get to loan you out like a lawn mower. You have useful skills, Irene, and you'll be compensated."

With a shock, Irene realized that Graciella was not simply being nice. She believed she was telling the truth.

☆

That was the great catch in her ability, the reason it hardly ever helped: she could only detect when people *knew* they were lying. If they believed what they were saying, she was powerless to determine the truth of it. The great lesson of her childhood was that most adults, but especially her father, believed much of the bullshit they generated. When she was ten, she went to him and said, "Something's wrong with Mom."

He was sitting on the couch in the basement, his headquarters since the car accident, watching the Cubs on channel nine, dressed in his uniform since the accident: undershirt, Bermuda shorts, black dress shoes. It was deep August, and that year they'd had nothing but the three Hs: Hot, Hazy, and Humid. The basement was slightly cooler than the rest of the house—but only slightly.

"Mom's fine," he said.

"She is?" Irene asked. Relieved, disbelieving, wanting to believe. Tears pooled hot behind her eyes.

"You're blocking the TV," he said.

Irene didn't move. "She threw up in the bathroom."

He finally looked at her.

"This morning," she said. "And last night." Mom had tried to keep it quiet, but the sounds were unmistakable.

"Huh," her father said. His hand came up and scratched his jaw, four fingers held together. His hands had become shovels since the accident.

"Do you think she has the flu?" Irene asked.

"I'll ask her about it."

"She shouldn't be working if she's sick," Irene said. "You should tell her to stay home."

He almost smiled. If he'd let the smile come on, she would have screamed at him. "You don't like Agent Smalls, do you?"

This was a month after Smalls had failed to lie to Irene. He was in love with her mother. The fact that she kept getting in the car with him every morning, kept working with him, was inexplicable to her. That her father let her mother do it infuriated her.

"What are you going to do about Mom?" Irene asked.

"I told you, I'll ask her." Irene thought, He believes that he's really going to do this.

"But she's okay?" Irene asked again.

"Madlock's up to bat," he said wearily.

Later, Irene started supper, with Buddy prompting her with the right ingredients from their mother's recipe. It was chop suey, an ultra-bland dish as Chinese as meat loaf. When Mom came home, she didn't try to take over as she usually did. She sat in the chair with Buddy on her lap, and told Irene that she was doing fine.

"How was work?" Irene asked. This seemed like an adult thing to say.

"Busy. And what did you do today, Mr. Buddy? Did you draw any pictures?"

They went on like that, talking about nothing as ground beef simmered in the skillet, until Irene called Frankie and her father to the dining room. Irene wasn't about to ask her mother what was wrong. She was terrified that Mom would tell the truth.

Once they sat down, Frankie was there to distract them. At ten years old he was a motormouth, before teenagerdom turned him sullen, and aging desperation made him a yammerer again. This was the summer he found the *Encyclopedia of Greek Gods and Heroes* at the Bookmobile and kept asking Dad which ones the Telemachus family should worship. He was the only one who could get Dad to laugh since the accident.

"No paganism," Dad said. "Your mom won't stand for it."

Mom had been moving the chopped celery and ground beef on her plate without eating any of it. When she thought no one was looking, her face went cold, as if all her energy had to be redirected elsewhere. But Irene was watching.

"Please stick to Christ and the Blessed Virgin," Mom said. She touched her napkin to her lips, and pushed her chair back. "Excuse me a moment." She was pale, and sweating in the heat. Buddy put his face in his hands.

Mom stood, and placed her hand on the chair back. But she put too much of her weight on it, and the chair tipped. She fell sideways, and the side of her head struck the linoleum with a sharp sound.

Everyone leaped up. Everyone except Buddy, who kept his face covered. Mom was embarrassed. "I'm all right, I'm all right, please everybody sit down, I just lost my balance." Dad helped her out of the room, and up the stairs, to the bathroom.

He returned to the table a long time later. "Mom's going to rest." He looked at Irene. "Everything's going to be fine."

Liar, she thought.

☆

Six in the morning and Matty was blearily awake, volunteering to carry Irene's bag down to the car and see her off to Phoenix. She knew he'd be asleep again before she left the driveway, but the effort touched her.

"I feel like I'm abandoning you to the wolves," she said to him.

"But it's my wolf pack," he said. "Awhoo."

The joking didn't fool her. For the past two weeks, ever since he quit on Frankie, Matty had been moody and tense.

From downstairs, Dad said, "We're twenty minutes late! Are we leaving or not?"

"Leaving!" Matty said.

"Give me a second," Irene said.

She didn't want to leave him. She'd already raised one set of feral children, her brothers, and knew the dangers. Was it any wonder she was so eager to find a man who'd take care of her for a change?

"So this Joshua guy," Matty said. "You're not *moving* to Arizona, right?"

"Did you pick up your room like I asked?" She'd learned to dodge questions by watching how others dodged hers. "That's what I thought. Do it this morning, okay? And c'mere." Before he could stop her she pulled him into a hug. "I love you, Matty. Don't forget to—"

She pulled back, frowning.

"What?" Matty asked.

She bent, and smelled his shirt again. He tried to step back and she grabbed his collar. Sniffed hard.

"Holy shit," she said. Matty's eyes went wide.

"Let's go already!" Dad called.

"Are you smoking pot?" she asked.

Matty opened his mouth. The lie died before it could break the surface.

"Currently?" he asked.

"Oh God. You're smoking pot. You're smoking pot. You're doing this to me right as I'm leaving town?"

"Doing what now?" her father asked. He stood at the bottom of the stairs, ready for duty: hat on, suit jacket buttoned, cuff links shining. He would have made an excellent limo driver, if not for his petulant attitude. "He's not to leave this room," Irene said. "All weekend."

"The *room*?" Matty exclaimed.

Dad looked at her, then at Matty, then back to her. "I'm supposed to ensure this incarceration how?"

"It's real simple," Irene said. "You watch him. Night and day. If he leaves the room, you beat his ass until he goes back inside."

"That sounds an awful lot like you're grounding *me*," Dad said.

"Jesus Christ!" Irene said. "Be an authority figure for once."

"Not really my strong suit," Dad said. "Now come on, don't do that." She'd burst into tears. "We're late already."

"Promise me," she said.

"All right, all right," Dad said. "I promise. Also, Matty promises. He will not leave his room except for necessary bodily functions. Can we go now? I'm meeting someone for breakfast."

"I promise, too," Matty said. He knew she'd want to hear it directly from him.

"You shut up," she said to him. She marched past him, heading for his room. He came after, emitting panicky squawks.

"Where is it?" Irene asked. "Where'd you hide it?" She kicked open his room. There were clothes littering the floor. To her newly drug-sensitized nose, the room reeked of marijuana. "Get it. *Now.*"

Any teenager with a normal mother would play dumb at this point. Wait her out. But Matty knew better than to lie or delay. She'd trained him from birth to accept the infallibility of her instincts. He walked to his dresser, opened the third drawer, and reached in. He handed the baggie to her without speaking. Two joints, one half smoked.

"If you miss your flight," Dad said from the door, "don't blame me."

"Where'd you get this?" Irene asked.

Matty flushed. Beet red, she thought, was the color of being beaten.

"Train's leaving the station," Dad said. "Off we go. Toodle-oo."

In the delay created by his grandfather, Matty found some words. "I bought it from an older kid."

"Which older kid?" Irene said. "Where? I want names!"

"I'll find out while you're gone," Dad said. "Irene. Look at me. I'll interrogate the boy to your satisfaction."

She looked at her watch. If she didn't leave now, she'd miss her plane.

She howled.

Eight hours later, she howled again, in a different key.

"Mmhmm," Joshua said, from somewhere south of her navel.

Both of them wordless. That was what she needed, and what he gave her. Skin, and sweat, and the urgent action of bodies, free from the interruptions of a frontal lobe frantically turning experiences into nouns and verbs and adjectives. Labeling. She needed the pure thing, fire and not "fire," heat and not "hot." His body was enough for her. She loved the smell of him, the tang of his skin. She adored the damp at the back of his neck. His hard, bitable nipples. She even liked the friendly pooch of his belly. They'd spent three hours in this hotel room without exchanging more than a handful of sentences, and all she wanted now was to live the rest of her life in this primitive, nonverbal state.

But of course that was impossible. As they lay side by side in the gigantic bed, feet touching, holding hands, breathing, Irene let slip an appreciative, exhausted, "Fuck."

"Past tense, honey," Joshua said. "We shall fuck. We are fucking. We have fucked."

That was the rub. She wanted *him* as well as his body: now, in person, not behind a screen, separated by satellites. But the only way to his mind was through a buzzing swarm of words. A more talented psychic could have reached straight in and grabbed the honey of his thoughts, but Irene had never been able to do that. Words, stupid words, were still required.

"Fucking is not an adequate name for what we just did there," Irene said. "We need a better word. Something more festive."

"Fucktivities?" he offered.

"Celebratio," she said.

"Funnilingus!"

Even though they were in Tempe, only miles from his house, he'd agreed to meet in a hotel, just as they'd done every time he'd come through O'Hare. (The word "layover" never stopped amusing them.) In Chicago she hadn't wanted to show him her house or introduce him to the family. And now that she'd traveled across the country to see him, she didn't want to see his home, either. Not the furniture that was no doubt better than hers, nor the clothes in his closet, or the dishes in the sink. Not his daughter's bedroom. If Irene saw how he lived, if she met his daughter, Jun, then there were only two possibilities: she would be repulsed and love him a little less, or she'd see herself in that house and want to move there. She couldn't risk either of those outcomes, not yet. Their relationship had blossomed in the greenhouse of Hotel Land. Why complicate it?

Yet this trip was all about complications.

"Do you need to go shopping?" he asked her. "For, like, shoes. Or an outfit?"

"You think I need an outfit?"

"If you were interviewing me, you wouldn't need any clothes at all."

"Answer the question."

He thought for a moment. "You did complain about your interview clothes being out of date."

Good dodge, she thought. "I went to Talbots before I came here. In fact, I need to hang everything before it gets wrinkled."

But still she didn't leave the bed. She didn't want to think about the interview. He'd set it up for her at his company, given her résumé to HR, and even made sure the interview could happen on Friday so they'd have the entire weekend after. This annoyed her, but she couldn't tell him that. He was only trying to help. And why mention it, when it might turn out, after the hiring process had run its course, that these people wanted her on her own terms, and she wanted them?

What trumped all intervening annoyances was her desperation to get out of her current life. Her father was toying with gangsters, her son was smoking pot, and she was flat broke and working a cash register for near–minimum wage.

She needed a game changer. She needed a home run. She needed the grand slam of all sports metaphors.

"I got something for you," Joshua said. He hopped up from the bed, and she admired his muscular buttocks in motion. The man loved to be naked. He became as free as a toddler as soon as they unlocked the hotel room door, and that allowed her to shed her own self-consciousness. The natives of Hotel Land knew no shame.

He retrieved something from his roller bag, hiding it behind his back, and then held it out to her: a gift-wrapped box, a little bigger than a shirt box, tied in green ribbon. When she didn't immediately take it, he swung his hips to waggle his penis at her, and she laughed.

It was this DNA-deep silliness that drew her to him, pushed her away, and drew her back again. She was a serious woman who'd grown up surrounded by frivolous men; by all rights she'd have no more truck with goofs, even gallant ones. Online he constantly poked at her, punned at her, and issued all-caps rants on her behalf that were directed at whoever had dared offend her that day. In person, where she had discouraged him from using words, he turned on the physical shtick.

"Nice bow," she said. "You wrap this yourself?"

"Mr. Johnson held down the ribbon for me."

She pulled off the shiny paper, opened the box. Inside was a portfolio, the brown leather glowing and buttery. Her initials were stitched into the front.

"You put your résumés in it," he said. "And look: Yellow notepad! Pen loop!"

"All this, and rich, Corinthian leather," she said. She pulled his face to hers, and was surprised to feel tears on her eyelashes. Tears, Irene? Really?

"I know you're nervous," he said. "But you're going to knock 'em dead. You know that, right?"

She loved him when he thought he was telling the truth. But did she love him enough, all the other times? They'd known each other for only two months and already he wanted her to cross the continent to be with him, his Internet-order bride. He talked as if this was No Big Thing. A grand adventure. A lark. He had no idea how hard this was for her. Mostly because she hadn't told him.

He grabbed her arm. "Come on. Up."

"What are you doing?"

She held on to the portfolio as he pulled her to the big wall mirror. "Stand in front of me." He placed his hand on her shoulders, put his cheek beside hers, and together they looked into the mirror.

"Repeat after me," he said. "I, Irene Telemachus, will get this job."

She narrowed her eyes.

"I, Irene . . ." he said.

"I will get this job," she said.

"Not to me. Say it so you know it's the truth."

Irene looked at the naked woman in the mirror, clutching the portfolio as if it could protect her. "They'd be lucky to have me," she said.

It was impossible to tell if Mirror Irene was lying. She gave nothing away.

Joshua slipped a hand under the portfolio and tweaked a nipple. "Damn straight."

The interview started out well enough. Amber the HR rep, a twentysomething nymph constructed entirely of freckles and positive attitude, led her on a tour of the building, highlighting the open-plan office where Irene would sit if she took the job. Her desk would be surrounded by more windows than anyplace she'd ever worked except for a Burger King drive-thru. Everyone was smiling and pleasant, and Amber enthused about how *friendly* the working environment was and how *laid-back* and *cool* everyone was. The girl believed every word she spoke. And it was certainly true that the dress code was relaxed. Everyone wore southwestern casual: polos and khakis, sundresses, even shorts and sandals. Only upper management seemed to wear anything with buttons, and Irene felt like an eastern stiff, dour as a missionary.

The interview proper began in a large, glassed-in conference room with a surfboard-shaped table. Amber introduced her to Bob, her potential boss, and Laurie and Jon, her potential colleagues. Those two had the same job title, though Laurie said she'd been there four more years.

Bob described the consulting business, the kinds of clients they worked with, the array of experts they had on staff, the kind of person they were looking for to fit into their "family." Jon and Laurie chimed in with details. Each of them took time to mention how they loved Joshua, Joshua was great, sharp as a tack that Joshua.

Finally it was time for the interrogation. The others opened their folders, pretended to study Irene's résumé, and fell silent.

Irene resisted the urge to open the portfolio. The monogram now struck her as pompous and ridiculous.

"So, Irene," Bob the boss said. "I'm not seeing a degree on here." As if he'd just noticed this.

"No," she said, "but I have experience in bookkeeping, accounting, and, well, money management."

"Right . . ." Jon said. Then he winced apologetically. "But you know the job requires at least an undergraduate degree? In business, accounting, or some related field?"

"I saw that," Irene said. "But we—I wasn't sure if that was a hard requirement." Joshua had encouraged her to apply anyway.

"Hmm," Bob said.

Another long moment of silence, as if they were mourning the death of her prospects.

"How about postsecondary schooling?" Bob asked. "Perhaps courses at a business school?"

Did he think she would have left that off the résumé if she'd taken any? "I plan on continuing my education as soon as possible," she said.

"That could be tough," Jon said, putting on a concerned expression. "I mean, while working here full-time, and taking care of a son."

Irene had not mentioned her son, and he wasn't on her résumé.

"Any experience with accounting software?" Laurie asked.

"I know how to use spreadsheets," Irene said. "The firm where I worked last used a homegrown system that was mostly paper-based."

"Aldi's uses a paper system?" Jon asked in mock surprise.

Fucker, Irene thought. He knew she wasn't talking about Aldi's.

"We have something a *bit* more complex," Bob said. Jon laughed an ass-kisser's laugh. Even Laurie chuckled.

The interview continued to spiral downward. She realized that they'd agreed to this interview only as a favor to Joshua, and now they wanted to make it abundantly clear that she didn't belong here, would never belong here. Amber the HR rep never asked a question, but scribbled and scribbled and scribbled on her notepad like a five-year-old in a church pew.

Irene's skin grew hot. She kept a smile nailed to her face. Held her voice steady.

Ten minutes or an hour later, depending on whether you were on the insulting or insulted side of the table, Amber finally spoke. She smiled and issued the obligatory words of benediction: "Do you have any questions for us?"

Irene remembered being onstage, blinking in bright lights, looking out into the darkness, where strangers were waiting for her to fail. She was so thankful when Archibald had debunked them and Mom had called an end to the act. She'd become disgusted with being judged.

Amber said, "All right, then, if you don't have anything—"

"There is one bit of work experience I forgot to mention," Irene said. The group regarded her blankly. Mentally they'd moved on to the next meeting, the next candidate. "When I was a girl, my family had a psychic act. Teddy Telemachus and His Amazing Family. It sounds crazy, I know, but we were famous for a while. We toured the country. We were even on national TV once."

Laurie said, "*Psychic* act?"

Bob the Boss said, "That sounds interesting, but I'm not sure that's relevant to—"

"Let me explain," Irene said. "We each had a talent. My brother could move things with his mind. My mother was clairvoyant. And I was the human lie detector." She smiled, and Amber returned the smile automatically, though her sunshine eyes were panicked. "At some point in the show, my father would call up someone from the audience and tell them about my ability. All they had to do was try to tell me a lie and not get caught. It could be something simple, like holding the ace of clubs and telling me it was the ace of spades. Or they could try to tell me their age, or their weight. Then Dad would ask them to write down two truths and a lie—just like the party game.

"Sometimes it got really interesting. If the crowd was right, Dad would prompt them into writing down embarrassing things, things that were a little risqué. I wouldn't even know what some of the sentences meant. I was only ten. But you know what?"

She had their attention now. More than twenty years since she'd been onstage, but the old skills were still there.

"I never made a mistake," Irene said. "Not once."

Bob and Jon exchanged looks. Laurie said, "Not once? What was the trick?"

"It's just something I could do. *Can* do."

Bob smiled uncertainly, not sure if she was kidding. "Well, too bad we don't have a deck of cards."

"I know," Jon said. He reached into his pocket, came out with a quarter. He flipped it, covered it with his hands. Then he peeked at it.

Irene waited.

"It's heads," Jon said.

"No, it's not."

Jon laughed. "Caught me. One more time."

Bob said, "Why don't we move along. If you don't have any questions, I suppose we can—"

"I do have a few questions," Irene said.

Bob took a breath. "Sure, sure. Fire away."

She pretended to glance at her notes. "Everything you've told me makes it sound like the perfect company," Irene said. "Have any of you looked for another job outside the company, say, in the last six months?"

No one spoke, until Amber the HR rep said, "I don't think that's a question that—"

"Of course not," Bob said.

"Not me," Jon said.

Laurie shook her head. "I plan on being here a long time."

"Huh," Irene said, as if mulling this over. "Bob and Laurie are telling the truth, but Jon . . ."

Amber's eyes went wide.

"Where did you apply?" Irene said.

Jon's smile was a little stiff. "I don't know what you're talking about."

"See, that's a lie, too," Irene said. "Bob, did you know Jon was unhappy here?"

Bob blinked in confusion. The interview had taken a hard left turn, and he was struggling to keep up.

"Never mind, new question," Irene said. "Bob, do you pay women and men equally for doing the same job?"

"Of course," Bob said.

It was a lie, but she was only setting him up for the fastball. She said, "How about Jon and Laurie, here. They're both assistant managers, but Laurie's been here longer. Is she making more than Jon?"

Laurie leaned forward and put her elbows on the table. A woman who already knew the answer.

"I have to warn you," Irene said to Bob. "I never miss."

"Who *are* you?" Bob asked.

"I take that as a no." To Laurie she said, "I think I'd get a new job. Or take Jon's when he leaves. Just make sure to ask for his salary."

She picked up the beautiful portfolio and stood. She felt dizzy, but didn't fall. Wouldn't allow herself to fall.

"I really enjoyed meeting you," she said. None of them were human lie detectors, but she was confident they'd be able to evaluate her statement. She walked off without waiting for applause.

Six hours later, Teddy met her at the curb at O'Hare. "I gotta tell you," he said. "I'm glad you decided to come home early."

Irene stared out through the windshield as they rode away from the airport. She didn't want to speak. She'd exiled herself from Hotel Land, but wanted to carry that wordlessness with her.

"I need your help with something. Something that'll help Graciella. You like Graciella, don't you? You two really seemed to hit it off."

Dad hadn't asked why she'd returned a day early, or seemed to notice that she was a hollow-eyed wreck. But why should that be a surprise? Before she left he hadn't asked her why she was going to Arizona or who she was seeing. He was oblivious to her nervousness and excitement, and now he was blind to her heartbreak. His sole interest in the trip was when it would start and end, and that was only because he wanted to know how long he was responsible for Matty.

My father is a narcissist, she thought. This was not a new thought. She'd learned when she was ten that if you're not part of the act, you're part of the audience.

He took the wrong exit off North Avenue and she gave him a look.

"One last errand," he said.

"Just take me home," Irene said. She'd taken too many car trips with her father recently, and she'd be happy never to take one again.

"I helped you, now you help me," he said. "I absolutely need you at my side for the next half hour."

"What scam are you running now?"

"I'm just trying to do something nice for a woman." His imitation of outrage was unconvincing.

"Sure, it's all for Graciella. Look at you. You're practically hopping up and down behind the wheel."

"I like helping people," he said.

She made a rude noise.

"What?" he asked. "Why are you acting like this?"

"Jesus Christ, Dad. I can't believe I'm still doing it. I'm a grown woman, and I'm still—never mind."

"Doing what? Please, enlighten me."

"I spent most of my life waiting for you to notice me." She shook her head. "What a waste."

"Notice you? How could I not notice you? You were the one scowling at me every time I did something that your mother wouldn't have done."

"There we go. It took you one sentence to get back to how you're the victim."

"You're making the same face. Right now."

"Did it even occur to you to ask me *why* I needed a babysitter for Matty?"

"I'm sure it was important."

"Unbelievable."

"If you wanted to tell me, you'd tell me! I'm sorry for wanting to respect your privacy. Now, here's the bar."

"A bar? We're going to a bar?"

"Technically, a tavern. Don't you remember this place? I used to bring you with me sometimes."

"You never brought me here. That was probably Frankie."

"Maybe so, maybe so."

He parked in the spot closest to the door, which happened to be a handicapped spot. Irene started to object, and he shushed her. "It's legal, it's legal. Open the glove compartment."

She found the handicapped tag and pulled it out with two fingers, as if it were a dead fish or a loaded gun. Dad rolled his eyes and hung the tag from the front mirror. "Come around and help me out."

"What?"

"Help me walk in."

"Help yourself out!"

"Damn it, Irene, it's a simple request. Hold on to my arm like I can barely walk. Help me sit down, fuss over me—"

"Jesus Christ, *why*?"

"I can't explain, not now. But rest assured—"

"I'm sure it's important," Irene said, throwing his line back at him.

"It is! It surely is!" He was oblivious to sarcasm. "Now remember, I'm feeble."

"Minded," Irene said, loud enough for him to hear.

They performed a geriatric mime on the way to the front door, Teddy placing one foot meditatively in front of the other, hand gripping her arm. He was pretty good at it. Irene could almost imagine the hip replacement.

"A cane would really sell this," he stage-whispered to her. "Maybe one with the three rubber feet?"

She couldn't believe she was participating in this.

"It's the saddest of the canes," he went on. "You can't even pretend to be stylish. Fred Astaire never danced with a tri-support."

Irene pulled open the door for him, and he hobbled inside. The dim interior smelled of stale beer and inadequate bleach.

"The usual, Teddy?" said a huge, indistinct shape behind the bar.

Teddy chuckled. To Irene he said, "Twenty years since I've been here, Barney still knows my drink." Somehow he'd made his voice shakier, as if it needed its own tri-support.

"Let's sit at the bar," Teddy said to Irene. There was no one else in the place. Maybe it was too early on Saturday for even the drunks.

"Sure, Dad," she said flatly. "Let me get the stool for you."

"Nothing for her," Teddy said to the bartender. "You been using the same bar rag since 1962. She doesn't have the antibodies for this place."

"I'll have a beer," Irene said. "In a bottle." Barney nodded. He was about the same age as Dad, but three times his size.

"So how's the place doing?" Teddy asked. He threw some extra quaver in his voice, an old man struggling to sound jovial. They started talking about people Irene didn't know and would, she hoped, never meet.

Irene watched Mirror Irene sip her beer. That woman lived in an alternate universe called Arizona, with a man who loved her.

When she came back from the interview, Joshua could see she was upset—unlike her father, he was no narcissist—and kept pressing her for answers. For words. She couldn't explain why she'd gotten so mad, and so couldn't explain why she'd all but set fire to the conference room. She couldn't tell him how angry she was at him.

"Never do me a favor again," she told him, and started packing.

He tried to talk to her all the way to the airport, kept talking as she exchanged her ticket. He even paid the transfer fee, all the while asking, "What are you saying?" As if she were speaking another language.

Only the gate stopped him. "You're never leaving Arizona," she said. Her anger had turned to sorrow, so that now she was a blubbering mess. "You can't leave, not with joint custody. And I can't just live off whatever crumbs you throw my way. There's no future for me here."

How could she explain? She loved their time in Hotel Land, but that wasn't a place you could live forever. The smart thing to do was to let him go now.

"So," Dad said to the bartender. "Is Mitzi in yet?"

Barney nodded over Teddy's shoulder. A woman whose age was in the same ballpark as the men's walked toward Teddy, her arms out. "Well, look what the cat dragged in," she said.

"That cat is my daughter," Teddy said with a grin.

"And you're an old dog." Mitzi kissed him on the cheek. To Irene she said, "Now I feel old. Your dad used to talk about you."

"Nice to meet you," she said to Mitzi.

"She's such a good daughter," Teddy said. "Takes me everywhere."

"It's good to have a strong woman at your side," Mitzi said.

"Talk about a strong woman," Teddy said to Irene. "You want a role model, look no further. Mitzi's run this place through fat times and thin."

"Charmer," Mitzi said. She was a scrawny bird of a woman, with a finch's glitter in her eye. Mitzi said, "You're not selling that UltraLife stuff, too, are you?"

"What's that?" Dad asked. He wasn't faking the confusion.

"Frankie started bringing it with him," Mitzi said. "Damn if it didn't straighten me out."

Irene shot her father a hard look. Was this visit about Frankie, and not Graciella? But no, Teddy didn't know what Mitzi was talking about.

"So Frankie's been stopping by?" Teddy said.

"Oh yeah," Mitzi said. "On a weekly basis. Mostly weekly. He's missed a few."

Dad seemed shaken. "I apologize if the boy's been pushing the stuff on you. Frankie's been so excited about it."

Mitzi said, "You want to come back in my office and talk about it?"

Dad hesitated, then said, "We can talk in front of Irene. She knows all about Frankie's business."

An outright lie. Irene had no clue what was going on. She wasn't reassured that Teddy seemed to have no idea, either.

"All right then," Mitzi said skeptically. She took the stool next to Teddy's. They were all sitting now, facing away from the bar. Barney had disappeared into the back room.

"So. Frankie's visits," Dad said. "How much are we talking?"

"You know I usually keep those numbers confidential."

"How much, Mitzi?"

"As of yesterday, forty-nine thousand, seventy-four dollars and twenty-four cents."

Irene suddenly realized what those numbers meant. Dad was shocked, too, to judge by his frozen expression.

Mitzi said, "I asked him not to bring you into this. He's going to talk to Nick next week. They'll work it out."

Fuck, Irene thought. Bad pictures flickered in her head from a dozen violent movies. She pictured her brother trying to talk his way out of trouble, the way he tried to talk his way out of everything. He'd never learned that when he was drowning he should keep his mouth shut.

"No," Dad said. "I'll talk to Nick." Irene watched her father. A moment ago, he didn't know about Frankie owing money, but now he was putting on to Mitzi that he not only knew about the situation, but had already put a plan in motion. Teddy Telemachus, world-class bluff. That poker face made him the only person in the family who could keep secrets from her. That, and the way he dealt his words as carefully as his cards.

"You want to talk to Nick?" Mitzi asked. "That might not be such a great idea."

"Your brother stands a lot better chance of getting the money from me than from Frankie," Teddy said.

"It's not that, and you know it."

"This is my son, Mitzi. Please. Make it happen."

Irene did not speak until they were back in the car. He let her get behind the wheel, for appearances.

"What the hell was *that* about?" she asked.

"I'm as surprised as you are."

That was the truth. He'd dropped the bluff now that he was out of the tavern.

"I wanted an appointment with Nick so I could talk to him about Graciella. But *this*?"

Still, she wanted to make sure they were on the same page. "Frankie's in debt to the mob for fifty K," she said.

"It seems so."

"That explains how he was able to keep Bellerophonics going so long with no customers."

"He kept coming to me for money," Dad said. "Third time, I told him I was tapped out and he should close up shop—work for somebody else and actually get paid. I didn't think he was stupid enough to go to God damn Nick Pusateri. The whole point of raising kids is to make sure they don't make the same mistakes as you did."

There was an entire story there that she was pretty sure she didn't want to know. Instead, she asked, "You're not going to pay it, are you?"

"Just drive me home, Irene. No. Wait. Drive me to Wal-Mart."

She raised her eyebrows.

"I need to buy a cane and a baseball bat," he said.

"I understand the cane."

"The bat is to whack your brother with."

"Let's buy two," Irene said.

14

Frankie

He could hear Loretta calling for him from the house. Eventually she thought of the garage.

The black hunk of metal nestled into the hood of her car like an egg on a pillow. The impact had also cracked the windshield. The safe door, however, was closed. Still fucking closed.

She walked toward him. He was sitting on a folding chair next to the front bumper of the car. The floor was littered by a garden of crushed Budweiser cans—and locks. Padlocks of every kind were scattered around the cement floor, none of them open.

"Can I help you, Loretta?"

She took in the sweatpants, the undershirt, the empty Doritos bag. She looked again at the Corolla and the black safe, then back at him.

"Are you going to work today?" Her voice was surprisingly soft.

"Sure," he said. "What time is it?"

"After nine."

"Huh." He rubbed his jaw. Normally he would have left a couple of hours ago. He probably should have gone. Work would have occupied him. Kept his mind off of what was waiting for him this afternoon. *Who* was waiting for him.

"I was going to go to the grocery store," Loretta said.

"Okay."

She stared at him.

"I think we're out of milk," he said.

"I was wondering about the car," she said.

He nodded slowly, as if this was a good point.

"So will it run?" she asked.

He pursed his lips. Thought for a moment. "Hard to say."

"I'll call one of the neighbors and see if I can borrow a car."

"Yeah," he said. "That's probably a good idea."

"Oh, and your father called. He wants you to call him back. Says it's important."

Like hell he was going to call back. It was Teddy's fault he was in this mess. He'd gone to his father for help when Bellerophonics was tanking, and after the bare minimum amount of financial assistance, his father had cut him off. No, the great Teddy Telemachus only bet on cards, never his own children.

"Did Matty call?" he asked. That was the Telemachus he needed right now. But Loretta was gone. What time did she say it was? He should have paid attention. There were only so many hours to fill until his appointment with Nick Pusateri Senior.

○

The first time Frankie thought he was going to die was in 1991, in a small room on the bottom deck of the *Alton Belle*, right after getting his nose broke. The guy whose fist did the damage was a wiry white guy with rabbit teeth and sun-cracked skin like a vinyl chair left in the yard. He was dressed like a janitor, but it wasn't clear if he was the official enforcer for the casino or just an employee whose job description included the line "Other duties as assigned." He certainly seemed to enjoy the hitting-people duty.

The two other men in the room—a floor boss and a slick-headed man whom Frankie took to be the casino manager—evaluated the janitor's work and found it good. "One more time," said the manager. He was a nervous white guy whose oil-black widow's peak made him look like a middle-aged Eddie Munster.

The floor boss, a black man in a shiny suit that looked more expensive than the manager's, said, "Tell us what you did to my table." Everyone seemed quite concerned about this. For the first half hour that Frankie had been held in the room, the men went over the video of the event using an ordinary VCR and small TV. They had declined to show the images to Frankie, but he picked up from their discussion of it that the tape showed from several angles that Frankie's hands were inches away from the roulette table when the ball, turntable, and chips flew into the air.

"Was it magnets?" the manager asked.

Frankie was too busy gasping in pain to deny it immediately. He lay on his side, watching an alarming amount of blood run across his cheek and pool on the floor. Magnets? he thought. Still with the fucking magnets? It was their first and last theory.

Frankie lifted a hand to his smashed upper lip, afraid to touch his nose. His fingers came away red, as if dipped into a paint can. Jesus. Where the hell was Buddy? Why the fuck didn't he see this coming in his vision of chips and riches?

A bad thought crossed his mind. What if Buddy *had* seen this, and didn't bother to tell him?

"It wasn't magnets," Frankie said. "Or if it was, they weren't mine." His voice sounded whiny in his own ears, due to nasal blockage. Mostly.

"Who do you work for?"

"I'm—" He spit blood. "Self-employed."

The janitor bent and gripped Frankie's shirt. Frankie put his hands on the man's forearms, smearing blood on one sleeve. He made protesting noises as he was jerked to his feet.

"Get him off the boat," the head manager said.

Oh thank God, Frankie thought.

The janitor and the floor boss grabbed him under each arm and frog-marched him out of the room and down a hallway carpeted, inexplicably, with Astroturf. The manager scooted ahead and pulled open a heavy door.

Frankie was pushed out onto a small side deck close by the glittering water. The paddle wheel churned away to their left, but the sound was almost drowned out by laughter, buzzes, bells—the jangling roar of a crowded casino. A large red-and-white motor launch bedecked in Christmas lights idled at the lip of the deck in a cloud of gas fumes. At the wheel was a man in a white shirt and black vest who looked like he should have been dealing blackjack. *Other duties as assigned.*

"Get him to the garage," the manager said. "And don't let anyone see you."

"Wait, garage?" Frankie said. They shoved him forward, and he stumbled into the boat and sat down hard on a bench. The janitor and the other man climbed in. "Where are you taking me?"

The janitor said, "Shut up or we gag you."

Frankie shut up. A coldness filled his stomach. He held on to the bench as the motorboat surged around the back of the riverboat's paddle wheel and pointed toward shore. They weren't heading back to the brightly lit loading area where he and Buddy had boarded the boat, but south of that, where a sporadic line of streetlights marked the edge of the river.

They're getting me away from the crowds, Frankie thought. Away from witnesses. In this "garage" they could do anything to him. All his life, Teddy had told stories about gangsters he'd known, mooks with knuckledusters, gun-carrying henchmen, molls with switchblades tucked into their garters. Movie characters. Teddy was the hero of these stories, a trickster with fast hands and a faster mouth. Frankie had longed to be that guy, the smooth-talking confidence man, but by the time he grew up, they weren't making movies like that anymore. All that remained were secondhand tales, you-shoulda-seen-it stories, and badly edited highlight reels.

So here he was, a failed casino cheat, in a boatful of mobbed-up thugs . . . and he couldn't think of a damn thing to say. He was going to die, whimpering, with his own blood smearing his shirt.

The boat charged toward a dimly lit pier. At the last moment the driver threw the boat into reverse, spun the wheel, and brought them alongside the wood with the slightest of thumps. Frankie decided that maybe he was a boatman first, blackjack dealer second.

The janitor gripped the back of Frankie's neck, and leaned in to his ear. "You're going to talk now, asshole."

The floor boss climbed up on the pier, then turned to pull Frankie up. A pair of headlights snapped on, turning the casino employee into a silhouette. A loud voice said, "We'll take it from here, boys."

A huge figure appeared in the lights. He waved a badge in the general direction of the floor boss, and then looked down in the boat.

The janitor's hand tightened on Frankie's neck.

"Who the hell are you?" Frankie said.

The man laughed. "Are you really choosing them over me?"

That was a good point. Frankie knocked aside the arm of the janitor and levered himself out of the boat.

The big man said, "I'm Agent Destin Smalls," and extended his hand.

The name rang a faint bell. Frankie shook the hand, and handcuffs appeared on his wrist like a magic trick.

"You're under arrest," Agent Smalls said.

○

He drove toward his father's house with the air-conditioning blasting into his face. "Embrace life," he said to himself. Embrace the fact that Matty had quit on him, forcing him to either give up on the heist or learn to do everything himself. Embrace the two weeks he'd spent trying to open locks with his mind, and failing to open a single one. Embrace his inability to get the safe dial to turn a centimeter.

Failure to accept reality led only to frustration, and frustration to rage. What did rage get you? A grown man picking up a safe in his arms and attempting to throw it down onto the concrete, before his back gave out. Rage got you a safe crashing into the hood of a Toyota Corolla that still had two years of payments.

Okay, forget about that. What's done is done. That's life. Embrace it.

But Frankie was after something more. And he very much needed to explain this to Matty.

At home the garage door was open and Teddy's Buick wasn't there, thank God. Irene's car was gone, too. Frankie marched up to the front door and its ridiculously tiled front step. A new fire extinguisher had been installed next to the door, the bracket screwed right into the brick. Why put a fire extinguisher *outside* the house? Who the fuck knows. That was Buddy. After all the crazy projects, maybe he was planning on burning the place down. If this was Frankie's house he would have kicked his brother out months ago.

It was cooler inside the house, but only marginally so. Teddy, the cheap bastard, had never installed central air, and had put a window air conditioner in one room: his bedroom. "Matty?" he called. No one was in the living room or the kitchen. Then he heard a noise from downstairs.

The door to the basement had been removed, everything torn out down to the frame. Inside the room, metal panels hung above the windows, ready to swing down, like plate armor for a Civil War battleship. Bunk beds were in construction against the far wall, waiting for ... crew members? Jesus Christ, if Buddy flooded the backyard he could re-create the battle of the *Monitor* and the *Merrimack*.

Matty, however, was engaged in an act of deconstruction. He knelt by the desk, pulling cords out of the back of the computer monitor.

"Matty, we gotta talk," Frankie said.

"Oh! Uncle Frankie. Hi." The kid looked miserable.

"What are you doing?" Frankie asked.

"Mom says I have to take it apart. Says she doesn't even want it in the house."

"I thought she loved that thing."

"Yeah, well, she's been pretty upset lately. Crying all the time. She broke up with Joshua."

"Who the hell is Joshua?"

"Her boyfriend? In Phoenix? Anyway, it's over, and she won't let me use the computer."

"Part of your grounding with the pot thing?"

Matty grimaced. "She told you?"

"Grandpa Teddy. And it's totally hypocritical, if you ask me. Irene used to smoke pretty heavy back in high school. Probably because Lev was practically a dealer."

"*What?*"

"That's not important now. Forget about the computer. We need to talk, man to man."

"Uncle Frankie, I'm sorry that I can't—"

"I'm not here to convince you to come back to work on the thing."

"You're not?"

"Come here." Frankie led him to the couch, which sat in a cluster of remaining normal furniture Buddy had pushed to the center of the room. "Sit with me, Matty."

The boy sat hunched on the couch, staring at his feet.

Frankie said, "I'm here to apologize to you." Matty started to protest and Frankie held up a hand. "No, no. I failed you. Something happened that made you turn away from me, and I want to know what it is—so I can make amends."

"You didn't do anything."

"Did your mother find out? Is she punishing you for more than the pot?"

"No! I didn't tell her anything. She has no idea about . . . our thing."

"Then I'm at a loss," Frankie said. "What happened to change your mind?"

Matty said nothing for a long moment. "I guess I got scared," he said finally.

"Scared of what?"

The boy didn't answer.

"Did you think you'd get caught?" Frankie asked.

Matty seemed to list away from him, which Frankie took for a nod.

"That's impossible," Frankie said. "You're not doing anything. You're just floating around, invisible. I'm doing all the work—and I'm the one taking the risk." Jesus, was it hot in here. He was sweating just sitting down. "You have to know, if I got caught, I'd never, never ever, tell anyone you were involved."

Matty looked up in surprise. Shit. That possibility had never occurred to the kid.

"What if there are people who can see me?" Matty asked.

"Who? What people?"

"I don't know, like, the government?"

"Okay, I get it," Frankie said. "This is my fault. I've been telling you all about Grandma Mo and her spy stuff. But what did I tell you? The Cold War's over. The government's done with that stuff."

"Is it, though?"

"Of course it is. But that's not what you're really afraid of."

Matty waited for it.

"You're afraid of using your powers! You know I'm right. You can't even say the word. P-O-W—"

Matty looked back at his feet.

"Say it. Try it out."

"Powers," Matty said quietly.

"Damn straight. You *have* powers, and you're power*ful*. What do you have to be afraid of? You can't go through life terrified of using what God gave you. You still want to help your mom, don't you?"

He didn't answer.

Frankie said, "She works at that shitty grocery store, wearing that shitty uniform, making shitty money. She can't even afford to move out on her own! How the hell are you supposed to go to college? How's she supposed to afford that? Because you're smart, Matty. You want to go to college, you better go. Or not. Your kind of power, you don't have to. The thing you *don't* want is to end up working some dead-end job, with a bunch of kids you have no control over, wondering what the hell happened to your—"

Frankie waved his hand as if clearing a chalkboard. "Never mind all that. Focus up."

"You want me to focus?" Matty asked.

Frankie wasn't exactly sure. One of them needed to.

"I know you want to help your mom," Frankie said, lowering his voice. "And I know you want to help me. But you've also got to think about what's going to help *you*. This is not just about the—what we've been practicing for. That's just the opportunity we have in front of us at this moment. Think of it as a first step. You're going to take a lot of steps, Matty, so many steps I don't even know where you'll end up. The other side of the moon, maybe! *However*—" He put his arm around Matty's shoulders. "You gotta think of who you are. You're a Telemachus."

"I know, but—"

"No buts. Do you know what today is?"

"Thursday?"

"The last Thursday of the month. Which comes right before the last Friday of the month. And you know what *that* is."

"Um . . ."

"Payday, Matty. The big payday. And due to circumstances beyond my control, this is the last time I—*we* will ever get a shot at what's in that safe."

"What's happening?"

"Too complicated to explain." Frankie glanced at his watch, then saw that he'd forgotten to put on his watch this morning. He jumped up from the couch. "I gotta go see a guy. I'll check in with you later. But while I'm gone, think about your future, Matty. Think about embracing who you are. You've got to embrace life."

"The UltraLife," Matty said quietly.

"Yes! Exactly! I knew I could count on you."

O

Frankie spent the first hour of his arrest alone in a motel room, trying to open the handcuffs with his mind. Agent Smalls had deposited him in the room and told him to wait "until we get set up." Frankie had no idea what he meant by that. Set up what, torture equipment?

He perched on the edge of the double bed closest to the door and stared at his wrists, willing the restraints to spring open. Or unlock. Or merely tremble. But all he could think of was chips flying into the air, and arms grabbing him. He doubted he could move a paper clip now.

His shirt was still damp, not from river spray, but from sweat. He'd been sure the casino operatives were taking him away to be beaten or killed. When Destin Smalls had shown up, Frankie had been relieved, but the longer the handcuffs stayed on, the longer he sat on this floral bedspread that smelled of industrial cleaner, the more he suspected that he'd made at best a lateral move: out of the frying pan and into the frying pan.

The door opened and Frankie jumped up. Agent Smalls filled the doorway. He was in his late sixties, but Frankie gave no thought to bum-rushing him. You could hurt yourself running into a wall, even an old one.

"I'd like to call my lawyer," Frankie said.

"Sure," the agent said, and grabbed him by the elbow.

It was near dawn, but there was no light in the sky except the small yellow face of the Super 8 sign. The parking lot was full of dark. Frankie felt another hope die. Not a person in sight to witness his illegal incarceration.

"You don't remember me, do you?" the agent said. "I came to your house dozens of times before your mother died."

"To do what, harass my dad?"

"That was a side benefit."

The trip was all of five feet, to the next motel room door. Smalls opened the door and nudged Frankie inside. "Do you remember *him*?" Smalls asked.

A bald gnome with a handlebar mustache sat behind a round table loaded with electrical equipment. The waxed, curlicued mustache had turned silver sometime in the past twenty years, but Frankie recognized him all right.

"Mother*fucker*," Frankie said.

"It's a pleasure to see you again as well, Franklin," said the Astounding Archibald. "Please, have a seat."

Agent Smalls unlocked the handcuffs and gestured toward the chair opposite Archibald. The devices on the table between them hummed and buzzed. Cables spilled onto the floor and snaked toward a stack of black metal cases. The air smelled of ozone and aftershave.

G. Randall Archibald lifted one of Frankie's hands like a manicurist and began slipping rubber-tipped thimbles over the fingers. Each thimble sprouted a bundle of wires that led to one of the machines.

"What's this?" Frankie asked. "Some kinda lie detector?"

"In a manner of speaking," Archibald said. "The items before you comprise a torsion field detector, mobile version. With it, I can measure psionic potential within two point three taus."

Frankie tried to snort derisively, but it came out a grunt. He had no idea what a tau was, but he was damn sure not going to admit it.

"I assure you," Archibald said, "it's *quite* accurate. Not as fine-tuned as the larger version in my lab, of course. That TFD prime is sensitive enough to pick up zero point three tau." The gnome spoke in the clipped, precise diction of a nerd. "There should be no need for such a sensitive measurement in your case. I understand you've already had a *pret*-ty active night."

"Whatever those guys said they saw, they're lying."

"Or," Archibald said, "they don't *know* what they saw. My job, tonight, is to determine whether that activity was truly psi-related, or mere flimflammery perpetrated by the son of a known cheat and fraud."

"Hey! I'm not gonna sit here and—"

Smalls put two big hands on his shoulders and shoved him back into the seat. "Stay."

"I thought you were a *skeptic*," Frankie said, almost spitting the word. In his family, there was nothing more despicable.

"I certainly am," Archibald said.

"I've seen you on Johnny Carson. What you did to that channeler woman from Australia? Humiliating her like you did us? That was cruel."

"It didn't seem to hurt her career. She went on to make a lot of money."

"And the thing with the faith healer, who knew what people's ailments were! People believed in him, and you destroyed him."

"He was using a radio in his ear to receive diagnoses from God, who happened to sound an awful lot like his wife. He was a fake. A fraud. Are you a fake?"

If I say yes, Frankie wondered, does that make me more guilty of attempted robbery, or less?

Archibald didn't wait for an answer. "I advise the government on using science, not blind faith, to separate the gifted wheat from the fraudulent chaff. Don't *you* want to know whether you have your mother's gift, Franklin?"

"I don't need you or your machines to tell me."

"Of course not. You believe in yourself! As your mother believed in you, transferring that faith to you in the manner of all family religions. However—" He leaned across a control panel festooned with gauges and dials. "—wouldn't it be nice to have objective proof, *scientific* proof of your ability? A stamp of approval, if you will. A diploma to hang on your wall."

Oh, Frankie did want that. More than anything. He'd grown up feeling like a prince in exile, his entire family denied their rightful place because of skeptics, rule-bound scientists, and a shadow government afraid of their powers.

"It won't work," Frankie said. The rubber thimbles were still attached to the fingers of his left hand, and he made no move to take them off. "The scientific method constrains our powers."

"You're quoting your father," Smalls said.

"A skeptical mind-set is like a jammer. That's how you got us to fail on *The Mike Douglas Show*."

"Is *that* what happened?" Archibald said. "Just me standing there onstage with you caused all your tricks to fail?"

"They're not tricks."

Archibald handed him another thimble. "Then let's prove it. I *want* you to succeed, Franklin. Agent Smalls certainly wants you to succeed. Ever since 1974, when your mother died, your country has been without its greatest weapon."

Frankie stared at him. "It's true?"

Smalls moved around the table and crouched so that he was eye to eye with Frankie. "Listen to me. Maureen Telemachus was the most powerful espionage asset in the world."

All his life, Frankie trailed behind his father, picking up each of the clues he dropped about his mother's government work: an oblique reference to the Cold War, a complaint about secret programs, a cryptic comment about submarines and psychonauts. Frankie assembled these scraps into a sci-fi spy movie that ran in his head. James Bond with a purse and mind powers, starring Maureen Telemachus. It thrilled him to think that even if his Amazing Family couldn't be publicly famous, it was secretly powerful. Only as he grew older, and Irene pointed out that many of their father's stories were not, in the strictest sense, true, had he allowed himself to wonder if Teddy might be exaggerating about their mother as well. Now he hated himself for doubting him.

"I knew it," Frankie said, his throat tight with emotion. "I knew she was great."

"But now she's gone," Smalls said. "And we need your help."

Did they not know that he had no talent for clairvoyance? He moved things around. *Little* things.

Archibald said, "We've come a long way, and all we need is five minutes of cooperation."

Frankie nodded at the machinery, this torsion field detector. "Is that how you found me?"

"Pardon?" Smalls asked.

"Tracked me down tonight. I mean, you could have found me anytime in Chicago, but you showed up tonight, way out here, right after I—after the problem at the casino." Which raised another question: How did they get here so fast? It was at least four hours' drive from Chicago. "Did you come from St. Louis?" Frankie asked. That was only a forty-minute drive.

Smalls and Archibald did not quite look at each other. "We've had our eyes on you for a long time," Smalls said. Which was not an answer at all.

"Come to think of it, how'd you show up at that exact dock in the middle of the night?"

Archibald said, "Why don't we do the test first, and then we can answer all your questions."

Headlights lit the drapes. Agent Smalls looked at the window, frowned. "Did you order the Chinese food yet?" he asked Archibald. The gnome shook his head.

Smalls reached behind his back and his hand came up with a pistol.

"Whoa now," Frankie said, and stood up.

"Stay," Smalls said again. Frankie was feeling more and more like a dog. "And shut up."

Someone pounded on the door. "Open up, God damn it! I know you're in there, Smalls!" It was Teddy.

"He's got a gun, Dad!" Frankie shouted.

Teddy didn't seem to hear him, because the pounding continued. Smalls opened the door, the gun at his side.

"Teddy. How in the hell did you find this place?"

"Out of the way, you God damn Kodiak. Is my boy here?" Teddy walked in, looking good despite the hour in a sharkskin suit and matching gray hat. When he saw the rest of the room, he stopped short. "*Archibald?* You're working with *Archibald?*"

Frankie hopped out of the seat and backed away from the table.

The Astounding Archibald stood up, which made only a marginal difference in his height. "Good evening, Teddy."

"I expect this kind of crap from you," Teddy said to the man. "But you, Smalls?" He wheeled on the big man. "You made a promise."

"I kept my promise," the agent said. "She said don't involve the children. But they're not kids anymore. Frankie is a grown man who can make his own decisions."

Teddy pointed a finger at him. "That's the most weasely, self-serving, bullshit sentence I've ever heard come out of that Easter Island face of yours. You should be ashamed of yourself, Destin, because one thing's for God damn sure—Maureen would be ashamed of you."

Smalls said nothing.

"Get in the car, Frankie," Teddy said. "We're leaving."

"We're not done testing," Archibald said. "Frankie, don't you want to know where you stand?"

"Where he stands?" Teddy said, mocking. "Where he stands is with me. Let's go."

Frankie followed his father out of the room. The morning sky glowed peach, but the sun was hiding behind the motel, waiting for the coast to clear. They walked to Teddy's latest Buick, a turquoise Park Avenue. The passenger's side door was locked.

Teddy made no move to get into the car or unlock it.

"What the hell were you doing with those bloodsuckers? In God damn southern Illinois?"

Frankie hesitated. Did his father know about the casino or not? "I don't know how they found me," Frankie said truthfully. "Smalls arrested me, brought me here, and the next thing I know Archibald is putting wires on my fingers."

"There's no such thing as a coincidence," Teddy said. "What did you do?"

"Wait, how did *you* find me?"

Before Teddy could answer, a white taxi pulled into the parking lot and stopped just behind them. Buddy climbed out of the back, and the driver rolled down his window. Buddy reached into his pocket and withdrew a pile of casino chips. He put them in the driver's hands. Then he reached into his other pocket and repeated the procedure. The taxi pulled away.

"Where the hell have you been?" Frankie said.

Buddy ambled toward them wearing a sleepy smile. He stood next to the rear door of the Buick and waited patiently, hands in his now-empty pockets.

"Jesus Christ," Teddy said. "I am truly blessed."

○

The back room of the Laundromat smelled of perfumed detergent and bleach and motor oil. Nick Pusateri Senior stood behind a large wooden table, a mound of loose quarters in front of him, and a stack of filled coin sleeves off to the side. At first glance Frankie thought Nick must be bagging the coins, but it was just the opposite; he was ripping them open and dumping them into the pile. He gestured for Frankie to sit in a plastic chair, then said nothing as he broke open another tube. Finally he glanced at him and said, "You got heat stroke or something?"

Frankie chuckled. It wasn't a convincing laugh, but it was the best he could manage. Was he really that red-faced? He felt himself sweating through his shorts. How was he supposed to go through with the plan if his body kept betraying him?

The plan was simple: delay, grovel, and charm. All he needed was for Nick to say he'd accept the money in four days. As long as he would agree to that, Frankie could abide all threats, consent to any punishment, acquiesce to any repayment terms, no matter how Shylockian—as long as they took effect after Monday. After Labor Day, Frankie's labors would be over, and he'd pay back Nick with his own God damn money.

"It's nothing," Frankie said. "Summer heat gets to me."

Nick snorted. "It's the humidity." He picked up another full coin sleeve, weighed it in his hands, and swore. He tore that one open, too, and dumped the quarters into the pile. "Chicago in August makes me want to move to God damn Iceland." Nick's pompadour was shot through with gray, but he was holding on to his Fonz look. He wore a robin's egg–blue Tommy Bahama shirt open to expose a gold chain tangled in gray chest hair. His arms were ropy, and his knuckles seemed abnormally large. He frowned at another sleeve, then tore that one open, too.

What the hell was up with the quarters?

"Your dad, he could do things with coins," Nick said. "Chips, too. Roll them over his hands, pull them out of the air. Hell of a man."

Frankie started to ask, Is there a problem with the coin bags? and then thought better of it. *Delay, grovel, and above all, charm.*

Nick said, "I'm surprised you didn't bring him with you."

"Who, my dad? Why would I bring him into this?"

Nick looked up. "You two don't talk much, do you?"

"We talk," Frankie said defensively. While another part of his brain loudly demanded, *What did Teddy say? What does he know about this?* "Just not about business. I don't involve him in this stuff at all. He's retired."

Nick nodded. "I hear he's pretty frail these days."

"I guess he's slowing down a bit," Frankie said. He wouldn't have described Teddy as frail, but hey: *charm.*

"Time catches up to all of us," Nick said. He picked up another sleeve, gripped it, then said, "Assholes!"

"What's the matter?" Frankie asked. He couldn't stop himself.

"These cheating motherfuckers," Nick said. "You got to check every single roll. Sometimes they short it a quarter, or put a nickel in there, or some Canadian shit. If you want something you gotta do it yourself."

"But—"

"But what?"

Frankie was going to say, Was it really worth your time to check every single roll of quarters, then rebag them yourself? Instead, he said, "But what else are you going to do, right?"

Nick stared at him. "Who would have thought little Frankie would be sitting here in that chair?" He wrapped his fingers around the roll.

Hot bile rose from Frankie's stomach to his throat. He clamped down, steadied himself. *Delay, grovel, and charm.* From the front of the shop came the hum of huge dryers. There were customers out there, customers who'd come running if Frankie started screaming. Or go running, out of the place. Either way, possible witnesses who could be tracked down by the police in case Frankie was murdered here.

Finally he could take a breath. "I want to say, right off the bat, I meant no disrespect to you or your sister for failing to make my payments. I know that was wrong, and I sincerely wish to make amends. I also want to assure you that I can pay you, in full, on Monday."

Nick squinted at him. "Really?"

Frankie nodded.

"Well, that would be incredible news." He set down the roll and ran his hands through the pile of quarters. "Where's this money coming from, if not Teddy?"

"I have friends."

"But do you have assets? That's what I'm interested in. Tell me about those."

"Assets?"

"That van you drove up in. I figure it's worth fifteen thousand Blue Book. You own it?"

"I owe sixteen on it."

"Ouch. Okay, but still. Inventory. How about the family car, what are you driving?"

"A ninety-one Toyota Corolla."

"Good shape?"

"It has a pretty big dent in the hood."

"I know a guy can do dents. Let's call it five K. And the house?"

Frankie tried to smile. "I don't know why the house matters. I'll have the money on Monday."

Nick made a hurry-up gesture. "How much do you think it's worth?"

"Uh, I don't know." He didn't like where this was going. "We paid sixty-eight thousand six years ago. So maybe seventy? Seventy-five if we got lucky?"

"How much do you owe on it?"

"Mr. Pusateri—"

"How much."

Frankie tried to think. A band had tightened around his chest, forcing open the pores across his body. He was full of holes, gushing like a lawn sprinkler. "Loretta's parents loaned us twenty-five grand for a down payment, so—"

"That's family. How much to the bank?"

"Thirty-five? Thirty-four, maybe."

"Well, there you go. Money just sitting around." Nick walked to a metal desk in the corner, picked up a phone.

Frankie tried to breathe. Abide all threats, he told himself. Four more days. After Monday, after Labor Day, none of this would matter.

Nick was saying, "It's me, Lily, let me talk to—no, Christ no, not Graciella. Put me through to Brett." Frankie stared at the tubes of quarters. Each one twenty-five bucks. Was he really so paranoid that he had to check them all? Or maybe he just liked to run his hands through them, like Smaug or Scrooge McDuck.

"Brett!" Nick said. "I need you to give me a ballpark figure." He looked at Frankie. "What's the address?" Frankie recited it, and Nick said into the phone, "Right, Norridge. Two-bedroom, basement. Frankie, is the basement finished?"

Frankie shook his head.

"Unfinished. One bath. I'm guessing 'fair condition.' Okay. Hurry it up, though."

Nick put the phone to his chest. To Frankie he said, "When my son first started the business, it was all in binders, but now they can look everything up in computers. My idea. Nick Junior, he didn't know what the fuck he was doing."

Frankie thought, So innovative he's on trial for murder.

Brett came back on the line. Nick listened for a minute, then said, "Ah, both of 'em are on the deed? Okay, still doable. So if we get it for sixty, spend as little as possible on carpets and painting . . . uh-huh. Right. Usual transfer fees. Got it."

Nick hung up. "I've got some good news and bad news," he said. "You'll be able to pay down thirty thousand of your debt. You still owe me twenty, but you get to keep your van and keep working—and keep paying me."

"You're taking my house?"

"No, I'm buying your house. And the Toyota. Now here's the bad news."

A sound escaped from Frankie's chest, part squeak, part hiccup. A noise he didn't know his body could make.

"You're wife's on the deed, so we're going to have to go pick her up."

"Okay, okay," Frankie said. He was having trouble breathing. "I can bring her by next week, and we can—"

"No, Frankie. Now."

"Now? But Monday I can—"

"Monday you can pay me the rest, when your *friends* come through with all their cash."

"Okay." He took a breath. "Okay."

"Why are you looking at the door?"

He was looking for Teddy. For Agent Smalls. For Irene. For anyone to arrive, in the nick of time, to pull his ass from the fire.

THE PRECIPICE

15

Buddy

+

He stares at the clock, waiting for the lozenges of light to recon-
figure and signal the final countdown to the Zap. The LEDs form
numbers—1, 1, 5, 9—that quiver with import.

Nothing happens.

What if he's stuck in this moment? What if his consciousness,
rebelling at last of its pendular existence, has decided to come to rest
here, in this second, forever? It would not be the moment he would
have picked—that would be September 1, 1991, at 11:32 p.m., almost
exactly four years ago, as he lay in a hotel bed—but some part of him
would be relieved to land anywhere. To not have to keep going, to
abandon his preparations for the apocalypse. To stop caring. Because
as soon as the clock ticks over into midnight, the Countdown to Nothing begins.

Four days until the anniversary of his mother's death. Four days
until the Zap.

He fights down the panic. He can't stop caring, so he can't afford to
lose track of the now. There's so much to do. Yet, and yet, the glowing
red lights of the clock refuse to move. Is it *still* now? The LEDs make
him think of electrons and electron holes and suddenly it's Novem-
ber 14, 1983. He's fifteen, hiding in a study carrel in the Elmhurst
Public Library, reading an article in *Scientific American* about how

light-emitting diodes work. The key step is when an electron is pushed into a gap in an atomic lattice, like one of Frankie's pinballs dropping into a kickout hole. This sudden plunge releases not bonus points but energy in the form of photons.

He flips a page, smiling to himself. Each drop is a quantum event. So beautiful—

And then he's back, staring at the clock. Not even the World's Most Powerful Psychic can know whether any one electron would fall into a particular hole, or ever drop at all. Electronic devices depend instead on statistical likelihood. Many holes, many electrons. Apply sufficient voltage, and *enough* electrons would almost certainly drop into place, causing the diode to emit light.

Buddy has tried to explain his job to only one person. Her name was Cerise. Is Cerise. *I can't know all the details, but I can spot trends,* he says to her. *And sometimes I give things a nudge.* Cerise doesn't understand. How can she? How can he make her understand what it's like to keep track of a trillion pinballs bouncing along an infinite number of paths? Everything depends on sending them into the right lanes, off the right bumpers, at exactly the right time. Is there any metaphor—using electrons or pinballs or roulette balls—sufficient to explain how stressful his job is? "Oh honey," Cerise says. "You're getting stressed out now."

He shakes himself back to 1995, the last few seconds of August.

11:59. There is no second hand on the digital clock. No way to know if 12:00 is coming soon, or ever.

Downstairs, the front door opens, and the sound reassures him that time is still flowing. (Unless—is this a memory of the door opening?) The visitor is Frankie, duffel bag in hand. A castaway, an exile, a refugee from the domestic homeland. Irene is up (she sleeps less than Buddy these days) and asks Frankie what the hell is going on. Frankie mumbles a reply, but it's okay if Buddy can't hear all the words right now; later they'll talk more, and there will be donuts, and coffee despite the fact that it's so late. Irene will raise her mug and say—

No!

He cannot skip ahead into the future. He has to stay on guard. Here. Now.

He glances back at the clock. A voltage knocks electrons into their graves, and suddenly it's—

SEPTEMBER

16

Buddy

$$\boxed{+}$$

—and he's walking downstairs, into the kitchen, where his sister and brother sit at the table, without donuts. Donuts come later. Irene is trying to get Frankie to tell her what happened to him tonight. Frankie is mute, struggling to find the words. Buddy watches them from the shadows for a full minute, his heart full, until Irene notices him.

"Buddy," she says. "You all right?"

But he's not all right. Who is? Nobody in this house, that's for sure. Frankie is staring into nothing, a lost man. Buddy drifts up to the table. Waggles his fingers palm up.

Frankie glances at him, barely seeing him.

"I think you're blocking the driveway," Irene says.

Buddy repeats the waggle. Frankie sighs—not a faked sigh, but a deep-down, Delta blues sigh—and reaches into a pocket.

Buddy walks toward the front door, Frankie's keys jangling, and behind him Irene says to their brother, "Just start with Loretta. Why did she kick you out? Is this about the money you owe?"

"You know about that?" he says in a small voice.

Buddy walks to the driveway, unlocks the back door of the Bumble-bee van. He rummages in the dark until he finds the box he'd once pictured himself finding, and then uses a key to slit it open. Inside are the expected four huge canisters of Goji Go! berry juice powder. He twists one open, exposing contents that look black in this light, and then dips a finger inside and puts it to his mouth, *Miami Vice*–style. It tastes like chalk and cough medicine. He spits several times to get the taste out of his mouth.

He feels bad about what he's about to do. He tries not to hurt anyone, and most of the time he remembers enough to know that he's not hurting them forever, or not as much as first appears. Like with Frankie. Yes, it was terrifying for him when the casino employees grabbed him, but nothing really bad happened, and Frankie had already learned how to take a punch. But this, this is different. He can't remember what happens after September 4. What if what he does tonight has far-reaching ramifications beyond that date?

And yet: he has to proceed, as his future memory dictates.

Buddy reaches into his pocket and brings out the packet of DUSTED insecticide. He pours it into the top of the goji powder, stirs it a bit with the big Magic Marker he's brought with him. Not too much stirring, though. The first dose will be scooped off the top. Then he screws down the lid and writes, *Embrace Life!*

It takes him only twenty minutes to make the delivery—traffic is light this time of night—and he remembers to stop at the Dunkin' Donuts. He orders a dozen, most of it chocolate sprinkles (he's partial to sprinkles), and adds a bear claw for the baker's dozenth. He's carrying the box toward the house when he remembers there's something he's supposed to do first. Something about the garage. Oh! Right.

In the garage, Teddy's big Buick is sleeping. Buddy opens the driver's side, and winces at the absurdly loud door chimes. Balancing the donut box in one hand, he leans down, fishes under the driver's seat. He comes up with his prize, a Ziploc bag containing two marijuana cigarettes, one half consumed. Best not mix that with the donuts. He tucks it into his pocket for later.

Frankie and Irene are still at the table, but they've gone silent. Frankie sits with his head in his hands. Irene stares at the tabletop, arms crossed on her lap. It's as if they're playing an invisible chess game and they've lost track of the pieces.

Buddy opens the donut box, letting Frankie have first choice. A quiet *oh* of surprise escapes his brother's lips. He reaches for the bear claw. Bear claws are his favorite. Always have been, always will be.

+

There are not enough donuts in the world to make up for what he does to his brother in Alton. It's an act of selfishness. Selfishness born of great need, true and burning curiosity, but selfishness nonetheless.

He lies in bed next to Cerise, whose hair is long and blonde and entirely artificial. What he's experienced in the past hour is real, however, the most real thing he's ever lived through. For long stretches of minutes he was entirely in his body, in the moment. His mind wasn't roaming through the past, or the future. He wasn't staring at a glowing clock frozen at 11:59.

"You feeling okay, honey?" she asks.

He says, "I've never felt better."

"I can tell by that goofy smile on your face." She chuckles, her voice low and sexy. She nibbles at the lobe of his ear and he laughs with her. Still close to his ear, she whispers, "Is this your first time with a girl like me?"

His ears burn. He's blushing.

She throws her head back and laughs. "I thought so! You were so *enthusiastic*."

"I've never met anyone like you," he says. "Yet . . ." He waits until she's looking at him again. Until her eyes soften. He says, "I've always known you. I've been waiting for you my whole life."

"Aw." She kisses his forehead, pushes his hair back. "Ain't you sweet."

He closes his eyes. "I just want to lie here forever," he says. "Back home I have to—well, my job is pretty stressful."

"What do you do?"

He wants to tell her everything, from the first guessed baseball score until the day his mother gave him the medal. "My job is to predict the future."

"Ooh. Are you a stockbroker?"

"It's kind of like that. I try to figure out what's going to happen, and find the way to the best outcome. It's impossible to know all the details—"

"Who can?" Cerise says.

"Right," he says. He sits up. "But I can spot trends. And sometimes I give things a nudge."

"Ah," she says. "You're one of those Master of the Universe types, aren't you?" Teasing him. "Doing a little insider trading?"

"It's not like that." But isn't it? Everyone else is on the outside of the machine, and he's running along under the glass, nudging the pinballs without being run over himself. He wants to tell her this. He wants to explain everything to her, but his own habit of silence is getting in the way. He wants to tell her that across town, his brother is being dragged from one boat to another.

"Oh, honey," Cerise says. "You're getting stressed out *now*. We can't have that." She takes his hand and puts it on her. "You have all the time you need."

"I wish that were true," he says.

She shushes him. "Don't be that way." She turns into him, and he feels Cerise's cock harden in his grip. Even though he's been picturing this night for years, he's amazed every moment by what it's like to be with another person. He thought it would be like masturbation, except a little better.

He was wrong. So, so wrong.

She says, "What else you want to try, your first day behind the wheel?"

"Everything," he says.

Slowly, she teaches him how to please her. Yes, they have similar equipment, but they're not the same. Cerise is Cerise. A miracle and a mystery.

+

He finds himself at a kitchen table, cards in his hands, three days before the Zap. Eventually they make enough noise that Matty stops pretending he's sleeping and comes downstairs. Nobody worries about waking Teddy. He snores like a man twice his size, and his sleep is impenetrable.

Irene has made a pot of coffee, but Frankie has switched to beer and Buddy's on his second tall glass of milk. Matty nabs the last chocolate frosted donut—that's *his* favorite—and says, "So we're having a party?"

"I thought you were grounded," Frankie says.

Matty shoots him a worried look, but Irene is not in a rule-enforcing mood. "The game is seven-card stud," she says to her son. "Low-high, nickel ante."

"Nickel?" Matty says. "Pretty steep."

"This is why you need a job," she says.

"To lose it to you in poker?"

"Or win big," Frankie says.

Matty looks away from Frankie, embarrassed. Covers it by hitching up his running shorts and affecting a world-weary voice. "Guess you gotta risk money to make money."

Irene laughs, charmed by her boy, and Matty doesn't hide his pleasure at this. Buddy's reminded again that those two were on their own for years, a self-contained unit.

An hour from now, Buddy disappears to the top floor. He retrieves the blue envelope from the locked box in his room, the one with Matty's name on it. Then he goes to Matty's attic room, strips the boy's bed, and puts on clean sheets. Frankie will have to take Matty's room, because the new bunk beds in the basement are too small for him. Matty will fit, though. Buddy goes downstairs and unwraps a set of Kmart sheets and dresses one of the four bunk beds. In the springs of the bed above, he places the envelope and the Ziploc bag.

Then he goes up to his own room. He hopes to sleep for a few hours before resuming preparations for the Zap, including installing a new fire door for the basement.

But that's in an hour. Now Irene deals him in. There's no money to risk, however; everyone's playing with handfuls of coins from Teddy's change jar.

Buddy's playing several games at once, in different eras. His mother asks if he's got any sevens. Teddy leans close, his hands covering Buddy's own tiny hands, as he shows him how to peek at the second card during the deal. A fourteen-year-old Irene, bored from babysitting duty, lays out a spider solitaire game while he watches. Frankie says, "You in or out?"

"I have two sevens," Buddy says.

"What?"

Wrong answer. Suddenly he's back in 1995, three days before the Zap. The end of history. There are no memories of future poker games.

This is the last he will ever play. He will never win another hand from his brother, or watch his sister frown over her cards. And he will never see Cerise again.

Irene touches his arm. "Buddy?"

He tries to focus on his cards. There are no sevens in this hand, merely a loosely connected series of cards that will never become a straight or a flush, and he knows better than to try to bluff Irene. He mucks his cards, folding.

That's okay. One less distraction. He can watch his family, all of them, play across the decades.

17

Matty

The blue envelope was tucked into the springs above his bunk bed. It was addressed to him, in black handwriting he didn't recognize. Inside was a single page, from a yellow legal pad. The ink was faint and scratchy.

Dear Matty,

We've never met, and to my great sadness, we never will. Alas and alack, as my Gran used to say. I suppose this is my one chance to sound like a grandmother.

My apologies for the pen. It's terrible, but I don't want to ask the nurse for another.

I regret that I know only a little about you. I've been told that you're quite the brain, that you work hard, and have a good heart. I also know that you're my daughter's son, and as such have been raised by a brilliant, caring, fiercely protective person who can be hell to live with. I hope she wasn't too hard on you. If my own mother could tell when I was lying I never would have escaped to meet your grandfather.

I've also been told that you've recently experienced something that I know a bit about. If you're worried about where your gifts might take you, don't be afraid. But I do have one piece of advice.

First, can I tell you a secret? I've only told it to one other person, your grandfather. But you deserve to know.

I worked for the government from 1962 to 1963, then again this past year (1974). I was a "remote viewer," though that title's not accurate. I wasn't remote at all. I flew. In the skies, deep in the earth, below the oceans. There wasn't anywhere I couldn't go. My job was to find out all the secrets of our enemies. I loved the flying. Do you? You must.

All of that is technically "Top Secret" but it's not the secret I want to tell you, which is this: I almost immediately came in contact with the other side. My Soviet counterpart, and fellow psychic, is named Vassili Godunov. He is—was?—a good man who loved his country as much as I loved mine. We realized that together we could pinpoint every missile silo in both of our countries, find every submarine, track every bomber. We also realized that if we gave our governments this information, they might destroy the world. I know this sounds melo-dramatic, but it's true. Neither superpower can ever be too confident. Neither can ever think they can strike first and wipe out the arsenal of the other. (Look up "Mutually Assured Destruction." Are the Encyclopaedia Brittanicas *I bought still in the house?)*

So, we lied. I lied to Destin Smalls, the man I worked for. Vassili lied to his superiors. We reported trivial sightings with great speci-ficity, to keep them impressed with our abilities. But for any high-value target, the details we reported were too vague to act upon. (I learned that trick from your grandfather.) We kept the world safe by keeping it ignorant.

I tell you this not to scare you, but because you deserve to know the stakes, and I'm the only one to bring the news. My advice is this: don't let the bastards use you. If later you want to use them, go right ahead. Teddy would approve. Your only duty now is to take care of yourself and your family, and to let them take care of you.

I have to sign off. I'm tired and scrawling this with a cheap Bic
from an uncomfortable bed, and I have one more letter to write
before I drift off.

    Safe travels,

Her signature was beautiful: a mountainous "M," a towering "T,"
with beautifully spiky characters after each.

At the very bottom of the page was this:

    P.S.

    How can I love someone I've never met? A mystery.

Also tucked into the springs was a plastic baggie that contained the
two joints Irene had confiscated: one full, one half consumed.

My grandmother, Matty thought, is delivering drugs from beyond
the grave.

How did she know about what was happening to him? Could she
travel into the *future*? Even if she could do that, who delivered the
all-too-physical envelope and Ziploc bag?

The letter and pot were freaking him out, but the message of their
simultaneous appearance was unmistakable: it was his duty to help
Frankie.

A half hour later he snuck out to the nest behind Grandpa Teddy's
garage and lit one of the joints. He needed to get as much of it into his
lungs before he was unable to keep smoking. He thought, This is not a
healthy life choice. And then: Duty calls.

He stayed out of his body for hours, his longest trip on record. He hovered in Mitzi's Tavern, in Mitzi's office, practically in Mitzi's shadow.
Friday, payday, made her office much more interesting than in previous visits. He watched her receive visitor after visitor, all men, most of
them white, who brought her envelopes of cash. Mitzi would put them
into the desk drawer, chat for ten seconds, then send the men packing.

As soon as they left the room, she moved the envelopes to the safe.
It was then that Matty would sweep in, push his ghost noggin close to

hers, and steal a glance at the dial. But Mitzi continued to make it impossible to read the combination. She leaned over the safe from her chair, her bird hand covering the dial, and spun it fast, barely looking at the numbers. For all he knew she'd kept the same combination for decades and could do it blind. After a couple of hours, he *thought* he had the starting number—28—but even that was a guess, because the dial was hash marks between every fifth number, and it could have been 27 or 29.

Mitzi barely left the room. Between visits she smoked, ate from a can of peanuts, read the paper, and drank coffee. Matty read over her shoulder, and mentally suggested solutions to the crossword puzzle. (He was usually wrong; Mitzi was really good at crosswords.) He killed time by floating around the room, peering into nooks and crannies. How malleable was his shadow body? Could he shrink down to mouse size, and go looking between the walls?

He also spent time pondering the morality of stealing from this old woman, and whether this was what Grandma Mo meant by helping his family. Frankie said Mitzi was a major criminal, but to Matty she seemed like a bored old lady doing a boring job.

A big change to her routine came when she filled a tumbler of water to make a drink that wasn't coffee. She opened up a canister of Goji Go! that was sitting on the floor and stirred in a healthy portion of powder. The canister wasn't here yesterday. *Embrace life!* was written in marker on the lid. Frankie, evidently, could sell this stuff to anyone, even his worst enemy.

Another man came in and paid. Matty again tried to see past Mitzi's hands, and again saw nothing. He felt his body—his real body—cramping up from sitting too long in one position. The pot was wearing off.

He was glad he hadn't told Frankie he was trying again. Another failure would kill the man. He'd seemed so sad last night. Loretta had gotten mad at him, thrown him out of the house. He didn't talk about it in front of Matty, but it clearly had to do with his money problems. Which sent Matty to bed feeling worse for his betrayal.

Then came the letter, and the means to help. What choice did he have.

Mitzi got up from the desk and walked down to the bathroom. This was her third visit in a half hour. He never followed her into there, no way. When she came back, she looked pale. She sat behind the desk just as another client, an old white guy with spiky gray hair, handed over his payment for the week. Mitzi barely seemed to be pay-ing attention as he talked, and didn't even bother to put the envelope into the drawer. When he left, she bent toward the safe.

Matty edged forward, eager to try a new idea. He thought of his body growing thinner. He spread out like Mr. Fantastic, thin as a slip of paper, and slid his transparent self between Mitzi and the safe. He was less than an inch from her hand when it touched the dial.

She turned the dial, and stopped. She'd never paused like this before, but he wasn't going to question it. He counted the hash marks and saw that the first number was definitely 28. One down! Then she turned the dial again, and paused. Her hand slipped down. A moment later, a red goo spattered the front of the safe.

Matty drew back in alarm. The rest of the room became visible to him. Mitzi had slipped off her chair, and was lying on the floor. Goji-vomit was everywhere. She'd stopped throwing up, but her mouth was still moving, calling out, though he couldn't hear what she was saying.

He moved beside her. "Are you okay?" he asked her, but of course she couldn't hear him. He couldn't yell for help, couldn't help her to her feet. He had nothing but a ghost voice and a pair of ghost hands. Useless! He'd have to go back to his body and call 911. But what then? *Hi, I know I'm several miles away, but I know for a fact there's an old woman who's real sick in a bar.*

The office door opened. The bartender, an old man with a huge, multi-chinned face like Jabba the Hutt, walked in, bent down, and helped Mitzi to her feet. He escorted her to the bathroom, and he and Matty waited ten, then fifteen minutes until she reappeared. She still looked horrible. Eventually the bartender guided her out the back door, to a car, and they drove away.

What was he supposed to do now? Mitzi had left without even put-ting away the last envelope. He knew exactly one digit of the combina-tion. The only person left in the bar was the waitress, and he was pretty sure she wasn't going to open the safe.

He'd failed.

He found Frankie in the basement, interrogating Buddy about the damage he was doing to the house. Then Frankie finally noticed him standing on the stairs, and said, "What?"

"It's about our thing," Matty said.

His uncle's face lit up, and that made Matty cringe inside. They went to the kitchen, out of Buddy's earshot, and Matty said, "I started again. Visiting Mitzi's. I was just there."

"Oh my God! That's fantastic! Did you get the combination?"

"That's what I want to tell you. I didn't get it. And I won't be able to. Payday's been canceled."

The telephone rang. Frankie ignored it. "What are you talking about?"

"There was a problem," Matty said. "Mitzi got sick, and she left."

"Sick? *Sick?* Mitzi's never sick."

"It was pretty bad. A lot of vomit." The telephone wouldn't stop. "Maybe I should get that."

"Don't pick that up. Could be anybody," Frankie said. "Just tell me what happened."

Matty didn't want to say what Mitzi had been drinking when she threw up. Instead, he said, "I don't think she's coming back. There's nobody there now but a waitress."

"Payday is never canceled," Frankie said. "It'd be like canceling—" He made a sputtering sound, looking for the word. "—*gravity.* Not possible in the realm of physics."

Buddy appeared at the kitchen entrance. He pointed toward the front door.

"*What?*" Frankie said.

The doorbell rang.

"Well, get it, dummy!" Frankie said.

Buddy slowly shook his head. Frankie stormed past him, heading for the door. Matty took advantage of the distraction and picked up the phone. Anything beat being yelled at. "Hello?"

A pause, and then a man said, "Oh! Hi. Is this Matty?" Matty didn't recognize the voice.

"Yes?"

"It's nice to meet you. Your mom's told me a lot about you."

"Uh . . ."

"I was wondering if she was home?"

"Can I say who's calling?"

"It's Joshua. Joshua Lee."

The boyfriend. Or, as Matty had started to think of him, the Penis from Phoenix. "She's not home right now. She's at work."

"She's hard to catch. Do you know when she'll be back? Or if there's a better time to call?"

"It's kind of busy here," Matty said.

"Right. Okay. I'll call back tonight." He sounded desperate. No, like a desperate guy pretending not to be. "If you see her, tell her— wait. No, that's okay. I'll just call back."

Matty hung up. Buddy was looking at him. "Has he been calling a lot?" Matty asked.

Buddy nodded.

"Is that Malice? I mean, Mary Alice?" He thought he'd heard her voice. Matty went outside, and Frankie was standing on the front lawn, saying, "Come on, Loretta. Please get out of the car!" Malice stood nearby, holding a lumpily full garbage bag. She saw Matty and walked up to him.

"Would you take this?" she asked. "He won't."

"What is it?"

"Clothes. Some other stuff he'd need."

"Wow, your mom's pretty mad." Matty didn't recognize the car, or the woman behind the wheel. One of Loretta's friends, it looked like. Loretta sat in the passenger's side, staring straight ahead, window firmly up. "What happened?"

"He didn't tell you? We have to sell the house. Like, today."

"What? That's crazy. Why?"

Malice gave him a half-lidded stare. "Like you have no clue. You want to tell me what you two have been working on?"

"I . . . I can't." He felt so embarrassed. "I wish I could."

Loretta had finally rolled down the window—but only to yell for Mary Alice.

"Wait," Matty said. He leaned close to Malice and dropped his voice to a whisper. "Do you have any, uh, pot on you?"

Malice stepped back. "Are you fucking kidding me?"

"I wouldn't ask, but I'm down to half a joint, and it's really—"

"Mary Alice!" Loretta yelled. "In the car!"

.   .   .

Matty held the stub of joint between his finger and thumb, flicked the lighter, and puffed to bring it to light. His last bit of rocket fuel . . .

He flew back to Mitzi's Tavern, wasting no time in transit. Inside, it was more crowded than it had been all afternoon, but it was Bomb Squad Silent. A dozen men of various ages sat at the bar or at the round, pock-marked tables, staring at their drinks as if trying to decide whether to cut the green wire or the red one.

Matty skirted and skittered around the edge of the room, anxious to leave, but knowing he couldn't face Frankie unless he at least figured out if payday was in progress. Jabba the Bartender had returned, but he wasn't talking to anyone, either.

Matty could feel the tug of his body back at the house. He'd made Uncle Frankie promise to keep his mom away from the backyard when she came home from work. He'd started to ask why, and then abruptly said, "Don't worry about it. I'll handle it. You do what you do."

The bar was depressing him. Mitzi's door was closed, and no one was making a move to walk in. He decided to take one quick pass through, just to make sure the safe wasn't hanging open, and then head home to face Frankie's wrath. He was drifting toward the door when the bar-tender pointed at a customer, and the man got up and started walking toward Mitzi's office. Was Frankie right after all, and payday was on?

Matty slipped through the wall into Mitzi's office and was surprised to see somebody new behind the desk. The man was at least as old as Mitzi and Grandpa Teddy, but looked like an Elvis left too long in the sun: gray pompadour, white teeth, beef-jerky arms. His clothing was period, too. His black short-sleeve shirt had flames on it, as if he were ready not so much to hop into a '57 Chevy but to become one.

The guy from the bar didn't sit down. He handed over an enve-lope, and Ancient Elvis pulled out the cash, sorted it in front of him, slapping the bills onto the desk as if sure he was going to catch the guy stiffing him.

Mitzi wasn't like that. She would barely glance at the money, just run her finger across it while it was still in the envelope, and then talk politely to the client. Sometimes everybody was all smiles. Sometimes the client had to start explaining.

Evidently the money added up. Elvis waved the customer away and turned toward the safe before the guy was out of the room. Then he picked up a scrap of paper, and started dialing.

Matty zipped forward.

Elvis pulled open the safe, still holding the scrap of paper. Matty stretched himself, willing his invisible eyeballs closer.

28. 11. And—thumb. Elvis's fat, grease-stained digit covered the only digit Matty cared about.

"Thumb, thumb, thumb . . ." Matty chanted.

The man swung his head toward the door—maybe someone had knocked?—and then dropped the paper. Matty swooped down, tried to focus on the digits, and the man snatched it off the floor.

"Oh come on!" Matty yelled. What he wouldn't do for a pair of spirit tongs. Anything.

The door opened, and Mr. Pompadour started talking to the next client. Matty looked forlornly at the safe—and then realized the door was still open.

Still open.

Matty flew a few feet and turned until he could see the face of the door. The dial was still resting at the last number:

33.

"Twenty-eight, eleven, thirty-three," Matty said.

He spun, held up his ghost hands. "Twenty-eight, eleven, thirty-three!" Pompadour and the new guest talked on, oblivious.

Matty zipped through the roof, chanting the digits to himself so he wouldn't forget. He stretched out his arms like Superman and headed for home. God, he loved flying. And now, he knew Grandma Mo had loved it, too. Screw Destin Smalls. Let the evil government agents come for him. He was going to save Frankie! Save his mom!

Two blocks from home, he zoomed low over rooftops, buzzed a series of parked cars. Something about one of the vehicles pinged on his cannabis-fogged brain. He hovered in the air, turned back.

A silver van was parked under a tree. Then the driver's side door opened, and a gray-haired black man stepped out. Cliff Turner. He put his hands on his hips, looked up at the tree, then turned—and locked eyes with Matty.

Turner nodded slowly, and then saluted.

Matty, in a panic, was snapped back into his body like a yo-yo. He shouted and opened his eyes and saw—

—Grandpa Teddy.

He sat in a lawn chair, legs crossed, hat on his knee.

Matty jumped up. "Grandpa!"

His grandfather held up a hand. "Settle down. You're not—"

Matty spun around. The silver van was so close. He could be here any minute.

"What's the matter with you?" Grandpa Teddy asked.

Matty tried to calm himself. "Nothing," he said.

"You know, marijuana can cause paranoia." Grandpa Teddy held the nub of the joint between two fingers. "I had to pinch it out. You don't want to waste it. It's expensive."

"I'm sorry. I know!" There were no sirens. No squeal of tires in the driveway. Just a quiet backyard, a couple of empty hammocks, and his grandfather. How long had he been watching? Long enough to pull out a chair at least. Thank God Matty hadn't been using his original travel method.

"Easy now, you're not in trouble," Grandpa Teddy said. "How long have you been at this?"

"I just tried it a couple times."

He chuckled. "Not talking about the smoke. I've seen that look before, Matty."

That look. Of course Grandpa Teddy would recognize a trance. He'd been married to the greatest clairvoyant and astral traveler of all time. He may have been the one to deliver her letter.

"You seemed pretty deep," his grandfather said. "How far away were you?"

"Not far." Matty didn't know what to do with his hands. Should he sit down? Lean nonchalantly against the garage? No. No way could he pull off nonchalant. Chalant was the best he could do.

Grandpa Teddy, though, seemed perfectly relaxed. "What's the farthest you've gone?"

"Uh . . ." Matty was having trouble concentrating. Were Turner and Smalls driving here, right now?

"Just estimate," Grandpa Teddy said.

"How far is the lake?"

"That's pretty good."

"Is it?"

"For a thirteen-year-old it's God damn amazing."

Amazing. He was amazing. He didn't even bother to mention that he was fourteen now.

"So tell me," Grandpa Teddy said. "Why are you still shaking like a leaf?"

Matty didn't want to say. But he was too terrified not to. "The government. They just spotted me. While I was, you know."

"The government? Who?"

"His name's Clifford Turner. He works with Destin Smalls? He looked straight at me. He *saw* me."

"Well I'll be damned. Cliff actually has some talent."

"You know him?"

"Oh, I know him. Good guy. Just didn't think he had it in him." Grandpa Teddy did not seem as shocked as he should have been. But wasn't he the master of the poker face? "And how did you catch their names? Did he talk to you?"

"Not this time."

"*This* time? This has happened before?"

"No, not like that." Matty quickly told him about meeting Smalls and Turner weeks ago, when they stopped him on the sidewalk. He talked fast, imagining SWAT teams converging on this location.

"Did Smalls threaten you?" Grandpa Teddy asked.

"No! I mean, not physically. He just said he could turn me off. Turn my power off. Like a light switch, he said."

"Jesus," Teddy said. "The God damn micro-lepton gun."

"What's a micro—?"

"A million-dollar boondoggle. Don't you worry about it. Does anybody else know what you can do?"

"Uncle Frankie."

"You went to Frankie with this? Your mother I could understand, but—"

"I could never tell Mom. But Frankie, I knew he would be . . . excited."

Teddy grunted in agreement. "Probably right about your mother, too." He looked at the joint in his hand. "And this helps, does it?"

Matty nodded.

"Someone should do some research into that."

"What do we do?"

Teddy smiled. Was it the "we"? He said, "Your cover's blown, kid. Destin Smalls is going to use you as his ticket back into the game."

"What game?"

"The only one men my age care about—relevance. But don't worry. I'll deal with him. Right after I go see a friend of mine." He handed Matty the joint. "Better hide that." Then he stood and brushed out the creases from his pants. "Meanwhile, you better get inside and change into fresh clothes—your mother's coming home."

Oh, right. Better take a shower, too.

Teddy left in his car. Matty went into the house and was stopped before he made it to the bathroom.

"Well?" Frankie said.

"Twenty-eight, eleven, thirty-three," Matty said.

18

Teddy

Somehow, without noticing it, he'd stopped throwing himself into love with a new woman every day. He'd forgotten his habit like an umbrella left behind in a restaurant, unmissed because the rain had stopped. It was absurdly late—late in summer, late in life—to realize that he'd abandoned his quest for a daily fix. Yet here he was, alone in a gleaming fortress of a kitchen on a Sunday morning, feeling like he was sitting in sunlight. All because of a random encounter with a woman in a grocery store.

Since Maureen had died he'd felt no need to get to *know* a woman, only to love her, briefly and intensely, and move on. And it was clear, after entering this house, that even if Graciella managed to love him, she wouldn't be happy sharing his ramshackle life. Just look at this room! A quarry's worth of granite, interrupted only by hunks of stainless steel, set on a plain of ceramic tile. His coffee cup rested on a slab of teak as big as a drawbridge. In these modern mansions, the kitchen served as both factory and showroom, like one of those Toyota plants staffed by robots. Even the phone he was talking on felt more expensive than one of his watches.

"That's my final offer," he said. "One test."

"I'm bringing in Archibald," Destin Smalls replied. "That's nonnegotiable."

A child ran into the room, yelling something about batteries, and stopped dead when he saw Teddy. It was the smallest one, about eight years old, the one he'd seen at the soccer game. Alex? No, Adrian. Teddy hadn't seen or heard the other two boys since entering the house. He doubted he could find them if he went looking for them; the estate spanned time zones.

"You're Teddy," Adrian said.

"Mr. Telemachus to you. And I'm on the phone." To Smalls he said, "So do we have a deal?"

The agent took a long time to answer. Smelling a trap? Maybe, but he was so hungry.

"Deal."

Teddy hung up the phone, satisfied. One task finished—or at least on hold for now.

"Mom says you do magic," the boy said.

"I do magic *tricks*. There's a difference. But I only do them for money."

"I don't have any money."

"Oh, you have money," Teddy said. "Just look at this house."

The kid didn't get it. "Can't you show it to me for free?"

"Sorry. No cash, no trick."

"That's mean."

"Yes, but it's the kind of mean that teaches you something."

Graciella reappeared from the basement, holding that green cartoon lunch box. The boy wheeled toward her and said, "He won't show me a magic trick."

"Leave Mr. Telemachus alone. We're going to tae kwon do now. Go get your uniform."

"What's in there?" the boy asked, reaching for the lunch box.

She lifted it out of his reach. "Robe and belt. Go!"

She watched him run out of the room. "He doesn't understand what's happening. I'm trying to do the right thing, but I'm never sure what they can handle. If they were older, they might be able to handle it."

"You never stop worrying," he said. "You never stop being their parent."

She sat down absently, still contemplating the damage. Being this close to her intoxicated him. He loved the way she smelled. The gleam of her tanned legs. Her painted toes. He even loved the way her brow furrowed.

"Take my grown son," Teddy said, to distract her from her nervousness. "He's got himself into a mess."

"Buddy? He did seem a bit . . ."

She didn't want to finish that sentence, and Teddy let her off the hook. "Naw, Buddy's just crazy, it's Frankie who's the trouble magnet. I'm just hoping his bad habits haven't rubbed off on Matty."

"He's in trouble, too?"

"He's been experimenting a little," Teddy said. "Got mixed up with the wrong kind of people, drew some attention from the authorities." This may have been the finest nonexplanation he'd ever delivered.

"Is that why Irene's upset?"

"Irene's upset? Did she say she was upset?" He'd kept his daughter out of all of the Matty business. He needed her focused on the Nick thing, not worrying about spies and agents.

"She hadn't called me since she came back from her trip, so I called the house," Graciella said. "She gave me an update on what she'd found with the company papers, but she sounded . . . wounded."

"Irene's touchy. I'm sure it's nothing."

Graciella's frown was there and gone in an instant. He didn't know how to interpret that. If they were playing poker, it would have telegraphed that she'd picked a bad card, and he would have bet against her. But in the game of Real Women, he was forever a novice.

He said, "She's sure working hard on those papers, though."

"I guess that's something." She handed him the lunch box. "Hold this, I need to round these boys up." She went to an intercom and pressed a button. "Adrian! Luke! We're going to tae kwon do! Julian, you better have your homework done before I get back!"

A burp of static, and a voice said, "It's a holiday weekend, Mom." He sounded bored.

"Done before Sunday night, that's the rule. The rest of you, I'm leaving in thirty seconds. Twenty-nine!"

She looked at Teddy. "Only a week into school, and Julian's already behind."

"He'll be fine. You said the new school was better, right?"

Graciella walked Teddy to the front door. She glanced at the lunch box, winced. "I don't like this, showing them to him."

"He's not going to believe unless he sees them. It's too crazy otherwise."

"So let's say he believes, and he makes his promise. How do I believe *him*?"

"That's why you've got to let me do the negotiating. I'll know if he's lying. I've got my secret weapon."

"I'm sure Irene is really happy you talk about her like this."

"You gotta admit, she's a pistol. And not just for the mind reading. That girl's a financial wiz."

"I need her," Graciella said. "No matter what happens in the trial Tuesday, the real estate office has to be clean from now on."

The defense was about to rest. Bert the German and several others had already implicated Nick Junior in the murder. If Nick Junior didn't testify against his father—and there was one last chance for him to take the stand, on Tuesday—then it was on to final arguments. The jury could hand back a verdict by the end of the week.

"Nick's going to jail, or his father is," Graciella said. "Either way, I'm not going back to him. I can't have all this follow my boys around for the rest of their lives like a bad smell."

Teddy wasn't sure a grandson of Nick Pusateri Senior was ever going to smell like roses, but he kept that to himself. "You're doing the right thing," he said.

She unlocked the front door, nodded at the lunch box. "You think if I held on to that, he'd break into my home?"

"Let's not think about that," he said. Because Nick Senior would have to come for it. He couldn't just let it sit in the house, waiting for Graciella to change her mind about the cops. "So . . . you got anybody living here with you?"

"Besides the boys? No. But I've got an expensive alarm system."

He nodded as if that would make a bit of difference. Nick Senior's guys had shot people in their own homes. They'd blown up cars by remote control, right in the suburbs. The *Sun-Times* had been running stories about suspected mob hits all through the trial.

Graciella seemed to know what he was thinking. "He'd never risk hurting his grandsons," she said.

"No, no. But still." And thought: Still, there's you.

"I need them out of this, Teddy. No more contact with the Pusateris, all that family business."

"I promise you, I'll make this work."

Adrian galumphed down the stairs, white robe open and green belt dragging behind him, followed by a lanky brother a few years older. That one was Luke. His uniform was cinched tight, and he wore a swoop of brown hair over one eye like a sixties cover girl. Adrian said, "That's him," as if ratting Teddy out. "He won't do magic."

"No tricks! We're late," Graciella said.

Teddy waved the smaller boy over. "Come here, your shoe's untied." Adrian reluctantly stepped forward and offered a scuffed, yet still garish shoe decorated with green cartoon animals wielding swords and such, each no doubt possessed of unique abilities and an elaborate backstory. Teddy went down on one knee. "I know people who can do magic. Real magic. And what does it get them? Nothing." He struggled to hold the shoelace between finger and thumb. His fingers had turned into rusty shears. Once—decades ago, before Nick Senior— they could make cards dance. Coins and papers and even engagement rings would wink in and out of existence, his touch as silent and quick as a mirror flicking sunlight. Once, he was a phantom of the card table. Maybe it was time for the phantom to strike back.

"Doing real magic," he went on, keeping up the patter like a professional. "That stuff makes those folk unhappier than if they had no magic at all, because it doesn't do 'em a damn bit of good. But if you can do a magic *trick*, you get paid. Do you want to get paid?"

Adrian nodded.

"Other shoe. Good. Now here's the thing." Graciella stood in the doorway, listening. "Magic's easy. It's tricks that are hard. You gotta be smart, you gotta be prepared, and you gotta be patient. Sometimes it takes a long time for a trick to pay off. Years even. Most people can't wait that long. They just want the magic, right now. Poof."

"I'm patient."

"We'll see."

"So when are you going to show me the trick?"

"You beg, borrow, or steal a fresh one-dollar bill, and then we'll talk."

Graciella laughed. "In the car! Now!"

Teddy stood up with an embarrassing pop of the knees.

"You can't tell a kid to steal money, Teddy. However . . ." She kissed him on the cheek. "I'm still glad I ran into you that day in the grocery store."

"I have a confession to make," Teddy said. "I didn't run into you by accident. I saw you, I thought you were a pretty woman, and I made sure I got close enough to do my mind-reading trick."

"Oh, I know about that."

"You do?"

"How many women have fallen for it?"

"I plead the fifth, my dear."

"Well, that wasn't the miracle. It was the fact you were there at all. That you turned out to know Nick Senior, and that you're willing to help—that Irene is willing to help, too. You two are my pair of pocket aces."

She knew he'd like that metaphor, and he liked that he knew that she knew. He strolled to his car, humming to himself, swinging the plastic box full of a dead man's teeth.

□

He used to have no problem making promises. When he proposed to Maureen, he said, "You'll never regret this." When their daughter was born, he said, "I'll be the best dad in the state of Illinois." And when Maureen told him she was sick, he said, "You're going to be fine."

It was a freezing morning in late winter. He found her in the bedroom, her face wearing that peculiar expression of the working clairvoyant: head tilted, mouth tight, eyes twitching under closed lids like a dreamer.

"There's a tumor," she said.

She'd discovered it on her own. She'd been feeling sick to her stomach for weeks, and had stopped eating. Then, following what she called "an intuition," she'd turned her attention to her own body. Not-so-remote-viewing.

He said, "You're not a doctor. Stop being dramatic." It wasn't the kindest he'd ever been. It was seven in the morning, and he was tired, unemployed, and in pain. He'd spent most of the night in the basement, watching the TV and doing physical therapy, which in this case took the form of repeatedly lifting a heavy bottle with his bandaged hands.

"I've already gone to the doctor." What she meant was "doctors." Weeks ago she'd made an appointment to see first their family physician, then her gynecologist, then an oncologist. She said, "I couldn't tell you until I was sure."

"But we can't know for sure until they do a biopsy. Did they do a biopsy?"

"It's scheduled for next week."

"Then it could be nothing."

After the test results came back, with undeniable evidence of epithelial cell tumors, he doubled down: the doctors were wrong, the tests were wrong, and even if they weren't, she could go into remission at any time.

She stood at the entrance to the basement, arms crossed, keeping her tears behind her eyes. "We need to talk about what to tell the kids," she said.

"Tell them what? There's nothing to tell," he said from the couch. "We're going to beat this."

In 1974, nobody he knew "beat" cancer. Half a dozen friends had caught the lung variety—they were a generation of chimneys—and had croaked in a few years. One died of colon cancer, another of some kind of melanoma. Ovarian cancer, that was something else. They called it "the silent killer" because early symptoms—stomachaches, the urge to pee, loss of appetite—were easily dismissed. The tumors grew, and it wasn't until the bleeding started that you knew something had gone terribly wrong. By then it was too late.

All through the spring and into summer, he avoided all mention of the Big C. Wouldn't have the conversation with Maureen. Her dogmatic belief that she was doomed infuriated him. It was surrender. Negative thinking. He knew that if they talked about death, if they planned for it, they would only give it power over them. Why invite the specter into their house, pour it a cup of coffee, let it put its bony feet all over their couch?

No. They'd beat cancer, by cheating if necessary. Teddy had been training for the job his entire life.

But even he couldn't remain blind to the changes in her body. She grew thinner through that summer. Their age difference once had bordered on the scandalous, but now she was catching up to him, aging at three times his speed, and angling to pass him. By August she was coming home from work exhausted. Irene was cooking then, and Maureen would sit with Buddy in her lap and look out the window as if she were already on the other side of it.

One night late in August, she roused herself to wash the after-supper dishes, and he watched her thin arms scrub the pots. That was the night she made him promise never to allow the children to work for any government. He'd made fun of her, and she'd shouted at him, wasting the last of her energy on him. He felt terrible. He apologized, and promised to do everything she asked—all without allowing himself to think there'd ever be a time he'd have to take care of the kids without her.

"I want you to come back," she said that night. "Back to the bedroom."

"Are you sure?" he asked.

"Jesus, Teddy." Exasperated. She leaned against him, and he put his hand around her shoulders. She seemed so light. A girl with eggshell bones.

They went into the bedroom and lay down side by side, on their backs, as if trying out burial plots. "I have to tell you something," she said.

His chest went cold, dreading what she'd say next.

"I've done something bad," she said.

He was relieved. There was nothing Maureen could do that was as bad as what he'd done, no weight as big as what he'd brought down, and he welcomed any shift in the scales. "You can tell me anything," he said.

What she told him was impossible to believe at first. She had to go through parts of it several times.

After she'd finished, he thought for a long minute, and then said, "You've betrayed the American government."

"Yes."

"And disrupted our nation's intelligence-gathering networks."

"Yes."

"And what else? Oh—allied yourself with a dissident Russian to also bring down the Soviet psychic warfare program."

"Uh-huh."

"My God, Mo, you're an international *criminal*!"

"Pretty much," she said.

They laughed together, like the old days.

"I'm so proud of you," he said.

She begged him to stop talking, because her stomach hurt. No, really hurt. He rolled onto his side to watch her face. That fast, her concentration had moved away from him, down into the pain.

A minute or so later, she spoke without opening her eyes. "We have to talk about what to say to the kids."

"Is this about the government thing? I promised you—they'll never work for them."

"I'm talking about me," she said. "Buddy already knows, but—"

"You told *him*?"

"He already knew. He drew my grave."

"Ah." He thought that had all stopped for the kid. But maybe there was still a bit of the talent there. He was so God damn unreadable, that one.

Mo said, "But Irene and Frankie have to know what's coming, too."

"I'll help you tell them," he said. He touched a scarred hand to her cheek. "Tomorrow, I promise."

He was so good at making promises, because he'd had so much practice.

□

From the basement came the high whine of a drill going full tilt into wood studs. Did he even want to look? For weeks he'd avoided going down there, afraid that he'd see the damage and burst an artery. But the mountain wasn't coming to Teddy, so he had to go to the mountain.

Buddy stood at the base of the stairs, using both hands to drill into the wall beside the basement door. The door frame was shiny new metal, and the old wooden door had been replaced by a steel one. A fucking steel door.

Jesus Christ.

At Buddy's feet lay an alarm clock, busted and sprouting wires. A spool of new wire was set beside it.

Teddy took a breath before he spoke. "Buddy. Buddy. Hey." The big lump finally heard him and released the trigger on the drill, but did not turn around. "Could you put that down for a sec?"

Buddy looked over his shoulder, drill tilted up, a cowboy holding his fire.

"I'm not going to ask you what you're doing," Teddy said. "I'm sure you got your reasons." Buddy said nothing. Waiting for the interruption to be over.

"I just want your advice on something," Teddy said.

Buddy winced.

"Come on," Teddy said. "Sit down with me, one God damn second."

Buddy reluctantly set the drill on the floor, and Teddy led him through the steel door into the basement. It was dark in there, darker than it should have been. The row of garden-height windows were all covered.

Teddy flipped on the lights. The windows had been sealed with sheet metal.

"What the hell did you—?" He stopped himself. He wasn't going to criticize. He wasn't going to question.

Buddy hadn't limited himself to remodeling and fortifying—he'd also been redecorating. A secondhand love seat and three ratty armchairs, all different colors, were set up around a twenty-six-inch TV, with a video-game gadget wired up to it. Lamps of various vintages were set up but not yet plugged in. The desk Irene had been using was pushed off to the side, the computer missing. And against the far wall were four unpainted bunk beds.

"Have a seat," Teddy said. Each of them took an armchair. "I gotta go somewhere this afternoon, talk to somebody I don't want to talk to. You know anything about that?"

Buddy looked off to the side.

"If it's going to go bad, I'd like to know. Are you getting any, you know, glimpses? Anything like you used to?"

Buddy refused to make eye contact.

"Okay, fine, you don't want to talk. I get it. You and me, we haven't talked much lately. I know I used to put a lot of pressure on you, back in the day. And I know that was wrong."

Buddy seemed to be holding himself to the chair through force of will.

"But I got a real problem right now, and the stakes are high," Teddy said. "So how about this?" He reached into his jacket pocket and held out a manila envelope. "You don't have to say a thing. Just nod or shake your head, okay? A nod or a shake." He leaned forward, watching his son's face. "Buddy, is this going to be enough?"

Buddy's eyes flicked toward the envelope and away, as if it were a too-bright light.

Teddy said, "All I'm asking is a nod or a—"

Buddy jumped up and fled the room. Teddy listened to him clomp up the stairs and bang through the back door.

"God damn it," Teddy said. He was going to have to do this blind.

He went upstairs to his bedroom, opened the closet door, and dialed open his safe. The top rack was piled with Maureen's letters, the top one being the one he'd opened last month, as Graciella lay in the hammock.

He'd drunk them in as they arrived over the years, each pen stroke like a scratch upon his heart, summoning her to life and killing her again in the same moment. Her words had coached him and soothed him and chided him, helped him navigate the minefield of years. Made him a better parent, a wiser man. Each letter was like a pocket ace.

But the letters hadn't told him what to do now, and no new letter had arrived today. He'd outrun the reach of Maureen's advice. Fallen off the edges of the God damn map. He'd have to go forward into the dark, steering by his own lights. Improvising.

On the floor of the safe rested a black velvet tray. He eased it out and set it on top of the bed.

Arrayed on the velvet were two sets of gold cuff links, Maureen's engagement ring, one diamond tie pin, and four watches of various worth: a Tag Heuer, a workaday Citizen, an Audemars Piguet Royal Oak, and the one he was looking for. It was a near twin of the watch he was currently wearing, a 1966 "Paul Newman" Rolex Daytona with a diamond dial, and a novice pawing through his collection would have thought a second one redundant. Teddy, however, had held on to the one in the safe for sentimental reasons. If he was going to go see Nick Pusateri Senior, there was only one watch he wanted to wear.

He wound it, set the time, and realized it was time to go.

He went looking for Irene, and it wasn't hard to find her. Whenever she wasn't at work, she was parked at the dining room table. She turned the room into the command center for her dissection of NG Group Realty's finances. File boxes were stacked on the floor, and her new computer was set up in the middle of the table, probably scarring the wood. Frankie was yammering at her while Irene kept her eyes on the screen.

"It wouldn't be just a video-game arcade," Frankie said to her. "We'd do food, beer, sports events—"

"I thought you were done with computers," Teddy said to Irene.

"This one's been disconnected from the Information Superhighway."

"The what?"

"Dad. Dad," Frankie said. "Tell Irene. You gotta invest your money rather than let it sit there, right?" He was talking fast, the mark of a desperate man. Loretta had kicked him out, and Teddy had a good idea why.

Teddy said, "What money? You're broke."

"But what if I wasn't, huh? What I'm talking about is an arcade, a whole family thing, like Chuck E. Cheese without the fucking robots and the dress-up characters." Frankie had always been scared of people in costumes. Never sat on Santa's knee, ran terrified from the mall Easter bunny. "We serve good food, good beer, play good music. And here's the clincher—no video games."

Irene finally looked up from the computer. "You're going to open an arcade," she said, her voice flat. "With no video games."

"Nothing but real pinball," Frankie said. "It's ready to make a comeback. Kids will eat it up."

"You're an idiot." She did not quite glance at Teddy. "Do you know what this family would do for you? You'd throw everything away, and you have no idea what any of us—"

"*Irene,*" Teddy said, interrupting. "Time to go."

"Where are you going?" Frankie asked.

"Out for an errand," Teddy said. "Delivering some food to a sick friend. Irene, you ready?"

"Let me get my shoes," she said. She did something on the computer keyboard, then stood up. "Don't touch my stuff," she said to Frankie. "And would you please wake up my son? He's going to sleep the day away."

"Let him sleep," Frankie said. "He deserves it."

"For what?"

Frankie hesitated. "For being a good kid who loves his mother."

She snorted and went up to her room.

Frankie said to Teddy, "That's Irene all over. Conventional. Not a risk taker. But you understand, right? I can't just keep working as a phone tech. How's Loretta supposed to respect me when I'm an *installer*? What are my girls supposed to think? I've got to work for myself. I've got to do something I'm passionate about. You wouldn't believe the ideas I have for this place. I was thinking of making it a real, old-style arcade, with, like, 1950s memorabilia. You could come in with me!"

"My boy, my boy," Teddy said. He walked forward, hands out, as if going in for a hug.

Frankie looked up at him eagerly. "You could be my partner! Silent partner, maybe, since you've never even gone to an arcade, but you could put in—"

Teddy gripped Frankie's head. "Stop it. Just—" He didn't know what to do with this kid. Never did know. He was the boy who wanted everything, and didn't know how to get it. Hours in the corner, trying to levitate paper clips. "Stop it."

Frankie tried to speak through squashed cheeks.

"No," Teddy said. "I love you, but you're killing me. Just killing me."

□

The morning after he drove Maureen to the hospital and stayed the night at her bedside, he came home to shower and get a few things she'd asked for. Mrs. Klauser, their neighbor, had stayed the night and had made the kids pancakes.

Teddy called the children into the living room and tried to sit them down, but Frankie wouldn't stay still, kept trying to explain the miracle that had occurred in their kitchen: "Best pancakes *ever*. Mrs. Klauser is the *best*. I want pancakes *every day*."

Buddy was quieter than usual, on his own planet, crouched over a Hot Wheels car, pushing it through the carpet. Only Irene seemed to understand what was happening. She was almost eleven, only a year older than Frankie, but she seemed a decade more mature, a full voting member of the Parliament of Seriousness. Teddy was pretty sure she outranked him.

"Is Mom in the hospital?" she asked. He'd been planning to ramp up to the "H" word, but Irene had jumped ahead in the script.

"That's what I wanted to talk to you about," Teddy said. "She wasn't feeling well, so we thought the doctor should—"

"Is she going to die?" Irene asked.

This wasn't in Teddy's script at all. "No, of course not! We're just checking some things out and—damn it."

Tears were already running down Irene's face. He should have known better.

"She's very sick," Teddy said. "That's true. But the medicines they've got today, the tools they have available—it's just amazing. They've got a machine there that zaps the bad stuff. Pow, like a ray gun."

"I know about radiation," Irene said. "She's been going for months."

"Yes, but—" Damn it, what didn't Irene know? "We gotta let all the medicines work. We're not giving up, because that's not who we are. Frankie, stop that." The boy was standing in front of Buddy, deliberately blocking the Hot Wheels car with his foot. "Leave Buddy alone. Did you hear what I was saying?"

"Mom's in the hospital," Frankie said.

"That's right. Now later I'm going to come back and pick you up. Mrs. Klauser is going to get you all dressed, and we can go down there for a visit, okay? I want you to wash your hair. All of you. And put on something nice."

Frankie said, "Could you tell Mom something?" Buddy drove his car in the other direction, his back to the rest of them.

"Sure, sure," Teddy said. He crouched down to look Frankie in the eye. "What do you want to tell your mother?"

"She should buy blueberry syrup like Mrs. Klauser. It tastes just like IHOP."

"Syrup," Teddy said.

"Blueberry. Can I go play now?"

Irene hadn't moved, not even to brush the tears from her face.

"I need your help," Teddy said to her. He stood up, and brushed the crease from his wool pants. "Can you help get the boys ready?"

She nodded.

"Good girl. I've always been able to depend on you."

☐

He was still leaning on her, now literally. He hobbled up to Mitzi's Tavern using the newly purchased tri-tipped cane, but for extra drama he made Irene keep a hand on his biceps, as if at any moment he'd pitch over onto the sidewalk. He'd told her to keep one hand on him at all times, and to not forget to be nice.

Another weekend morning, another empty tavern. Barney locked the door behind them. "Don't want the drunks wandering in," he said. He nodded toward the open door of the office. It took Teddy and Irene a while to get there.

Nick Pusateri Senior sat behind the desk. Unlike Barney, who looked like an air mattress that had been inflated and deflated too many times, Nick was essentially the same man, only more weathered. Teddy thought, God preserve us from the longevity of assholes.

"Great to see you," Teddy said.

Nick came around the desk and shook hands, his grip deliberately crushing. Teddy didn't have to fake the wince, and he saw Nick enjoy that sign of weakness. Teddy didn't let on that his only desire was to jam his tri-cane down the man's throat. Yes, it'd be more work than a regular cane, but so worth the effort.

"And you must be little Irene," Nick said.

Irene smiled a tight smile. Teddy hoped she could pretend to be the dutiful daughter through this meeting. She was innately honest, like her mother. Deception was Teddy's department.

They took their seats on opposite sides of the desk. Nick had six pencils lined up on the cherry surface, all perpendicular to the edge, all sharpened to exactly the same length. So, Teddy thought. He's stressed.

Nick's OCD always kicked in when he was stressed. It had to be the pressure of the trial.

Nick said, "You're looking well, Teddy."

Irene's hand tightened on his arm. Teddy smiled, kept his eyes on Nick. "And that haircut never gets old." He leaned toward Irene. "Literally, it cannot get old."

Irene kept her smile in place.

"Because it's a fake," Teddy said.

"Uh-huh," she said without moving her lips.

"A *toupee*."

"I get it, Dad."

Nick laughed like it was a thing he'd seen people do in movies. "Still giving me the business, after all these years. Glad you still got some balls, Teddy."

Teddy shrugged. "Mitzi not coming?"

"She's feeling under the weather. Caught a bug."

"I'm sorry to hear that," Teddy said sincerely. "She seemed fine the other day."

"She'll snap back. She's a tough bird."

They agreed on this. Teddy told the story about Mitzi hitting an unruly drunk on the side of the head with a telephone. "What was his name? Right on the tip of my tongue." He made a shaky gesture with one hand, playing the doddering old man, the scatterbrained ancient. The name of the victim was Ricky Weyerbach, and he used to be an electrician at the Candlelight Dinner Playhouse before he hurt his back. "Anyway. Big guy, twice her size, and bam, right on the temple."

Nick laughed, and it nearly sounded human this time.

"This was one of those Bakelite monsters that weigh ten pounds," Teddy explained to Irene. "Put the guy in the hospital."

Nick liked that, Teddy saw. He liked any story about the fearsome Pusateris. At least any story that wasn't on the front page of the *Sun-Times*.

"So," Nick said. He frowned at one of the pencils, and made a microscopic adjustment. "I'm meeting with you out of respect for our history."

"I appreciate that," Teddy said.

"But your boy has already been in here, and we've worked out a payment plan."

Frankie came on his own? God damn it. Teddy had deliberately not told Frankie what he was up to, so the boy wouldn't do something stupid. And now he'd gone and stupided it up anyway.

Teddy let his annoyance show. "I told Mitzi I wanted to be the one to work out a deal."

Nick shrugged. "He's a grown man. And if you're here to get back the house, that's not going to happen."

This was the first Teddy had heard about a house. But it might explain why Frankie had moved into Teddy's.

"Why take a man's home, when you can take cold hard cash?" Teddy asked. He reached into his jacket pocket—a move Nick paid close attention to. Teddy's arthritic fingers came away with the envelope. Teddy set it on the desk, being careful not to disturb the pencils. "That's fifty thousand. Mitzi let me know the full amount when I saw her."

"The full amount," Nick said. Putting a skeptical spin on it.

"Is there a problem?"

"Just that you saw her over a week ago."

"Ah," Teddy said. He pretended to just now understand that over a week meant that interest was due. "How much?"

"It's not just the vig," Nick said. "A lot has changed. The real estate market, for example."

"How's that doing?"

"It's booming, Teddy. Fucking booming."

Irene squeezed Teddy's arm. "How much to make it all right?" Teddy asked. "The house, Frankie's remaining debt, everything."

"You don't have that kinda weight, Teddy."

"Try me."

"A hundred K."

Teddy let his face fall.

"And the watch."

"What?" Teddy's hand fluttered near his wrist, as if unconsciously protecting it.

Irene looked shocked. "What do you mean, his watch. That's— that's his pride and joy."

"He owes it to me," Nick said. "He's owed it to me for twenty years. I should have taken it back then, but I fastened it to his fucking wrist, and let him go."

"We're leaving," Irene said. "Come on, Dad."

"No."

Teddy lifted his head. He withdrew a second envelope, put it on top of the first. Then, without looking at the watch, he unlatched the steel band and slid it over his fingers. He dropped it onto the middle of the desk, sending the pencils rolling.

Nick quickly caught the pencils. Only when he'd lined them back up did he pick up the watch. "Jesus, that's beautiful. Paul Newman used to wear one of these when he raced."

"You don't say," Irene said.

"It was worth twenty-five grand when your pop won it in a poker game. And now? Who knows?"

"Right. Let's go, Dad."

Teddy put his hand over hers, so she wouldn't move it from his biceps. "There's one more thing," he said.

Nick raised his eyebrows.

"It's about your son," Teddy said. "And your daughter-in-law."

"Graciella?" Nick seemed genuinely confused.

"She never wants you to see her again. Or the boys."

"What the fuck is that to you?"

"I said I'd speak to you on her behalf."

"Are you *talking*? To *my family*?"

"And she wants you out of Nick Junior's real estate company. It's not going to be your front anymore. No more money laundering."

Nick still didn't seem to understand. "Graciella said this to *you*. A stranger."

"We're not strangers. I met her at the grocery store. By accident." He held up a hand. "It doesn't matter. The thing is, she's offering something in return."

"And what the fuck would that be?"

"Your freedom." He nodded at Irene. She opened her purse and took out the lunch box. Nick looked impatient. Then Irene lifted out the clear-plastic container of teeth and set them next to the envelopes of cash. She was polite enough to not disturb the pencils.

"Those once resided in the mouth of Rick Mazzione," Teddy said. "Before you evicted them. Nick Junior says that some of the blood on 'em is yours, though the FBI wouldn't have to take his word for it. They've got labs for that kind of thing."

Nick picked up the bag. He tapped the bottom of it, as if testing whether the teeth moved realistically.

"Graciella will take no action against you," Teddy said. "She hasn't talked to the cops. All she's asking is that you promise never to contact her, or the boys, again."

Nick couldn't take his eyes off the teeth.

"She wants them out of the life," Teddy said.

"The moron kept them," Nick said in a faraway voice. "Why would he do that? Why would he fucking keep them?"

"Why do kids do anything?" Teddy said. "They disappoint us. Half the time they're trying to win our approval, half the time they want to bury us."

Irene dug her fingernails into his arm. That wasn't a signal, except if the signal was "I'm pissed at you."

"So what do you say?" Teddy said.

Nick rubbed a hand across his face. "Where are the other teeth?"

"I don't know," Teddy said. "I told her to put them in a safe place, not in her house."

"You've got them, don't you?"

"I'm not that stupid," Teddy said.

"Oh yes you are. You're an idiot if you think you can come between me and my grandchildren."

"That may be so, but I felt I had to help her out. She was afraid to talk to you."

"Why would she be afraid of me?" Nick asked, distraught. "I'm Pop-Pop. I'm God damn *Pop-Pop*."

"All she wants is your word," Teddy said. "If you promise to give up your interest in the real estate company, and promise that you won't come after the boys or try to hurt her, she'll give you the rest of the teeth."

Nick shook his head in disbelief.

"Just your word," Teddy said.

Nick leaned across the table. Teddy could see tears forming in his eyes. The old Nick never cried. The old Nick didn't even own tear ducts. So maybe Graciella was right, and his grandsons had wrought a change in the devil. He hadn't wanted to tell Graciella that he thought it was impossible, but he was willing to be proven wrong.

"I swear on my mother's grave," Nick said, voice hoarse with emotion. "I would *never* hurt Graciella. She's like my own daughter. But if she—" His voice broke. "If she doesn't want me to see the boys, if she thinks that's really the best for them? Then I'll do it. I'll do it for them. Because I love those boys."

Irene squeezed Teddy's arm, hard.

"I'm so happy to hear that," Teddy said. "I'll let her know the good news."

Nick didn't shake their hands as they left. He was staring at the desk. At six pencils, two envelopes, and a collection of souvenirs.

Irene helped him into the passenger seat. Neither of them spoke.

He'd set up the feeble act back at Mitzi's a couple of weeks ago, just so he'd have an excuse to have Irene in the room with him when he met with Nick. He needed her there, listening to the man talk. Every squeeze on his arm from her had meant a lie from that bastard.

They were two miles from the tavern when Teddy finally said, "Well?"

"He's lying, top to bottom," she said.

Teddy sighed. Of course he was. What a shame to be proven right.

"Let's go," Teddy said. "We need to warn Graciella."

19

Irene

In the end, there was only one place to take them. Irene opened the front door to the house, peeked inside to make sure Buddy wasn't naked or something, and said to Graciella, "As it turns out, we have a lot of spare beds."

Graciella hadn't wanted to leave her house. Dad, however, managed to persuade her without inducing panic. He'd presented the idea of a sleepover at his house as a lark, a bit of fun for the kids, while somehow getting across the idea that her sociopathic father-in-law might indeed want to break into Graciella's home, kidnap his grandchildren, and shoot her in the head. Graciella took this implied news better than Irene expected. The woman's primary emotion, however, seemed to be not fear, but anger. She was mad at Teddy, or else mad at herself for going along with him. Irene knew exactly how she felt.

Plus, who would want to leave that palace? Irene had known that Graciella had money, but she hadn't realized just how much until she saw that home.

And now, unfortunately, Graciella was seeing theirs. Irene ushered her inside. Buddy was nowhere in sight, but he'd left a sawhorse in the middle of the living room. Sawdust coated everything.

"Uh, we're doing a little renovation work."

"I know," Graciella said. "I was here earlier."

"Right? Then come on in."

Her sons looked around at the room, saying nothing. It hadn't been easy to get them out of their house, either. The two younger boys, Adrian and Luke, didn't have the first clue how to pack a bag, and the teenager, Julian, seemed to think that if he hid in his bedroom then they'd somehow forget about him and let him stay home. Fortunately, both Graciella and Irene knew how to herd young males.

And summon them. "Matty!" Irene called. "We have company!"

There was no answer from the basement. Was he sleeping again? How much downtime did a teenager need?

Dad came in through the back door. "The wagon's all tucked away," he said. He'd wanted to take the precaution of parking Graciella's Mercedes in the garage and out of sight. "I know, it's a silly thing, probably not necessary at all, but why not? No sense advertising your presence."

Adrian, the youngest, held out a dollar bill to Teddy. "*Now* can you do a magic trick?"

Dad took the dollar from him. "You think you've been patient, eh?"

The boy nodded.

"All right, then. Ever hear of the shoe bank?" Dad sat down on the ottoman and pulled off a shiny black oxford. "The first step, so to speak, is to make a deposit." He folded the bill with his stiff fingers and placed it inside the shoe. Even crude tools could do crude work. Enough to fool a child, perhaps. "Then we wait for interest to develop. Don't worry kid, these are all jokes you're going to get someday and just *laugh*." He slipped the shoe back on and stood up. "Now the tricky part. How to make a shoe-to-shoe transfer?" He slid the money-laden shoe forward. "Let's go toe to toe, shall we? No, the other foot—right foot to right. Press the tip against mine. This, you see, allows us to combine our digits. No? Nothing? Okay, now we order the money. This is called a money order."

Graciella groaned.

"As I mentioned, someday, hilarious. Are you ready?" Adrian looked at his brothers, then nodded. Dad said, "Repeat after me: Money! Order!"

"Money order," Adrian said.

"Transfer!" Dad said, and kicked his toe against Adrian's. The boy hopped back as if he'd been shocked. Dad said, "Now let's see if the wire went through. Take off your shoe, my boy."

Adrian dropped onto his butt and pulled off his shoe. "Under the insole," Dad said. "That's right, pull it right out."

The boy pulled out the foam insole. Underneath was a folded bill. "It made it!" Adrian shouted. He unfolded the bill. "And it's a five!"

"Holy shit," Graciella said.

"Mom!" Adrian said.

Graciella laughed. "How did you do that?" she asked Dad.

"He'll never tell," Irene said. She'd never seen that one before. It was a pretty good gag. He hadn't touched the kid's shoe, except to tap it with his foot.

"Now the best part," Dad said. "You boys like video games? Because we've got a whole setup down there."

"What kind of video games?" Adrian asked.

"A brand-new whosit whatsit."

"An SNES?"

"Undoubtedly," Dad said. "Right that way."

Irene said, "If there's a boy down there, wake him up."

Adrian, one shoe off and one shoe on, jumped down the stairs. The older ones followed.

Dad was excited by all this drama, despite the danger. Or maybe because of it. Irene had always known that her father was once a gambler, what Frankie euphemistically called a "risk taker." She'd thought that was all behind him. After Mom died, he was at first depressed and unengaged, then frustrated and unengaged, and finally just unengaged. All this time, she'd thought he didn't like children, but maybe it was just that he didn't like *his* children. Only an audience of strangers would find him entertaining.

"What are we doing for supper?" he asked Irene.

"Don't look at me," she said. "Where's Buddy? And Frankie?"

"Buddy's out back, cleaning the grill. Frankie, no idea." He clapped his hands. "I guess we're ordering out. What do the boys like?" His eyes lit up. "What about fried chicken? Boys love any food that comes in a bucket. I'll get it. You girls get comfortable. Make her a drink, Irene. Graciella likes Hendrick's." And then he was gone.

"Wow," Irene said.

"I think he's enjoying this," Graciella said.

"And a little afraid to be in the room with you."

"You think so?"

"He doesn't want to disappoint you," Irene said. "Don't worry. He will, sooner or later."

Graciella gave her an appraising look. "How about that drink?"

They sat at the dining room table, among the file folders and boxes from NG Group Realty. Graciella picked up one of the listings that Irene had marked up with red pen. "How bad is it?"

"Could be worse," Irene said. She walked her through what she'd found in the last two years of files. Going by the number of properties being handled, most of the business was legitimate. But the cash flow was seriously weighted toward the suspicious house trades—and almost all of those were done by one agent.

"If you're going to run this clean," Irene said, "you've got to fire this Brett guy. And if you're going to make a profit, the other agents have to sell a lot more houses."

"I appreciate that you're not sugarcoating it."

"Who has time?"

"I'll drink to that."

They both did. "To fucking Nick."

"Junior *and* Senior," Irene said.

"And how about your guy?" Graciella asked. "How's that going?"

"Down in flames," Irene said.

"I thought you seemed down after your trip. You broke up with him?"

Broke up. With Lev, her almost husband, and with other boyfriends, the phrase felt right; she broke them off from her, let them fall away like the spent stage of an Apollo rocket. She was stronger without them and never looked back. With Joshua, though, it was as if she'd left a piece of herself behind. She was the one who was damaged, incomplete, adrift. Destined to grow cold and die alone.

She needed a story to tell Graciella, however, so she invoked a different destiny. "It was never going to work," she said. "He can't leave Phoenix. He's got a daughter, and they have split custody. He wanted me to move out there, get a job with his company, but I couldn't even get through the interview."

"What happened?"

"I found out they'd instituted a uterus tax."

Graciella laughed. "Oh, one of those places."

"Let's just say that I'll never work for those fuckers. I just hope I didn't get Joshua fired."

"Is he mad at you?"

"No! He feels guilty. Says he should have known more about what he was putting me into. He thinks I'm great and everybody else isn't worthy."

"Sounds like you're up on the pedestal, right where you belong. What's the problem?"

"The problem is that he's delusional."

Graciella put two fingers to her pursed lips and bent forward—the signal used by sane people to indicate that they *would* have spit their drink in laughter, if only they were a teenager or Lou Costello. Irene appreciated the gesture. Graciella swallowed and said with a smile, "Explain."

"We've only known each other for a couple months," Irene said. "We've barely spent time with each other. He hasn't even met the family!" And I haven't met his, she didn't say. "He keeps talking like everything's going to be so easy, so wonderful, nothing but unicorns in the garden. He has no idea what it would be like to live with me on a daily basis."

"The psychic thing?"

"Ah. Teddy told you about that?"

"He's not a bit ashamed of it."

"Well, I just know I wouldn't be able to handle it when he started lying to me."

"You'd be surprised what you can handle," Graciella said. "I knew what Nick was when I met him. It was part of the attraction. And for almost twenty years, it was fine. I didn't have to think about what he did with his father. I knew he was still doing things, not-so-nice things, but *our* family was good. If he hadn't been arrested, I'd still be the happy homemaker."

"Must be nice," Irene said.

"To be happy?"

"To live like that. To not notice the lies."

"Oh, I noticed them."

"Really?"

"You haven't been married, have you?"

"I got threatened with it once."

"Here's the secret. You both have to lie sometimes to make it work. He says, 'You look great in that outfit.' You tell him he's right about Clinton. And when he comes home at three a.m. with a bag of fucking teeth, you make sure not to ask him who they belong to."

"Jesus," Irene said.

Graciella stared at her glass. "You're right. That's awful. How did I live like that?" Her eyes shone. Irene had never seen Graciella get emotional.

"I knew when Nick wasn't where he said he was," she said. "Or when he made up some story when he was working for his father. And I just . . . let it go."

"You had the boys to think about," Irene said.

"I was thinking of myself. All the things I had."

"It *is* a pretty good house," Irene said.

Graciella shrugged, admitting it. "Is Joshua well-off?"

"Better off than I am."

"And you've known him for all of two months."

"Almost three. We met online."

"Online. I don't get that. How much have you been with him in person?"

Irene tried to count the days. "Maybe a week's worth? Ten days?"

"That's crazy, Irene! Ten days and he wants you to move to Arizona?"

"I know. It's not like me."

But what *was* like her? Stay home and take care of the boys, for sure. To be the Designated Adult in the room. To put herself second. She said, "I'm just not sure what person I want to be anymore."

"Stay here, then," Graciella said. "Work for me. Take care of the money."

"You want me to be your bookkeeper?"

"We'll hire a fucking bookkeeper. I need you to be the chief financial officer. Someone who knows where all the bodies are buried."

Irene made a face.

"Monetarily speaking," Graciella said.

"You're serious?"

"Dead serious." Then: "I really need to find a different way of expressing myself."

"I'll think about it," Irene said.

"I see. This is you being an adult. Non-impulsive. Let's drink more."

A few minutes later, Dad's Buick slid past the picture window, heading for the driveway. Irene said, "Let's get the boys."

But Matty wasn't in any of the bunk beds. Irene went up to the attic and knocked on his bedroom door. "Supper, kid!" After no answer, she knocked again. "Matty?"

She tried the knob. It didn't turn—which meant that Matty had locked it from the inside—but the door wasn't sitting flush in the frame. She pushed it open.

Matty lay in bed, unmoving, hands under the covers. Jesus Christ, not again, she thought. She started to back out of the room, then realized his eyes were wide open.

"Matty?"

She waved her hand in front of his eyes.

"Matty. You hear me?" He didn't move. She put her hand to his neck and verified that he was still breathing.

"God damn it," she said. Her son was an astral fucking traveler.

☆

It was in the limo ride to the cemetery that she thought, Maybe now we'll be normal. At the end of the service she realized: Nope. Never gonna happen.

On the way there, Dad seemed to be in a trance. He sat in the backseat, his hat beside him, watching the telephone poles slip by. It was Irene who had to keep Frankie and Buddy in line. Buddy had refused to sit on the seat, and was lying on the floor mat, drawing in crayon on his big pad of paper. Frankie kept putting his feet on top of him and saying things like "Wow, is this footrest comfortable!" Buddy would slap his feet away, and Irene would yell at both of them, and as soon as she looked away the whole process would start all over.

Dad ignored them. This only made her more angry with him. She was furious that he'd never come back from the hospital to bring them to see Mom. Mrs. Klauser had gotten them all bathed and into fancy clothes, like they were getting ready to go onstage. Then they'd been forced to hang around the house, not allowed to go play outside because they'd get dirty. After three hours of waiting the phone rang. Mrs. Klauser told them they weren't going to the hospital. Only Irene knew what that meant.

Dad should have taken them that morning. Mom wouldn't have cared what they looked like. But because he was so worried about *appearances* Irene wasn't allowed to say goodbye to her mother. None of them were.

Well, at least now the act was over. There was no Amazing Telemachus Family without Mom. Now they could be just like everybody else.

The graveside service wasn't nearly as crowded as the viewing the night before, or the church service that morning, but there were still over a hundred people gathered around the coffin. Dad got out of the limousine without looking back, leaving the boys to Irene. "Put the coloring book in the car," she told Buddy. "Tuck in your shirt," she said to Frankie.

"You're not the boss of me," he said.

"Stop it," Irene hissed at him. "This is Mom's *funeral*."

"Is it? I hadn't noticed." Frankie had been a jerk from the moment they'd made him put on a tie.

The funeral home worker led them into a tent over the grave site, then to the front of the crowd, right next to the hole. They sat on white folding chairs while most everybody else stood.

Someone put a hand on Irene's shoulder. She glanced up and saw that it was a red-haired woman she'd never seen before. "I'm so sorry, honey," the woman said. "If you need anything, you can call on us."

"Anything at all," said the man beside the red-haired woman. It was Destin Smalls, huge as ever.

Later, Irene wished she'd said, "All I want is for you to leave our family alone." But at the time she only said, "Thank you," and turned back around.

The priest said yet more words, but Irene was beyond listening. What was left to say? Mom was gone, and Irene was trapped here, the next available adult in charge.

Finally it was time for the coffin to be lowered into the ground. Irene took Buddy's hand, for herself as much as him. A couple of funeral home workers in black suits squatted beside the metal frame that surrounded the coffin and flipped some latches. The priest kept talking as the men worked the thick straps that held up the nickel-colored coffin. The box lowered a few inches, then stopped.

The funeral workers looked at each other. They lowered the straps some more, but the coffin wasn't going down. It hovered, unsupported. A murmur ran through the crowd. Dad didn't seem to notice anything was wrong. He was looking off in the distance, chewing at his lip.

Irene turned to Frankie. Tears coursed down his cheeks. He was standing stiffly, fists clenched.

Irene leaned close to his ear. "Stop it," she said.

Frankie shook his head.

"It's okay," she said. "It's okay. Just . . . let her down easy, okay?"

The coffin suddenly plunged two feet, and the metal frame shook. Someone in the crowd shrieked.

"Stop telling me what to *do*!" Frankie shouted, and ran for the car.

☆

There was nothing to do but shut the door and wait for Matty to come back into his body. Graciella saw that something was wrong. "Everything okay?"

"He's going to be eating later," Irene said.

Dad dealt out chicken parts. "A leg to the gentleman with the Ninja Turtle shoes! A breast to the strapping young man across the table. And a lovely pair of thighs to Cool Hand Luke."

Irene grabbed him by the arm. "Could you step outside for a second?"

"Wait your turn, my dear, these boys are—"

"*Now.*"

Dad finally looked her in the face and twigged to her mood. "Uh, Graciella, could you introduce your lads to the miracle that is Brown's coleslaw? We'll be right back after this brief interruption."

Irene led him into the backyard. Buddy was unspooling a red cable, laying it across the lawn as if he was installing a sprinkler system. When he noticed them, he dropped the cable and walked toward the garage.

"Stop!" Irene said. "This is for both of you. Did you know about Matty?"

Buddy put up his hands and backed away.

"Come back here, Buddy." He slipped into the garage via the side door. "Damn it!"

"What are you talking about?" Dad asked.

"Astral travel," Irene said. "Remote viewing. Whatever you call it—Mom's old stunt."

"You're saying Matty is psychic?"

"Don't you Trebek me, Dad."

"What are you talking about?" he asked innocently.

"You're still doing it!"

Dad glanced at the house. "Perhaps we should keep our voices . . . ? I mean—ahem—let's keep our voices down."

"Did you know about this?"

"I've recently learned that, yes, the boy has some ability. He's had a few experiences, evidently."

"He's up there right now—" She waved in the direction of the attic room and the air above it. "—flying around in space! When the hell were you going to tell me?"

"Soon. Matty thought you wouldn't take it well. He asked Frankie's advice, and then I—"

"He told *Frankie*?" Suddenly those sleepovers made sense. "What's next, getting the act back together?"

Teddy raised his eyebrows. "Do you think Matty would be willing to do that?"

"No!" Irene shouted. "It doesn't matter what he wants. He's fourteen!"

"You were nine when we started. Buddy was only five."

"You do not get any parenting awards for that."

Graciella opened the back door. "Chicken's getting cold."

"We're not done talking about this," Irene said to her father. "Not by a long shot."

Irene stormed into the house. "Graciella. I want to start Monday afternoon. Because Monday morning I'm moving out of this house."

"Okay . . ." Graciella said.

"Monday's a holiday," her oldest son, Julian, pointed out.

"I work holidays," Irene said.

"Who's moving?"

Matty had appeared at the doorway to the kitchen. Heads swiveled.

"What?" he asked. "What did I miss?"

"You, me, outside," Irene said. "Now."

"Can I get some chicken first? I'm starving."

Irene took a breath. "One piece."

Irene sat on the front porch—the new front porch, with its too-smooth tiles—and wished she had one of her son's joints to smoke.

Matty's father liked a good smoke. Irene did, too, back in the day. But that was just another bad habit she'd given up along with Lev Petrovski. She'd never told Matty why she didn't marry his father. Maybe it was time to remedy that.

She'd only wanted two things from the man. (*Man*. Hardly. He was nineteen then, not even drinking age except in Wisconsin.) The first was a certain quality of DNA, by which she meant normal, unexceptional DNA full of dominant genes that would swamp whatever wild-ass trait the child might inherit from his mother and grandmother. She didn't want a gifted child, an Amazing Telemachus. She wanted a normal son or daughter who would never be tempted to show off on a national talk show.

The second was Lev's presence. His continuing presence. It seemed a low bar to require that he merely stick around after the child was born, but Lev couldn't even manage that. The night she went into labor he was nowhere to be found. One a.m. and he was off with his buddies, unreachable. She'd told him to get a pager, but of course he hadn't gotten around to it.

Dad was the one who drove her to the hospital. He wasn't about to come into the room, however. "I'm not cut out for that," he said, as if a glimpse of his daughter's functioning cooch would send him spiraling into madness. She went in alone and lay down alone in a room that to her pregnancy-enhanced sense of smell was a steaming bath of disinfectant.

She'd never missed her mother so much. There'd been other milestones—birthdays, the death of her cat, her first period, her eighth-grade graduation—after which Irene would steal away to stare at her mother's picture and hold one-sided mother-daughter talks. But that night in the hospital, pushing out a child into the hands of strangers, made her ache with longing. Even when they finally tucked her son beside her, she was wounded a second time, because she couldn't show him to her.

Lev showed up later that morning. He apologized over and over. He expressed wonder at the baby. He said all the right things you should say after doing all the wrong things, but something had closed in her heart. He'd come straight from the bars, clothes thick with cigarette smoke, and she could barely tolerate him holding her son. Before he left the room she decided that he would never hold Matty again.

His presence was no longer required. And fourteen years later, it turned out that Lev had botched even the DNA portion of the test. The Petrovski genes were no match for the McKinnon magic.

It was time to have the talk she'd been dreading. Explaining the birds and the bees was nothing compared with the psychos and the psychics. Irene was thirty-one years old, the same age as her mother when she died, and a part of her had always believed that she'd be dead before she had to face this moment. But no.

Lucky her.

She was about to go back inside and chase down Matty when Frankie's yellow Bumblebee van swung into the driveway and screeched to a halt. A moment later, a twenty-foot U-Haul eased up to the curb and parked in front of the house.

Loretta came out of the van and marched up the ramp, scowling like a demon. The twins scampered after her.

"Hey, Loretta," Irene said. "What's going on?"

"We're moving the hell in is what's going on. We're God damn refugees."

Irene stepped out of her way before she was run over. The twins threw themselves into Irene with a four-armed hug. "Auntie Reenie! We got kicked out of our house."

"Some guys came and they put all our stuff on the lawn!"

"Dad got a truck!"

"You don't say? Well, go in, and get yourself some chicken, girls."

Mary Alice climbed out of the U-Haul and crossed the lawn.

Frankie followed her, looking not so much like he'd driven a truck as been hit by one.

Mary Alice caught Irene's eye, then shook her head and went inside.

Frankie looked up at her. "A temporary setback," he said.

"Who kicked you out?" Irene asked.

"It's complicated. Is Matty inside?"

"Stay the hell away from Matty."

"What now? Why?"

"You heard me. You're not his fucking *coach*. You wait right here. Do not move."

"You can't tell me what to do. I'm a grown-ass—"

She slammed the door behind her before he could finish. Matty stood in the hallway with Mary Alice, talking in a low voice. He was holding a white foam plate loaded with too much fried chicken and a pile of mashed potatoes.

"You," Irene said, pointing at him. "Upstairs."

"I thought you wanted to talk to me."

The kid didn't know what a stay of execution looked like. "To your room!" she said.

"Can I bring the food?"

"Consider it your last meal," she said, her voice icy.

Matty traded a dark look with Mary Alice, then went upstairs with his heavy-duty plate.

Irene raised her voice. "Dad! I need you out here!"

He stepped out of the kitchen, still joking with someone she couldn't see. He saw Irene's face and frowned.

"You got to hear this," she said, and went back outside.

Frankie was on the porch now. "Don't bring Dad into this," he said. "I'm handling it."

"You have no idea," Irene said.

Dad stepped out, which forced Irene and Frankie to move down the ramp. "What's going on?" he asked.

"Nick took his house anyway," Irene said.

"Well, you said he was lying through his teeth," Dad said.

Frankie was bewildered. "You know about Nick?"

Graciella had followed Teddy out of the house. "Which Nick?"

"We've got a problem," Dad said.

"We're going to need more chicken," Graciella said.

"Jesus Christ," Irene said quietly. "I'm done."

"At least forty-eight pieces," Graciella added.

"Done with the whole God damn show," Irene said.

Dad seemed to have finally heard her. "Everybody calm down," he said. "I'll fix this."

"Nobody needs to fix anything," Frankie said. "I've got it handled. Handled!"

Irene screamed without words. Everyone looked at her as if waiting for a translation.

Surely they understood: it wasn't reasonable to raise a son in this house, under these conditions. He was going to be normal, damn it. He was going to be *boring*.

She said to Frankie, "Where'd you rent that moving truck?"

20

Frankie

The plan was simple. Pretend to fall asleep. Sneak out of the house. Empty Mitzi and Nick's safe.

Step one fell apart when he found himself unable to lie still. It wasn't just nerves, it was the fucking humidity. He'd been exiled to the living room couch, where there were only windows to cool him off.

It took forever for everyone in the house to settle down. The twins were supposed to be sleeping with Loretta in one of the attic bedrooms, but they were too keyed up by the excitement of being in Grandpa Teddy's house with all these strange kids running around. They kept making excuses to get up. Each of them visited the bathroom, then came down to the kitchen for "cool water" (because bathroom water was too warm?), and then they appeared beside his couch to ask him to make "chocolate milks." The girls were desperate to find out what the other kids were doing in the basement. Irene and Graciella had gone down there at eleven and told them to turn out the lights, but it was impossible to know from here if they'd obeyed. Buddy had installed some kind of vault-like door, and when it was closed no light or sound escaped.

Twenty or so minutes passed without interruption from the twins. He wanted to wait till midnight, which was about forty-five minutes from now. Midnight seemed auspicious. No one except Matty knew what he planned—and the plan was going forward, damn it. Yes, his father had "talked" to Nick Pusateri. Dad wouldn't tell him what they talked about, but it obviously hadn't worked. Outfit guys had still shown up at his house and thrown out his family, then started dumping their belongings on the lawn: furniture, kids' toys, pots and pans, piles of clothes. Frankie had shown up just in time to pull Loretta away from a guy. Frankie knew better than to try to interrupt or argue with the "movers"; mixing it up with presumably armed thugs was a quick way to get killed. Loretta's rage had made her fearless, however. Only the presence of her (bawling, scared) children had stopped her from murdering them. And him. Oh, she hadn't forgotten that this was his fault.

Another stretch of minutes crawled past. His eyes had adjusted to the gloom, but he still couldn't make out the face of his watch. He listened to the house, and was relieved that the upstairs bedrooms were quiet.

He sat up, the back of his shirt a damp rag despite the sheet that Buddy had thrown over the leather cushions.

"Are you ready?" he whispered to himself. "It's time, Frankie. Time to—"

He almost said, "Embrace life." But he was done with the Ultra-Life. If he tasted another goji berry anything he'd heave his guts up.

Using guesswork and clues from dim shapes, he foraged for pants, socks, shoes. His pants pocket held the all-important piece of paper. The empty tool bag was in his hand. There were only two more things he needed before he left the house.

He went down the stairs, and nearly tripped over the huge industrial drill Buddy had left on the floor—even though Frankie had been looking out for it. His brother had been using it to screw a digital clock to the wall beside the basement door. Why? Who the hell knows. You'd get more answers from a chimp. But at least the red letters told him the exact time: 11:25. Jesus. He hadn't even made it to 11:30.

He pushed on the metal door. It scraped open with a sound that he wouldn't have noticed in daylight, but whose Night Volume went up to eleven. The room inside was lit only by the glow of Super Nintendo indicator lights. Somehow that made it darker.

"Matty?" he whispered. He stepped into the room. The new bunk beds were stacked against the far wall, but which one was his nephew's?

"Hey. Matty." His foot caught on an invisible power cord, but he righted himself.

"He's over there," a tiny voice whispered.

"Thanks," Frankie answered. Wow, was it cool down here. Had Buddy installed AC? Why the fuck was he sweltering upstairs?

"Hello?" a familiar voice called.

Frankie swung toward it. "Marco."

"Polo," Matty said.

Everybody was still whispering. The boy seemed to be on the lower bunk. Frankie bent low and crept forward, his hand hovering before him in the dark to stop him from cracking his skull against the wood.

"I need you on overwatch," Frankie said.

"What?"

"You know. Watching over me. Up there."

"You're still going to do it?"

"Yes, I'm going to do it. Of course I am. Are we not Telemachuses? Telemachi?"

"Yeah, but—"

"I need you, Matty. You're my—" He tried to think of a great side-kick from Greek myth, but Castor and Pollux were the only dynamic duo he could think of, and Frankie really didn't want to think about his daughters right now. "You're my lookout."

The room lights flashed on. Frankie stood up, and whacked the back of his head on the bunk frame. He fell back, and nearly dropped onto his ass.

"What the hell are you doing?" Irene stood by the door, in shorts and a T-shirt, her hand on the light switch. The oldest of Graciella's sons sat up in his upper bunk, and the youngest one, who'd spoken to Frankie in the dark, automatically covered his head with the blanket.

"I'm *trying*," Frankie said, mustering his dignity, "to have a *conversation*."

"This is not the time," Irene said.

"I just wanted to—"

"*Out.*"

"All right, all right," Frankie said. He tried to shoot a significant look at Matty, but the boy's eyes were on his mom. "I'm going. You don't have to *look out* for me."

Irene caught up to him as he was heading out the front door.

"What's the matter with you? Where are you going? And what's in the bag?"

"Nothing. It's hot, Irene. I can't sleep."

"I want to talk about Matty. Give me two fucking seconds."

"I've really got to go."

"Where?" she said, exasperated. *"Outside?"*

He groaned.

"I can't have you talking to Matty right now," she said. "Not until I figure out what's going on." The porch light was on, and her face was half in shadow. She looked both older and younger at the same time.

"Come on," Frankie said. "You know what's going on."

"No, I don't. But when I get to talk to Matty, when we don't have fifty people in the house—"

"Are you really going to take him away from us?"

Irene blinked at him.

"To Phoenix?" he asked.

"No," she said. "Probably not. But I can't stay here. Not with all . . . this."

"See, this is why Matty couldn't talk to you. You hate everything about our family."

"That's crazy. I don't hate everything."

"Just the important parts. Listen—Matty wanted somebody to talk to who wouldn't make him feel ashamed, okay? This is something to be proud of. He's really good at remote viewing, maybe even better than Mom someday. But it's scary, and when it happened to him, he came to me, because he knew that I'd think it was *great.*"

"And I'm glad he did."

"What?"

"I'm glad he talked to you. He needed somebody, and if it couldn't be me, I'm glad it was somebody in the family."

"Okay . . ." Frankie couldn't think of what to say.

"But that's over," Irene said. "No more filling his head with the glories of extrasensory perception until I get the whole story—from him."

"Right. The whole story."

Irene's eyes narrowed.

"Because that's what you need!" Frankie said. "Everything. Start to finish."

"You gave him the pot, didn't you?"

"Are you using your power on me, Reenie?"

"I don't know, are you Trebeking me?"

He laughed. "Okay. Listen to me. I did *not* give your son marijuana. Do you hear that? Didn't happen."

"I hear it."

"Good. Now, if you'll excuse me, I'm going to take in the night air."

He stepped onto the porch and nearly slipped on the tile, now slick with condensation. The night air, it turned out, was as moist and thick as swamp gas. "Jesus, this humidity," he said. "It's . . . what's the word? Cloying."

"Like a Sally Struthers infomercial," she said.

"Exactly." Irene, she always knew the clever thing to say.

"I'm sorry about your house," she said.

"Temporary setback," he said, and climbed into the van.

That Irene. Always the smart one. She was only a year older, but he always felt like she understood things he didn't, spoke in a language he didn't understand. The language of adults. Of women. When they were little, Irene and Mom would exchange a look and it was like they were beaming information at each other in some frequency available only to the females of the species. He'd grown up with two moms, and he'd been unable to please either of them.

Not like Buddy. Buddy was an emotional wreck, yet somehow beloved. Mom and Buddy especially shared something inaccessible to him. Frankie would see them cuddling together, whispering to each other, and know there was no room for him there.

He moved his attention to Dad. A tough nut to crack, but the man with the keys to all the locked rooms. Frankie didn't want to be *like* his father, he wanted to *be* him. He wanted to dress in a fine suit, pull a fedora low over his eyes, and set a roll of cash on the table. Teddy Telemachus was the opposite of invisible. He drew your eyes, and at the same time directed your attention to whatever he wanted you to see—an empty hand, a diamond-encrusted watch, the brim of a hat— while he made his magic.

Irene used to say that the only thing Dad cared about was the act.

But that didn't mean he didn't care about the family. The family was the act and the act was the family. But back when they were touring, Frankie knew, deep down, that he was failing as a performer, and as a son. He couldn't bend a paper clip. He couldn't levitate a water glass. It shouldn't have surprised anyone when the Astounding Archibald had revealed Frankie's ability to be nothing more than Dad kicking the table to life. Dad had been doing all of Frankie's tricks since they started performing. Irene needed no help; she had genuine ability. Buddy, when he wasn't having a meltdown, could call every shot on the Wonder Wheel. And of course Mom was the best of them, a world-class talent in a second-rate vaudeville act.

And Frankie? Frankie was the faker.

It wasn't until Mom's funeral that he finally moved something, but even then he couldn't take credit for it. The power seemed to come from outside himself, arriving of its own accord while he watched his mother being lowered into the ground. Then nothing, for years, until he found pinball, and again he felt like he wasn't so much controlling the table as communing with it. The bond could break down at any time. His power was not something he possessed, but a skittish companion he had to woo to his side, and who'd vanish as soon as he showed fear.

He would have spent his whole life chasing that feeling, if he hadn't walked into that bar on Rush Street and met Loretta. She was the first person who thought he was special. The morning after they first made love, he started to pull on his pants and leave, but she grabbed him by the waistband and pulled him back into bed. "Maybe you don't understand," she'd told him. "You're my man now."

He didn't know how to respond to that. And she said, "You'll come around."

He did come around. And stuck around. Loretta was ten years older than him, but by designating him as her man she'd promoted him to full adulthood. She wanted him to help raise her girl, and make more babies. She wanted her children to be Telemachus children. And when he told her he wanted to create his own business, she believed him. And when he said he wanted to do something great, she believed that, too. She fell for his con.

That was *her* mistake. His was that he fell for it, too. Now the only way out of this predicament, this clusterfuck he'd created, was to make all the lies into truths.

He had to do something great.

The paranoia that accompanied an act of greatness, however, was exhausting. Headlights seemed to be following him. On North Avenue he was certain a police car was on his tail, but then the vehicle passed him, and he saw it was just a sedan with a luggage rack. A luggage rack! How were those things legal?

Frankie parked on the street, about fifty feet from the mouth of the alley that ran behind Mitzi's Tavern. It was out of sight of any video cameras Mitzi might have up, yet within a hundred yards of the back door. Not far to run, even with a bag of money. His tool bag would do for that.

The thought of video cameras reminded him of his disguise. He reached under his seat and pulled out the White Sox baseball cap he'd bought at Osco. Nobody would suspect it was Frankie Telemachus in a fucking Sox cap. He went through his mental checklist again. Disguise, tool bag . . . and what else? Right. The keys to the kingdom. He turned on his Bumblebee-issued Maglite and checked the slip of paper he'd been carrying with him. There were two sets of numbers on it: one for the door alarm, and one for the safe. Matty had provided them both.

He addressed the area above the van. "You on overwatch, Matty?"

There was no answer. And that, in a nutshell, was the major defect of remote viewing; it only worked one way. Somebody needed to invent a mobile phone for clairvoyants. You could call it—

A 1960s Chevelle passed him, going slow, and turned at the next street.

Too slow?

No, he thought. The paranoia was messing with him. Making him procrastinate. And worse, the name of the clairvoyant phone service was gone. A really good pun had been right on the tip of his tongue, and he'd lost it. He sat for a moment, trying to recall it. It was a company name . . .

Damn it! Procrastinating again.

"Okay, Matty," Frankie said to the ether. "I'm going in. If I get in trouble, do *not* call the cops! Go find Grandpa Teddy. If he won't get up, find Uncle Buddy. Last resort, your mom."

He really should have said all this before he left. Stupid nosy Irene.

He pulled the cap low across his eyes, grabbed his tool bag, and marched down the alley, flashlight off. The alley grew so dark that he was afraid he'd trip and impale himself on something. Finally he switched on the flashlight. So bright! Burglar bright. He hurried to the back door of the tavern and aimed the light at the lock.

This was the diciest part of the plan, the step that gave him the terrors. He took a breath and gripped the doorknob.

Stealing from Mitzi required three things: the alarm code, the combination of the safe, and a way past the back door lock. When Matty confided in him about what he could do, the first two pieces of the puzzle were solved. All Frankie had to do was get past the door.

He spent weeks practicing in his garage, just like he had before the *Alton Belle*. He focused his mind on padlocks, concentrated on the innards of door locks, stared down doors of all kinds. He summoned every ounce of psychokinesis in his body.

And failed. Every fucking time.

Buddy Telemachus, in that one night in the casino, had destroyed his last shred of confidence. And without confidence, he was nothing. But if Buddy had taken that from him, at least Frankie could take one thing from Buddy.

He opened the tool bag and brought out his brother's gigantic drill. The drill bit looked like a World War II artillery shell. He pulled the trigger, got the metal spinning at maximum velocity, and jammed it into the lock.

The shriek nearly made him let go of the drill and run, but he knew if he stopped now he'd never get another chance. He held the shaking device with both hands and bore down. With a clunk the drill bit punched through.

Fuck yeah. If he couldn't depend on his power, he could at least depend on Black & Decker.

He reached into the hole with two fingers and pulled the remains of the lock bar free of the notch. Then he tugged the door toward him.

The door didn't move, until suddenly it did.

And there was the alarm console. Two feet from the door, the keypad was lit up and beeping.

He threw himself inside. The bar was dark, but he knew this hallway well. And the alarm code was simple, so simple he'd memorized it. Or thought he had.

On the console a countdown was showing: 28, 27 . . .

Where the hell was the slip of paper? The paper was gone. It began with a four, he thought.

Then he found the paper in his other pocket and held it under the flashlight. 4-4-4-2. Seeing it, he remembered.

He punched in the numbers. The box considered his entry, then blinked twice. He aimed his flashlight at the LCD panel. The countdown continued: 18, 17 . . .

"Shit," he said. He looked at the paper again. 4-4-4-2, just like he'd typed. He punched the number again, going slowly.

He stared at the alarm console, panic blinding him. What the hell was wrong?

"Jesus, Matty!" he said aloud. "Did you fuck this up? Did you fuck me?" The console showed 8, then 7. So many God damn numbers!

Then he noticed the enter key.

He pressed it.

The countdown was replaced by the words READY TO ARM.

He collapsed against the wall, breathing hard. Then he lifted his shirt and mopped the sweat from his face.

"I'm in," he said to Maybe-Matty. "I'm sorry about the swearing."

He needed to play it cool for Matty, but he knew in his heart that he could never do this again. Maybe real thieves got off on the danger. Maybe people like his dad could sit at a poker table and rob gangsters while looking them in the eye. But Frankie wasn't that guy.

If he left, this very second, he'd get away a free man. But then what? If he bailed out now, he'd never get his house back, and Loretta would never forgive him. He could lose everything: his marriage, the twins, and most definitely Mary Alice, who resented his presence. He wanted to be that presence. He wanted to be the guy who stuck around even when she wanted him to leave, because he wanted to be better than her deadbeat dad.

No. The only way out of this was through it.

He put the drill into the bag, then followed the light of his Maglite down the hallway to the main room. The Bud Light sign glowed in the window, casting a red smear across the surface of the bar. Did they keep beer taps on at night? He should at least take a bottle of scotch before he left.

The door to Mitzi's office was unlocked. He moved around the desk and pointed the light at the black safe.

"Okay, Matty," he said. "Here we go." He crouched down beside the safe, and held the piece of paper up to the glow of the flashlight. The second set of numbers was the safe combination: 28-11-33. His ears were roaring.

"I apologize in advance for any cursing," he said.

He spun the dial to clear it, then dialed each number, left, right, left. There was no indication that the combination was correct. He pushed down on the handle, and tugged.

The door swung open.

"Thank you fucking Jesus," Frankie said. Happy curses were allowed, he decided. "And thank you, Matty."

Suddenly he remembered the name of the imaginary phone service: Astral Travel and Telephony. AT&T! Ha! He'd have to tell the kid that one.

He aimed the flashlight inside the safe. He couldn't quite process what he saw. He swung the light away, then back, then played it all around the interior, as if looking for false bottoms, for mirrors. From the back of his throat came a high whine, like air being squeezed from a balloon.

The safe was empty. Or almost: a kid's lunch box sat on the top shelf. It was too small to hold what he needed.

The inside of his head clanged with the same three syllables, over and over: *NOMONEY NOMONEY NOMONEY* . . .

He pulled out the lunch box, a soft-sided Teenage Mutant Ninja Turtles model. *Money?* he asked the box. He yanked open the zipper. Inside was a plastic container holding the remains of some popcorn, or maybe white Chiclets.

No money.

Not even a fucking thermos.

"God damn it!" he shouted. "Give me a fucking break! One fucking break!"

. . .

There was one thing he'd learned this summer while practicing breaking locks, and failing: if he got really, really frustrated, he had the strength to pick up a safe and hold it over his head. Of course, he'd also learned that if he lost his balance he might accidentally drop it on his wife's car.

This time when he picked up the safe—first hauling it to waist level, and then up to his chest—he picked his target. He tossed the thing onto Mitzi's desk, and the explosive crack of wood was so satisfying it almost calmed him down.

Then he thought: I should get out of here.

He hurried down the hallway to the back door. Why would Mitzi move the money? It was already in a safe! That's why they called it a *safe*. The stacks of money were supposed to be there, waiting for him. He was supposed to buy back the house—no, buy a new house, with two bathrooms, with AC installed. And a new car, too. He'd come home like a Greek hero in his Toyota chariot, and the twins would run to him. Even Mary Alice would smile. And Loretta—Loretta wouldn't leave him.

The back door wouldn't lock, of course. He pulled it shut as best he could, then strode down the alley, still fuming. He had to talk to Matty. When had the Pusateris moved the cash, and why wasn't the kid watching when they did it? Maybe he could spy around Nick's house, find out where he kept the dough. No way was the mobster putting that much money into a bank.

The wall beside him was suddenly lit by a swipe of headlights; even his silhouette looked surprised. The cops! For a long moment he was paralyzed, expecting strobe lights to erupt behind him, the whoop of a siren. But nothing, nothing except the clank of a car door opening. The sound unlocked his legs. He ran pell-mell for the street, the tool bag clanking at his side, and threw himself around the corner.

He reached the driver's side of the van and smashed his elbow against the big mirror trying to brace himself. He yanked open the door, threw the tool bag and the fucking lunch box inside. Where were the keys? He searched one pocket, found nothing. Did he drop them? Where was his flashlight? He pushed a hand into the other pocket.

Keys!

He started the van and checked his rearview mirrors. The driver's-side mirror was knocked askew, but the passenger's side showed the shadow of a giant walking out of the alley. He turned, and his arm raised. If he didn't have a gun, it was a very convincing mime.

Barney, Frankie thought. How the hell did Barney get here so fast? Why was he here, even?

Frankie peeled out, his head clanging with the same three syllables, all the way home:

No money.

No money.

No money.

SEPTEMBER 4

⊞ 〰 ⊡ ☆ ◯

21

BUDDY

⊞

The World's Most Powerful Psychic stands before the calendar with a crayon in his hand. Each numbered square, by convention, is a box to hold everything that will happen in those twenty-four hours. The boxes fill the page, but there's no use looking back, or ahead. Not for him. The only square that means anything now is today's.

A purplish pink circle already surrounds that square. He made the mark months ago, with this very crayon.

Zap.

He feels dizzy, as if he's standing at the edge of a swimming pool, blindfolded. The endless chain of days past is jostling behind him, nudging him forward. Is the pool full, or empty? When he falls (and he will fall, he knows that much), will he smash into cement, or be cushioned by water? He doesn't know. He doesn't know and the not-knowing fills him with dread. This must be what it's like for everyone else, every day, and he doesn't know how they stand it.

It's 6:30 in the morning, and he has so much to do before the future ends at 12:06 p.m. Some of these things he's been thinking about for years. Images of the day's events he's saved like snapshots in a wallet. Some he drew years ago, at the kitchen table, while his mother encouraged him. But there are other events that are in shadow. He hasn't looked too closely at them, because by remembering them clearly he'll turn them from possibilities into certainties, and he doesn't want everything locked down.

But oh, those shadows are scary. The idea of ricochets haunts him.

He lifts his hand, and isn't surprised that it's shaking. He steadies himself by focusing on the crayon. It's his favorite color, a particular shade of pink. When his hand is steady again, he draws an X through the box that holds the day.

"You're up early," Irene says.

He puts the crayon away. Irene is still sleepy, still tired. Probably didn't sleep well up in the attic room. She had to share the bed with Mary Alice. Irene puts a filter into the Mr. Coffee and reaches for the canister.

"I was thinking we should have a picnic," he says. "Right here. Hot dogs for the kids. Hamburgers and brats for the adults."

She looks over at him, a curious smile on her face. "Look at you, talking and all."

"I was thinking two packs of hot dogs," he says. "Then three or four pounds of ground beef, but . . . I don't know. I don't know how much people will eat." The picnic, if it happens at all, will occur on the other side of history.

"Could you make Mom's lamb sausage?" Irene asks. "You know, the ones with the feta and the mint?"

"Oh." He'd remembered making patties out of ground meat, but had assumed he'd been making hamburgers. Huh.

"You don't have to, if you've got your heart set on burgers," Irene says.

"No, that's fine." Mom had learned a few Greek recipes, mostly at Frankie's urging, and Buddy had memorized them. It would be good to do this on the anniversary of her death. "Could you go to the grocery store for me?"

He writes out the ingredients, tripling the usual recipe for the number of people in the house. And then he starts writing out the instructions. "Just in case," he says. "I might not be able to . . ." He doesn't finish the sentence.

"You look so nervous," Irene says. "Don't worry. It's all going to work out."

"What did you say?" He looks up. His eyes are awash in tears. Unexpected, uncalled for. One of the first surprises of the day.

"Oh, Buddy." She reaches up and puts a hand on his neck. "I'm sorry. I know having lots of people around stresses you out."

He takes a breath. There are so many plates to keep spinning, and some of them are beginning to wobble. "It *is* a lot to manage," he says.

MATTY

He was flying over water. The slate blue water stretched to the horizon, into a golden smear of the rising sun, and he moved toward it along the brilliant, rippling path of the dawn road. He could feel nothing, hear nothing. There was no *speed*. It could be that he was not moving at all, simply hovering in place while the planet rotated beneath him. And at the thought of the planet, there it was, a blue-green orb glowing beneath his feet. So pretty. He glanced up, into the black of space, and noticed a star winking at him. Or was that Mars? He moved closer—

—and woke with a yelp.

A dream. Or was it? Could his astral self slip away while he was sleeping? What if it couldn't find its way back? Another thing to worry about.

God he needed to pee.

He lay in the bunk bed, staring up at springs and slats. No new deliveries, thank goodness. The room was dark except for a crack in Buddy's new metal window shades. What time was it?

Finally his bladder nudged him out of bed. When he climbed out of the bunk, the entire frame creaked and swayed. So maybe these weren't the most permanent structures Buddy had built.

"Oh come *on*," a voice above him said.

"Sorry," Matty said.

Julian, the oldest of the Pusateris, made a dismissive noise through his teeth. Even in the dark he could roll his eyes. Matty had decided last night that he didn't like him, and not just because the older boy had kicked his ass in Super Mario. Every time Uncle Buddy had walked in, Julian made a face. When Malice came down, he frowned at her and said, "Of course. A Goth."

The other bunks, containing the two youngest Pusateris, were to his right, which meant the basement bathroom was off to his left. He started for it.

Julian said, "What's the *matter* with you?"

"Nothing," Matty said without looking back. He'd learned to deal with the random aggressions of older boys. School was a dog park, all the big dogs off the chain, the pups fending for themselves, and the teachers distant and useless. The trick was to keep your head down and keep moving.

"I mean *all* of you," Julian said.

"Hey." Matty wheeled to face him, propelled by a flash of anger. "You don't know us."

"I know *what* you are." But he didn't sound so sure. He seemed as surprised as Matty that someone younger and poorer would dare disagree with him.

"You don't know shit. We were on TV. We're the Amazing Telemachus Family."

"Yeah, well do something amazing." Julian hopped down. "I'm serious. Do something. Now."

Matty stood his ground. "Ask me if I've got change for a five."

"What?"

"Ask me. Then hand me a five-dollar bill."

"Fuck you."

Matty shrugged. "Fine. Forget it."

"No, wait." He reached into his jeans and brought out a nylon wallet. "I've got a ten. Will that do?"

Matty pretended to consider this. "All right. Now ask the question."

"Do you, dick-muncher, have change for a ten?"

"Sure, mister fuckwad." Matty folded the ten, palmed it, and unfolded the two-dollar bill. He gave it a snap and showed it to him. It was a blast to watch his face.

"What the fuck! Where's my ten bucks? How'd you do that?"

"I'll teach it to you for twenty," Matty said.

"Deal."

"Later," Matty said. "I gotta pee."

After the bathroom, he went upstairs. Uncle Buddy stood at the stove, twisting wads of cinnamon dough onto a cookie pan. "These will be done in a few minutes," Buddy said. "Your mom went to the grocery store."

"Thanks." It was weird to have Uncle Buddy talk to him unprompted. Weird, but nice.

The house was quiet, everybody except Buddy still in their bedrooms, which was good, because Matty needed a little privacy. He went into the living room, where a half-naked Uncle Frankie lay on the couch like a drowned sailor tangled in sailcloth. Matty squatted next to him and touched his shoulder. Then he poked him.

Frankie opened one eye. It took a long time for consciousness to spread to the rest of his face.

"So?" Matty said.

"No money," Frankie croaked.

"What?"

The second eye opened. "No. *Money.*"

"But the safe—"

"Empty. At least . . ." He shut his eyes again. "Anything useful."

"No money," Matty said wonderingly.

"What time is it?" Frankie asked.

"I don't know. After eight?"

"Fuck." Then: "Sorry." He sat up, coughed hard. Then he looked Matty in the eye. "You didn't see them move it or anything?"

"No! Every time somebody paid, he put it in the safe. I swear."

Frankie looked at the floor. After a while, Matty said, "What are we going to do?"

"We're not going to do anything," Frankie said. "There's nothing *to* do. We're fucked."

All this work, Matty thought. All this trouble, and there was nothing to show for it? Nothing he could give Mom?

Frankie was looking at something over Matty's shoulder. Matty turned, and Malice was staring at them. She looked so much younger without her makeup, more fragile.

"Who are these guys?" she asked, and nodded at the window.

Matty stood up. A silver van had pulled into the driveway.

"Don't let them in!" Matty said to Malice. He ran upstairs, thinking, They've come for me.

TEDDY

Someone pounded on his bedroom door. "Grandpa Teddy?" Matty said, his voice frantic. "Are you in there? Agent Smalls is here!"

Already? Teddy thought. They'd agreed on nine. "I'll be right down," he said. Fortunately he was already showered and dressed. He'd put on one of his best bespoke suits, a charcoal and black pinstripe merino, handmade downtown by none other than Frank DeBartolo. The tie was a purple paisley, the tie pin diamond. The gold cuff links were an award for distinguished service that he'd won from a Shriner in 1958. The final accessory remained to be chosen from the black velvet tray. But really, there was no choice at all.

He picked up the Daytona Rolex. It was the twin of the one Nick Pusateri had taken from him. The thing about twins, though; they were never truly identical, even if they looked it at first glance. One of them might be worth twenty grand, the other twenty bucks. Hard to tell unless you knew your watches. Nick didn't, obviously. But it wasn't just the fake diamonds that had fooled him. The man had trophy blindness. All Teddy had to do was act wounded when it was taken from him, and the gangster felt like he'd won something priceless, because of how much it had cost his enemy. He'd never suspect it was a fake, because that would mean admitting that his victory was fake. Once a man had committed emotionally to the con, it was near impossible to claw his way back to objectivity.

He fastened the watch to his wrist and felt the quality radiate up his arm. Trophies couldn't blind if you knew exactly what they were worth.

He returned the tray to the safe, and tucked it below Maureen's letters.

Downstairs, Frankie stood at the front door, blocking Destin Smalls from entering. Matty nervously hovered behind Frankie. "Let 'em in," Teddy said. "Let's get this over with." He patted Matty on the shoulder. "Nothing to worry about. Trust me, all right?"

Frankie stepped aside, and Smalls ducked through the door. "We won't take long," he said.

"You knew Smalls was coming?" Frankie said, outraged. "With *him*?"

Him being G. Randall Archibald. The magician entered carrying a metal suitcase. Cliff Turner came in behind him with more cases in hand and a loop of electrical cable slung over one shoulder.

Archibald held out his hand to Matty. "A pleasure to meet you. I assure you, the entire process is painless."

"What process?" Matty asked.

"A simple test of psionic potential," Archibald said. "We'll set up here by the couch."

Buddy came into the room with a tray of cinnamon rolls drizzled with white goop, just like the ones in the mall. He set them on the coffee table and vanished without a word.

"How about some coffee?" Teddy asked. "Cliff?"

"That would be great, Teddy," the man said.

Archibald raised his bushy eyebrows.

"Okay, you too," Teddy said. To Frankie he said, "Son, could you tell Buddy to get some coffee for these boys, and a cup of warm water for Agent Smalls? Also, and this is just a suggestion, put on some pants." Frankie looked like he was hungover. He wouldn't have blamed the kid if he'd drunk heavily last night.

"I'm going upstairs," Frankie said.

"Fine. Matty, could you talk to Buddy? And then why don't you wait in the basement until we're ready." The boy was only too happy to skedaddle. Mary Alice went with him.

Cliff ferried in more cases from the van, and Archibald hopped about the room, stringing cables, plugging in devices, and turning on colored lights like a Christmas elf. Teddy took a seat to watch the show. God he wished he could smoke a cigarette, but the place was too full of disapproving women and impressionable children.

Graciella came down, looking casually elegant as always, wearing a light summer dress with her hair pinned back. She surveyed the living room and said, "Are we filming a documentary?"

Teddy introduced Graciella to Cliff, who didn't know who she was, and Smalls, who pretended not to know. Archibald kissed her hand.

"Oh, I've heard of *you*," Graciella said.

"Alas, my advance publicity cannot help me now," said the little white gnome. "I've retired from the stage. And yet"—he vanished his handkerchief, and made it reappear—"I can't help but perform in the presence of grace."

"You're worse than Teddy," Graciella said approvingly. "Don't let my sons see you do that, they'll pester you all day."

She pulled Teddy aside. "What in the world are they doing here?"

"I made a deal," he said. "One test. If Matty scores well, Destin gets to report the results and keep his program running until Matty turns eighteen. Then, Matty gets to make his own decision." He didn't mention that he'd promised to keep the children away from Smalls, because that would require more explanations about how he wasn't really breaking his promise.

"I mean *today*," Graciella said. "If Nick shows up—"

"He won't be able to do a thing. Look at all these people! So many witnesses! Plus, that man?" He nodded to Destin Smalls. "That man there is a government agent. There's no one better to have hanging around the house in case your criminal-minded father-in-law shows up."

She didn't look reassured.

"I promise you," he said. "No place safer."

As Archibald and crew set up, children started popping out of the woodwork, many of them carrying squirt guns. The young ones kept asking what the men were doing. Teddy made up a different story each time: recording insect songs; freezing time; setting up for karaoke. That last was a mistake. The three little girls went crazy.

Three? Teddy thought.

"Where's the microphone?" the Asian girl asked.

She could have been any age between seven and twelve. Teddy paged through the roster of children he knew to be in the house, sorted them by gender, age, and race, and came up empty. Graciella and Irene weren't in the room.

"And who might you be?" Teddy asked.

"June," she said.

"Hi, June."

"June," she said, slightly differently.

"June."

She was already bored trying to correct him. "It's not really karaoke, is it?"

"No, it's not," he admitted. "It's for highly advanced psychometry. Do you live in the neighborhood?"

He didn't get an answer. One of the twins shrieked in joy and sprinted from the room, and Not-Exactly-June gave chase.

That's when Irene walked in the door, carrying two paper sacks of groceries.

IRENE

☆

"What the *fuck*?"

The living room had been turned into a laboratory: black cases sprouting wires and cables; half a dozen small satellite dishes on tripods, like inverted umbrellas; control boxes on the coffee table and the floor.

Destin Smalls greeted her with a cheery hello, and G. Randall Archibald—the Astounding Archibald himself—waved at her from near the couch.

Teddy ushered her toward the kitchen. "Nothing to worry about, Irene. Just a little science."

"Where's Matty?"

"Downstairs, playing. Perfectly safe."

She gave him a dark look. "You're on top of this, right?"

"I'm offended you even asked. Off you go."

Buddy passed her carrying a tray of coffee cups. Irene went into the kitchen with the groceries, where someone stood at the counter, chopping vegetables. The someone was Joshua.

He set down the knife and lunged forward, just in time to grab a bag as it slipped from her grasp.

"Hi," he said.

Her body was having a full-on chemical reaction. She wanted to throw herself on him. She wanted to run away. She wanted *him* to run away, and then she'd catch him, tackle him, and squash him into the ground.

Her mouth eventually managed to make words. "What are you doing here?"

He set the bag on the counter. "You didn't know I was coming?"

"Why the hell would I know you were coming?" Anger, even fake anger, was good. It gave her something to hold on to.

"Your brother invited us to a picnic," he said.

"Buddy?" And then: "Us?" She flashed on the unknown child in the pack who'd run past her. "Jun is here?"

"Yeah. It was my weekend, and I figured, hey, adventure."

She couldn't think of what to say.

"He didn't tell you," Joshua said.

"Nope."

He blew out through his lips. "Okay. I'm so sorry. We'll go."

"You can't," she said. "I've got four pounds of ground lamb shoulder in the car."

"Four pounds?"

"I thought Buddy was overestimating, but it turns out, he may be right on target."

"Right," he said. "Us and the karaoke guys."

He helped her carry in the groceries and put the perishables into the already crammed refrigerator. During the process she tried to figure out what was happening in her body and in her brain.

"So . . ." he said.

She stopped him. "Where's Buddy?"

"Outside?" he said.

She took Joshua's hand and pulled him outside. Buddy was in the yard, crouched over the same device he was working on yesterday. Two cables, one red and one blue, ran from it for a couple of yards, then vanished into the lawn.

"Buddy," she said. He didn't respond. "Buddy, look at me."

He stood up reluctantly. The thing he'd been fiddling with was an orange canister. The cables terminated at a junction that was topped with a big red button.

"What is that, a bomb?" she asked.

Buddy's eyes went wide. Then he shook his head.

"I'm kidding," Irene said. "Buddy, I wanted you to meet Joshua in person. See, he and his daughter came all the way from Arizona."

"We met," Joshua said. "He was in the street when we pulled up."

"That's awfully nice," she said.

"Don't be mad at him," Joshua said into her ear.

"Is there anyone else coming I should know about?" she asked Buddy. "Anyone else dropping by? You know, in case we need more lamb shoulder."

Buddy grimaced.

"*Who?*" Irene demanded.

"Surprise," he said quietly.

"Jesus Christ."

The kids ran through again. Somehow they'd acquired water pistols, and the older kids were carrying giant Super Soakers, the AK-47s of squirt guns. Jun was grinning and yelling with the rest of them. Sooner or later, someone would be crying, but for right now they all seemed happy. Buddy eyed them, then covered the red button with a metal cap that snapped shut.

"The garage," she said to Joshua, and took his hand again. There was no logical reason she needed to physically drag him around. It's that she got a charge every time she touched him, fizzing up in her bloodstream.

Graciella's Mercedes wagon took up most of the space. Irene popped the back hatch and gestured for him to sit beside her.

"Nice car," Joshua said.

"It belongs to the mob," she said. "Long story."

They said nothing for perhaps half a minute. The air warmed between them.

"You left kind of suddenly," Joshua said.

"I hope I didn't get you fired," she said.

"Me? No. Others, though . . ."

"Really?"

"The gender gap struck a nerve. The manager you interviewed with, Bob Sloane? Already gone. Technically he's on leave, but that's just until they finish the paperwork."

"Wow."

"I still don't think they're going to hire you, though," he said.

"Thank you for being honest."

"I'm trying."

Do not kiss him, she thought. Kissing him would ruin everything.

"What are you doing here?" she asked.

"I've been trying to call. Did you get any of my messages?"

She looked away, embarrassed. "A few."

"And you haven't been online, either. You didn't leave me any choice. I had to come."

"I told you we were done."

"But that's all you said! You were so mad after the interview. You started packing, and all you'd say was that it wasn't going to work out, we didn't have a future, and you had to leave."

"Because it's true," she said. "We're just messing around. You're not leaving Phoenix. You can't. I don't blame you for that."

"So come to me."

"I've got a job here," she said.

"*Aldi's?*"

She didn't like the way he said that, even though she usually said the name with the same tone of disbelief: *Aldi's?* "No. I've got a job offer with a company. As a—" It sounded ridiculous to say chief financial officer. "As head of finance."

"Really? Irene, that's great!"

"And I want to do it."

"Of course you do," he said. "I mean—" He took a breath. "I'm really happy for you."

He was telling the truth. Even though it meant that she was choosing the job over him.

"I just want you to be happy," he said. "You deserve to be happy."

Also the truth. And she felt horrible.

"What we had was fun," she said. "Those nights in Hotel Land—I loved that. But it wasn't real life. It wasn't serious."

"I thought it was pretty damn serious," he said.

"You need to find someone who can be with you and Jun. And I need someone who can handle me and Matty. This was never going to work out." She kissed his cheek. "I enjoyed every minute of it, but it's over."

"Over?"

"I'm sorry," she said. She kissed his cheek again. "So sorry."

FRANKIE

Frankie had become a ghost to his wife. Loretta made up her hair as he talked, did her makeup. Ignored him as he dressed. Then she walked straight through him—or near enough.

He followed her downstairs. She said hello to Teddy, asked about the men in the living room ("Radon testing," Teddy told her). She poured herself a cup of coffee and then walked out to the backyard.

The entire time, she'd never looked at Frankie, even as he said, over and over again, "Loretta, I'm sorry."

Buddy had turned the back patio into an outdoor kitchen. Ground lamb sat out in big stainless steel bowls, and a plate held a mound of freshly chopped mint. God he loved Mom's lamb sausage. Buddy was at the grill, wrapping potatoes in aluminum foil. Loretta thanked him for the breakfast rolls. He nodded and kept working.

Loretta lit a cigarette—her first, and favorite, smoke of the day. He stood beside her and they pretended to watch the kids playing. The medium-sized Pusateri boy had lost his Super Soaker and climbed a tree, and the younger ones were trying to shoot their smaller water pistols at him. Luckily they were ignoring the orange canister that sat on the lawn only a few feet away from the tree. Left over from one of Buddy's projects no doubt. And knowing Buddy, it could have held anything, from compressed air to mustard gas.

After two minutes, Frankie broke—and broke the silence. "Come on, sweetie," he said. "Please say something."

If she'd just talk to him, he had a chance of winning her back. She'd been mad at him in the past—God yes, a hundred times—though never as completely, as thoroughly as she was now. But if she listened to him, he could find a crack in her anger, and slip in a few words. He could crowbar his way into her heart.

His greatest fear had always been exile. The day Loretta decided she'd had enough and left him, taking her love, and the girls, away from him. He knew that on his own he was nothing. Less than nothing: A subtraction. A black hole. A taker. If all that taking served no purpose, if he couldn't turn around and pour it all back into his family, he was lost.

He said, "I did this for you, you know."

That got her. She looked at him, and her disgust sliced through the smoke.

"For you and the girls," he said.

"You lost the house," she said. "For *us*."

She spoke! He tried not to show his relief. "That's true," he said. "But the reason—"

"You made your children *homeless*."

"Temporarily," he said. "I'm going to make this right."

She shook her head, her eyes on the middle distance. Took a drag on the cigarette. Exhaled. He'd become invisible again.

"Loretta . . ."

"No one would blame me if I left," she said quietly. "When you went bankrupt and lost the business, my friends said I should leave. When you spent a year pretending to run a casino in our garage, I said nothing. I stayed silent even when you dropped a safe on my car."

"The casino thing was only a few months," he said. "And the safe was an accident."

"But this. You borrow money from the mob? For what, Frankie. What the hell are you trying to do?"

Polly noticed them, and ran over, followed by Cassie and an older Chinese girl. They all carried bright-colored water pistols. "Can we sleep in the basement tonight? With Jun?"

"Jun lives in the desert," Cassie said. "She sees scorpions all the time."

"When's the picnic?" Polly asked.

"Didn't you just eat cinnamon rolls?" Loretta asked them.

"We want hot dogs," Polly said.

The youngest Pusateri boy, who seemed to be the same age as the twins, gave up on trying to shoot his brother and ran over to them. "*When* are the hot dogs?"

Frankie said, "Go play, kids. The adults have to talk." Smalls and the rest of the family were in the house, and Buddy wasn't moving. He nodded toward the garage. "Give me two minutes," he said to Loretta. "Please."

He went in through the side door. He was surprised to see a long Mercedes station wagon—with the hatch up.

Loretta closed the garage door. She surprised him by talking first. "I know you love the girls. Mary Alice as much as the twins."

"That's true. And I love you. I'm going to make this right. I have plans. I'm going to get the house back, and things are going to be great."

"I don't need great," Loretta said. "I don't need *you* to be great. I just need you to be *here*."

"I am here! I'm here for the family!"

"No, I don't know where you are. And I'm not going wherever that is. I can't live like this," she said. "I can't take—" They'd both heard the noise. An animal grunt.

Loretta frowned at the side window of the vehicle. Frankie turned. In the back of the wagon were two shapes. He leaned forward, put a hand on the glass.

Irene and some Chinese guy looked out at him. They were stretched out in the cargo area, and the skin-to-clothing ratio was higher than he would have expected.

God damn it. Was there nowhere in this place to be alone?

Loretta walked out of the garage.

"*Now* you decide to get laid?" Frankie said. "Jesus, Reenie." He followed his wife into the yard, and hoped she'd still be his wife when the day was over.

⊕ 〰 □ ☆ ○

22

BUDDY

⊕

The World's Most Powerful Psychic will never be twenty-eight years old. He wonders if it's the stress of the day that will kill him. For example: the damn window shades! The garden-level windows run along the patio, and yet again, the metal blinds he installed have been hauled open.

He'll also never get to eat these lamb sausages. With Joshua's help he managed to chop all the garlic, and on his own blended four pounds of ground meat and another pile of the mint-feta mixture, but now he's almost out of time, and he has to make all the patties. He's preparing the food outside because this is where (a) there's enough room, and (b) he remembers doing the cooking for the morning.

Loretta walks out of the garage, looking sad, and Frankie comes out after, talking talking talking. He wants to tell them both that it will all work out, but he doesn't know that, not really. After 12:06 today, they'll be in uncharted territory.

He's having trouble concentrating as time rolls closer to zero hour. And zero minute, and zero second. Though which second has always been a mystery. What knowledge he has is accurate, but it's not precise. Exactitude escapes him.

He takes out his crayoned checklist and goes over it for the third time in ten minutes:

✓ *clean grill*
✓ *squirt guns*
✓ *drill (F's bag)*
✓ *compressor*
✓ *window shades*
✓ *potatoes*
  lamb patties
  front door
  potato salad?
  basement door
  hot dogs
  other dog
✓ *window shades AGAIN*

At the bottom, he scrawls an addition:

LOCK WINDOW SHADES!!!!

He checks his watch. The patties will have to wait. He goes inside to the kitchen sink, washes his hands, and walks into the living room.

Graciella spots Buddy and says, "Are you sure I can't help?"

He waves her off, then remembers something. "When the doorbell rings, have Teddy answer it." Then he grabs his toolbox from the hall closet and retrieves his drill from Frankie's tool bag.

"Can we have the boy?" Archibald asks.

"Try to sound less ominous," Teddy says. He calls for Matty, and he comes up from the basement, freshly showered and changed, but wary.

"Sit over here," Archibald says. "Right here on the couch." To Buddy this sounds equally ominous.

Destin Smalls says to Matty, "Remember what I told you about your grandmother? Later, you'll look back on this as the moment you stepped into her shoes."

"What, high heels?" Teddy says, and Graciella laughs in her low, throaty way. Teddy does love an audience.

Archibald tapes electrodes to the backs of Matty's hands, humming as he works. Matty sits very still, like a prisoner being prepped for the electric chair. Buddy has much to do, but he wants to see this part. And because he remembers seeing it, he knows he has enough time before he has to go downstairs to the fuse box.

"Now please, I want you to concentrate," Archibald says to Matty. "Focus your attention on the silver van outside. Can you see it?"

"I can't," Matty says.

"Close your eyes, and do what you normally do when you're remote-viewing."

"That's what I'm saying—I can't do that." He looks at Teddy. "I have a . . . routine I've got to follow."

"What kind of routine?" Smalls asks. "Meditation? Some of our operatives—"

"You don't need him to leave his body," Teddy interrupts. "Just record his resting tau state and we can get down to business."

"Will that give us what we need?" Smalls asks Archibald.

"One way to find out," the tiny bald man says. He flips two switches on the control board, and puts his finger over a third button. "Beginning measurement . . . now."

He presses the button. The needle of the biggest gauge slams into the red zone and stays there. A whine starts in one of the machines, and grows higher in pitch.

"Huh," Archibald says.

A flash erupts from one of the devices. A loud pop! sounds from below, and all lights in the house go out.

Buddy hustles to the basement, where Mary Alice and Julian, Graciella's oldest son, sit in front of the now-blank TV, holding game controllers. "What happened?" Mary Alice asks.

Buddy goes to the far wall, flips open the fuse box, and resets the circuit breakers. Lights come back on, as does the TV.

Buddy walks past them and sets to work on the window shades with the drill that he's retrieved from Frankie's tool bag. Each shade has a flange that rests against the wood. He doesn't have time to be clever, so he drives screws directly through the flange into the wood. He really wishes he'd remembered this earlier. He could have made locking hooks. (Except he wouldn't have made hooks, because he didn't remember doing that. He was so tired of Future Buddy being such an idiot.)

After he's finished, Julian says, "That was . . . loud."

Buddy puts away the drill.

Julian says, "And it's pretty dark in here."

"It's perfect," Mary Alice says kindly. "Less glare."

Buddy goes into the laundry room and gets down the supplies he bought a few weeks ago. One of them is a shallow metal dish. He fills that up at the utility sink and brings everything out to the big room. He sets the bowl on the floor, and hands Mary Alice the plastic bag. The girl looks confused.

Buddy's sympathetic. For the longest time, this was the memory that most confused him. But now, it makes perfect sense. "I'll be right back," he says.

He hurries to Mrs. Klauser's house and knocks on the front door. He can hear Miss Poppins barking in excitement, and a second, even higher-pitched noise. The yipping increases in intensity when Mrs. Klauser opens the door.

"I was wondering if I could borrow Mr. Banks," he says.

She laughs. "Take him all day! I don't know how you talked me into this. He's a terror!" But she's smiling. She's more energetic than she's been in months.

Buddy acknowledges Miss Poppins with a pat to the head, but then scoops up the ball of white fluff next to her. Mr. Banks is barely two months old, all head and paws, and his puppy coat is so soft. Buddy holds the little creature's face to his own, and it licks his face. Mr. Banks still has that lovely puppy smell.

He carries the dog back to the house, and as soon as he enters the backyard he has the attention of every child. They rush him. Squealing.

"Don't scare him," Buddy says. "This is Mr. Banks. I wonder if you could take care of him for me, for just a while?"

This is a rhetorical question. They follow him as if he's the Pied Piper, and he walks them into the basement. Even Matty, now freed from the smoking devices and the attention of the government men, has been attracted by the commotion.

Buddy says to Jun, "Have you ever taken care of a pet?"

She nods excitedly. "I have a cat."

"Then you're in charge. Don't let them squash him." He puts the puppy in her arms.

He does a quick head count: three Pusateris, the twins, Mary Alice, Matty, and Jun Lee. Eight is the correct number, so that's a relief.

The children don't notice him leaving, and no one squawks when he closes the steel door. He checks his watch. 11:32. So little time! He sets the timer beside the door to thirty minutes and presses enter. The magnetic locks engage with a reassuring thunk.

MATTY

He was still shaky after frying the house's electrical system, but he had to admit that the puppy helped calm him down. When the lights blew, Grandpa Teddy had rushed over and unplugged him, over the objections of Destin Smalls. "One test!" Teddy said. "That was the deal." They kept arguing, and Matty escaped to the basement with the other kids to play with the dog.

Even Malice was enjoying herself. Somehow she'd gotten possession of a bag of pet toys. Inside was a real bone, a rubber ball, and a selection of squeaker toys in the shape of small animals that Mr. Banks would supposedly be happy to kill. She distributed them to the younger kids, and they seemed more excited by them than the dog was.

After playing Santa, Malice sat down beside him. He realized that the smell of her also calmed him down.

"So," she said, in a voice pitched so that only he could hear. "My mom and Frankie are probably getting a divorce."

"Whoa. Really?"

"It doesn't look good."

"I'm so sorry."

"Can you tell me *now* what you and Frankie have been up to?"

"Uh . . ."

"Because whatever it is, it got our house taken away from us."

"I don't know what he's been—"

"Don't say that. Don't. If you fucking lie to me, I won't be able to take it."

"I don't want to lie to you," he said.

"So don't. Just tell me. Please."

He was not about to tell her about her dad, and the mobster thing.

But it would be such a relief to have one person his own age know what he was going through. Especially if it was Malice.

He looked around. The room was full of kids, but they were all paying attention to the puppy.

"He was helping me," Matty said. "Helping me do stuff."

She waited for him to explain.

"I'm like Grandma Mo," he said. "I can travel outside my body, and see things."

"Are you fucking kidding me?" That might have sounded harsh from someone else, but the way she said it, it meant *That's amazing.*

"You believe me?" he asked.

She rolled her eyes. "Jesus, Matty. I'm in the family. The shit I've seen?"

Relief flowed through him like cool water. He didn't know what she meant by seeing shit; he hadn't *seen* anything until something happened to him. Before that it was all family stories and rumors.

"I thought I was going crazy at first," he said. "I'm getting better at it, but I still need . . . help. To make it happen. Psychologically, and uh, physically."

"So *that's* where I fit in," Malice said.

He felt himself blush.

"It's okay," she said. "There's nothing to be ashamed about. True, you're a little young . . ."

"You think so?"

"Sure. But now it makes sense why you were so desperate. You needed to get high."

It took him a moment to process this. "Right," he said. "*That's* where you came in."

"Though I have to tell you, I've never seen someone smoke up and get such a boner."

His throat seized, and he coughed.

"At the playground?" she said, oblivious to his distress. "Man, Janelle and I looked over and you were like, shwing!"

He covered his face. She leaned into his shoulder. "It's okay, man. Janelle thinks you're just a natural born perv, ever since the night in the attic." He was so glad she was keeping her voice down.

"That was the first time," he said.

"The first time you jerked off?"

He uncovered his face. "No!" Wait, did that make him sound more like a perv, or less? "The first time I left my body. And traveled."

"Really? And to think, I was there."

"Sometimes that's the thing that gets me to travel," he said. He couldn't believe he was telling her this, but she was being so frank with him, so unfreaked out, that he wanted to tell her everything. "Certain emotions happen, and boom."

"Sexual emotions."

"Uh . . . yeah."

"So you're like the Hulk, but with hard-ons."

"Oh God."

"Horny Hulk."

"Stop, please."

She grinned at him. "It's nothing to be ashamed of."

"You're being so cool about this," he said.

"I just wanted to know what was going on," she said. "All you have to do now is explain how Frankie helping you got us kicked out of our house."

And just like that, the trap snapped shut.

"Spill it," she said.

TEDDY

Give this to Destin Smalls: he was persistent. Even as Archibald and Cliff unplugged and disassembled equipment, he was arguing for a second test.

"Not going to happen," Teddy said. "Not today."

The doorbell rang. Graciella said to Teddy, "I think that's for you."

"Then this week," Smalls said. "You and the boy, come to my office. We need a score, Teddy, a proper tau rating. This time we'll do it with an industrial electrical system."

"I promise you, we'll come," Teddy said.

"You can trust him," Graciella said. And oh, that warmed his heart. A woman defending his honor. She was a much better woman than his honor deserved.

The doorbell rang again.

Smalls said to her, "Don't you remember how you met? He was conning you. This is Teddy the Greek. He took his name from the Greek deal, his specialty. He only changed his name when—"

"Enough of that!" Teddy said. Smalls had never lost his urge to expose him, embarrass him. Well, Teddy got the girl, didn't he? Everybody fell in love with Maureen, but he was the only one she loved back. That was a trump card Destin could never beat.

Teddy opened the door, and the air in his chest turned to ice.

It was Nick Pusateri Senior.

He stood on the tile step, looking sweaty, eyes glittering like a crazy man. That toupee probably trapped heat like a World War II helmet. Behind him, Barney loomed unhappily.

Teddy struggled to put on a smile. "What can I do for you, boys?" Only long training kept his voice from breaking.

"Mind if we come in?" Nick asked.

"I'd love to invite you in," Teddy said, lying desperately. "But we're having a family event."

"That's who I've come for," Nick said. "Family." He shoved Teddy in the chest, palm out, and sent him stumbling. Teddy regained his balance and Nick said, "You're moving a little better now, looks like."

Oh God, he was in the room. The devil had never gotten into the house before. Of all his failings over the years, Teddy had never allowed that to happen.

Smalls and Graciella had gotten to their feet. Archibald was watching from beneath his big eyebrows. Barney was trying to count heads and count threats. Nick, though, was staring at Graciella.

"What the fuck is she doing here?" Nick said. His voice was strangled by outrage. Teddy had never seen him this angry, this out of control.

"*She* is standing right here," Graciella said.

"She's my guest," Teddy said. His mind raced. If Nick wasn't here for his family, then he was after Teddy's. "What do you want, Nick?"

"I'm here to return something," Nick said. He nodded to Barney. The big bartender lifted his hand, and Teddy tensed. But it wasn't a gun; it was a large yellow flashlight with a bee logo stamped on the side. Nick said, "This looks familiar, don't it? A lot like the fucking bee on little Frankie's fucking van."

Teddy put a befuddled smile on his face. *What had Frankie done?* Did he go to the tavern and say something stupid? Threaten something stupid?

"Well, I thank you for bringing it by. I didn't know he'd lost it, but I'm sure he appreciates—"

"You think I'm a fucking idiot?" Nick asked.

Destin Smalls stepped forward. He was the only one in the room bigger than Nick or Barney, and Teddy was happy to have him there. Barney and the agent locked eyes like two steam engines on the same track.

"I don't know what you're talking about," Teddy said. "Honestly."

"You think you can fucking break into my bar and I won't know it's you? The fact that you sent your fuckup son doesn't make a difference."

"I didn't send Frankie anywhere. Calm down, Nick, let's discuss this like—"

"Fuck you, Teddy."

"—gentlemen." The only problem being that Nick was no gentleman, he was a sociopath. With a gun. His shirt covered the bulk of some kind of pistol tucked into his waistband.

"There are kids here," Teddy said, lowering his voice. "Your grandsons among them."

"Give 'em back!" Nick shouted. His eyes were jumping, and his hand had moved to rest on that lump under his shirt. What was he thinking, showing up here in broad daylight, ready to blow? He was losing it. Maybe it was the stress of waiting for the feds to knock at his door. The threat of his business—no, his entire way of life—vanishing with the bang of a gavel. "Right fucking now!"

"Give what back?" Teddy asked. "I'm being honest, here. I don't know what you're talking about."

"The fucking *teeth*."

"Teeth?" Archibald said.

"It's a long story," Graciella said. She walked up to Nick, and Teddy was proud of how calm she looked. She was terrified of the old man—she'd told him so—but you couldn't tell.

She opened her purse, and took out a plastic bag. "Here. The other half. Now you have them all—all the evidence. I just wanted my sons to be kept clear."

"Now the rest of them! Bring me my lunch box!"

Teddy said, "That's all of them. The ones we brought you, and those. That's it."

"Frankie," Nick said. "Bring his ass in here, *now*."

"I'm not going to do that," Teddy said.

Destin Smalls had moved around the edge of the coffee table. "It's time for you to leave," he said. "Now."

"Who the fuck is this guy?" Nick said.

"Destin Smalls, federal agent," Smalls said. "I repeat, it's time—"

"Shut up," Nick said. He raised his arm, and the bang shook the walls. Smalls fell back onto the coffee table with a crash. Cliff shouted and Graciella screamed, though Teddy could hardly hear them over the ringing in his ears.

"Fuck this," Nick said. He did not put the pistol away. "I'll get him myself."

IRENE

"What the hell?" Irene said. Teddy's yell had carried into the garage, followed by a loud pop. Now there were more angry shouts—from men whose voices she didn't recognize.

"And everything had been going so well," Joshua said.

It *had* been going well—very well—at least until Frankie and Loretta had interrupted them. Then suddenly it was the night back in high school, in the backseat of the Green Machine with Lev Petrovski, when the patrolman tapped on the window. Joshua, however, was magnitudes better at making love than Lev had ever been. After the interruption, they picked up where they'd left off—no sense stopping the race when they were that close to the finish line—but now this. It sounded like a fight had broken out.

Of course there could be no such thing as a normal picnic with her family. Why expect sane behavior on the one day her boyfriend came to visit? Joshua would never want to get tangled up in this nonsense. He'd never want to expose Jun to these people. He'd leave Irene, no matter how good the car sex.

"This changes nothing," Irene said. She tugged on her shorts. Outside, Loretta screamed.

"Of course not," Joshua said. He managed to pull up his pants before she opened the garage side door.

The yard was full of angry. Loretta was shouting at a couple of men whose backs were to Irene, and Frankie was trying to step between them. Then she realized who the men were.

"Holy fuck," Irene said. "That's Nick Pusateri." Before she could explain to Joshua who that was, the kitchen door burst open, and more people rushed out: first her father, then Graciella, and a moment later, G. Randall Archibald.

There was something in Pusateri's hand. Then he stepped forward and smashed Frankie in the face with it, and her brother went down.

"He's got a gun!" Joshua said to her.

Oh God, she thought. Where were the kids? She needed to make sure none of the kids came out here.

"Go around to the front of the house," Irene said to Joshua. He started to object and she said, "*Listen.* Round up Jun and the girls. Shit, all the kids."

"Right," he said. He ran for the gap between the garage and the house.

Too late, she thought. And call 911!

Nick Pusateri aimed the pistol at Frankie, who lay on his side, covering his bloody nose.

"Hey!" Irene shouted. She marched across the lawn. "Pusateri! Look at me!"

Nick glanced behind him. "Jesus, not you too."

"Just tell me what you want, and we'll get it for you."

"I want what this motherfucker stole from me." She kept walking toward him slowly. "Do that, and nobody gets hurt."

Nick Pusateri, to her complete lack of surprise, was lying again.

FRANKIE

It was as if someone had thrown a bucket of paint into his face, and the shade was named Blinding Pain. He'd read the term "pistol whip" in crime novels and never imagined precisely what that meant. He certainly never imagined it would happen to him.

What stung even more than the blow was the unfairness of it. He didn't have any of Nick's money, so how could he pay him back? Frankie had stolen nothing, yet everything was going to be taken from him. He was back in the parking lot of the White Elm, after the Royal Flush had been yanked away from him. Nick and Barney were just like Lonnie. Bullies.

But worse, this time his humiliation would be witnessed not just by his sister and brother, but by the woman he loved. He only hoped that the girls weren't seeing this, too.

Loretta crouched and put her arms around Frankie. Irene and Nick Senior were yelling at each other, something about teeth. It made no sense.

Nick yelled, "Shut up!" at Irene, then shook the gun at Frankie with renewed vigor. "Where is it?"

"Where's what?" Frankie said. His voice was muffled by blood and damaged cartilage, but he tried to sound sincere—because he sincerely had no idea what Nick was talking about.

"My fucking lunch box!"

An idea dawned. "Lunch box?" It came out *lun bod*, but Nick got the idea.

"What did I just fucking say?"

"Put down the gun," another voice said. It was Archibald. He'd drawn his own pistol.

Nick blinked at it. "What the fuck is that, a toy?" He looked at Barney to make sure he was seeing it, too. "Some kinda Buck Rogers shit?"

"I assure you, it's no toy," Archibald said. "This, my friend, is a micro-lepton gun."

Nick said, "What the fuck is a lepton?"

"The micro-lepton gun," Archibald said, in a calm, teacherly voice, "disrupts torsion fields, the medium by which psychic energies propagate. When targeted at a psionic individual, it permanently destroys their ability to generate such fields. But when aimed at a non-psionic, it causes instant stroke and paralysis."

Nick stared at him. "You guys are fucking nuts."

Frankie couldn't disagree with that. "Look, I don't want the lunch box," he said to Nick. "You can have it. It's in my van." At least, that was where he last remembered seeing it. He was pretty distraught last night.

"I'll get it," Buddy said. He'd stepped out from behind the tree. Frankie didn't even know he was there.

"Do it," Nick Pusateri said. To Frankie he said, "But not you. You stay put. Anything happens, you get shot first, you prick."

That's when Loretta started screaming at the mob captain of the western suburbs.

23

BUDDY

He hurries past the van. He told Nick Pusateri Senior that he was going to the vehicle to get the Teenage Mutant Ninja Turtles lunch box, but that's a lie. In the driveway is a yellow Super Soaker. He picks it up, and it's as full of water as he remembered. Thank goodness.

He didn't think the end would be this hard. Mostly because he didn't try to think about it all. A gift of his final moments being so hectic, so crammed full of detail, was that it made it impossible to ruminate. To brood. Even now, there are so many things he has to do, he barely has room in his head for thoughts of the Zap.

But it's there. He can hear the noise, and it's the last thing he remembers before the future goes black. His heart shrivels in despair. The world is going to go on without him.

He checks his watch. 11:55. Eleven minutes to go, or maybe less. He can only remember the position of the minute hand. Why didn't he pay more attention in that final moment? It would be *really really useful* to know the exact second that history stopped.

At the front door he aims the Super Soaker at the tile and starts squeezing the trigger. Empties the whole tank onto the tile until it's gleaming. The water doesn't run off. He'd laid the tile slightly concave, just enough to hold a shallow pool.

He tiptoes over the water and goes into the living room. Clifford Turner is crouched over Destin Smalls, pressing his wadded-up jacket against the man's shoulder. Smalls is moaning in pain. Buddy feels terrible about Smalls. But he could see no way around that—it was a fact of the day that was impossible to change.

He goes back to the kitchen wall phone and dials. Before anyone picks up, Joshua Lee runs into the room. He's sprinted all the way around the house, come in through the front door. "The kids!" he says, nearly out of breath. "Where are the kids?"

"Safe," Buddy says, then holds up a finger for silence. The operator, a woman, says, "Nine-one-one, what is your emergency?"

He wants to say, The future is dying. He wants to tell her, I'm about to be erased.

Instead, he repeats what he remembers saying: "There's been a shooting. The gunman's still here. Please send the police."

Joshua says, "Where's Jun? Where are the children?"

"Downstairs," Buddy says. In fact, he can hear one of them banging on the basement door. He hands the phone to him. "Tell the operator whatever she needs to know."

He walks out to the backyard, circling around the clump of angry people without looking at them. Nick Pusateri says, "Hey! Where the hell is the bag?"

Buddy marches toward the tree, ignoring him. His heart thuds in his chest. Finally he reaches the spot he remembers, beside the air compressor. He's part of a special triangle. On one vertex stands a septuagenarian mobster holding a .45 automatic. On the other, a retired stage magician aiming a psi-based beam weapon. And at the third point of the triangle, the World's Most Powerful Psychic, and a tank of air.

In the middle of this triangle stand Irene, Frankie, and Loretta. Loretta is threatening to cut off the balls of the mob boss of the western suburbs.

Buddy flips open the metal guard to the pressure switch, exposing the button, and checks his watch. It's 11:57, and the second hand is swooping down the right side of the dial.

MATTY

"It won't open," Julian said. "What's the matter with this place?"

"Shut up, Julian," Malice said. She was at the window, her ear pressed to the metal shades. They'd all heard the bang from upstairs. Matty had told the older kids that it was Archibald's equipment blowing up again, but now he wasn't sure. Malice said, "There's a bunch of people yelling, and I can't tell what it's about."

"Don't scare the kids," Matty said. But he didn't have to worry about them. All five of the younger kids were fascinated by Mr. Banks—and the puppy was fascinated right back. It stood on Luke's chest, aggressively licking his face, which made Adrian and the girls fall out with laughter. Cassie and Polly seemed especially giddy, bordering on the manic. A Beanie Baby come to life! It was a Labor Day miracle.

Matty twisted the door handle and pulled, but the door didn't budge. "That's weird," he said.

"Told you," Julian said. He pushed Matty aside and tried again.

Malice said, "We've got to get out there." She looked worried. He'd never seen Malice like this. Her default mode, except when she was with her friends, was Profound Disinterest.

"I'm sure somebody will hear us eventually," he said.

"Fuck that." She pushed him into the laundry room and closed the door behind them. "You need to go look. Out there."

Then he realized what she meant. "I can't just go," he said. "It takes . . . preparation."

"They're hurting my dad!"

"Okay, okay. Do you have some pot?"

"We don't have time for that," she said. "Give me your hand." She took his palm and jammed it against her left boob.

"Whoa!" he exclaimed.

"How's that?" she asked. Pretty great, he thought. But that wasn't what she was asking.

She studied his face. "Don't worry, I'll hold you up."

"Okay, but I still can't just—"

She grabbed his crotch.

He jumped in surprise. His body, however, hadn't moved. Suddenly he was floating three feet away from it, his psyche intermingled with a shelf full of cleaning products. Malice still had her hand on his crotch. His body's jaw went slack, and then it began to slump. Malice grabbed it around its chubby waist and lowered it to the floor so that its back was propped against the washing machine.

"Get out there," Malice said to it. His eyes had rolled back in his head, but his face retained an expression of amazement.

He spun in midair and zipped through the room full of children, through the metal blinds, and into the backyard. His family was gathered by the tree. Mom and Frankie were trying to hold back Loretta, while Buddy hovered nervously behind them, his hand resting on a machine. Across from them stood two men: the bartender from the tavern, and the old guy with the fifties hairdo who'd been in Mitzi's office. Ancient Elvis. He was waving a gun, and Matty thought: He's going to shoot Loretta.

Then Teddy stepped in front of the men, and Matty thought: No, Elvis is going to shoot my grandfather.

TEDDY

When he was younger and stupider, Teddy thought that getting gunned down would be the perfect capstone to his career. The *Sun-Times* would write up his life story, and the world would finally learn about the greatest card mechanic in Chicago. But that was before he met Maureen, before she gave him these children—who, unfortunately, had all decided to congregate in front of a madman.

"You can't win," Teddy said. "You're outgunned."

Nick laughed. "You mean *that* guy?"

Archibald still aimed the micro-lepton gun at Nick. But the weapon was less than useless to a non-psychic. He'd been lying when he said it caused stroke and paralysis. Teddy believed in the power of suggestion, but Nick was beyond suggestion, and well into the realm of mania.

"No, I mean—" A flash of light, like the reflection off a watch crystal, distracted him. It flickered from the house to a spot in front of him. Which made no sense, because light had to reflect off something to be seen, and this will o' the wisp—was already gone. A trick of the light. Or of his aging mind.

"He means us," Irene said. "We're the Amazing Telemachus Family, asshole. And you're screwed."

"Step aside," Nick said.

"No dice," Teddy said. Suddenly Graciella was beside him. He said, "Honey, let me—"

"Honey?!" Nick shouted.

"Go home," Graciella said to Nick.

"Oh, I'm going home. Go get the boys. They're coming home with me."

"That's not going to happen," Graciella said.

"I'll kill you where you stand," Nick said. "I'll kill all of you."

Without turning his head, Teddy said, "Irene?"

She put her hand on his shoulder—and did not squeeze. Not a bluff, then. Nick really was that crazy. Teddy would have to appeal to a higher power.

"Barney," he said. "You really going to go to the electric chair for this guy?"

The bartender sighed deeply. Then he said, "Come on, Nick. Let's go."

Nick wheeled on him. "What did you say?"

Barney grabbed the pistol in both hands, and yanked it out of Nick's grip. It was the bravest thing Teddy had ever seen.

"We're done here," Barney said.

"God damn it!" Nick screamed, and he threw himself onto the bartender.

Both men had their hands on the pistol, Barney at the grip, Nick with both hands around the barrel. Nick wrenched it sideways, and for an awful moment the gun was pointed at Teddy. Then for a worse moment it jerked toward Graciella. Teddy pulled her to him—

—and the ground exploded beneath their feet.

He didn't have time to even shout.

IRENE

☆

Later, when she had time to think it through, she still wouldn't be able to decide what had occurred in what order. In the moment, however, everything seemed to happen at once: she screamed, her father and Graciella vanished, a gun fired.

The gun. Nick and Barney were still fighting over it, grunting like bears. She couldn't tell who was winning. The men had become a tangle of arms, a furious, tumbling mass.

What the hell had happened to her father? A hole had appeared where they stood.

No, reappeared. Buddy had dug it early in the summer. But hadn't he filled it in? Irene and Frankie and Loretta stood frozen. Two more feet closer and they'd have fallen in, too. And Buddy—

Buddy lay on the ground behind her.

For a long moment, her body was paralyzed. Then, with no memory of moving, she was on her knees beside him. Buddy lay still, his head turned away from her. Frankie and Loretta hadn't noticed he was down; their attention was riveted to the fighting men.

The gun went off a second time, followed by another sound. She flinched, and then realized the second sound was the sha-ring of metal on metal: a ricochet.

Buddy's eyes were open. He was looking at the orange canister. His hand rested against its side as if it were a dog that needed soothing. His other hand lay on his chest.

She touched his face. "Are you okay? Talk to me."

"I'm not sure," he said. "Was anyone else hit? I couldn't remember everything. I couldn't see it all. I'm so sorry."

Anyone else? Irene thought. She looked down at his hand, the way he was pressing it to his shirt.

"It's almost time," he said.

She realized that he wasn't looking at the canister, he was looking at his watch.

Someone screamed in rage. She looked up. Nick Pusateri had gotten the gun. He held it up as if it were a starter's pistol. His toupee had been pulled back from his scalp, but it was still stitched to the back of his head; it hung over the back of his neck like a pelt.

Barney lay on the ground, holding his throat.

"Fuck you all," Nick said. The barrel of the gun jerked in his unsteady hand. Pull the trigger, and he might hit Frankie or Loretta. Point a few degrees higher, and only the tree would get it. Drop a few degrees, and Irene and Buddy could be shot.

Irene had time to think, Yes, he's telling the truth. We are all fucked.

FRANKIE

He couldn't take his eyes off the gun. It twitched and weaved, commanding his attention like a pinball. The fact that a man was holding it was almost immaterial.

Buddy lay on the ground behind him, probably shot. Irene perched over him, talking, though he couldn't hear what she was saying. The gun was everything.

When he played pinball, there'd been many moments when the ball was moving too fast, pinging around the table, responding only to the physics of bumper and rail. Every game, no matter how good it had been up till then, ended the same way: the ball dropping between the paddles, heading for the drain, and not a thing he could do about it. The waiting almost made him drowsy.

He sensed Nick's hand tensing on the trigger. He saw the gun nose toward him. It was a relief, really. Then the mouth of the barrel moved a few centimeters, and he realized that the bullet would miss him.

The gun fired. And fired again, and again. That quick.

Loretta said, "Oh." She looked down, and her eyes widened.

A wad of silver hovered in the air a few inches from her chest. The bullets had nestled together. As she watched, they became mercurial, smoothing into a perfect little ball bearing. Then gravity resumed, and the ball dropped to the ground.

"Jesus fucking . . ." Nick stepped back, mouth slack, unable to fin-ish the curse. He was afraid. Afraid like Lonnie. Then he turned and ran toward the house, still holding the gun.

Irene said, "Frankie."

He glanced behind him. Irene crouched beside Buddy, who lay on the ground holding his chest.

"The kids," she said.

Oh God. The children were in the house.

"Get that fucker," Loretta said.

Nick had reached the back patio. Archibald stepped forward and Nick shouted and pointed the gun at his face. Then he yanked open the door and vanished inside. Frankie heard a second shout a moment later.

"Take care of Buddy!" Frankie yelled to Loretta, and sprinted for the house. He lurched inside and had to stop short. A dark-haired man knelt on the kitchen floor, holding a hand to his bloody mouth. It was the guy Irene had been having sex with in the station wagon.

"Guh," the boyfriend said.

"He's got a gun. I know."

"No. *Guh.*" The boyfriend lifted his hand. He was holding Nick's pistol.

"How the hell did you do that?"

"That way," the guy said, and pointed toward the living room.

Nick had reached the front door. Were the kids out front? Then Nick pushed through the door—and went tumbling. His feet flew into the air, and he hit the ground.

People used to say to Frankie, You look like a wrestler, ever do time on the mat? And Frankie would tell them fight stories, about how it was nothing like professional wrestling. Nobody flies off the ropes. Nobody throws "atomic drops." No, a real wrestler puts you on the ground and chokes you out.

Frankie had never been a wrestler, real or otherwise. But he'd watched a lot of TV.

Two seconds later, he launched himself from the front door and dropped onto Nick Pusateri like Andre the fucking Giant.

24

He's trying to concentrate despite all the distractions. The pain in his chest is terrifying, and Irene's tearful face makes him want to soothe her, but there's no time.

He squints at his watch. The second hand is climbing, climbing. Finally it reaches the notch that stands for the twelve. It's 12:02. He imagines the sound of the magnetic lock disengaging on the basement door, but he's too far away to hear it. Worse, he has no memory of the children emerging safely from the bunker he built for them. He only can remember the next sixty seconds.

It's not an interesting memory. Mostly it involves him lying here on the ground, with Irene crying over him. And he remembers his father calling out for help.

So far, the plan is working, if obeying the dictates of faulty memory can be called a plan. For the last seven months he's lived in a state of stress, constantly worried that he was forgetting a key detail, or that he'd misunderstood some part of the vision. The rest of the time he was afraid that he was remembering too much, locking in the future when he needed to leave more in the shadows, allowing free will to . . . be free. Either way was a trap. When he was a boy, he saw so much, and changed nothing. Nothing to the better anyway. What if, by trying to see less, he made everything worse?

BUDDY

Irene brushes the tears from his eyes. "It's okay," she says. "I'm here."

"I'm glad," he says.

Loretta, weeping mascara, leans over him and says, "I'll call nine-one-one." He doesn't tell her he's already called them. It will make her feel useful if she can help.

Irene puts her hand on his. "I'm going to need to take a quick look, okay?"

He remembers this moment, so how can he stop her? Soon she'll do whatever she wants. He moves his hand out of the way.

She sees the hole in his shirt. She frowns.

"It's okay," he says. Meaning it doesn't hurt, too much.

She undoes a button, then another. "What is this, Buddy?"

"Mom gave it to me," he says.

She lifts the medal from his chest. He winces, because the impact has bruised him. Then she looks at his skin. There's no blood.

"You're one lucky son of a bitch," she says.

"No," he says. "I'm not."

MATTY

He slammed back into his body so hard that it shook the washing machine. He opened his eyes, and Malice was squatting in front of him, her worried face inches from his.

"I heard gunshots!" she said. "What's happening?"

Oh God, what *wasn't* happening? "There was an explosion, and Grandpa Teddy fell, and then your dad got shot—"

"What?!"

"But not shot! Now he's in the front yard, and they're fighting—"

Julian yelled, "The door opened!"

Malice bolted from the laundry room. Matty pushed himself to his feet, feeling dizzy. The kids had stopped playing with Mr. Banks. Jun cradled him in her arms. The other kids looked scared.

Malice ran out the door, and Polly and Cassie chased after her. "Front yard!" Malice yelled.

"Don't go out there!" Matty said.

Julian gave him a scornful look and left the room. Matty turned to Jun. "You're in charge. Don't let Luke and Adrian go up there, okay?"

"I'm older than she is!" Luke said.

Matty ran up the stairs, and saw Malice, the twins, and Julian running toward the front door. "Stop!" he yelled. "They have guns!" They ignored him and ran to the front lawn.

Frankie straddled Nick Pusateri, punching down. Nick had his forearms up, protecting his face.

The twins screamed. Frankie glanced over his shoulder. His face was covered with blood, as it had been when Matty had seen him in the backyard. The girls screamed again. "Get back," Frankie said.

And in that moment Nick hit him hard across the jaw. Frankie fell onto his side. Nick pushed himself to his feet. He looked twice as old as he had a few minutes ago. The toupee had vanished, exposing a skull that was hairless except for a fringe at the temple.

"That's the guy who shot your dad," Matty said. Shot *at*, he should have said. He hadn't had time to explain what he'd seen.

Nick stepped to Frankie. Malice yelled, "Get the fuck away from him!" The twins resumed their miniature screams. Nick raised a boot. The pants pulled up, showing the red flames stitched onto the black leather.

Behind Matty, Julian said, "Pop-Pop?"

Nick glanced at the door, lowered his boot. Maybe it was seeing his grandson. Maybe it was finally hearing the sirens. Either way, he stepped back, breathing hard. Then he looked around as if getting his bearings. He turned and shambled toward a gleaming, finned sedan that looked like it had just driven off a Plymouth showroom in 1956.

Frankie moaned, tried to sit up. Matty said, "He's getting away."

Malice said to the twins, "Girls. Look at me." Cassie and Polly were crying, but they listened. "Girls, you know that thing that you're never supposed to do?"

Cassie nodded. Polly pushed a hand across her nose.

Malice pointed at the car.

"Really?" Polly asked.

"Do it," Malice said.

"Okay," Cassie said.

Nick got within twenty feet of the Plymouth when the hood catapulted from the frame in a shower of sparks. It spun away, end over end. The car battery was on fire. And then the entire engine burst into flame.

Nick stopped walking. He stared at the car for a long moment, and then he sat down in the grass.

TEDDY

Dying by gunshot was one thing. But he'd never expected to be blown up.

There'd been a whump, and then the ground opened beneath their feet, and he and Graciella had plummeted. They landed, tangled in each other—and bounced. Then they came down again, and her elbow slammed into his ribs. It was the pain that convinced him he wasn't dead.

They'd landed on a stack of mattresses.

Dirt pattered upon their faces. Before they could get the air back into their lungs, they heard gunshots. He'd never used the word "fusillade" before, but he'd just experienced it. Then Frankie had run past the hole without looking down, and there was no noise except for the distant peal of sirens.

Finally they wiped the dirt from their faces, and got breath back into their lungs. Graciella asked the obvious. "What happened?"

"Buddy," Teddy answered.

"We've got to get out," Graciella said. "The boys are up there." Even covered in dirt, even wild with anxiety for her sons, she was beautiful.

He looked for a way up. The hole was more than a hole; it had *structure*. The dirt walls were lined by four-by-fours, spaced every few feet and cross-braced. A wooden frame at the mouth anchored an array of hydraulic pistons. Those had been keeping the door closed, until they suddenly, and violently, weren't.

It was a God damn tiger trap.

Teddy had known about the hole, he'd watched Buddy dig it, but he'd thought the kid had filled it in, not covered the trapdoor with turf. Somebody could have been killed!

"Can you climb out?" Graciella asked him.

"Hmm," he said, as if seriously considering it. If he were younger, he might be able to scamper up those cross-braces until the handholds were blocked by the door, then leap manfully and pull himself up. He wondered if he'd ever been that young. Or manful.

Instead, he yelled for help. And again. Eventually two heads appeared at the lip of the grave: Archibald and Clifford.

"Is everyone okay?" Graciella said.

"I was going to ask you the same question," Archibald said.

Clifford said, "The shooting's over. The police are here. Destin's wounded, but he's fine."

"The children are fine, too," Archibald said.

Graciella didn't look relieved. "Get me out. Now."

"Is there nobody under seventy up there?" Teddy asked.

"Do you want help or not?" Archibald said.

Teddy made a basket of his hands, and stooped to allow Graciella to step into it. The men above hauled her up and out. Goodness, she had lovely legs. He was almost sad that they hadn't spent more time down here, trapped like miners after a cave-in. They could have bonded while they waited for lunch to be lowered on ropes.

Archibald and Cliff had to lie on their bellies to reach him. "Just a moment," Teddy said. He plucked the Borsalino from where it had come to rest against the dirt wall. He brushed it off and set it firmly on his head.

"Now," he said. The men pulled him up by both arms, and he felt the stitches of the sleeves of the DeBartolo popping at his shoulders.

Archibald and Cliff hauled him onto the grass like a porpoise from a tank. By the time he got to his feet, Graciella had reached the house, calling her sons' names.

Then Teddy saw Buddy. Irene sat beside him, tears in her eyes.

Not Buddy, Teddy thought. He couldn't take it if Buddy was hurt. He was their innocent. Maureen's most beloved.

Teddy glared at Archibald. "I thought you said—"

"I meant the little children," he said.

IRENE

She saw Dad and Graciella being pulled from the hole, and everything clicked. The evidence was laid out across the house and grounds. The instant sinkhole. The metal, ricochet-proof window blinds. The medal around his chest.

She leaned close to her brother. "You did this, didn't you? You saw it all."

"Is everybody okay?" he asked desperately.

"Everybody's okay," Joshua said. She looked up. He was studying her with a desperate, worried expression. Jun was at his side, holding a white puppy. Where the hell had that come from? And why hadn't Joshua run? All this craziness, and he was worried about her. He'd come looking for *her*.

"How about Dad?" Buddy asked.

"He's fine, Buddy! He's fine!"

He burst into fresh tears.

"It's okay, it's okay," she said, holding him. "You did good. Look, Dad's coming." He was marching toward them, scowling. Dad's worried face was a lot like his angry face, so it was hard to read his mood.

"I saved one of them, at least," he said.

"You saved them all, Buddy. All the—"

Oh. He meant one of his parents.

"I think I want to rest now," he said.

"Just don't go to sleep."

"It's not that kind of tired," he said. "I can't keep on like this. *Knowing*. I'm worried all the time."

Oh God. All the time? This explained so much about Buddy.

"I'm so sorry," she said. "I didn't know. Watching out for you guys—that was supposed to be my job."

"You don't understand," he said. "I can't take it anymore."

She heard the truth of it in his voice—and recoiled from it. "I know it feels that way right now," she said. "But someday soon—"

"I don't want to know about *someday*. I don't want to know about any of it anymore. I just want it to . . . stop. There's something you're going to do for me now, Reenie."

Dad said, "What the hell is he talking about?" He loomed over them, grimacing. Up close, there was no ambiguity: Buddy was distraught.

"Don't pretend like you don't know," Archibald said.

"That thing," Irene said to the magician. She glanced at his hand. "Does that work?"

"Absolutely," Archibald said.

"You're telling the truth," Irene said. She wanted Buddy to hear that.

The pistol, this micro-lepton gun, looked like something she'd find at the Ben Franklin dime store when she was a kid. Irene reached up, palm open. Archibald's eyes narrowed. Then he placed it in her hand.

The gun was surprisingly heavy. Buddy watched her as she weighed it.

"This is irrevocable," Archibald said to Buddy. "Do you understand?"

He looked at the weapon wistfully, as if he'd found an old photograph of someone he'd half forgotten. She'd assumed for years that Buddy's gift had vanished with Mom's death. After the funeral he never called another Cubs game, never wrote another lottery number. If he'd ever missed his moments at the Wonder Wheel, waiting for the applause of the crowd, he never spoke of it. In twenty years, he'd hardly spoken at all. But the wheel never stopped spinning. He'd carried the knowledge of it, alone, silently.

She pointed the gun at his head, where she imagined his great power came from.

Buddy looked at his watch, then held up a finger. "Wait," he said.

FRANKIE

His daughters stared down at him as if he were a strange fish washed up on the shore of Lake Michigan. He wondered how bad he looked. His nose was certainly not where it ought to be. Several teeth were jostling for new positions. One eyelid had closed for the season.

"You were brave," Cassie said.

"And so strong!" Polly said.

Red and blue lights flashed against the side of the house. Mary Alice crouched beside his head.

"Did we get him?" Frankie asked. His voice didn't sound at all normal.

"Oh, we got him, Dad," Mary Alice said. "The government guy just put a knee in his back."

"That's good," he said.

They were still broke. Still homeless. But Mary Alice had called him Dad. So that was something. He felt like Odysseus, returned home at last, to find his family waiting for him.

Then he remembered.

"Buddy." He sat up—and almost fell back again when a rib stabbed his side. "Help me up."

"What about Buddy?" Matty asked. The kid held a fire extinguisher. He'd been putting out flaming patches of grass and the stray bits of burning auto parts.

"Now. Please."

Frankie hobbled through the house, Mary Alice and Matty holding him up. In the backyard, his family surrounded the spot where Buddy lay. "Is he okay?" Frankie yelled. "Answer me!"

G. Randall Archibald stepped back, and he could see Irene holding the micro-lepton to Buddy's temple.

"Reenie!" Frankie said. "What the fuck are you doing?"

Irene ignored him. Buddy looked at him and smiled. "You're okay," he said.

"Ready now?" Irene asked Buddy.

He glanced at his watch. "Twelve-oh-six," he said. "Perfect."

Frankie said, "Would somebody please—"

Irene squeezed the trigger. The gun discharged with an electrical buzz and pop:

Zap.

OCTOBER

25

FRANKIE

He was surrounded by women. At least two, and possibly all three, were about to be annoyed with him.

"I'm not going to sign," he said.

"What, the price is too steep?" Irene asked.

"It's the paperwork," Frankie said. "It's all wrong."

Graciella leaned across the conference room table. "Trust me, it's all in order. The bank forms, the insurance, everything's pretty standard. We don't often have a closing like this, but it's all in order."

Loretta said, "Just sign it, Frankie."

He put down the pen. "Nope. Not going to do it. The name's wrong."

Graciella frowned. "Franklin Telemachus and Loretta Telemachus. Your name's not Franklin?"

"His name's Franklin," Irene said.

"I don't want my name on there at all," he said. "Just Loretta's."

"What are you talking about?" Loretta asked.

"I want it to be yours," Franklin said to her. "Just yours. Nobody's going to take that house away from you again."

"Well technically," Irene said, "if you're married, in some cases the court can—"

"Shut up, Irene," Frankie said. "It's hers. I don't want any piece of it."

Loretta put her hand on his. "You don't have to, Frankie."

"My mind's made up."

Irene said, "You couldn't fucking tell me this before I did all this paperwork?"

"That was a mistake, and I'm sorry." Truth was, the idea only came to him when he saw both their names on the paper.

"Right." She picked up the stack of documents. "I'll get a couple of the secretaries to help me. This is going to take a few minutes."

Graciella said, "Who wants coffee?"

They sipped coffee and talked about raising kids. All of them, it turned out, wanted a puppy. Then Frankie said, "So I guess we'll see you at Nick Senior's trial."

"Eventually. These things take longer than you think."

"Sorry about Nick Junior," Loretta said.

"The important thing to remember is that thirty years is not a life sentence," Frankie said. "They've got excellent health care inside."

Loretta said, "Jesus, Frankie," but she was laughing.

"What? They do!"

"It wasn't as bad a sentence as it could have been," Graciella said. "And at least he didn't have to testify against his father."

"That's considered worse than anything," he said. Then he realized that his own testimony against Nick Senior might cause him problems. The smart thing, he decided, was to never talk to anyone in the Outfit again, including Mitzi.

After almost twenty minutes, Irene returned with a newly printed stack of documents. "We're not changing another word," she said.

It took several minutes for Loretta to sign and initial each page, with Graciella and Irene explaining what she was signing and why.

"Now the last step," Irene said. "Payment."

"Don't look at me," Frankie said. "It's all on her now."

Loretta shook her head and opened her purse.

Irene said, "Usually we accept only certified checks—"

Loretta slid her a crisp dollar bill.

"But in this case, cash is acceptable."

The girls were waiting for them in the foyer, where the twins were cutting up magazines. "Malice said we could!" Cassie said.

"I asked for old ones," Mary Alice said.

"Let's go see our new house," Frankie said.

"You mean our old house," Polly said.

"Same thing," Frankie said. The feds had been this close to seizing the house. Irene had hinted, though, that Graciella had made some kind of offer of cooperation on the other properties the Pusateris had been pushing through the company, and that had eventually cleared the house for purchase. Now they owned it, free and clear. Not even a mortgage.

They piled into Irene's Festiva, a car that won the award for most ironic distance between name and driving experience. Not that he could say this out loud; Irene was loaning it to them until they found a replacement for Loretta's Corolla, and he wasn't about to look a gift car in the grill. Fortunately, the family was in such a good mood that the cramped cabin couldn't dampen their spirits. That was, until he went left on Roosevelt instead of right, and Loretta gave him a hard look.

"Just one stop," he said.

He pulled into the parking lot, carefully avoiding the potholes, and parked in front of the warehouse-like building. The walls were still notionally white, but the years had painted them with grime and rust.

"What are we doing here, Frankie?" Loretta asked.

"We want to go home," Polly said.

"Come on, take a look, girls." He went to the metal front doors and fished for the set of keys Irene had lent him. NG Group was handling the property.

"This was quite the hangout back in the day. People in the fifties used to come dressed in ties and skirts. The White Elm was not just a skating rink, it was a destination." He pushed open the door. A dank smell rolled out.

"It's a destination for something," Mary Alice said.

"Picture it," Frankie said. "The largest, most complete pinball arcade in Chicagoland."

"Pinball?" Mary Alice said. "No video games?"

"Absolutely not."

"No teenager is going to come in here if you don't have video games."

"I tell you, kid, pinball is poised to make a comeback."

"We're not buying this," Loretta said.

"Let's take a look around, and then we can talk about it."

IRENE

☆

"What am I forgetting?" she asked.

"That we were supposed to leave a half hour ago?" her father said.

"Funny man in a hat."

Graciella and Dad both laughed. They found her distress amusing, maybe because she was usually the most organized person in the building. "Traveling makes me nervous," Irene said.

"Right, *traveling*," Graciella said, and the two of them laughed again. They sat on the couch in the waiting room, leaning into each other. Irene couldn't figure them out. Graciella swore there was nothing sexual going on, but the two of them went out to dinner together, saw movies, and, most disconcertingly, hung out at her father's house with all her kids running around. She was happy for her dad, but it struck her as unhealthy for Graciella.

"I know there's something," Irene said. She'd loaded her suitcase into the trunk of Dad's Buick this morning, so that was taken care of. It had to be something from the office.

"Phone charger," Irene said. She went into her office and unplugged the charger from the wall. Her Motorola had quickly become indispensable. Of course Matty wanted one. She told him to go back to work and save five hundred bucks.

"I've got appointments, you know," Dad said. "People to see."

"I'm ready, I'm ready," Irene said.

Graciella hugged her goodbye, and then turned to her father. They kissed. On the lips.

"Thanks for all the help with Frankie," Dad said.

"The least I could do," Graciella said. And kissed him a second time.

"Christ," Irene said. "I'll be in the car."

Irene and Dad didn't talk on the road. They were ten minutes from O'Hare when Dad said, "You're doing that thing with your face."

"It's just my normal face."

"You used to scowl like that when the boys misbehaved. Or I did. Don't worry about Matty. I'm going to keep him on the straight and narrow. No marijuana or cocaine, and hardly any hookers."

"It's not you I'm mad at," she said.

"You don't have to go see him," Dad said.

"Oh, I do." She felt like she'd die if she didn't. This was her third trip to Phoenix since Labor Day.

"I mean he could come here. He's a hero! Took the gun right out of Nick's hands."

"Nick barreled into him and the gun went flying."

"Sure, but Joshua grabbed it. That's hero material, my girl. Tell him to come back and we can double-date at Palmer's."

"That's not going to happen, Dad." She didn't want Joshua coming back to her house, not yet. If anything non-normal happened—anything at all—he'd have permanent PTSD.

"Fine. Move there, then," Dad said. "You're young."

"I love my job."

"Pfff."

"I don't think I can live *with* him, either. We can hold it together for a weekend, but after that—the little lies just start piling up. Every day there's a slipup, and I get more and more paranoid."

"So you've got to forgive him every day. How's that different from any couple? Your mom? Hoo boy. She had to forgive me five times before breakfast."

"You're a hell of a role model, Dad."

He pulled up to the curb, then reached down to pop the trunk. "Good luck out there, kid."

"I just wish I knew where this was going."

"Who does?"

"Well . . ."

"Not even your brother, not anymore."

Poor Buddy. Irene hoped he was happy, walking around in the dark like everyone else now. "Have you heard from him?" she asked.

"Not a word, not a word."

"I don't know if that's good or bad."

"Me neither."

She pulled the bag out of the trunk, and was surprised to see that Dad had gotten out of the car. He never did that.

"There's only one thing you need to know," he said.

"Yeah?"

"When your man says he loves you, is he telling the truth?"

"That is so profound, Dad."

"Answer the question. Is he?"

"Every time," she said. "Every damn time."

TEDDY

New love walks up and slaps you on the butt, demands your attention, gets your pulse racing. Old love lies in wait. It's there in the evening when your eyes are closing. It slides into bed beside you, runs its ghost fingers through your hair, whispers your secret name. Old love is never gone.

The envelope, this time, was delivered by Mrs. Klauser, his neighbor. "Buddy gave this to me a month ago," she said. She held leashes for two dogs, one a puppy. "He made me promise not to deliver it until today. I hope it's okay."

Multiple hands had been involved—a jagged ink for his name, and blocky pink crayon (*crayon!*) for today's date—written decades apart, he guessed.

"Oh, and this, too," she said. An orange and white box, addressed in that same crayon, to Matthias Telemachus. Teddy walked into the house, set the package on the table, and then stopped, stunned.

The house was quiet. No sawing or drilling. No elementary school girls squealing over stuffed animals. No one loudly complaining about who drank all the milk.

Huh.

It was a relief when he heard a thunk above him. He went upstairs and rapped on Matty's door. "You ready?" he asked.

"Almost," he answered.

Teddy went into his bedroom. He held the envelope to his nose, trying to catch a scent of her. Not a thing. The paper was old, and had traveled through machines and mail bins to reach him. Any whiff he caught now would be imaginary. He held the envelope to the front of the hat, in the traditional manner, and then opened it.

Dearest Teddy,

I hope you get this, out there in the future. Buddy says he can't see anything after September of that year, and I'm so afraid for what this means. If your heart is broken now, as mine is, then the world is even crueler than I feared.

I've been sneaking home to watch the children. It takes a lot out of me, but it's worth it. How did we make such beautiful children? Our best trick. I'm so sorry for leaving you alone with them. There's no sleight of hand that will get us out of this one. I know my body's never leaving this hospital.

I have no more warnings for you, my husband, my one true love. No more advice, except this—be happy. You were always better at it than I was.

I think I'm going to go for a swim now.

> *Love,*

> *Mo*

> *P.S.*
> *Sooner or later you're going to have to tell the kids they're not Greek.*

"Like hell," Teddy said.

He didn't try to get up. He let the weight of years roll over him and hold him there.

He wiped old man's tears from his cheek, coughed to clear his throat. There were people to see, games to finish. He dialed open the closet safe and placed this final letter atop the stack.

Matty was waiting for him in the living room. He looked nervous.

"Don't worry, kid," Teddy told him. "You're going to do fine. You're a Telemachus."

Matty grinned shyly. "Descendant of demigods."

"Yeah, well, don't believe everything you hear."

He drove down Route 83, toward Mount Prospect. After a while he said, "So, Matty, when you're up there, flying around, have you ever seen anyone?"

"What do you mean?"

"Other minds. Spirits, maybe. Souls."

Matty thought about it. "You're talking about Grandma Mo."

Teddy sighed. "I suppose I am."

"I'm sorry," Matty said. "I . . . I don't know if it works like that."

"Fair enough, fair enough."

"But I'll keep looking."

Teddy laughed. "You do that. That would be swell."

They walked into the building where Destin Smalls had rented an office. Smalls, his arm still in a sling, met them at the door. He shook hands awkwardly with each of them, solemn as a wounded soldier greeting his troops. "I appreciate you coming in."

"You didn't give us much choice," Teddy said.

"The boy's still better off under our protection," Smalls said, not denying it. "I have only his best interests at heart."

"And yours."

"They happen to coincide."

"Fine, fine. Let's get this over with."

G. Randall Archibald waited in the next room, presiding over an array of humming transformers and control boards. The familiar Advanced Telemetry Inc. logo was stamped on the biggest pieces.

"Matthias!" the little bald man said. "Good to see you again. We'll be using the large-gain detectors instead of the portable set—no danger of blowing up this time, I assure you." He had the boy sit before the machine as before, and began wiring him up to the electrodes. "We're just going to take another crack at the torsion field distortion. As you know, there'll be no discomfort for you."

"Right," Matty said. The kid looked twitchy and nervous.

"Let's try a little OBE, shall we?"

Matty closed his eyes and breathed deep. Almost instantly the detector needle bounced to the right.

Smalls gasped.

"Don't get a hard-on," Teddy said. "That's my grandson."

The needle hovered in the five thousand tau range. "Yes!" Archibald said. "Highest on record!"

"You don't know what this means to the country," Smalls said.

"Please," Teddy said. "You're just using him to get Star Gate re-funded."

"We'll make sure we keep his identity secret."

"Just like you kept Maureen's secret? How many people up at the Pentagon know her name? Know *our* name?"

Matty sat very still, his lips tightly closed. The needle edged even higher.

"We have to get the psi-war program back on its feet," Smalls said. "Now that we have Matt, that's possible."

"Nope, sorry, not buying it," Teddy said. "I don't think you can ever keep someone like him safe. Not someone so valuable."

"You think *you* can keep him safe, better than the government can?"

"Actually, no."

Smalls seemed exasperated. "Then what are we arguing about?"

"Nothing," Teddy said. "Nothing at all. Matty?"

The boy opened his eyes. He looked shocked at the gun in Teddy's hand.

Smalls said, "You wouldn't. Buddy made his own choice, but Matty has so much potential! You can't do this."

"To save his life, I can. I'm sorry, Matty." He pulled the trigger. The micro-lepton gun whined, higher and higher, and then the capacitor discharged with a loud snap. There was no visual sign of the distortion ray. Teddy thought, This thing would be more impressive if there was some kind of laser effect.

The effect on Matty, though, was immediate. The boy shouted and gripped his head. His body began to shake as if he was having a seizure. Then suddenly his head fell back, and he slumped in the seat.

"What have you done?" Smalls exclaimed.

Archibald studied the main control panel. "There's no signal. No field." He looked up in surprise. "He's inert."

Teddy knelt in front of the boy. "Matty, talk to me. Are you all right?"

He looked around in a daze. "I feel . . . different," he said.

"Do you realize what you've done?" Smalls said.

"We're going home," Teddy said. "Don't bother us again."

MATTY

He was afraid to speak until they reached the interstate. "So," he said finally. "Did I overdo it?"

Grandpa Teddy laughed. "You, my boy, are a born showman. The shaking was a nice touch."

"It just sort of came to me, so I went with it. But then, I wasn't sure how the gun affected Uncle Buddy, and I worried that—"

"No! No! Kid, when a mark's as committed as Smalls, it's almost impossible to oversell. You reeled him in, my boy. Reeled him."

Matty's laugh turned into a giggle. He kept thinking of the look on Destin Smalls's face when the micro-lepton gun went off. It was like *he* was being shot.

"I think you deserve a drink," Grandpa Teddy said. "Something tropical." They pulled off 294 and drove down Grand Avenue. "I had a pal loved the tropical drinks. I grew up with him, both of us loved the magic, wanted to be Blackstone. Both of us the shortest kids in class, a pair of pipsqueaks. Anyway, he turned into a pretty good escape artist, then started building tricks for people. A magician's magician, you know? Great mechanical mind. Anyway, he never liked the hard stuff, but by God, give him a drink the color of Kool-Aid, stick an umbrella in it, and he'd drink you under the table." He parked in front of a wooden shack with a gaudy sign out front: THE HALA KAHIKI LOUNGE. "You're gonna love this."

The inside was a movie set for a late-night jungle melodrama on WGN: walls of grimacing island gods, plastic leis and paper lanterns, and enough bamboo to build an Indonesian aircraft carrier. "Don't worry, the Pusateris don't have a piece of this." Matty didn't know he should have been worried about that until he mentioned it.

They took a table at the back of the room. The waitress, a plump, dark-haired woman in her fifties, greeted Grandpa with a kiss on the cheek. "Patti, this is my grandson, Matty. We're celebrating. How about a piña colada? You like coconut, kid?"

"Virgin?" Patti asked Matty.

He felt his face heat. "Uh . . ."

"Semi virgin," Grandpa said. "Give him a taste. Like I said, big day, big day." He rapped his hands on the table, as full of energy as Matty. "So. How's school?"

How's school? He barely thought about school, even when he was there. Nothing seemed as real as the things that had happened to him this summer. After Nick Pusateri Senior, who could fear a high school senior? What could a math teacher possibly do to him?

"It's good," Matty said.

The drinks came. Matty's was some kind of white slushy with a huge slice of pineapple riding the side of the glass. He sipped at it through the straw and felt the tingle of incipient head freeze. Or maybe it was the alcohol. Matty had no idea what was in the drink, or what it would do to him. He'd only smoked pot.

Grandpa waved at someone at the door. "And here's my pal now."

G. Randall Archibald strode across the room. "Mai tai, my dearest Patricia! And a platter of calamari!" He slapped Matty on the shoulder. "What a performance! We should go on the road!"

Matty was so confused. Archibald shook hands with Grandpa Teddy and plopped down in a seat. "Whew!"

"So Smalls bought it?" Grandpa asked.

"Literally. He's planning on big orders. Once he got over the disappointment over losing Matty, he realized the defense possibilities. The micro-lepton gun is the greatest weapon ever created to combat psi-spies, foreign and domestic!"

Matty couldn't figure out what was going on. It was as if Hitler had sat down at the table with them, and Grandpa was asking about the weather in Berlin.

"So he's in, then," Grandpa said, and he couldn't hold back a grin.

"*In?* He's already talking RFPs, taking the gun straight to the military," Archibald said. "He's fired up to get us a contract, no matter if Star Gate's canceled. The safety of these United States depends on it."

Grandpa was nodding. "I was thinking we need to add a visual component. The sound effects are great, but a laser doodad would really sell it."

"Wait wait wait," Matty finally said. "You guys are *working* together?"

The men regarded him with amusement. He was not amused. Everything he knew about his family was not wrong, exactly, but turned sixty degrees. It was like the big red Picasso statue downtown—it became something different when you found a new angle.

"How long's this been going on?" Matty demanded.

"Since the beginning," Archibald said. "Before there was even a Telemachus Family." His circus-animal eyebrows arched their backs. "Or a Telemachus."

"But you destroyed us! On TV!"

The magician looked chagrined. "That was regrettable."

"Regrettable? You wrecked everything."

"That wasn't Archie's fault," Grandpa Teddy said. "He was following the plan. Your grandmother was supposed to come out and do her best trick. The audience would have eaten it up. And then he—"

"And then I," Archibald put in, "the world's most notable debunker of psychics, would have eaten crow. Loudly, chewing openmouthed. My endorsement of authenticity, my imprimatur, would have catapulted them over the heads of that Israeli faker himself."

"May he burn in hell," Teddy said.

"But that didn't happen," Matty said.

"Fate intervened," Grandpa said. "And your grandmother refused to try again. I must admit, I sulked for a while. But in the end, it was for the best. What would fame have gotten us?"

"Jail, perhaps," Archibald said.

"Heartache," Grandpa said.

"Better to take the money," Archibald said.

Grandpa put his hand on Matty's shoulder. "The company Archie and I started—ATI? It was built from the start to milk as much money from the government teat as possible. That milk was running dry, what with Smalls's retirement. But now that the ol' boy is jazzed up—"

"We're back in business," Archibald said.

"Sorry I couldn't tell you about what was up," Grandpa said. "Didn't want you to tip our hand."

Patti set down Archibald's drink, a tall orange-colored thing decorated with a sprig of something green, a slice of pineapple, and a pink parasol. Archibald raised it high. "To ATI!"

"Archibald and Telemachus Incorporated," Grandpa answered.

"Okay, but, but . . . ." The number of questions in Matty's head was turning into a multivehicle pileup. "Is the micro-lepton gun fake or not?"

"Oh, it's real," Archibald said.

"And totally fake," Grandpa said.

"Ever hear of a placebo?" Archibald asked.

Matty nodded, even though he wasn't exactly sure what the word meant.

"The gun, my young friend, is that dark cousin of the placebo, the *nocebo*. If a placebo provides false benefits, the nocebo imparts false harm. The damage to the patient is psychogenic, but no less real."

"If you believe in it," Grandpa explained, "it hurts."

"We've tested it on several 'psychics,'" Archibald said. "Once we explain what the gun does to the torsion field, they lose all ability to function. Of course, half of those people were fakers—"

"Unconscious fakers," Grandpa put in.

"—so we're faking the fakes."

Matty took a moment to think about this. "So Uncle Buddy . . . ?"

"Buddy needed to be normal," Grandpa said. "It was a mercy killing."

Matty took a sip from the frozen drink, thinking. The two men started talking about the details of government contracts. When the calamari arrived, Grandpa noticed him and said, "What's the matter, my boy?"

"Nothing," Matty said. "I was just wondering about . . . me."

"You?"

"My power is real, right?"

"My boy, my boy," Grandpa Teddy said. "Just because there's a lot of cut glass in the jewelry case doesn't mean there aren't a few diamonds. You, Matthias, are descended from greatness."

"I know, I know, demigods."

Archibald snorted.

"I mean Maureen McKinnon," Grandpa said. "The World's Most Powerful Psychic. I made that medal for her for Christmas one year. A joke between us, but *not* a joke, because let me tell you, Matthias, she was, indisputably, the real deal."

"To fair Maureen," Archibald said, raising his glass again.

"To the love of my life," Grandpa said.

Matty lifted his piña colada. "To Grandma Mo."

⊞

He turned the plastic-coated pages in a slow simmer of panic. Each picture was more luscious than any pornographic photo he'd ever seen: seductively crossed chicken strips; gleaming pot roast; wet, juicy quesadillas; steaming piles of spaghetti. Too many choices. Far too many. The Build Your Own Burger section made his heart race. For years he'd known what to order, because he remembered ordering it. It was a causal loop that had long ago stopped feeling strange and become reassuring: remembered meals were the ultimate comfort food. But to be set loose in an environment where not only could almost anything be ordered, but if that failed, could be assembled from a vast number of ingredients? Madness.

Then he turned the page, and a squawk escaped his throat. *Breakfast Any Time.*

The waitress appeared. She was shorter than Buddy and ten years older, with a narrow chin and a nose that was a bit loo large for her face. "See anything you like?" she asked.

For a moment Buddy couldn't speak. He took a breath and said, "Denny's is a hellscape of unfettered free will."

The waitress laughed. "I'm with you on hellscape. Can I start you with a drink?"

"Just ice tea, thanks."

The waitress smiled cryptically, then walked away. Buddy had asked to sit in her section. For the past four weeks, he'd been engaged in his own experiment in choice. Could he really do anything now? Travel anywhere? Talk to anyone? He'd become that terrifying and terrified thing: a free agent. And yet it was thrilling. He was responsible for no one but himself, and he could do anything he wanted. At least until his money ran out. He'd traveled to Alton, Illinois, then to St. Louis, Missouri, and then, following rumors and referrals, to two other small midwestern towns. At each step, the number of decisions he'd been required to make was nearly paralyzing. But he'd made them. He'd made them without knowing if they were right or wrong. Finally he'd arrived, at nine-thirty at night, at an all-but-empty chain restaurant in Carbondale, Illinois.

He was so nervous.

To soothe himself while he waited, he took out his crayon and drew a line across the paper place mat. He'd drawn this line several times during his trip, on napkins and hotel stationery, to remind himself of where he'd come from and where he was going. Call that his lifeline. He made a mark near the right end of the line that was September 4, 1995. Until that date, his mind had wandered up and down the line, remembering in both directions. But now he was on the tip of the line, which crept forward moment by moment. He never knew when it was going to stop. He kept doodling until the waitress returned with the tumbler of tea.

"Pretty color," she said. "What happens then?" She nodded at the numbers Buddy had absentmindedly drawn far to the right of the line: 11 2 2016.

"No idea," Buddy said. Suddenly he was embarrassed. He must look like a little kid. "Do you remember me?"

The waitress glanced toward the woman working the cash register. "I'm not in that line of work anymore."

"No! I didn't mean that! I'm so sorry. I just wondered—"

"I looked you up," she said. "That story you told me. You really were famous once."

"It didn't turn out well."

"What does?" The woman at the cash register walked into the kitchen, and the waitress seemed to relax. "So you stalking me, Buddy?" Then she quickly said, "Just kidding. It's okay."

Oh, but he had been stalking her, across two states and four weeks. Buddy said, "I wanted to—" What did he want? This moment was so different than he imagined. He had no memory to guide him. The script was blank.

"I just wanted to say thank you. You were very nice to me."

"And you were a sweet kid." She extended her hand. "I'm Carrie."

"Carrie," Buddy repeated, as if he hadn't found out that name early in his search. "Glad to meet you."

"So," she said. "Have you decided what you want?"

26

MATTY

The World's Most Powerful Psychic is fourteen years old. He sits on his bed in the attic bedroom, eyes closed, with an orange and white box beside him. The box is empty now. The gift, the inheritance, hangs around his neck, the steel cold against his bare chest.

He's a little disappointed that it's not real gold. But not too much. He runs his hand across the jagged chunk carved out by the bullet, and the dent makes him feel simultaneously more vulnerable and more mighty.

That's a helpful state of mind, it turns out.

He rises out of his body, and keeps rising. The rooftop falls away. The treetops become a blur of orange and red. He turns in the air, wondering where he should go. South, he decides. There's someone he'd like to check in on.

He's not that great at Chicago geography, but simply by thinking of the place he wants to go, his ghost self finds the way. He slips into the building, then down to the basement.

Princess Pauline stands in her royal stall, chewing hay with solemn dignity. She pays no mind to the tubes running into her body, and ignores the uninvited guest hovering near her.

He floats down to look into the Plexiglas window in her side. In June it was difficult to see the artificial heart that powered her, but now he can get as close as he wants. He nudges his point of awareness forward, letting his ghost head and ghost eyes slip past the window.

The World's Most Powerful Psychic thinks, This is the grossest thing I have ever done. Still, it's pretty cool. The heart is far larger than he expected, a hunk of plastic nestled in the tissue of the cow. Her Highness doesn't seem to mind the intrusion.

He feels a sense of professional camaraderie. She's his partner in transparency; he can't be seen, and she reveals all. "Glad you're doing okay," he says to her, though of course she pretends not to hear.

He levitates through the layers of cement, through plumbing and phone lines, until he's back in the sky above Downers Grove. The sun is setting, and the clouds are glowing a peculiar shade of pink. Interesting. He zips up to see them, and then he's inside the water vapor, blinded by white.

Higher, then. Navigation, he's been learning, is an act of imagination.

He rises above the cloud layer. Far above him, the sky deepens from purple to black. The moon is a quarter in shadow. Somewhere on its surface is an American flag. He wonders if it's still standing, and what it looks like up close.

In an instant, he's there.

Acknowledgments

Many people read drafts of this book and offered advice and encouragement. My undying thanks to Liza Trombi, James Morrow, Gary Delafield, Matt Sturges, Dave Justus, Andrew Tisbert, Fleetwood Robbins, Nancy Kress, and Jack Skillingstead.

My children, now inexplicably grown up, were in my heart on every page. Thank you, Emma and Ian Gregory.

My thanks to my editor, Tim O'Connell, who saw what this book needed—and what it didn't. It should be illegal to laugh so much while doing such hard work. Richard Arcus of Quercus and Kiara Kent at Penguin Random House Canada provided valuable notes on the penultimate draft. My agent, Seth Fishman, as well as the entire team at the Gernert Company, has been magnificent from start to finish.

There are others who helped me without knowing it. The Chicago Cubs taught me everything I needed to know about fate, faith, and suffering. You bastards broke my father's heart year after year—until you didn't. My thanks as well to the gullible members of Congress who funded Project Star Gate for decades, and provided so much material for this novel.

I owe an apology, however, to one of my heroes, James Randi, aka the Amazing Randi. His lifelong crusade to investigate psychics, faith healers, mediums, and frauds of all paranormal stripes inspired a story that might provide aid and comfort to the enemy. And so, though it seems ridiculous to have to say this in the twenty-first century: none of it's real, folks. There are no mind readers, no remote viewers, no water dousers, no one who can warp kitchen utensils with the power of their mind—except in fiction. But isn't that enough?

A NOTE ABOUT THE AUTHOR

Daryl Gregory is the author of *Afterparty*, *The Devil's Alphabet*, and other novels for adults and young readers. His novella *We Are All Completely Fine* won the World Fantasy Award and the Shirley Jackson Award. He grew up in the suburbs of Chicago and now lives in Oakland, California.

A NOTE ON THE TYPE

This book was set in Janson, a typeface long thought to have been made by the Dutchman Anton Janson, who was a practicing type-founder in Leipzig during the years 1668–1687. However, it has been conclusively demonstrated that these types are actually the work of Nicholas Kis (1650–1702), a Hungarian, who most probably learned his trade from the master Dutch typefounder Dirk Voskens. The type is an excellent example of the influential and sturdy Dutch types that prevailed in England up to the time William Caslon (1692–1766) developed his own incomparable designs from them.

Typeset by Scribe,
Philadelphia, Pennsylvania

Designed by Soonyoung Kwon